D0421954

SKULLDUGGERY

Other works by Peter Marks:

Collector's Choice
Hang-Ups

SKULLDUGGERY

A NOVEL

PETER MARKS

Carroll & Graf Publishers, Inc.
New York

Best Books for Public Libraries

First Carroll & Graf edition 1987

Carroll & Graf Publishers, Inc.
260 Fifth Avenue
New York, NY 10001

Library of Congress Cataloging-in-Publication Data

Marks, Peter.
  Skullduggery.

  I. Title.
PS3563.A667S6   1987   813'.54   87-754
ISBN: 0-88184-319-9

Manufactured in the United States of America

To my parents

Things are seldom what they seem,
Skim milk masquerades as cream;
Highlows pass as patent leathers;
Jackdaws strut in peacock's feathers.

W. S. Gilbert, *HMS Pinafore,* Act II

Chapter I

THE FARTHER THE FRIDAY AFTERNOON TRAIN SPED OUT OF London, the more Kenneth Oakley felt the tension of the week ebbing. He had purposely taken a midafternoon train to Oxford to avoid the evening rush, to give himself a well-deserved, generous hour of being alone, without telephone calls, without questions or insistent requests for interviews. As a geologist, an unglamorous specialty in the consciousness of the public who only knew about scientists who cured things or split atoms, Oakley had thought that even if he ever made a significant contribution in his own field, it would be noted only within the small world of science. It had never occurred to him that one day his name would be in the papers, having precipitated the greatest scandal in the annals of the British Museum of Natural History.

The train slid past the blackened factories on the edge of the city, past new buildings and council flats. There were few signs left of the Blitz. Oakley looked at the mud-colored brick backsides of row houses with brief, passing glimpses of derelict backyards, one a disarray of unidentifiable rusting iron, another overgrown with the withered and neglected aftermath of the autumn, another hung with stiff gray wash. A light rain made oblique scratches on the window. The train then reached more open country, November pastures, soggy town commons, empty playing fields. In the far distance, where the pewter sky met the earth, was an irregular stripe of brightness Oakley hoped spread over his destination.

Kenneth Oakley had recently completed a series of tests on the remains of Piltdown Man, the most precious set of fossils in the museum and one of the most celebrated hominids in the world. The specimens had been discovered in 1912 at Barkham Manor, a farm near the village of Piltdown, Sussex, by a local amateur archaeologist, Charles Dawson, and Arthur Smith Woodward, then keeper of the Department of Geology at the museum; they had been assisted by a young French Jesuit priest, Pierre Teilhard de Chardin. After forty-one years of being kept in the museum's vaults as the crown jewels of British paleontology, the skull fragments proved to be recent and the apelike jaw a modern orangutan's mandible. The fossil animal remains found with the skull fragments had been imported and salted at the site. The flint tools were recently made. The whole collection had been stained dark brown to match the gravels at the find site and to simulate their origin in the Ice Age. Five days before Oakley departed for Oxford, the British Museum had publicly announced his findings. Piltdown Man was a fake, and there was no denying Oakley had revealed the most grotesque scientific fraud ever perpetrated.

The announcement had been made to the press at the museum. Sir Gavin de Beer, the museum's director, gave the briefest possible statement before offering up to the assembled journalists Dr. Kenneth Oakley, Department of Geology, the scapegoat to whom the sins and ill luck of the museum might be ceremonially attached.

Oakley had carefully rehearsed his answers to probable questions: No, there had been no delay in making the public announcement; yes, the cast of the skull would be removed from the exhibition gallery immediately; no, there had been no suspicions regarding the fossils prior to his investigations; no, the revelation did not reflect on the countenance of the museum. As to why it had taken the museum forty-one years to uncover the fraud, it was better late than never. And in response to the inevitable question: "Whodunit?" Oakley declared, "It would be unfair and premature to make groundless accusations at this time,'' implying that the museum was continuing its investigations, which it wasn't. It only wanted to forget.

Sir Gavin had stood silently at his elbow throughout like a referee who thought it entirely fair for Oakley to absorb all the body blows to the museum's prestige and reputation. Occasionally they exchanged glances, or rather Oakley noted Sir Gavin's expressionless face, offering neither sympathy nor support. Sir Gavin was bald, with rosy unlined skin his wife envied. Whenever Oakley turned in his direction, Sir Gavin would lower the lids over his slightly protruding eyes, making it clear that it was Oakley's mess, and he could damn well sort it out. At the moment the value of the scientific truth did not weigh heavily against the fact that the museum had been put in an extremely awkward position. There were times when the truth was highly overrated. During the months of Oakley's re-examination of the Piltdown specimens, Sir Gavin, the only person at the museum who knew what was going on, had thought privately more than once that he wished Oakley's revelations about Piltdown Man might have been postponed until some time in the future, after his retirement. As director he had avoided drama, even in the displays. Two entire galleries were filled with cases of mollusks, systematically arranged in rigid geometric grids and identified in a nearly medieval minuscule. The pride of lions in the diorama of the African veldt was posed under the shade of a thorn three in attitudes of postprandial languor, like an upper-class Edwardian family at a picnic. Sir Gavin did not welcome having to preside over a scandal. Every time he lowered his eyes in denial, Oakley, looking at his otherwise immobile pink face, thought of a giant antique doll with a bisque head that had lost its wig. He half expected the director to bleat out, "Ma-ma!"

Oakley hadn't thought that the press conference would entirely satisfy the newspapers' appetite for information or the public's relish at institutional embarrassment. But he was surprised how quickly the story spread over the international wire services. Newspapers across Europe, in America, carried it as front-page news. He knew he would have a lot of calls, but there were so many that he was forced to beg sanctuary across the hall in Fossil Fish while Geology's secretary, Miss Ogilvy, took messages. Miss Ogilvy's emotional commitment to Geology did not exceed shorthand and typing. Her life's passion was the cinema. Each Monday morning, to whomever would listen, Miss Ogilvy would retell, in detail, the plots of the two films she had seen on Saturday night and Sunday afternoon. But she was no passive cinema slave. She would not tolerate plot absurdities or badly motivated characters, and more than once delivered the opinion that although certain love stories were obliged to have happy endings, after the final kiss and fade out, the marriage would just not work.

Miss Ogilvy followed the Piltdown scandal in the newspapers, and out of the various speculations over who the culprit or conspirators might be, she came into the museum every day with a new version of the solution, as complete and complicated as her cinematic plot synopses. By the end of the week Miss Ogilvy had indicted everyone who had ever come near the bones.

When she was not speculating on whodunit, Miss Ogilvy went through the avalanche of mail. Some envelopes contained pages rudely torn from paleontology textbooks that discussed Piltdown Man. Many had halftones of the Piltdown skull or fleshed-out reconstructions of the simian man himself with comic-book bubbles drawn from the mouth. The gamut of sentiments ran from the blunt—"You bloody arseholes"—to the donnish—" 'The truth is great, and shall prevail/When none cares whether it prevail or not' "—which also seemed a challenge from the world of letters to the world of science to identify it as a quote from Coventry Patmore. A mother from Blackpool wrote to Oakley that her eleven-year-old son, Maurice, had just been studying Piltdown Man at school, and said that he, Oakley, ought to be ashamed of himself. A great many letters came from antievolutionists and the biblical fundamentalists who were overjoyed that the obscene and satanic idea of man's hominid ancestors had finally been revealed by science itself for what it was—a fraud. Hostility was not confined to the public. A number of Oakley's coworkers gave him narrow looks as if he were a child molester; because of him they were having to endure the tedious jokes, suspicious sarcasm, and probing questions, especially about Arthur Smith Woodward, from colleagues at provincial museums and universities, many of whom could not conceal their pleasure at seeing London's British Museum, in its panoply and perceived arrogance, brought low.

As the train snaked its way across the flat countryside, the increased distance from London worked its analgesic effect. No one could accuse him of escaping. Besides deserving a respite from the malestrom at the museum, he had legitimate work to do, work that he had put aside too long. He hadn't even told Joe Weiner, his partner in the Piltdown investigation, that he would be in Oxford.

The compartment contained only two other passengers. The elderly woman directly across from him had placed her overcoat on the seat to the right of her, and a brown paper parcel to the left, rather than on the overhead webbing of the baggage rack, as if to protect herself from the possibility of contact. Her hair was arranged in a meager roll the color of veal sausage, which ran from one temple to the other across the nape of her neck. She sat stiffly reading a pamphlet Oakley surmised was a religious tract. The other passenger offered better possibilities for erotic musings. She sat by the window dreamily absorbed in the passing countryside. Early twenties, a student perhaps. The old, baggy Aran sweater and fully cut twill slacks she wore obscured the outlines of her body. Oakley did not look directly at her until her eyes fluttered shut. She had a lovely Northern Renaissance face in perfect repose, her long lashes resting on her sculptured cheekbones. From her hands resting in her lap he could see she was fine boned; her breasts would be small, white, with tea rose nipples.

The older woman across from Oakley had looked up from her reading and fastened him with a pitiless indicting stare.

Piss off, Oakley nearly said. Instead, he reached for his briefcase on the neighboring seat. It had a wide accordion bottom that could take his papers and assorted scientific periodicals. Battered and scratched, it had done heavy service since his graduate school years. The handle had recently been repaired again with black electrical tape. The briefcase was crammed with research notes and sections of a paper, as well as a pair of pyjamas he had worn for more nights than he cared to think about, a clean shirt, and a toilet kit. He wondered what the older woman would do if he took out his pyjamas. Oakley withdrew a sheaf of papers.

Seeing him respectably employed, the woman dropped her eyes again to her reading. It was the barest hint of a self-righteous smile on her thin lips that made Oakley bridle at his acquiescence to her disapproval. He'd had a bellyful of ac-commodation in the last week, dealing deferentially with the unsatisfied, antagonistic press and trying to be tolerant of the coolness of his colleagues. He'd only wanted a small holiday on the train to Oxford, and, damn it, he'd have one. Stuffing the papers back into his briefcase, he got up impatiently, slid open the door to the compartment, and went out into the passageway.

He wore a reversible raincoat, tweed side in, and a knitted scarf loosely twisted as a cowl around his neck. A blue blazer, threadbare at the cuffs, showed an inch or two at his wrists. A number of men stood smoking, watching the land-scape slide by. Oakley hoped he wouldn't meet anyone he knew. There was usually somebody from the university on the train to Oxford, and ordinarily he would welcome the chance to catch up on scientific gossip and the state of work in progress. He liked the fraternity, the shared feeling of curiosity, skepticism, and the sense of quest. Ever since he was a boy, he'd wanted to be a scientist.

When Oakley was ten, he had a significant shock. Leaving church with his parents, he saw that Canon Harcourt, who was shaking hands with his father, had hairs growing out of his nose. Not just a few, but two snorting, prolific clusters. It was not that he hadn't noticed them before; he had in fact wondered at the extravagance without coming to any conclu-sion. But at ten he confronted God's servant made in God's image. God with nose hairs? Surely not. In a single moment, God ceased to exist. The little boy in his Sunday suit became a materialist. Later he realized it was the start of his scientific career. Oakley still had a residual nostalgia for the notion of divine perfection in the universe and had spent the better part of his adult life trying to find a measure of it through science. In the recent years after forty, he occasionally thought that whatever was responsible for the miraculous farrago in which that order was embedded might have nose hairs after all.

The childhood shock had a ripple effect. Oakley tended to question pieties and catechisms in general. Not all of them succumbed to his examination, but at least he was satisfied that those remaining had withstood his test. He became a close reader, particularly of footnotes. He reveled in little-known facts, collecting them as an eighteenth century savant collected curious objects for a Kunstkamer: the first flush toilet was invented in 1596 by Sir John Harrington, a godson of Queen Elizabeth. One little known fact in particular had a profound effect on his life as a scientist, and was the prime cause of his being on a train fleeing from London to Oxford: In 1892 a French minerologist, Carnot, published a paper reporting that fossil bones accumulated fluorine from water in the ground. Oakley realized that knowing the rate of accumulation and measuring the deposited fluorine would provide a reliable date for fossil specimens. Before the Piltdown inquiry— before he had applied his technique to the Piltdown specimens— Okaley had been working with Ian Carr, a paleontologist at Oxford, to establish the validity of fluorine dating. Carr had wanted to run tests on fossils he was certain were misdated. But instead of beginning by attacking what he believed to be long-cherished errors, Oakley decided to test firmly dated fossils; by confirming what was already known, he would prove he was not a dangerous upstart. His results would be uncontroversial and reassuring. They'd already published a series of papers that had been well-received. Oakley was now even more convinced that his cautious approach was good scientific politics, considering the events of the previous week. When Carr had called to invite him down for a week-end of serious work on their joint paper, Oakley grabbed the chance to get away, to get back to the sober business of cross-checking their data, and the invigorating business of scientific discourse. His only condition to Carr was that the subject of Piltdown Man would be taboo. Perhaps the week-end would mark the end of a bumpy and rutted detour, and he would find himself once again standing on the main road of his scientific life.

If Oakley had one regret that clouded the prospect of resuming his former life, it was losing the opportunity to work closely with Joe Weiner. As an anatomist, Weiner's interests lay far from his own, but whenever their scientific lives intersected, they would fall into an easy rapport, an agreement of temperaments.

They had run into each other at the annual dinner of the Wenner-Grenn Foundation for Anthropological Research, a catchall event for several hundred specialists in a variety of natural sciences. It was a crusty black tie affair at the Reform Club.

"Do I look as much like a penguin as you do?" Weiner said to Oakley as they met at the large polished doors of the banquet room.

"I didn't see you at dinner," Oakley said. "I thought perhaps you'd been locked up for unseemly behavior at the university."

"Not quite. But I was sharply reprimanded at a faculty meeting for returning my students' papers too promptly."

They descended the thickly carpeted stairs and went together across the marble and gilded hall.

"Which way are you headed?" Oakley asked.

"Paddington. There's a late train. But I could use some air after all those speeches and cigar smoke."

Strolling down Pall Mall, they passed the dark masses of trees in St. James's Park.

"Interesting, McClellan's talk about surviving Neolithic cultures and the technology of early *Homo sapiens*," said Weiner. "Not a mention of our own flint maker from Piltdown."

No one mentioned him anymore. Piltdown Man's career had had its ups and downs. Between 1912 and 1916 there had been a simmering controversy over whether the Piltdown remains represented the fossil skull of a human and the fossil jaw of an ape, brought together by a geological accident. But four years after the initial discovery at Barkham Manor, Charles Dawson made another remarkable find. Two miles away, at Sheffield Park, he had unearthed a tooth and a skull fragment of a second, identical hominid—Piltdown Two. The two-individuals faction was finally silenced. In the next decades scarcely a conference was convened, or a book written concerning human paleontology, that did not cite the Piltdown remains as supremely important to the understanding of early man. Then, by the late thirties, the accumulation of hominid fossil evidence from China, Java, and Africa made Piltdown Man seem an evolutionary oddity, then a pariah, hanging far out on a branch of the tree of man with no apparent ancestors or evolutionary progeny. He was a puzzle that defied solution. Most human paleontologists had put him in what was called a suspense account.

"We know he's there," Oakley said, "but it's not polite to talk about him in public."

"Rather like somebody's mad uncle locked in the west wing."

"The essential problem is this: Either Piltdown Man is Dawson's weird creature with a human skull and an apelike jaw, or we're back to two individuals—parts of a fossil ape and a fossil man. Now, one aspect of the problem is that every time new hominid fossils are discovered, like Leakey's, the brain case is primitive while the jaw has developed human qualities, exactly the opposite of what Piltdown Man is. Anyway, a creature as primitive as Piltdown living in the Pleistocene has become difficult to accept, even though he's firmly dated to that period of the faunal remains."

"All right. Let's chuck him out and be done with him," Weiner said.

"Then we're stuck with two individuals, the jaw and the skull brought together by geological shift in the Piltdown gravels during the Pleistocene or later. The problem is, could such an accident happen twice, once at Barkham Manor and again at Sheffield Park?"

"Obviously not. So we've got to bring him back. Piltdown Man is an anomaly, or seems so now. Maybe the whole thing will eventually be resolved by new evidence. New excavations."

"The site was reopened three years ago when the Nature Conservancy set up some sort of shed. They've dug a cross-section and glassed it in, showing the gravel stratification. Very educational for the schoolchildren they trot out there. They've removed tons of earth, sieved everything, and found nothing."

By then Oakley and Weiner were walking up Duke Street, past galleries showing flower paintings and proper English landscapes. In the window of an antique shop was a beautiful Tudor church pew of burnished oak with a high linen-fold back. Oakley stopped before the window and began to think of Canon Harcourt, then Canon Harcourt's nose hairs. Oakley stood for some moments staring through the window and then said to himself, "Surely not," with the same intense feeling of certainty he remembered from his childhood. Turning to Weiner he said, "I am having a grotesque epiphany."

"Perhaps it was something you ate. A blot of mustard, a crumb of cheese, a fragment of an underdone potato."

"I suddenly realized that, to resolve the Piltdown problem, we have to change our mental set. We must look at the specimens from a completely different point of view."

Weiner waited as Oakley looked steadily at him in the soft glow of the illuminated window.

"Neither natural exlanation of Piltdown Man is satisfying," Oakley continued. "Therefore we are left with an unnatural explanation."

"Unnatural?"

"Suppose Piltdown Man was put there by a person or persons unknown?"

"My God, Ken. That's unthinkable."

"That's exactly why you must think about it."

"Someone buried the fossils at Piltdown and Sheffield Park," Weiner said, trying to make it sound like a statement of fact but shaking his head in disbelief.

"Buried the what?"

"The fossils."

"What if they're forgeries," Oakley said.

"The skull, the jaw, the flints . . . everything?" Weiner began to pace slowly back and forth in front of the antique shop and finally sat down on a ledge under the window. "You're saying Piltdown Man is a complete forgery."

"All I want to do is look at Piltdown as a forgery and see what happens."

"But you must have seen the lot at the museum a thousand times."

"I have never seen the Piltdown specimens," Oakley replied evenly, "and I don't know anyone who has. I've only seen plaster casts of the bones. As far as I know, anyone who's worked on the Piltdown problem has used casts."

"But the bones are at the museum."

"Oh, they're at the museum, in a vault. But one can't get to them."

"Why not?"

"It's always been that way since Woodward's time. As if they were holy relics."

Weiner looked up at Oakley. "Piltdown Man is as English as steak and kidney pie. We've all been brought up on him."

"If he is an artifact, we can stop wasting our time fretting about him. Instead, we could be out there," Oakley said waving his arm dramatically, "running after women."

" 'Bone Man Assaults Shop Girl,' " Weiner read from an imaginary headline. " 'The latest in a series of sexual attacks by randy paleontologists occurred at a sweet shop in Earl's Court. . . .' Listen, Ken, it's not going to be fun and games if you pursue this. You're going to have to take a lot of flak."

"I'll take the flak, but I'd like to work with you. You're an anatomist; you're essential to my plan."

After a moment's reflection Weiner said, "It's irresistible." He got up, and he and Oakley continued slowly up Duke Street.

"What was found at Piltdown Two?" Weiner asked.

"Bits of a skull, a molar tooth. And an animal's tooth, a fossil rhinoceros, I think."

"Which dated the finds at the second site to the same period as the first."

"Right. But although we know all about the first discoveries at Barkham Manor—they're well-documented in correspondence between Dawson and Woodward on file at the museum—we know next to nothing, archaeologically, about Sheffield Park except that it's about two miles from Piltdown.''

"Who dug the site?"

"Dawson and Woodward, I suppose."

"You suppose?"

"Who else could it have been?"

"Didn't anybody else ever visit Sheffield Park after the discovery of Piltdown Two?"

"How could they, when they didn't know where it was."

"Didn't anybody ask?"

"What for? After all, Piltdown Two confirmed Piltdown One. Everyone who had thought the jaw and the skull didn't match had to admit the same thing couldn't possibly have happened again two miles away. And Piltdown supporters didn't see any point in digging anymore. They'd found what they were looking for.''

"An archaeological site that everybody knows about, without knowing where it is, which may not even exist. It's inconceivable, but it's so. Are we all idiots? Ken, it's going to make a very big noise if you're right about this.''

"I'll do a fluorine test on the specimens."

"But how are you going to get to them? You said yourself they're kept like holy relics. Do you know any church that would let us do a chemical analysis of their particular bit of the True Cross?''

"We'll have to get Sir Gavin to insist," Oakley said.

"I don't know him well," said Weiner, "but he doesn't seem to me susceptible to epiphanal revelation.''

"We aren't going to appear before him in a blazing effulgence.''

"What a relief. I don't have an asbestos lab coat.''

As they walked, Oakley thought what effect an admission of having overlooked the greatest scientific fraud ever would have on the museum and its director. "We'll have to get Sir Gavin to insist," he repeated. "The only way we can do that is to present a very strong case for the forgery of the Piltdown specimens before we look at the specimens themselves. I mean the cast of the skull. It's available for study at the museum. People look at it all the time; we won't arouse suspicion. We'll present a persuasive prima facie case. That's where you come in. Stay over at my flat, and tomorrow we'll go to the museum and have a look at Piltdown.''

They walked to Piccadilly for a cab. Across the street was Burlington House, the iron gates shut across the arched entrance.

''That's where the public announcement was made in 1912, at the Geological Society,'' Oakley said. ''I wish we could get in. They've got the Piltdown portrait there, a great brown group portrait.'' He squinted, trying to remember the picture. ''They're all at a table. Arthur Keith, the skull man. Dawson and Woodward are on one side; Grafton Elliot Smith, I think, is on the other with Lankester, the museum's director, taking up pretty much the whole other side. There are others; I forget who. It's all rather murky. Oh, and there's a portrait within the portrait. Hanging on the back wall is a picture of Charles Darwin.''

''Let's go to Westminster Abbey and see if we can hear him turning over in his grave.''

The next day Oakley and Weiner sat in one of the museum offices examining the cast of the Piltdown skull. They faced each other, the skull lying between them on a piece of green baize. They were equipped with a magnifying glass and a high power loupe.

''I wonder how good this cast is,'' Weiner said.

''They have the reputation of being remarkably accurate as far as surface detail is concerned.''

Weiner was looking intently at the skull through the magnifying glass. ''Right,'' he said, marshaling himself. ''We have to remember that, if it is a fake, it was made shortly before 1912. So whoever made him had very little to go on. How many fossil men were known forty-odd years ago?'' Weiner asked himself. ''Bits and pieces of Java Man, who some people thought was an extinct gibbon. The Heidelberg jaw. And extensive Neanderthal remains from Germany and France. That was it. The forger couldn't predict the Java series, Peking Man, and the rest. Whoever concocted Piltdown Man was clever, but he wasn't clairvoyant; he can't be faulted for being a man of his time and making a forgery of his time. Paleontologists had predicted that hominid development toward full humanity would occur through enlargement of the brain. And that's exactly what we see here,'' he said running his hand over the top of the skull. ''The absence of brow ridges was a nice touch, so nobody would say he was a Neanderthal variation. Our forger wanted to create another species. But to establish an early date he combined the avant garde brain case with a primitive jaw. Unhappily for him, subsequent finds prove that human evolution didn't follow that model.''

''That was very well done, Joe. You get a gold star. His being a forgery satisfies the simplicity principle. You see how easily an explanation springs to your lips? One doesn't have to clutch at straw theories of parallel lines of development—every other fossil man over there, and Piltdown Man over here, hanging on for dear life to an evolutionary bough that is about to break.''

''And down will come Piltdown, theory and all.''

''Let's see.'' Oakley picked up the reconstruction of the skull. The casts of the actual pieces of bone were colored chocolate brown, as in the originals, while the reconstructed sections had been left plaster white. ''These are the pieces from Barkham Manor,'' he said, ''and these are from Sheffield Park,'' he noted, pointing out another skull fragment and a molar. ''Notice that the finds from one site fill in the gaps of the other. It's possible that two sites could yield either complementary pieces as we have here, or duplicates, say, two left parietal fragments, or both. The complementary pieces here don't prove it's a forgery, but if it is, it suggests the forger used leftovers from Piltdown One to salt Piltdown Two.''

''Waste not, want not.'' Weiner removed the skull from the jaw, looking at it inside and out and using his fingers as calipers. "The brain case is completely human except for its unusual thickness."

"Could it be old?"

"Possibly. But the question is: Does it belong to the jaw?"

"If not, we would be back to the two-individuals theory. If it's a fake, the theory's correct, but the two individuals were not brought about my two geological coincidences, but by one human design."

Weiner turned his attention again to the skull. "Christ!" he snorted, half in mirth, half in vexation. "I don't believe it. I simply don't believe that we've all been looking at this thing for years without noticing. . . ." Weiner interrupted himself. "Look at me, Ken." He opened and closed his mouth mechanically, like a ventriloquist's dummy.

"Hot tea and honey is the best thing for laryngitis."

"The jaw articulates in the cranium by means of the condyle, a knobby structure at the end of the jaw that fits into the temporal bone," Weiner recited, demonstrating on himself. "You can feel it," he said, putting his finger next to his ear.

"And it's missing on the Piltdown skull."

"Exactly. There's only half a jaw for a start, but the most critical feature, the condyle, is missing too. The whole world has been looking at the Piltdown jaw only for what's there, rather than at what's not," Weiner said. "The forger needed to give his creature an apelike jaw, so he used an actual ape's jaw, which is what this is—a chimp or orangutan. But there was no way for him to adapt an ape's condyle to a human skull. He couldn't carve it to fit without destroying the integrity of the bone's surface. So he gave us only half a jaw and broke off the condyle."

"There's another item on the agenda, ours and the forger's: the teeth," said Oakley. "The two molars were supposedly found about the same time as the jaw. The canine tooth came later. And the third molar came from Piltdown Two. The sequence of finds suggests that perhaps the forger thought he'd done enough by 1912. Then perhaps success went to his head, and he decided to have another go at it—the canine tooth. And when that went down as easily as the rest, he felt utterly secure in giving us Piltdown Two.''

Weiner examined the canine tooth. ''It's the right size for a transitional hominid—smaller than an ape's canine, and worn properly. But it's awfully scratched. Oh, Christ, I don't know. It looks like such an abortion to me now,'' he said.

''Good.''

Weiner bent toward the cast again. ''The molars. The salient feature of these teeth that brings them close to the human side is that the crowns are worn flat, unlike what is found in either fossil or living apes.''

''If it's an ape's jaw, they're ape's teeth,'' Oakley said. He took the loupe and looked at the molars. Then he ran his fingertips across the surface of each tooth and then lengthwise back and forth between the two. ''The molars have been filed,'' Oakley said giving the loupe to Weiner. ''You can plainly see the transverse marks of the file. Also, if you rub your finger back and forth as I did, you feel a slight difference in the height of the first and second tooth. That wouldn't occur if the wear resulted from natural chewing.''

Weiner followed Oakley's instructions and leaned back in his chair. ''Why are we so brilliant? Why hasn't anyone else seen any of this? It's so obvious.''

''We're not that brilliant, and there are certainly other skeptics. But they have only confined their questions to interpreting the evidence as genuine. Whatever questions were generated by that interpretation were answered with another interpretation based on the same fallacy. Nobody's thought to resolve the Piltdown puzzle as we have because, as you said yourself, the idea of forging scientific evidence is unthinkable. There's another thing,'' Oakley continued. ''Something to do with being able to make an objective test. Fluorine dating will give us an objective reading. It gives us a new kind of power. Perhaps that allows one to think more radically.''

''I can't believe the specimens were never tested,'' Weiner said. ''Any time after 1912 samples of the skull and the jaw would have at least shown two individuals, regardless of whether they were real or fake. I feel somehow personally embarrassed, almost as if it's my fault.''

"It's all our faults, really. Science is thought of as iconoclastic, but we have our own sacred cows. Piltdown Man was one of them. So were the men who built their careers around the discovery. So were the eminent scientists who studied the problem so seriously. Men of reputation. The Piltdown bibliography is yards long. Reputation and bibliography, two more sacred cows. Piltdown Man was an idea whose time had come. Now it is an idea whose time is up.''

Sir Gavin listened to their case, looked at Oakley as if he were an incorrigible schoolboy, and then insisted that immediate full-scale tests of the specimens be made. The samples were taken in the strictest secrecy in the vault where they were kept. Until the announcement no one at the museum was aware that Piltdown Man was even under suspicion.

The fluorine tests proved the jaw and teeth were modern and the cranium considerably older, a partially fossilized bone. The brown patina of the specimens, including the flints, associated animal remains, but with the sole exception of the canine tooth, was found to be a stain of potassium bichlorate. The patina of the canine tooth was a flexible film, that looked as if it had been painted. It was analyzed as ordinary Van Dyke brown paint from a tube. Oakley briefly wondered why the tooth had been patinated differently from the other artifacts.

Oakley's investigations at the museum went beyond the physical examination of the Piltdown specimens. He spent hours excavating in the files.

"There is nothing in the museum's records of Woodward's papers that says anything more about Sheffield Park," he told Weiner.

"What about Barkham Manor?" Weiner asked.

"The Dawson-Woodward correspondence covers the years 1908 to 1912, giving the dates of each find and who the finder was. The early pieces were found by Dawson who sent them to Woodward at the museum. There was a period when they excavated together and then they were joined from time to time by Teilhard.''

"What about Teilhard?"

"If you're asking me if I suspect him, the answer is yes. He's the best suspect, in a way, because he's the only one alive. Besides, the Dawson-Woodward correspondence is so convincing—the enthusiastic amateur the prudent professional, the long months of digging between finds, Woodward's discovery of the jaw. You should read his notes on the possibility of its being an ape's mandible. He really seemed to have his doubts."

"I have my doubts about his doubts."

"I read everything through for content, and then again to try to get the tone. It's completely convincing. Woodward is unfailingly cautious. He suspended final judgment on the finds until the last possible moment when the evidence was overwhelmingly in favor of a hominid at Piltdown. And you can't fault Dawson for his hopes and optimism," Oakley continued. "It's quite charming, in fact. But neither man in any way suggests they're playing out a preconceived script. At least not one that they wrote."

"Then the author is Teilhard?"

"Why not?" Oakley said. "When I started, I was pretty sure Woodward was deeply involved."

"With Dawson?"

"Yes. But I'm not as sure about either of them as I was. It's possible that Dawson deceived Woodward, and Woodward was reacting honestly, and less likely that Woodward contrived somehow to get Dawson to dig up objects that he, Woodward, had planted at Barkham Manor for Dawson's benefit. If you reject the idea that Dawson and Woodward were co-conspirators, or that one duped the other, we're left with Teilhard."

"Except if it was a conspiracy of three."

"I consider that unlikely."

"Why? Apart from his scientific interests, Teilhard is a devout Catholic. He'd be fond of the idea of a trinity."

"The dates of his being in Sussex are bracketed by the first and last Barkham Manor finds. But what about Sheffield Park?"

"All Woodward says is that the Piltdown Two specimens came to him from Dawson in 1915."

"Was Teilhard in England in 1915?"

"No. It was the middle of the war. He'd gone back to France."

"If Teilhard was the sole perpetrator, he'd have had to salt Piltdown Two before leaving England and then contrive at a distance to get Dawson to dig there in 1915. That is, assuming that there actually was a find site in Sheffield Park."

"Or, if Teilhard and Dawson were conspiring to dupe Woodward, Teilhard gave Piltdown Two to Dawson to send on to Woodward at the appropriate time."

"Or, if Woodward and Teilhard were coconspirators, Teilhard gave Piltdown Two to Woodward, who salted the site at Sheffield Park so Dawson could dig them up. Which is too far-fetched."

"Maybe Woodward's 1915 date is wrong. Maybe he's lying."

"Every time I begin to think of this as a whodunit, I feel as if I'm putting my foot in a bed of quicksand. I'm losing my objectivity in a mire of speculation and suspicion. We've proved Piltdown is a fraud; why don't we leave well enough alone."

"Because you know you're dying to get in touch with Teilhard and find out if he knows anything. You may be losing your objectivity, but not your curiosity. It would be irresponsible of you," Weiner said with a slightly mocking tone, "not to ask the one surviving excavator if he had anything to tell us."

"Is he still active?"

"I come across papers of his from time to time. Mostly on early man. They're very good."

"Where is he?"

"In New York," Weiner said. "I think he's got an office at the Wenner-Grenn. I hear he's gotten quite fragile—his health—but I understand he's very social, turning up at receptions, meetings. He's very much of this world; there are several women who rather look after him."

"Why not?"

"Why not, indeed," Weiner said. "He's definitely not your simple parish priest. I've also heard that apart from his scientific work he's done some remarkable philosophical writings, but they've never been published."

"A man of many mysterious parts. He gets to be a better suspect by the moment."

"Which means you must call him."

"Sir Gavin has sworn us to secrecy. I'd have to get his clearance."

"Get him to insist. Tell him there are indications that Teilhard might have a deeper connection to the fraud than we originally thought. When you give him the dates of Teilhard's stay in Sussex, that'll do it. If there's a chance of deflecting suspicion from Woodward, he'll even dial the number for you himself."

Not only did Sir Gavin dial the number; he spoke to Teilhard personally. On the day before the museum made the announcement to the press, Sir Gavin called Teilhard in New York. Oakley sat across from Sir Gavin, trying to fill in Teilhard's responses to the one-sided conversation.

"Father Teilhard . . . I can't hear you very well," Sir Gavin shouted. "Oh, I thought it was the line. Sorry to hear that. I hope you'll be feeling better. . . . Fine. Well, actually I'm not. We've having a very serious problem here. Piltdown Man . . . I know it's a ghost from the past. But we've finally got conclusive evidence that it's, well, not right. What I mean is, everything's fake, the whole kit." There was a long pause. "Father? . . . Of course it does. . . . Of course it is. . . . Tests. Ken Oakley's fluorine dating . . . yes, he's one of our best." Sir Gavin looked at Oakley as if he begrudged him the compliment. "We're making a formal announcement to the press tomorrow, and I thought it would only be fair to let you know beforehand, so that you might, well, collect your thoughts. There may be questions. . . . There's so little actual evidence, but in any case, we wouldn't dream of making accusations or appointing ourself judge and jury. We'll have enough to deal with simply bringing out the facts as we've been able to determine them. . . . I'm glad to hear you say so. I admire your loyalty to them. Their reputations are above reproach. . . .'' Sir Gavin, who had the receiver nestled between his neck and shoulder while doodling nervous geometric patterns on a note pad, listened, then threw down his pencil and raised his hands in a symmetrical gesture of disbelief. Oakley sat with increasing frustration and suspense, and couldn't keep himself from taking the pad and scrawling ''Piltdown Two?'' Sir Gavin bobbed his head irritably, signaling Oakley that such things could not be confronted head-on.

''Well, you can help, as a matter of fact,'' Sir Gavin said, pursing his lips at Oakley in an approximation of a smile. ''Our records for the second site aren't all they should be. . . . Yes, Sheffield Park. . . . You did?'' he said smoothly. ''With Dawson. When was that? . . .'' Another silence. ''The exact chronology may be terribly important. . . .'' After a moment Sir Gavin wrote under Oakley's note, ''1913.''

Sir Gavin listened again, and looked unhappy. ''That is a bore, isn't it? We were hoping to get a precise location for Piltdown Two. . . . I'm sorry too. And I'm sorry to be the bearer of bad news. But I didn't want you to wake up to it without any warning. . . . Not at all. Will you be in London soon? I'm always at your disposal.'' There was an exchange of politeness before Sir Gavin hung up. ''Dawson showed him the Sheffield Park specimens at his home,'' he said.

''So the site is as ephemeral as ever,'' Oakley replied, looking at the date Sir Gavin had written.

''He says he can't believe that Dawson or Woodward forged the specimens. I'm glad to hear him say so, but, good God, doesn't he realize where that leaves him? Does he think being a Jesuit priest puts him above suspicion? What's he up to?''

''Teilhard said he saw the specimens at Dawson's in 1913, but Woodward said they came to him in 1915.''

''Teilhard was lying. But why?''

''It's possible that Woodward was lying,'' Oakley replied.

''Look here, Oakley. I've given you free rein with this investigation, but I don't understand why you'd be prejudiced in favor of that crafty French Jesuit. You are trying my patience."

"I'm trying to be objective."

"I suggest trying a little institutional loyalty. So far as we know, there's no reason to assume Woodward didn't get the Sheffield Park finds when he said he did, except for Teilhard's statement, self-serving, no doubt, for reasons I cannot fathom or care to know. I have never burdened you with an official position during the whole of your efforts to uncover the truth about Piltdown Man. And you have done that, admirably. But now we are in the gray area of conjecture, and there is no reason to involve the museum or its trustees to a degree not indicated by the facts. It is my recommendation," Sir Gavin said, stopping to get his breath and give his statement particular weight, "that if, and I repeat, if, Woodward was involved in the Piltdown fraud, it would be better to consider him a dupe—a fool, rather than a forger. Is that clear?"

Oakley went back to his office. Rereading the draft of the statement he would give to the press the next day, he checked every qualifying adjective and made sure that all his allegedlys and purportedlys were in place. He would be detached, noncommittal, as dry as cold toast. But what did happen between 1913 and 1915, if anything? Woodward published Piltdown Two in 1917; so there were two possible two-year gaps in the record. Why were specimens withheld, and by whom? Dawson? Woodward? Or both by agreement between them? What did Teilhard know? Did he actually see the specimens or was he lying? Was he the forger, or was he an accomplice of Dawson? Woodward? Both? Or somebody else? Oakley's mind spun in dizzying circles. Why was it, he wondered, that the Piltdown skull seemed to grin more broadly than others?

There was a lazy curve in the tracks, and Oakley could see the train's engine pointing toward Oxford. The sky had split open for a moment and despite the season, the sandcastle spires of the university were lit by a warm light. Oakley took it as a good omen. Before the train arrived, he went into the compartment for his briefcase. The older woman was gathering her belongings while the younger one, awakened by the movement, looked briefly out the window and recomposed herself for sleep.

Oakley got down, giving his scarf a pull and another turn around his neck, and went to the red double-decker parked by the station. Presently, the bus ostentatiously cleared its throat as if to begin a lecture, and set out down George Street, then Broad Street, past Baliol on the left, the Bodleian on the right, through the architectural hodgepodge of the university. A Tudor quadrangle had an Italianate entrance stuck to it; a Renaissance chapel was sliced in half by a Georgian addition, if not in fact, then by the angle of view as Oakley passed. He knew enough about architecture to be aware that none of these buildings were necessarily what they seemed. The work of a nineteenth century revivalist, given a hundred or so English seasons, might have attained a patina of grime, moss, and ivy's tentacles as convincing as a building four times its age. Oakley had never bothered to distinguish between Gothic or Pugin, but after Piltdown he resolved not to be like the thousands of tourists who traipsed through Oxford with the fatuous assumption that every trefoil ornament or pointed arch spoke to them in authentic Middle English.

Oakley got off the lumbering bus and walked the few blocks to the entrance of the mews where Ian Carr lived. Each house facing the cobbled street had nearly identical narrow facades designed like a child's drawing—a door and a window with two windows above and a peaked roof. Oakley pressed the bell and heard it ring inside. After a long moment Carr opened the door and gathered him into the front hall with a brawny arm around his shoulder.

"Hallo," Carr bellowed, as if shouting across a valley. He was a serious trekker and mountain climber, well over six feet with what looked like four Yorkshire hams attached to the end of each extremity. Oakley often thought his oversized friend made the place look like a doll's house.

"I won't ask you anything," Carr said. "I won't even ask you how you've been. Did you bring your notes?"

Oakley thumped his briefcase.

They went down the narrow hall toward the rest of the

house. As Ian Carr opened the door to the study, Oakley saw a half dozen men in full black-robed academic regalia in a line across the room. Quickly scanning their faces, he saw Joe Weiner grinning sheepishly among the members of Oxford's department of paleontology. One of them hummed a pitch and the group delivered the soulful chorus of "Nearer my God to Thee," in as close harmony as could be achieved without the benefit of rehearsal. Then the center of the line parted. Behind them was Piltdown Man. A cast of the famous skull had been placed at one end of a library table. The body was a lab coat stuffed with pillows, the arms folded across the chest. The rubber-glove hands held a cricket bat, a cardboard cross-piece added with the inscription "1912–1953." Carr had contributed a pair of moleskin breaches and climbing boots, lying toes out in a Chaplinesque position. Candles burned at the head and feet, and pennies had been placed in the eye sockets.

One of the men wearing his mortarboard tassel hanging over his face stepped to the head of the table. "We are gathered here today to pay our last respects . . ."

"Oh, shut up, John. Let's have a drink."

There was a general movement toward the bar set up on the desk, where the usual unruly load of books and papers had been pushed aside. Weiner took Oakley in hand, seeing he had not yet resigned himself to a party, and drew him toward the whiskey.

"This wasn't my idea," Weiner said.

"You bastard," Oakley replied in a tired, not unaffectionate tone. "If you'd warned me, I would have gone to Land's End for the weekend."

"Don't be too cross with me."

"It's been a nightmare at the museum. And don't say you warned me about that."

It was a small room with not much space to move around, with the large desk, two overstuffed chairs, a broken-down couch, and the library table catafalque moved to the center. John Hobhouse backed into Oakley and turned around. He had an owlish face underneath his academic headgear and two bits of kinky hair stuck out above each ear like rusted scouring pads.

"I'll pour the first one," Hobhouse said, measuring out two oversized drinks and holding one to Oakley as a toast. *"Requiescat in pace,* Piltdown." After a first swallow he continued. "Well done, Ken. But you haven't told us who the culprit is."

"Leave him alone," Weiner said. "He's had enough of that all week."

"You picked a fine time to be protective of me," Oakley replied. He began to back away from Hobhouse, but the space was immediately filled by Lester Knowles. He was a specialist in copralites, fossilized animal droppings, but he never hesitated stating his opinion on any subject.

"Piltdown is such a poor forgery, *qua* forgery," Knowles said.

"Only after the fact," said Hobhouse.

"I've always had my doubts."

"When did you publish them?"

"I am very careful only to publish in my own field."

"Your interest in bullshit, fossil or fresh, is well-known."

"Gentlemen," Carr interposed. "This is a wake, not a colloquium. And let's have pity on poor Ken," he added, feeling guilty, seeing Oakley was not doing well.

"How can we not talk about it?" Knowles said. "There he is," he said pointing to the effigy. "Besides, that's all any of us have been doing all week."

"Whodunit?" Hobhouse said insistently.

"We'll never get anywhere on that score," said Carr, trying again to deflect the conversation. "We're just a lot of armchair detectives."

"We need a professional. We need Sherlock Holmes," said Hobhouse.

A reedy voice was heard from the corner of the room. "What about Sir Arthur Conan Doyle. Not as a detective. As a suspect." George Brewer's beard would have looked excessive even on a man of ordinary height. But he was so short his robes bunched around his toes and completely hid

his small hands. His students were convinced he was a
Hobbit.

"What's he got to do with it?"

"He lived near Piltdown and knew Dawson rather well, I
think. He would have had the imagination, the wit to carry it
off. And he started as a doctor, so he'd have had the knowledge of anatomy I maintain was necessary to perpetrate the
forgery."

"What was his motive?"

"Doyle became much involved with Spiritualism, and that
could have led to a deep antipathy toward science, to scientists who were always saying what a lot of nonsense it
was—all that rot about extrasensory powers, the spirit world.
Doyle was a Spiritualist fanatic, so he decided to make his
adversaries in science look ridiculous by making fools of
them."

"That doesn't make any sense," said Hobhouse. "I don't
recall ever hearing that Doyle expressed an opinion about
Piltdown Man. If he had, he would have said something
detrimental about the fossils, which would have been an
interesting twist, since he would be trying to expose his own
forgery. But he didn't. The specimens had to be convincing
enough to be accepted as genuine, which they were," he
continued glancing pointedly toward Lester Knowles. "And
they remained accepted without a peep from Doyle or anybody else. Having gone to the trouble to fake Piltdown, he
wouldn't have stood about enjoying his private joke, waiting
passively for someone else to discover what the fossils really
were."

"Well, if Doyle was right about Spiritualism, perhaps he's
enjoying his last laugh posthumously," Brewer said. He
looked up at the ceiling. "I say, Sir Arthur. What about it?
And remember, anything you say may be taken down in
evidence and used against you."

After a silence, Carr said, "He's not prepared to make a
statement until he's talked with his solicitors."

"I favor the other sir Arthur," Brian Phillips said, looking
directly at Oakley. It was said of Phillips that the adage,
"Anatomy is Destiny" explained his obsession with ptero-

dactyls. Everything about him was long, thin, and angular, and he flapped his arms when he walked.

"Arthur Smith Woodward? That pokey little person?" Hobhouse said.

"My strange cousin Cecil is a police inspector in Liverpool, and he told me once about this chap who cut his wife up and posted her in boxes all over England. And strange cousin Cecil said he looked like anybody, a pokey little person."

"I haven't seen your wife about lately, Brian," Brewer said.

"Dr. Woodward and Mr. Hyde," said Hobhouse. "The idea is preposterous."

"Not at all. Your analogy defeats your objection," said Phillips. "The idea of a secret, unsuspected life in fact or in literature isn't my invention. I find the idea appealing. From nine to five Woodward is the meticulous paragon of the British Museum. And as the fog settles over London, he sets out—a shadow in the night—to Whitechapel, or Limehouse, to a secret laboratory where he makes fossils, and heaven knows what else. There could be something to it."

"Woodward couldn't have done it. He didn't have the skills or the knowledge of human anatomy," Brewer said.

"Dawson wasn't an anatomist either. That's why he decided to include Woodward as his dupe—someone who wouldn't question the specimens right away."

"It doesn't matter whether either of them were specialists in human anatomy. If either of them did it, they would have known that the specimens would eventually be subject to the closest scrutiny by those who were specialists."

"So what? The specialists did accept them as genuine."

"It doesn't matter whether the forger was a specialist in human anatomy or not," Hobhouse said with irritation. "Piltdown Man wasn't a whole skull, let alone a whole skeleton. Nowhere near. In fact, whoever made the specimens was very clever. He made a few pieces and let the specialists fill in the rest with all sorts of reconstruction and theories. The specialists were the ones who actually accomplished the forgery—anyone who ever mentioned Piltdown."

"I resent that," piped Brewer from beneath his beard.

"When did your Piltdown paper appear?" asked Knowles.

Laughter drowned out Brewer's protests that his reference to Piltdown Man had been parenthetical within the text, not even dignified by a footnote.

"You're in good company," Carr said, trying to comfort him. "There's a vast literature on Piltdown, in part because it was a puzzle. Every paleontologist wanted to have a go at solving it."

"I like the idea of somebody forging Piltdown Man as a way of ridiculing not science, but some particular scientist," said Phillips. "The forger isn't someone like Doyle, outside the inner circle, but somebody inside it. I think somebody was out to get Smith Woodward. I used to hear that Elliot Smith up at Manchester couldn't bear him."

"I've heard he was a terrible fart. Nobody could stand him."

"I thought he was quite nice," said Henry Keene. He was considerably older than the rest, and had been sitting in a corner listening with detached amusement to the collective effort at detective work.

"You met him?"

"Yes. It was during the war. There weren't many of us left here, but Woodward came up once—some kind of research. Well, there we were, sitting around in our scruffy corduroys and moth-eaten sweaters, and there was Woodward, like some escapee from the Edwardian era, wing collar and all. And he was very self-effacing. He was much more interested in what we were doing than talking about his own work."

"I shouldn't wonder," said Brewer.

"The idea of professional revenge as a motive assumes that the forger wanted his work exposed. But any forger wants his work accepted," said Lester Knowles with characteristic finality. "Any forger—literary, artistic, whatever—thrives emotionally on the idea of contempt for his audience, the feeling of omnipotence. It's a question of ego. Dawson had an ego as big as a house. And Dawson's the logical suspect."

"Too logical, in my opinion," said Hobhouse.

"He found the first specimens."

"But that doesn't mean he put them there. Circumstantial evidence."

"Nevertheless, he had an excellent motive. He was an amateur and wanted the kind of recognition that was only possible for a professional. The only way he could accomplish that was to one-up his professional colleagues with something all of them hoped to accomplish and none had achieved."

"I think you're making a mistake," said Carr. "Dawson grew up in the age of the Victorian amateur. There were local societies for the advancement of everything all over England, like the geological society in Sussex Dawson belonged to. Some of the finest contributions to science, particularly the natural sciences, were made by dedicated amateurs who made great reputations, equal to those of professionals. Dawson was famous in scientific circles long before Piltdown. They called him the Wizard of Sussex."

"We've all been speaking ill of the dead—Dawson, Woodward, Doyle. Would anyone like to speak ill of the living?"

"We will, Brian, as soon as you go to the loo."

"I mean Teilhard. Did you get in touch with him in New York, Ken?"

"Sir Gavin talked with him."

"And? Come on. Did he make a complete confession?"

"We had hoped to get some more specific information about the finds at Sheffield Park, but he'd never been there."

"Or so he said."

"And that's all he said?"

"He said he didn't believe either Woodward or Dawson was the forger," Oakley replied.

"Why would he want to put himself in such a position of jeopardy?" said Brewer.

"I wonder whether Catholics consider professional suicide a sin?" Hobhouse asked.

"With Woodward and Dawson dead, he knew he would be the prime suspect if the fraud was ever uncovered," Knowles declared. "He'd had a lot of time to think it through."

"Assuming he knew about the fraud," Hobhouse warned, with an admonishing finger. "But if he didn't, when Sir Gavin told him, he wouldn't have had any time to think about it. If Teilhard is completely innocent, then his initial reaction might be to suspect them, or suspect someone else, as we have. Both Woodward and Dawson were extremely important to his early career; he wouldn't want to irresponsibly malign either of them."

"But it is equally true that he was important to their careers," Knowles said, wanting to punch a hole in Hobhouse's theory. "Before the discovery of Piltdown Man, Dawson had a local reputation in Sussex; Woodward was a drone in the hive of the BMNH. They only became famous after the Piltdown discovery. Consider this: Teilhard needed a start. It would have been too dangerous for him to do the forgery alone; his youth, his nationality, his religion were against him. He had the best motive in the world. Ambition. But he was clever enough to realize it would be better to put himself on the periphery of events. A relatively small step for a beginner was better than no step at all. It's not unfair to say that Teilhard's subsequent career was built on the cornerstone of his connection to Piltdown."

Carr glanced at Oakley, who sat on the couch staring morosely into the bottom of his half-finished drink. "Enough," Carr declared. "We're no closer to solving the mystery now than we were at the start. Case dismissed for lack of evidence." He went up to Phillips and began telling him some university scandal, ripe enough so that several other guests joined them, and soon they were engaged in the usual exchange of academic trivia. At last, even Oakley began to brighten, accepting a refill from Carr.

Phillips had been drinking steadily, taking tiny but frequent birdlike sips from his glass. His speech was slurred, and he was making a terrible muddle of it trying to explain to Brewer the principle of reptilian flight embodied in his beloved pterodactyl. To illustrate more graphically, Phillips began to move his arms in odd, jerky motions, flapping the long sleeves of his academic gown, and to hop about making high-pitched squawkings. In his enthusiastic demonstration he stumbled against the table where the Piltdown corpse lay in state. The skull fell to the floor and broke into pieces.

The only sound was the hissing of the gas fire; the shocked silence continued while everyone stared at the smashed cast until Ian Carr stepped forward and picked up the top of the plaster skull.

" 'A fellow of infinite jest, of most excellent fancy,' " he said, striking a theatrical pose. He laughed ironically, but the guests remained silent. Rueful looks were exchanged in common agreement that the Piltdown forger had duped them all, that Piltdown Man had been the subject of incalculable wasted time and effort, that the forgery was the grossest perversion of the quest for truth. The party was over.

Chapter II

CHARLES DAWSON GATHERED HIS GREATCOAT CLOSER TO him and sank back in the seat of the cab as it pulled away from Victoria Station. It was late in the afternoon, already dark, a week before Christmas, a time of expectation. Dawson's own movement of fulfillment was only hours away, not from something he would receive, but rather something he was about to give—to the holiday shoppers struggling with parcels, the clerks and company managers making their way to the station, even the shivering boys hawking papers. Dawson's great discovery would belong to all of them.

Next to him in the traffic jam a horse-drawn van fought with a motorcar, the horse's breath mixing with the acrid exhaust fumes, the van's driver shouting insults from beneath his muffler. The shops across the broad intersection of streets facing the station blazed with electric lights, silhouetting some shoppers, illuminating others. Women picked up their skirts as they tiptoed in the half-frozen mud of the street. A few hardy omnibus riders who couldn't elbow inside the lurching double-deckers sat huddled on the open tops, the sky above them threatening snow, livid in the glow of the city.

Dawson watched out the taxi window. With profound satisfaction he thought that by the next day, these Londoners and every Englishman to the last village yeoman would have a common ancestor, the father of their race, of Man himself.

The newspapers would call the national progenitor Darwin's Missing Link, but Dawson's discovery, the great patriarch, bore the scientific name *Eoanthropus dawsoni*, Dawson's Dawn Man.

The cab made its way behind the Palace. Dawson didn't know George V's views on evolution, but he pictured his sovereign the next morning, a dozen goose-down pillows behind his head in a gigantic gilt bed hung with scarlet Venetian damask, sipping tea and reading the paper, mulling over the fact that he too had descended from an ape-man. Dawson allowed himself to think of the possibility of a royal audience. As the cab picked up speed through the grandiose vistas of Pall Mall and then turned into St. James's toward Piccadilly, he lay back in a delicious reverie of fame. He was not foolishly beguiled by the idea of celebrity for its own sake, although perhaps more than other men Dawson craved attention. The value of fame, like money, depended on how one used it, and for what purposes.

"A'right, Guv. Burlington House," said the cabbie over his shoulder.

By the time the program was about to begin at the Geological Society, every seat in the large lecture room was filled, with the overflow audience standing at the rear. Geologists, paleontologists, distinguished invited guests from the scientific world and representatives of the press already knew for some weeks of the sensational fossil finds made at Piltdown. December 18, 1912, was the occasion of the official announcement of the discovery of the earliest and most significant hominid fossil known, the first evidence that humanlike creatures lived in England. The stage was set with a lectern and a slide screen. As Dawson and Woodward entered from the wings, the audience began to applaud. Each spectator, singly or together, seemed to realize the momentousness of the event, and the applause, instead of dying away, increased until the hall rose to its feet.

As both Dawson and Woodward were Fellows of the Society, they were accompanied by Sir Geoffrey Stills, its president, and Woodward's professional affiliation was represented by Sir Ray Lankester, superintendent of the British

Museum of Natural History. Both attendants had decided that no other supporting players were needed to share the stage, to avoid hurt feelings of those left out of a larger group, and to conserve whatever advantage accrued to themselves from proximity to the speakers. It was an unavoidable ritual that each would make introductory remarks, the former acting as guide on an overlong trot through the history of British science—adding Dawson and Woodward to the company of Newton, Darwin, Farraday, and others—while the latter recapitulated the achievements of the museum since it had become a separate entity from the British Museum in Bloomsbury. A restive sigh through the auditorium brought Sir Ray back to the events at hand.

Arthur Smith Woodward stepped to the lectern to further applause. He was middle-aged, wearing a white goatee and gold-rimmed pince-nez glasses that seemed as much a part of him as his beard. His bald head gleamed in the overhead light as he bent to arrange the pages of his written talk in a neat pile, slightly feathered so that the pages could be turned without hesitation as he spoke. The white wing collar of his shirt was a trifle too large for his neck, but his suit was well cut, almost black worsted. He was a model of Edwardian scientific probity.

"Lights please," he said, and the clusters of milk glass globes on their curved brass sconces were switched off. Then he squeezed a little metal device in his hand that made a sharp click-click, and the first slide appeared on the screen. The reading light on the podium reflected off the white typescript. In the darkened room he was nothing but a head and shirtfront.

Behind Woodward was a projection of a fossil hippopotamus tooth, the first of a series of animal remains, including the teeth of a deer, beaver, and horse found at the site, that dated the Dawn Man of Sussex to the Early Ice Age. Woodward quickly flashed photographs of fossil elephant, mastodon, and rhinoceros teeth, completing his Pleistocene menagerie. He spoke in a monotone, only looking up from his paper to check that the correct slide appeared on the screen. His voice never varied, even when he came to the hominid remains themselves: nine cranial pieces and the jawbone, a fragment broken off at the middle of the chin and just above and behind the two remaining back molars which were still in place.

Each piece of the skull was carefully considered, Woodward pointing out that the pieces were unusually thick. The jaw was essentially apelike, except for the particular condition of the molar teeth. They were worn flat, Woodward pointed out, and had "a marked regular flattening such as has never been observed in apes, though it is occasionally met with in low types of men."

Finally Woodward presented a picture of the skull restored. The cranium rose in a smooth curve from the brows in an obviously human manner. The lower part of the face was clearly snoutish. The reconstruction of the brain case was provisional, but the brain capacity was well within the human range. Owing to the secure dating through association faunal remains, the thick though humanoid skull, and the transitional nature of the jaw and teeth, what they had before them was a new genus and species of man, which would be named in honor of its discoverer, Charles Dawson.

Woodward looked up briefly at his audience and nodded several times to show he had finished. Then he stepped away from the lectern to applause as Dawson took center stage.

Dawson would often fall into physical attitudes that looked like poses, as he did on the stage, grasping the sides of the lectern as if taking command at the wheel of a ship. But his stances came from a natural physical self-assurance rather than from studied theatricality. He was a big man with square shoulders and an athletic torso, rugged and rough-hewn. Dawson filled the space around him with the largeness of his gestures and the resonance of his voice. Looking directly at the audience, and speaking without notes, he began in an easy, anecdotal style.

"I was walking along a farm road close to Piltdown when I noticed that the road had been mended with some peculiar brown flint nodules not usual to the district. And I was astonished to learn that they had been dug from a gravel bed at Barkham Manor. The workmen there had found no bones or fossils or anything of the sort, but I urged them to preserve anything they might find.'' He paused to listen to the eager silence that begged him to continue. ''The discovery of *Eoanthropus dawsoni* began on a false note of hope, because the first find at the site given me by the workmen proved to be a piece of a modern skull. But the flints, which I recognized as paleoliths of human manufacture, gave me hope that hominid remains might be found. I pressed forward with my own digging, and at last I was rewarded. The moment is forever fixed in my memory. It was at the end of another fruitless day. My back ached, and the cold rain blowing from the southern coast chilled me to the bone, seeming to reproach me for my vainglorious hope. But there, in the gathering darkness as I sifted another spade of gravel, I saw it: the first cranial fragment. I held the great treasure in my hand,'' Dawson continued, stepping away from the lectern to be fully visible to the audience, and looking down into his cupped palm, ''and I began to shudder—not from the cold, but from inexpressible excitement, from the sense that I had, in an instant, been carried back through eons of time, to the beginning of humanity. This then was the first man, the first Englishman. I do not know how long I remained thus, heedless of the rain. It was only the bell from a nearby church ringing evensong that brought me back to my own world.'' Dawson could see the first few rows in the lecture room where the men in uniform gray suits looked up at him with the rapt attention of children listening to a fairy tale. He then stepped back to the lectern and continued. ''Dr. Woodward, to whom I sent my first discoveries, concurred in my opinion as to their age and importance, and agreed to work with me. His optimism never wavered, nor did his energies flag during the long hours working with me in the gravel pit, even when nothing came to light. I also wish to thank the other participant in the dig, Pierre Teilhard de Chardin, Society of Jesus, whose youthful enthusiasm buoyed us throughout; the flint he discovered will be among the group I am about to discuss.''

Dawson's analysis of the Piltdown flints was brilliant in detail, impressive in the depth and scope of his experience as an archaeologist and collector. The Dawn Man's flaked tools were compared with examples from his own extensive collection, analyzed as to the method of manufacture, use, and their relationship as prototypes to other specimens of later periods. By the time Dawson was through, he had made a convincing case that the Dawn Man was a veritable Daedalus. Dawson smiled with unconcealed pleasure as the waves of applause swept toward him and broke like a warm surf.

As was usual at such occasions, questions were invited from the floor by Sir Geoffrey. After a silence, there were a few nit-picking queries about the faunal remains and the flints; the Dawn Man, by some unspoken agreement was beyond question, above criticism. Sir Geoffrey looked complacently into the lecture room and was about to adjourn for refreshments when a man rose near the rear of the auditorium.

"If I may raise a point?" Grafton Elliot Smith said. The celebrated professor of anatomy from Manchester University answered his own question by saying, "I was struck, as we all were, by Dr. Woodward's and Mr. Dawson's presentation. It almost seems as if the Dawn Man of Piltdown stands among us, so vividly has he been conjured. But I would recommend caution before any of us attempt to reach out and touch him. The restoration of the skull fragments is, I admit, inventive, but I would like to suggest that there may be two individuals here. Not one, but two. That is to say, a human cranium and ape's jaw, two fossils brought together in the Piltdown gravels by a geological accident." Elliot Smith looked around the murmuring audience. There were hostile eyes on him, but there was also the level gaze of his allies, whom he had already told of his planned attack.

Dawson rose quickly to his feet and approached the podium. "The academic side of anatomical paleontology has much to contribute, but all paleontology begins in the field, in this case the gravel beds at Piltdown, which my learned colleague from Manchester has yet to visit, a situation I hope he will rectify at his earliest convenience. Such a visit would add immeasurably to his knowledge and afford an opportunity to enjoy the outdoors. Geological accidents such as he describes do happen, but the proximity of the jaw to the skull fragments found in the same stratum absolutely preclude such

an explanation. Moreover, I must point out that all the specimens recovered at Piltdown are identically colored by the
iron-rich gravels and the fossils are in the same state of
mineralization. There is no doubt that they form a geological
unity.'' There were sibilant whispers of agreement from the
audience. ''But I must, in the final analysis, address myself
to the physical characteristics of *E. dawsoni* himself,'' Dawson continued. ''It is an irrefutable fact that the molar teeth
are worn in a manner never seen in apes. And this hominid
transitional feature of the teeth is reiterated in the skull—its
human form contrasted with its thickness.'' Dawson leaned
forward over the reading light and squinted toward the back
of the room in a way that suggested Smith's intellectual stat-
ure made him difficult to see. ''This is not the time to make a
more detailed rebuttal to my learned colleague's remarks, but
if he would be kind enough to put his objections to paper and
is able to find a journal that will print them, we will read his
comments with the sort of attention they deserve.''

Sir Geoffrey looked anxiously at Dawson and brought the
discussion period quickly to a close by announcing that mulled
wine and punch, in honor of the occasion and the holiday
season, would be served in an adjoining reception room.

As Dawson and Woodward were leaving the stage, Woodward said quietly to him, ''I don't think you should have
been so antagonistic.''

''To whom?'' Dawson replied with a look of wide-eyed
innocence. ''I was simply stating the facts fairly and squarely.''

''You should have let me do it.''

''What rubbish, Arthur. You would have made a mess of
it.'' They were walking down a corridor to the reception
room.

''Smith is dangerous enough without being provoked.''

''Controversy is good, especially when one's on the right
side. One always wins, and that's lovely. Let him babble in
the wilderness about his two individuals.''

Dawson entered the reception room and immediately attracted a crowd of well-wishers, who trailed after him like
the wake of a ship as he saluted others to the right and left.
Woodward was momentarily abandoned at the threshold but

was approached by Ray Lankester. The superintendent was mountainous, one of the wonders of Savile Row, a street largely inured to the ostentations of human form. His large head was mounted on a squat plinth of jowls and a neck that all but covered his collar. Only his features were small, crowded into the center of his face by the surrounding flesh. He took Woodward in hand, grabbing him by the forearm, holding him like a trophy.

That evening, for the first time in Woodward's professional life, he did not have to make his way like a needy vagabond, peering over high fences of backs and shoulders. It was not that he lacked respect for his knowledge or scientific achievements, but rather it was his manner that palled. He did not know how to be comfortable with other men. Now a renowned paleontologist from Cambridge, who scarcely acknowledged him a month before, was speaking to him with sudden familiarity. Woodward listened, knowing that others hovered nearby waiting like moths to get closer to the flame of his new distinction. Woodward had never shrunk from exercising his authority at the museum strictly within the limits that bureaucracy defined. But his eminence would set him apart from the structure of power and hierarchy, now that others of greater professional status sought him out. He was cautious in his response, taking his pleasure inwardly, hoping that his associates might report to each other that his celebrity had not gone to his head. He knew they had found his reserve and correctness unattractive, perhaps even unmanly. Now they might accept his primness as a personal quirk, in the English tradition of friendly tolerance toward great eccentrics; Woodward didn't like admitting he sought affection as well as esteem.

Dawson staked out a position close to the wine and punch. He occupied himself exclusively with the newspaper reporters, who could interview him and refill their cups without inconvenience. He was more expansive and hail-fellow than usual, democratically attentive to the tabloids and to the closely set newspapers that disdained headlines and halftones. Whether the story would be read over coffee sipped from a Spode cup in Belgravia or eventually used to wrap a pound of onions in Covent Garden made no difference to Dawson. He meant the public, high and low alike, to be an operatic crowd in the spectacle of his success. As the reporters' questions came too fast to be answered properly, Dawson got out a small appointment book and scheduled private interviews.

The room was filled with the loud rumble of male talk and laughter, groups forming, then breaking apart, re-forming, except for Elliot Smith and his faction, who remained aloof. Many of the Piltdown supporters thought they had a lot of cheek to attend a celebration they meant to spoil by taking an untenable and mean-spirited position contradicted by every bit of evidence the earth had finally yielded to Dawson's and Woodward's heroic efforts. It was bad science and shockingly bad taste.

One man stood sulkily against a fluted half-column that rose between the windows of the room, grinding his teeth in resentment. Arthur Keith had managed a fixed smile as he had offered his most cordial best wishes to both Dawson and Woodward. As keeper of the paleontological collections of the Hunterian Museum, Royal College of Surgeons, Keith was furious that Dawson hadn't brought the Piltdown specimens to him, rather than to Woodward. He would have stood at the podium that night instead of that goateed little martinet. The way Dawson preened was beyond bearing. What a pair, Keith thought bitterly, unable to decide which of them he most despised. Woodward had deliberately slighted him by telling him of the important finds a mere two weeks before the official announcement, and then had only allowed him a scant twenty minutes with the fossils before whisking them back into the museum's vaults. Keith felt cheated and humiliated, yet he also knew that there was great professional advantage to be gained by close association with Piltdown Man. As an expert in fossil human skulls, he would find a way to make himself useful. He would toady to Woodward now, ingratiate himself, swallow his wounded pride.

As the reception ended with final handshakes and congratulations, Woodward realized that he and Dawson hadn't exchanged a word. Looking around the room, Woodward

saw Dawson leaving with a theatrical gesture and an exit line
he was too far away to hear. Knowing Charles, Woodward
thought he had some motive for ignoring him all evening,
but Charles would say, if accused of negligence, "But my
dear Arthur, you had only to come up to me. If only you had,
I might have had some relief from those newspaper fellows. I
did all the work tonight for both of us while you feathered, or
fouled, your academic nest; don't deny it, you ungrateful
wretch."

Woodward got his black Chesterfield from the cloakroom
and stepped into the courtyard of Burlington House, surrounded on three sides by Neo-Georgian facades, soot-streaked
and clammy. The great black cast iron gates to the street
were closed. A watchman in a brown oilskin touched his cap
to Woodward and let him out a small side gate into Piccadilly. It wasn't until Woodward had gone a considerable
distance toward Green Park underground station that he allowed himself to turn up the collar against the cold. He was
let down, depressed to become an anonymous figure in the
night. Maud would be waiting in Fulham.

When Arthur Smith Woodward married Maud Seeley, there
was some speculation among their acquaintances. That the
bride's father was a scientist of considerable repute was
regarded either as a natural consequence of Woodward's
professional life or an astute political maneuver by the groom.
A prim bachelor matched with a formidable spinster, who
was her widowed father's companion and housekeeper, had a
certain symmetry, but it remained unclear who benefited
most: Woodward from the domestic convenience and professional connections, or Maud, married at last with all the
inestimable, if tardy, advantages. "Well, after all, why not?"—
or some variation, was the comment most often heard. But
there were a few acquaintances, a shade more acute, more
curious about uninteresting events, who allowed to themselves (because they were sure no one else would care) that
there was something more between Arthur and Maud, a
matching beyond appearances.

When they first met, Maud looked to Arthur magnificently
threatening, wearing an oversized hat the chief ornament of

which was a large bird, its wings set in flight as on the helmet of a valkyrie. He'd wanted to talk with her father, but there she was. Maud was certain she saw him shrink from her, and then she held him in an orbit, manageable, acquiescent at a distance.

The fire was inadequate in the Woodwards' parlor, and Maud wore a paisley wool robe pulled high at her throat over a flannel nightgown. While she waited for Arthur, she occupied herself with her needlework, her workbox beside her on a japanned table inlaid with mother-of-pearl. As she studied the skeins of colored silk, the intensity of her gaze, resolved one moment, uncertain the next, emphasized the severity of her features—a beak nose, heavily drawn eyebrows, a wide thin mouth. Her hair was loosely bound so that the gray at her temples looked like wisps of smoke.

Soon after she married Arthur, Maud bought a delightful puppy, which quickly grew into a mastiff, aggressively male in his physique and trained to unquestioning devotion. Samson lay beside the armchair, opening his eyes to look at the coals in the grate whenever the wind rattled a shutter or the house creaked.

Maud didn't do needlework as an idle pastime. There were no worked cushions in the parlor or stitched mottoes in the kitchen. As a child she had learned the art only to satisfy the requirements of her genteel education. She had mastered a little simplified Schubert for the piano and memorized high-toned poetry without a whimper. But she had cried with frustration when the needle refused to follow the printed outline on a sampler or when the thread caught in perverse and maddening tangles. Her mother tried to comfort her by saying that one day she would be thankful for the skill. Maud hadn't dared express her doubt, and she was glad she hadn't. The maternal advice had been correct, but her mother couldn't have foreseen to what ingenious end Maud's adult needle would be put as she made determined little stabs at the drumhead of white linen stretched on a round embroidery frame.

It was a tea cloth, thirty-six inches square, that lay across her lap. Whenever the Woodwards entertained scientific visitors, some of them were asked to sign their names on it. Then Maud stitched over the signatures. She used a simple running stitch for the small ones, to get the fine curves and flourishes just right, and a thicker chain stitch for the larger ones. She had long discussions with Arthur about who would be allowed to sign and who would not, and having decided that, she tormented herself and him about the color of the embroidery silk. The color was based on her insight into the signer's character. After discussing the implications of green or red for a particular guest, Maud might choose blue, telling Arthur he had neither taste nor psychological insight. The matter didn't rest there; the question of what sort of blue carried even greater weight. Blue people might have affinities, like those under the same sign of the zodiac, but the small niceties of character—and manners—expressible in Wedgewood, turquoise, or robin's egg, were what really mattered. And since once signed and stitched, the signatures could not be erased, her choices and decisions were made with the greatest care. After the Piltdown announcement, Maud looked forward to being more selective. She could imagine the tea cloth as a social register and she the sole arbiter of acceptability.

When Maud heard the key in the lock, she set aside her work. Samson stirred.

Woodward entered, sniffing back the wetness of his nose and reaching for his handkerchief as if she had admonished him to use it.

From her seat Maud gestured to a decanter of sherry on a cabinet. Woodward poured two glasses, giving her one and then sitting down some distance from her on a settee.

"Sir Ray was very pleased."

"In what way?"

"You know Sir Ray. It's not what he says, exactly."

Maud nodded. "What about the department? Now is the time to get more money for research publication."

"But the trustees don't meet for months."

"I know when the trustees meet."

"Charles was having a field day with the press," Woodward said.

Maud disliked Dawson. It offended her, the way he lounged
on the furniture, as if it were made for comfort. Arthur and
he had often worked together in Fulham during the last
months before the announcement. As Dawson came and
went, he spoke to her with loud familiarity, showing no more
deference to her than to their Irish servant girl. Maud would
occasionally find him looking at her with something resem-
bling amusement, as if she were of no consequence, as if, for
all her corseted bearing, commanding profile, and firmness
of manner, she was powerless. She couldn't risk asking
Arthur whether Dawson spoke to him of her without acknowledging she was concerned.

Maud ignored the mention of Dawson as irrelevant. Instead, she pressed Arthur, questioning him closely about the
tone and quality of what had been said to him. Her questions
were coldly stated, as if she were reading them from a
prepared examination, ticking them off before moving on to
the next. Her voice was even, her responses noncommittal.
Woodward replied with carefully worded answers, anxiously
watching her from across the room.

There was about him, he sensed, an aura of guilt, of
having grossly erred. Inevitably he would incriminate himself. He felt in the presence of a grand inquisitor, blocking his
escape, meeting every protestation with an implacable indict-
ment. If he said he believed, the quality of his belief was
flawed; if his sincerity of belief was unquestionable, he had
nevertheless committed grave doctrinal errors; if he thought
himself both devout and doctrinaire, then his supposed excel-
lence was a delusion of ignorant pride.

"What about Keith?"

"He was cordial enough, considering."

"You spoke to him?"

"I had to. He came up to me."

"Was Hennessey there?"

"It was the first time he talked to me."

"What did he want?"

"He wants me to come down to Cambridge to give a
lecture."

"And what did you say?"

"I said . . ."

"Yes?"

"I said I would be delighted," Woodward replied, making an effort to keep looking at her.

Maud sat as straight as a Byzantine icon, her hands resting symmetrically on the arms of the chair. A fragile ghost of a log in the fireplace collapsed, revealing its inner orange glow. Woodward's gaze flicked toward the embers, then back to Maud. She rose, the deep folds of her robe falling from her broad, square shoulders.

"You should have extracted an acknowledgement of your work from Sir Ray. Then you could have asked for an expansion of the department and its activities—and of your own authority. Allowing Keith to speak to you was a serious error. You must learn to cut people. They will respect you for it. As for Hennessey, and anyone else who wants you to speak, you must not commit yourself without a formal request in writing."

Woodward dared not tell her of the applause in the auditorium, and later the pleasure of being sought out, courted.

It seemed she read his mind. "They may have considered you a very great man tonight, but I know the truth."

"Yes, you know the truth."

"That you are weak and feckless."

"I am weak and feckless." He accepted as an inevitability her determination to nullify his triumph. She nodded in agreement, but he knew she was not yet satisfied.

Maud moved across the room, through the double doors, and up the stairs with the dog at her heel. As Woodward followed, he watched Samson's waggling haunches and the sack of egg-sized testicles swinging between his sinewy thighs.

There were two bedrooms, a master bedroom and another that Woodward occupied. Instead of going to his own room, he accompanied Maud.

The zigzag pattern of the bedspread of the four-poster imitated flame stitching. There was a large armoire of tigerwood veneer, the door slightly ajar. A tall baluster urn with a mottled, liverish glaze filled with dried cattails stood on the floor. The room was chilly and damp despite the heavy brown velours curtains drawn across the window. The air smelled of stale talcum and underwear.

Woodward remained standing in the middle of the room. Maud, with a deliberate stateliness, went to the dressing table, removed the few pins from her hair, and fanned the coarse mane through her fingers. She turned, approaching Samson, bending toward him as she indulgently scratched behind his ear and stroked the sleek hair of his neck. He yawned, stretched languidly, and composed himself on the floor at the foot of the bed. Woodward had not moved as she removed her robe, draped it over the counterpane, stepped out of her slippers and got into bed.

"Kneel," she commanded.

Woodward dropped to his knees.

Maud satisfied herself that, apart from his posture, he wore an expression of complete subservience and contrition; then she reached for the bed lamp and lay back on the pillow.

The room went black, but after a while Woodward could make out the dim form of his wife lying in state like a stone tomb figure perfectly composed with her hands folded outside the sheets. He must kneel there until she was asleep. He knew when she slept by her regular breathing, then the slow crescendo of her snoring to which Samson was a nightly long-suffering audience.

Kneeling in the dark, Woodward wondered, as he had before, whether Maud had the imagination to take her domination of him to the farthest extreme, to rewrite the drama in its true form, to act out fully the encounter they only hinted at to each other. He could make out the form of the vase with its jutting cattails. He had counted them once. There were nine, and he wondered whether Maud was making a sinister little joke, a pun, a promise. He hoped she would eventually become dissatisfied with alluding to their potential. He wanted to believe that her full capacity for domination lay just beyond the horizon of her consciousness.

At last he got up, backed toward the door, and with the stealth of a burglar, went to his own room.

It was so difficult to imagine pain—so vivid and immediate in actuality, so abstract in memory. Methodically, with his characteristic attention to detail, he adjusted a looking glass on a stand to a slightly downward angle. Going to a bookshelf, he removed three volumes and took a small bottle and a cotton swab from the hiding place and put them on the floor.

Woodward took off his trousers and carefully folded them on a chair. He left on his shirt, tie, and collar, his jacket and vest. Owing to the season, he wore long knit underwear, with black lisle socks and garters over them. He kept them on with his polished black shoes. The underwear hung loosely and sagged at his crotch.

He stood with his back to the mirror, quite close, and went down on his elbows and knees. Then, reaching back with one hand he unsnapped the back flap, exposing the white globes of his buttocks. Everything was in readiness.

Uncorking the bottle, Woodward dipped the swab into it, and wiping off the excess on the rim, he reached back and drew the swab across his buttocks, repeating this again and again, feeling the thin, cool stripes of wetness. Quickly closing the bottle, he got down on his elbows, his rump high in the air, and turned to observe himself in the mirror. He began to breathe deeply with excited anticipation. It would be a few moments before the solution of caustic soda would begin to work.

First a tingling, an irritation. As he watched with lewd fascination, the pale pink slashes appeared, etching his white skin, gradually deepening to rubicund, tumid welts with an intensification of pain, burning with the sting of a thousand nettles. His exposed buttocks began to throb with pain, as if under the rhythmic blows of a whip. He watched the shameful, obscene, and putrid vista that begged chastisement—his butt, his bum, his fundament, his shithole. Behind him in the reflected darkness the walls of the small room seemed to dissolve; there was a tremendous clamor, a roaring crowd of taunting voices damning him, demanding submission. Finally, a towering figure emerged from the teeming nocturnal obscurity to the edge of the light that shone on his exposed twin orbs. Maud wore her hat, and the bird was alive, a falcon, its glossy wings twitching, its eyes glittering malignantly in expectation of tearing at his flesh. Maud's square shoulders and muscular arms were bare,and she wore a black costume flashing with sequins and jet beads, a lurid apparition he'd called up out of a dream circus. The brim of her hat partially obscured her face, but he could see her mouth set in a thin line under her magnificent black moustache.

The searing pain intensified, nearing the point where he knew it would be transformed by erotic alchemy. The vision in the mirror took another step forward, and she raised her brawny arm to show him the cat-o'-nine-tails. She tested it once in the air, making a sound like the sharp intake of breath. His cheeks flamed with shame and expectation. Fixing him with obsidian eyes, Maud raised the scourge above her head. He could see the thick patch of hair in her armpit every time she poised for the blow, before the whip cut into his flesh.

Chapter III

THE LANDSCAPE OF EAST SUSSEX BETWEEN LEWES AND Uckfield is heaven as private property. Even the county locals, who may never have seen anything as foreign and as beautiful as Surrey, are certain that other claims to perfection of earth and sky are misguided and parochial chauvinism. One of the hills on the rolling downs may rise inordinately, but only to afford a perfect view from its crest of the decorous grandeur of the rest of the countryside—receding pastures woven back and forth with dark hedgerows as if by a shuttle. Herds of Southdown sheep, dense white packages attentively munching at the grass, wander like woolly angels in the meadows. East Sussex may seem like a work of Nature in a felicitious mood, but the downs owe their open and inviting placidity to generations of woodcutters, herdsmen, and plowmen who cleared the gentle slopes and shallow valleys of virgin forests since the arrival of Neolithic farmers some six millenia ago.

It was from the continuing works of men that Charles Dawson had his livelihood. As a solicitor, a partner in the firm of Dawson & Hart in Uckfield, he skillfully attended to the conflicts and misunderstandings arising from deeds and land titles, drew contracts and prepared for the legal consequences of mortality among the prosperous landowners, tradesmen, and industrialists of the neighborhood. Sir Percy

Maryon-Wilson, lord of Barkham Manor, had appointed Dawson steward, with responsibilities of general management and yearly accountings. Sir Percy and the Kenwards, the chief tenant family who lived in the manor house, were among the many clients who looked upon Dawson with respect as a solicitor and with puzzled interest at his passion for anything dug out of the ground. When the workmen at the manor found what they thought was a piece of a coconut shell, an agricultural object exotic to the countryside, it was natural that they saved it to show Dawson when he made one of his periodical visits.

Dawson practiced law with his partner, John Hart, in commodious offices just off the top of the High Street. In the beginning they had faced each other across a large partners' desk, but Hart, a man with neat ways, was continually encroached upon by Dawson's mess of law books, crumpled sheets of foolscap, small floods from overturned inkwells and dirt-encrusted geological oddities. After Hart realized that he would forever have to work from the narrow edge of his side of the desk, he retired from the field with good grace to an adjoining office formerly occupied by several clerks. Hart knew that Dawson brought business to the firm with his forthright manner, his ability to talk with easy familiarity to landowners and bricklayers alike, while Dawson knew he needed Hart to dot the I's and cross the T's. Hart never objected when Dawson left the office to pursue his geological interests, while Dawson never needed to tell Hart of his absences.

Each workday morning Dawson set out from Lewes to Uckfield, eight miles away on a short trunk of British Rail's Southern Region from London, which terminated at the seaside less than an hour further south at Brighton. The station master, lanky in his rusty frock coat and top hat, with a schedule on a clipboard and pocket watch as the emblems of his dominion, looked after the passengers under the cast-iron loggia while they waited for the train, and his adolescent assistant in a lesser uniform of cap, jacket, and Eton collar swept the platform and stoked the waiting-room stove in bad weather. Once out of the station the locomotive and its few carriages passed the lumberyards and sawmills by the bridge over the River Ouse. In the distance were signs of the newest industry in the county—the chalk pits cutting deeper every year into the sides of the hills, white wounds where the chalk had been carried away in three-wheeled carts to be burnt for lime, plaster, and cement. Between the towns Dawson knew the acreage and boundaries of every field and pasture, and who owned them. At one time or another he had been in every cottage and manor house, and attended every church, not from religious scruples, but only to witness the rites of a late client whose survivors would note his presence.

Dawson was a paleontologist by avocation but was not a scientific dabbler whose later eminence was considered a stroke of luck. He knew the country's eons of history below the surface as he knew it lying comfortably green and fertile against the sky. Where the workmen blasted and gouged at the chalk pits near Lewes and the limestone quarries as far as Hastings, Dawson made fine collections of fossils. He knew the courses of the narrow rivers that dawdled southward toward the Channel as he knew their ancient beds now far afield, sites strewn with smooth riverine flint nodules, some as big as melons, some gravels smaller than cherry pits. The glass-front vitrines in his study contained an encyclopedic collection of ancient artifacts made from these flints—scrapers, hand axes, and weapon points. For years before the discovery of Piltdown Man, Dawson had trekked with an observant eye back and forth between promising geological sites in Sussex. At twenty-one he had been made a Fellow of the Geological Society, and by 1908 he had already donated a significant collection of fossils to the British Museum in South Kensington, including several new species of dinosaurs and an early mammal, species which bore the philogenic surname *dawsoni*. These fossils were given into the safekeeping of the young Arthur Smith Woodward, who had been named a Fellow of the Society the same year as Dawson.

Dawson woke up one summer morning to a bright cloudless sky and decided that he would devote the afternoon to geology. After a morning of case law and codicils in his office, and an unusually large lunch of rabbit pie, a thick slice of cheddar, and some greengage plums to fortify himself for his walk, he changed from his business suit into a soft collarless shirt, linen trousers, and a pair of stout walking shoes he kept in a cupboard. The rucksack he slung over his shoulder contained a small pick, a magnifying glass, a leather case of rather surgical-looking steel tools for delicate work, some soft brushes, and wrapping material for specimens. He also put in a crock of lager against the heat. His destination was east of town, a chalk outcropping, too small for commercial exploitation, that was a trove of fossil sea urchins, bivalves, and antediluvian fish.

Dawson stepped out onto the cobblestones and turned into the top of the High Street. He briefly looked down the hill past the row of shops to the railway to Lewes. Then he turned and continued in the opposite direction. Within a few blocks he was on the unpaved road flanked by woods and pastures. Soon he sidestepped between some brambles into a small rutted lane and cut across the downs toward higher ground. Thoughts of the Party of the First Part vanished as he strode in the thick grass. Standing in the middle of the hill to gauge his progress, he could see below him the ribbon of buildings along the High Street, the towers of the Low and High churches, and the smoking stacks of the factories beyond the station that reminded him that others were still at work. Dawson continued on with an expectation of finding something wonderful. The sky was cerulean with occasional feathers of clouds. The air hummed with summer insects; grasshoppers fled in panic from his hiking boots.

He walked for the better part of an hour, sometimes making his way across pastures of bleating sheep, or following the narrow dirt roads. At the edge of a lazy stream overhung with pale cascading willows and opulent arrangments of ferns, Dawson paused in the shade. Rolling up his sleeves, he splashed his arms and face with water and sat in the hissing silence with his crock of beer. He drank and watched a ladybug going about an inexplicable errand, and then with unthinking contentment he leaped the stream in one bound and made his way through the filigree of leaves and vines once more into the sunlight.

The sweat trickled down his open collar as Dawson made his way to the top of a knoll. Unexpectedly, in the shade of a row of trees was a woman. He knew Arabella Spence by sight from Uckfield and had always thought her attractive when they had nodded to each other in the street. She sat on a small folding stool, her head bent toward a tablet of paper balanced lightly on her knees, a half-finished watercolor view of the countryside. Next to her was a paint box and a jar of water. Her dress, gauzy yellow muslin, fluttered in the gentle breeze, and the golden ringlets of her hair, usually well-coiffed in town, blew freely, a miraculous fleece about her shoulders. Dawson thought her the loveliest thing he had ever encountered. If he had known French painting, she would have been a Fragonard, spit and image. He was transfixed, not daring to move, so that he might hold the moment everlastingly.

Arabella was startled, then recognized him. "Mr. Dawson!" Getting up, she knocked over her water.

At first he could not speak, but finally rushed to her. "Oh, Mrs. Spence. Look what I've made you do."

"There's a bit left. Enough to finish my picture. But what are you doing so far in the country?"

Dawson wanted to say that fate had brought him to that spot. "I was on my way to the chalk pits near Buckham Hill."

"Ah, yes. I have heard of your interest in digging."

"I didn't know you were a painter," Dawson replied, thrilling that she knew something of his life.

"My amateurish daubs."

"Not at all. You've got it exactly." He moved closer to be more specific about her artistic skills. "Those birches, the way they, I don't know, stand out."

Arabella smiled approval of his critique. She seemed to emanate a warmth, even in the heat of the summer afternoon. He noticed that her muslin dress clung to her breasts and a few strands of wet hair made bronze whiplash curves and volutes against the column of neck. Looking more closely at the picture, Dawson brought his face as close to hers as he dared. A sudden breeze drew a lock of her hair across his cheek. He wanted to say something more about the picture, but his throat tightened, and his mouth was dry with longing.

"The hardest part is there," Arabella said to the horizon, then to her unfinished picture. "The way the earth and the sky blend in a mystic union."

"Let me watch you work."

"Oh, I couldn't possibly."

But Dawson prevailed and sat beside her on the ground. He watched as Arabella worried at the leaves of a tree she had placed in the left foreground, according to the laws of landscape painting. Occasionally she would cock her head at her work, frown, and look out over the green and golden vista. After a time, she said, "I can talk and work at the same time."

Dawson, marveling at her cleverness and the perfectly modulated flush of her cheeks, asked, "Did you walk all the way from town?"

"Heavens no. My dog cart is just there," she replied, pointing down the hill. "On the road, beyond those trees. Colin rather disapproves of my excursions. He says that he would suspect I had gypsy blood in me, if I weren't so fair."

Dawson thought: Behold you are beautiful, my love, behold, you are beautiful! Your eyes are like doves. And then she would say to him: The voice of my beloved! Behold he comes, leaping upon the mountains, bounding over the hills.

Arabella reached up with one hand and lifted up the thick fleece of her hair, exposing the damp nape of her neck to the cooling breeze. The whiteness of it curved down into the filmy stuff of her dress, and Dawson followed the contour of her spine downward to where her buttocks swelled on the camp stool. He had been sitting with his arms clasped around his knees, but shifted his position, feeling his trousers binding at his groin.

"It is so very warm," she said. "Even for summer."

"I wish I had brought something suitable for you to drink, but I'm afraid I only have lager."

"That would do quite well."

Dawson looked at her with surprise.

"We cannot make tea out here in the wilderness. Besides," she admitted, "I like the taste of lager, even though it might be considered a low taste for a woman. You mustn't mention it to anyone."

"It will be our secret, Mrs. Spence," Dawson assured her, reaching into his rucksack.

"If you were not a solicitor, Mr. Dawson, I would not trust you. But I know that discretion is the alpha and omega of your profession."

He offered her the crock after uncapping the top, and she put it to her lips, tilting her head back at a masculine angle. She must have known he had drunk from it as she put her mouth to the rim of the opening. Her lips glistened before she blotted them with the back of her hand. "Most refreshing," she said.

The drumming whisper of the insects in the grass filled his head as he took the crock from her and drank as deeply as she had, thinking that if he could not taste her lips, at least his were where they had been.

"How wicked I am," Arabella said, "distracting you from your work. Your rocks, your buried treasures."

"Those fossils have lain in the ground for millions of years. They can wait a little longer."

"So you will not reproach me for staying the march of science?"

Dawson answered her by lying back in the grass with his hands clasped behind his head. He looked at her through half-closed eyes. "I will not impede the progress of art."

"There is no progress in art," Arabella said with great seriousness. "We can only imitate the past. Everything in art was discovered by Joshua Reynolds. But not in science. Scientists are the heroes of the new age. The new adventurers, the new explorers. Do get up now," she teased. "Discover something!"

Dawson raised himself up on one elbow and looked at her squarely. "I have."

He thought she might lower her eyes in modest retreat or blush, or protest that he had gone too far. But instead she returned his gaze with a look as direct and wanton as his own. Dawson recalled the last time he had seen that bold

look—on the boardwalks and amusement piers by the seaside, where whores paraded up and down fastening their eyes
on him, thinking he might be a potential customer.

Dawson looked at Arabella with open admiration, as a
lover. Framed by the ringlets of her hair, Arabella's face was
as oval as the face on a cameo with a longish aquiline nose.
Her dark eyes were prominent in the gilded fairness of her
complexion. There was a crooked smile on her small, delec-
table mouth as she sat quite still, inviting his close inspection. He could look at her as long as he liked, and he made
no attempt to conceal from her what he wanted. He realized
she was being as frank with him.

"Well, that's settled, then," Dawson said.

Arabella could see that it would not be long before he was
on top of her, naked between her thighs, rooting until he
found the soft wet entrance. "Yes, it is settled." She was
acquiescent and triumphant, as if it were inevitable. "Do you
know why? Because of the way you looked at me. You made
no excuses."

Dawson looked at her a moment longer, still not entirely
believing the serendipity of the afternoon. Then he got up
and started toward her.

"No. Not yet."

"Are you testing my love already?" Dawson said with
some annoyance.

"Nothing of the sort," she said. She spoke slowly, in a
low-pitched voice. "I am going to heighten your lust."

"I shall be nothing but a cinder if we wait too long."

"I am not flirting with you, Charles. I may call you
Charles, mayn't I? Unless there is another endearment you
prefer."

"Arabella!"

"You may rest quite assured that you will have me in a
week's time—and that I will have you. But let us pretend for
the sake of romance that I have my doubts. You, of course,
have none whatever, which is as it should be, although you
are married."

Dawson reflexively took a step backward.

"Surely you must have known that I knew. And you knew

about me. You are a man," she said, sighing, "and Mama used to tell me that all men are beasts. If only all of them were. But you are, and that is what makes you so wonderful."

"I have never met anyone like you," Dawson said. He had begun by being completely open with her, but now he was trying to mask his bewilderment.

"You probably think I'm silly. But I want to move restlessly about the house, asking myself whether I should or shouldn't let you have me. And I want Colin to ask why I seem so distracted. And I want to lie in bed listening to the sounds of the summer night and watch the white curtains blowing gently in the moonlight; and I will think of you as restless as I, yearning for me, wondering if we will ever meet again."

"I will live for the possibility."

"I am like a bird of summer. I go here and there with the wind. I think next week at this time the wind will be blowing toward Ringles Cross."

Dawson walked into the sun, back across the downs to take the train back to Lewes. To the advent of Arabella and the certainty that they would become lovers he attached no moral significance, no ulterior motive. He hadn't, after all, been hunting the countryside like a fox. He had happened upon her, like a sovereign dropped in the street, waiting to be found. Not being the least introspective, Dawson concluded that his unspoken explanation that fate had led him to her might be correct—if justification were needed.

"What a pity, dear," Helene commiserated when Dawson told her he had returned home empty-handed. "You must be so disappointed."

"Not a single specimen," he said, kissing her lightly on the forehead as she stood in the doorway of the parlor at Castle Lodge.

"Well, you've collected so many specimens, it must be difficult to find something you don't already have. You'll feel better once you've had a wash. There's soap and a fresh towel for you upstairs."

Knowing Dawson had spent the afternoon in the country, Helene had prepared a cold dinner, being uncertain of when he would return. The servant, Mary, hearing the master come in, took a small ham and a potato salad from the larder and put them on the dining room table, returning for a pitcher of cider and a cut glass bowl of lettuce.

The dinner was laid on a round table that stood in the center of the small, but comfortable dining room. The windows looked out on the thick foliage of the garden, black in the ebbing twilight. There was a sideboard with a garniture of Cantonese ginger pots, silver candlesticks, and, on the cornflowered wallpaper, a large chromolith of a Landseer elk. Above the table was a good eighteenth century English brass chandelier fitting with electric bulbs.

Helene Dawson was a pretty woman in her middle forties, who, like the town of Lewes, had not given much thought to the twentieth century. Her clothes were not at all in style, not out of neglect, but rather, like other women in Lewes, she had her dresses made by a seamstress who catered to that conservative taste. In all things, Helene didn't like to call too much attention to herself. When they sat at the table and Dawson busied himself cutting the ham, Helene lowered her head and said a hurried, silent grace, knowing Dawson's views about the Deity and taking the opportunity to acknowledge Him without vexing her husband. She told Charles who she had met at the market that day and the shocking price of carrots, and knew he wasn't listening. She also knew she shouldn't and didn't mind. Charles was a man and a scientist, and therefore doubly deep. As he cut another slab of ham and laid it on his plate, Helene thought him exceedingly handsome and herself an exceptionally lucky woman.

"Are you still hungry? Would you like something else?" she asked.

Dawson shook his head, and when Helene saw he had finished, she rang a silver bell on the table so that Mary would know it was time to clear.

Helene waited for Dawson to get up and followed him out of the dining room. As was often the case, he went into his study while she went to the parlor to read or attend to some work.

Dawson turned on the desk lamp with its green bread-loaf

shade that cast a dim glow in the room. The walls were lined with vitrines containing all sorts of objects he'd collected, tokens of ideas and theories he meant to pursue, incomplete collections that represented momentary enthusiasms. There were boxes of early mammalian teeth that he had either collected in the gravels of Sussex or bought at taxidermy auctions in London. And there were bones and artifacts he had bought from dealers that were interesting to him without any particular notion of their exact significance. He had free-floating intuitions.

Dawson drew a stack of papers toward him and, taking the first batch in hand, tried to read the last minutes of the Sussex Geological Society, at which there had been a heated discussion over whether or not certain early flints were naturally broken objects or artifacts. But the words went out of focus as he conjured visions of Arabella. He pushed his chair away from the desk and went to the threshold of the parlor.

"I think I'll go up to the Castle for a bit," he said to Helene, who was seated in a wing chair with her sewing on her lap.

She looked at him with sympathy. "I'm sorry it was such an unsatisfying day. The next time will be better."

Except for the ruined Norman battlements of Lewes Castle, Dawson's home stood on the highest point of the town. Although it was right off High Street on a narrow road that passed under the turreted barbican, the neighborhood had the look of a park. There were few houses and a spacious bowling green that had been a jousting field in medieval times. Castle Lodge was not a big house, but it had Gothic distinction—four little fake turrets at each corner with slits for defense in times of attack, mullioned windows, and an oversized front door strapped with iron hinges that should have led to a great hall rather than a narrow vestibule. Like the Castle and more recent masonry buildings of the county, it was built of smooth, water-washed flints cleaved in half and set in mortar with the glassy cut surface showing. In the darkness that obscured the paraphrased aspects of its architectural style, the Lodge might have been part of the Castle itself.

Dawson crossed between the rows of lettuce and French beans in the small kitchen garden at the back of the house and entered the precincts of the Castle. Although it was a historic site that attracted tourists at two pence a head through a ticket gate at the bottom of the street, Dawson merely sat on a low wall, threw his legs over and began to climb to the castle keep. The ruins were open to the sky. Enough weeds and intruding vegetation had been left and the walls had only been partially restored, to satisfy any tourist's appetite for the melancholy and the picturesque.

The wind was damp, blowing from the Channel, and the sky, packed with clouds, was only faintly lighter than the irregular silhouette of the crenellated tower. Dawson paced back and forth on the broad flagstone platform. His life with Helene had been adequately satisfying, no more or less than a High Victorian marriage. He might have spent the rest of his life in bland contentment with her, for whom, even now, he bore no ill feeling, although she had metamorphosed from a wife into an inconvenience. Arabella's lifeline and his had intersected, and he stood at the crossroads without the slightest hesitation about which way to go.

Tumultuous thoughts of Arabella kept Dawson pacing the worn flagstones of the castle tower and preoccupied him the following week. Sometimes he hated her for being the cause of his delicious, agonizing expectations, but then he thought that if he'd already had her rather than her promise, he would want her even more.

He had never made love in the sunlight, in the open, in the grass. Arabella was painting when he saw her again, a nymph in white copying the view of the woods that seemed to be her Arcadia. She made good her promise with a passion beyond anything Dawson had imagined in his most lecherous fantasy. In the beginning he was even a little frightened at her easy and utterly uncomplicated sexuality, her animal enjoyment, as if she had never been burdened with the knowledge of constraint, modesty, or disingenuousness. As he explored her body, she reciprocated, letting her hands roam in the hair of his chest, down past her navel, fondling his cock and balls, or lightly stroking his back and delving between the cheeks of his ass. They coupled in every posture and position they could think of and laughed at the idea that they'd invented ways until then unknown. Every week they met in another part of the country. One day, to their added delight, some sheep came to watch. Once, twice, three times in an afternoon they would make love, sometimes in a fury of passion, sometimes with childish delight or languorous delectation. And in between they would play with each other's naked bodies.

"What a wonderful thing," Arabella said, holding the object of her adoration to her lips. "It goes up, it goes down; it goes up, it goes down."

He could almost not believe her. "The phoenix rises again," he observed. He had begun as his mother's darling, with the potential of a manly body, nobility of mind and success written on the top of his otherwise blank slate. Then as a crude and ruddy youth he was good at games, idolized by his peers, and was cruel but not unjust to his inferiors. He had a masculine penchant for science and the law. Later, as a man, he was robust, confident, and easy with his fellows, and picked a wife that praised him to the skies. All of that history fell away under Arabella's spell. In the meadows and woods where they played and fucked as maenad and satyr, Dawson finally discovered what it was simply to be male.

Summer was subsiding into autumn as Arabella hurriedly painted a stand of cypress by a stream at Buxstead Park, to have something to show for her day in the country.

"My paintings are getting awfully sketchy. I will have to say I've decided to change my style." She washed her brush and dabbed at the tab of blue in her paint box. "What about your specimens?"

Dawson reached for his rucksack and took out a nautilus-shaped ammonite. "I take them from home and bring them back." He lay beside her as she tipped the tablet of paper to help the blue of the sky wash down toward the horizon. "Put me in the picture," he said.

"You are so vain," Arabella replied.

"It would give some human interest. You must."

"With or without clothes?"

"Just there, in the background," Dawson said, indicating a brush stroke that was meant to represent the trunk of a tree.

"I don't do figures. They are too hard," she said, but she made the small addition.

"You've made me into a large ant."

"You are not pleased with me," she said, pouting at him.

"I have never been more pleased in my life," Dawson declared.

When the weather became unpredictable, Dawson found that legal business took him to Eastbourne and Brighton. They strolled on the nearly deserted sea fronts beside the foggy beaches and made love in small, genteel hotels, where the beds sagged in the middle. Arabella would be deliciously satiated, while Dawson could only think of when they would be together again. Finally he could no longer contain himself.

"I want you to go away with me," he said.

"Away? Where?"

"Anywhere."

Arabella was naked and warm beside him under an eider-down cover. She noticed that the chintz-patterned wallpaper of the hotel room had ugly stains by the water stand.

"I'd go anywhere with you," she whispered, and he embraced her again. "But how?" she added in a practical tone, extricating herself from his arms.

"Never mind how. Say yes. Once you have a goal, you can make a plan."

"I'll pack a picnic basket of cold duck and champagne, and we'll fly across the Channel to Calais in a balloon." After a moment, Arabella said, "Oh, my darling. If it were only that simple."

"It is," Dawson insisted. If he had stopped long enough to consider their circumstances, he might have concluded that they were well-matched as they were—adulterous lovers who could design their lives for self-indulgence to a degree that would be the envy of others in the same position. But while Arabella might revel in his rutting need of her and enjoy the languid satisfaction of their lovemaking, Dawson felt only deprivation as they went their separate ways to Uckfield and Lewes.

"You are a solicitor whose bread and butter is confidence and trust. You wouldn't be able to survive the scandal of having stolen me away. Who would trust you, believe you? No, Charles, we could go as far away as Edinburgh, and they would find you out. I could not be the cause of your ruin."

"We'll go to Europe."

"How could you practice law there? Do you speak fluent French, German, or, God forbid, Italian? I don't have a penny of my own. We must be practical."

Dawson looked like a child who had been told he would not be going on a holiday as planned, and for reasons that were arbitrary and senseless.

"And then there's Colin, and my boys," Arabella continued. "And there's Helene." They rarely spoke of their lives away from each other. Dawson turned away from her in the bed, but she put her hand on the back of his shoulder and spoke quietly. "Colin could get along quite well without me, and I only see the boys when they're home from school. But still . . . Oh, Charles, I need time. I'd follow you to Timbuctu, but for now we must make do with Brighton." She rubbed her warm breasts against him.

Arabella had been married for thirteen years to Colin Spence, the owner of a large lime-burning kiln. She had been passionately in love with Colin, who had courted her with a wild fervor, writing poems to her in the manner of Browning, throwing pebbles at her window at night so that he might get one last glimpse of her after a party. She had been in a state of secret, feverish anticipation belied by a tremulous, girlish demeanor. Her wedding night had been a dream of pleasure, contrary to the warnings of her mother, and in the months that followed, Arabella was finally able freedly to express her erotic, romantic nature. Over the years, however, romance gave way to matrimony. She lived in a stagnant fog of disappointment. Not that Colin mistreated her; he was kind and attentive. An ideal husband. But a husband, nevertheless. A lover no more. Gone was the poetry in word and deed. No more baskets of fruit out of season, or furtive kisses. There was snoring, soiled underwear, head colds. Even her children began to disappoint. They'd been perfectly plump and rosy as the baroque putti she'd seen in Italy on her honeymoon, but they'd become real, raucous boys, Liam and Mark, the elder of whom had come home from school with the shadow of a mustache on his upper lip. The years marched in tight formation. Arabella was thirty.

For the rest of the year Arabella kept Dawson at bay, pleading for time, urging him to be realistic and to be happy with what they had. She had already learned how romance turned into tedious domesticity, and she had no intention of letting that happen again. Charles was her lover, and she determined he would remain just that. Then, without explanation, he stopped asking her to go away with him. Since the fever of his lust never broke, Arabella had no anxiety that he no longer wanted her any less than the first day they had met. She was only immensely relieved that he was being sensible, and she continued to enjoy, as Dawson seemed to, their frequent assignations.

But Dawson had not given up the idea of complete possession.

Chapter IV

THE AMATEUR ARCHAEOLOGISTS AND PALEONTOLOGISTS of East Sussex were as motley a collection as the objects they had unearthed. A jeweler, a grocer, the headmaster of a boy's school, Dawson the solicitor, and others, men whose work and graded positions within the middle class would have otherwise kept them in their own social spheres, found themselves regularly together at meetings, where they debated, quibbled, read papers, and proudly showed their discoveries to one another. They all had their collections, theories supported by their collections, and their well-worn, annotated copies of Darwin and Huxley. Like Dawson, they had walked many miles to promising sites, and they were fortunate that their turf contained such a rich variety of treasures: Cenozoic sea creatures from the dawn of time, Jurassic dinosaurs that had left their footprints in the primordial mud, Pliocene mammals and early man, full-fledged *Homo sapiens* whose distant descendants left Norman and Saxon kitchen middens and other detritus of human life, including their own bones, for those amateurs who preferred to investigate more recent events. One had only to turn to whatever page one wished in the history of the earth of East Sussex, and begin to read. One page was missing, still to be written. No early form of man had been found there or in the whole of England.

No one in scientific circles questioned the Darwinian idea that man had developed from some sort of ape with human-like characteristics, a hominid. His fossil remains, when found, would place him at the very threshold of humanity, hirsute but erect, perhaps looking at the rising sun of a new day with the barest glimmer of a thought that the dawn was beautiful, that the day would end and another begin, and that one day he would die.

The Sussex amateurs were not alone in their hope that this hominid would eventually be found in England, and the geology of Sussex offered particularly tantalizing possibilities. The strata dating to the Pliocene and Pleistocene, periods ending about 500,000 years ago, had yielded abundant evidence of primitive mammals, which were thought to be contemporary with the elusive ape-man. Their hope, and the hope of every English paleontologist, of finding this creature was sharpened on the whetstone of chagrin: The French had had their finds of the bestial, shambling, but undeniably early Neanderthal Man since 1857. English human paleontology was in the doldrums.

Dawson and his cronies often spoke of their hopes as they sipped Madeira or port after their formal meetings.

"It would be a pity if he turned out to be a Neanderthal variation."

"Impossible."

"He's got to be here somewhere, the shy little beggar," someone would say with vehement frustration.

"And he'll be the earliest known."

"Of course," Dawson said. "It's the only way to explain why we English are such a superior race." He spoke with such a slight touch of wry that most of the group responded with a rousing, "Hear, hear!" of agreement and self-satisfaction. Britannia ruled the waves and countless millions of colonial peoples. The Empire had been formed and burnished by Victoria and was held in Edward's palm like a royal orb. The pride of Empire might be seen by others as national hubris, but the discovery of the first man would reveal the history of Empire as predestination. England was meant to rule; we only do our duty; we were first on the planet.

The "coconut shell" from Barkham Manor was a piece of a human skull—a recent one—stained chocolate brown by natural absorption of iron salts. As Dawson rode home from his visit to the manor, he held the skull fragment in his pocket, thinking that the idea of finding the remains of an early hominid individual in England was held with such conviction that the discovery of the evidence seemed only to be waiting for the intervention of Divine Providence in the form of a lucky or persistent man with a spade and a sieve.

Dawson made up his mind to be that man. If fate would not lead him to the find site, as it had to Arabella, then he would have to take matters into his own hands. He would find a creature of his own making. He would be famous, as famous as the fossil itself. He would write, tour Europe giving popular lectures, serious, but for the masses. His book would become as classic as *The Descent of Man*. He would get financial sponsorship for expeditions, from private philanthropies, from the Royal Society. It would be a new life of discovery, far from the narrow confines of provincial and professional obligations, which were like a suit of clothes he had outgrown. It would be a new life, and Arabella would be with him, his paramour and his muse.

He sat at home, dining on mutton and potatoes, thinking of another appetite. Arabella would put no impediment between them once he had become the instrument of England's destiny. Why not he? With his distinguished credentials, no one would be surprised. The theory had been universally accepted. He would only anticipate what would eventually be corroborated by someone else's genuine find. But the glory would be his, along with Arabella. Until the moment of his triumphant celebrity came, he determined to put no pressure on her. Once he had accomplished his brilliant paleontological trick she would bend to his will.

"Shall we play rummy tonight, Charles?" Helene asked.

"I must work. I've got to sort out the Barkham Manor accounts. Bob Kenward doesn't keep the books as he should."

"Then I will darn your socks. You are so hard on socks, with all your walking."

"I may be late. Don't wait up for me."

"You work so hard."

Dawson shut himself up in his study sanctum. He appeared to be doing what he had done many times before: opening his vitrines and cabinets, closely examining the objects, reviewing their rarity and condition with the pride of a collector, and reliving the pleasure and excitement of discovery. His own hypotheses had been formed by the consideration of evidence. But this time he searched his collections for evidence to fit his hypothetical creature.

His hand first rested on his storage box of early mammalian teeth. He moved them about with his forefinger and was satisfied that he had enough specimens to suggest a Pleistocene menagerie as big as the London Zoo. His imaginary man had lived intimately with animals and was nearly an animal of the forest himself. Besides, Dawson thought, returning from his reverie of his stalking creature, the faunal remains would provide an incontrovertible early date.

Establishing a date for his Dawn Man was a long way from creating the man himself. Unfortunately, in the category of human remains, Dawson didn't have too much in stock. His collection contained neither examples of great antiquity nor anything unearthed in Sussex. He couldn't go now to any of the regular auction sales of miscellaneous bones at Gerrard's in London, or visit bone dealers or taxidermists who turned up interesting things. At some point any one of them might remember a recent acquisition and match it to the great discovery regardless of how Dawson might transform it for his own purposes. Like the battlefield chef who had concocted chicken Marengo for Napoleon out of the ingredients at hand, Dawson searched his larder.

Over the years he had put together a disparate group of fragments, showing various human pathologies with the idea of eventually collaborating with a doctor on the history of diseases in ancient times—cancer, arthritis, vitamin deficiencies. At a London auction, years before, he had acquired a partially fossilized skull he noticed had unusually thick walls. The provenance in the sales catalog stated that it had been excavated in Nubia, Upper Egypt, at an archaeological dig and was dated by the artifacts in the tomb to the Coptic period. A pathologist friend at St. George's Hospital opined that the thickening of the skull showed clear evidence of Paget's disease. Placed in the theoretical context of a hominid, the thickness of the cranial dome would be the unmistakable mark of an early type. But to discover a cranium of such great age intact might be too dazzling an achievement, even for himself, Dawson concluded. So there would only be some judiciously selected fragments, but which ones? He traced the curve of the skull with the tips of his fingers, from front to back along the midline. What a lovely, noble curve, he thought. The Dawn Man of Sussex would not resemble the brutish, continental Neanderthal, with his jutting, superciliary brow ridge. Instead, the man from Piltdown would have a patrician English forehead, declaring his intellectual superiority to all other hominids. He would give his countrymen what they wanted. His creature would conform to scientific expectations of cranial development as well as national prejudice. Piltdown Man would be nothing less than a benevolent and thoughtful lord of his estate and, though understandably rustic, to the manor born. Pieces of the Nubian skull would do admirably. No one need know that the Dawn Man of Sussex was an immigrant.

Skull fragments alone, however convincing, would not clearly establish the transitional position Piltdown Man would occupy in the evolutionary tree. Having not yet struggled out of his simian past in his striving toward humanity, he would have an ape's jaw, suitably altered to show transitional features comparable to those of the skull. But Dawson had nothing in stock. And he realized again that going marketing for a likely specimen from a chimpanezee or an orangutan the way Helene bought a soup bone at the butcher, would be too risky.

Dawson sat brooding at his desk, one hand under his chin, the other drumming a tattoo of frustration on the dome of the skull before him. Without a jaw, there would be no moment of glory, no Arabella.

After several hours, and with the greatest difficulty, Dawson reluctantly concluded he would have to share his discov-

ery with someone else—someone who had access to a jaw.
Once having made his decision, and being a man with an
excessively pragmatic nature who could always find his advantage and make the best of a bad bargain when his own
self-interest was at stake, Dawson came to the conclusion
that it would be best to have a partner. He was contemptuous
of his academic colleagues, thin-blooded pedants who sat
timidly theorizing at their desks, rarely venturing out into the
field or beyond the narrow scope of their specialties. Still, as
an amateur, Dawson admitted there would be definite advantages to having professional bona fides attached to such an
important discovery.

Rising and going to a bookshelf, Dawson searched through
his bound copies of the transactions of the Geological Society
for a list of Fellows. He would confine himself to possible
candidates who worked in London, foreseeing that events
would require them to be together often; for his part, Dawson
wouldn't have minded long train rides in any direction, considering what was to be achieved. But working with an
ordinarily desk-bound academic would be difficult enough
without his being cranky and overtired. And whoever he
proposed to himself would also have to be connected profes-
sionally to a collection containing the necessary ape's mandible. This narrowed the field to only two possibilities.

Arthur Keith was Dawson's first choice. The Royal College's collection was enormous, and Keith, an anatomist,
was a specialist in fossil human skulls. His opinions were
highly respected. He would have a natural enthusiasm for the
project and would be able to make critical evaluations of the
hominid brain size and extent of intelligence based on the
few fragments of the skull Dawson would allow him.

Arthur Smith Woodward. The collections of the Museum
of Natural History were even more extensive. Woodward
worked in fossil fish, yet it was possible that his ignorance of
human anatomy might be used to advantage. But what a stick
he was, what a bore. Dawson shook his head in disbelief at
the idea of Woodward digging in a ditch beside the road at
Barkham Manor.

As Dawson thought about Keith and Woodward as possible alternatives, another problem presented itself that applied to both: how to get either of them involved. They couldn't be bribed by him, and there was no lure of money from the enterprise itself. There could be no immediate financial rewards for either Keith or Woodward. It would be unseemly and ethically improper of them to profit from such a discovery. The papers and articles for learned journals which he, Dawson, would co-author would bring them fame, no doubt, and Dawson, who never underestimated the power of egoism, could offer that. But he wondered whether the spur of fame alone would drive either Keith or Woodward to compromise his scientific integrity. Was either of them, Dawson wondered, ambitious enough, hungry enough for the kind of international recognition that the discovery of the man from Piltdown would confer, to make them take a daring and irrevocable step into the dangerous world of complicity and fraud? And if not, could Dawson devise some way of duping them, as he planned to dupe the entire world of science? He wondered whether or not he could make Keith or Woodward an innocent accomplice. If the discovery of the remains at Piltdown were made over a long period, perhaps Dawson, establishing himself as a familiar and frequent visitor to the Royal College or the British Museum, might find some way of stealing the necessary jawbone right from under the nose of his colleague without anyone being the wiser. There was much to think about and much to do before the world would know that the Dawn Man had once strolled the greenswards of Sussex.

In the middle of the afternoon, Dawson sat in his study at Castle Lodge. The large window faced south. Outside there was a little path and a planting of well-behaved flowers against the top of a wall, which dropped on the other side into the courtyard of Lewes Castle. For the better part of the afternoon, in all seasons, the day gave the room as much light as it had.

The glaring south light fell directly on the top of his desk. Dawson liked working best in the sunlight; it was pitilessly revealing. It challenged him to produce a patina on the skull fragments before him that would convince even his most skeptical critics that they had been buried in the iron-rich gravel bed in Piltdown for five hundred millenia.

Sheets of newspaper were spread over Dawson's blotter and on it were several fragments of the Nubian skull he was using as trial pieces, keeping careful notes of various chemical recipes. Arranged on the table were bottles and apothecary jars containing acids and solutions of metallic salts. There were also brushes, bits of cotton wool, swabs, and small sponges. The aging experiments involved bathing the bone in a variety of weak acids to etch the bone surface to erode its softer structures and to round off the broken edges to give the impression of its being naturally rolled in the Piltdown gravels. The color of the patination had to match these gravels that were colored with iron oxide, and Dawson had collected a small sack of them to duplicate. He had tried a number of combinations of iron salts and oxidizing agents at the effects of bichromate of potash and ferric ammonium sulfate. Never far from his consciousness was the problem of the jaw.

Mary was busy in the vestibule. The missus was out, and Mary worked without much dedication, dreamily moving a broom over the ghost of a Turkey carpet, when there was a loud knock at the front door. When she opened it, she didn't know whether to look at the man standing there or his car parked at the front gate. They were both equally magnificent. The visitor stood four-square in the doorway, a commanding figure in cavalry twills, a loud houndstooth coat, madder foulard at the throat, and a port velvet waistcoat across the wide expanse of his chest and belly. The vehicle was an ostentatious Sunbeam Mably touring car, maroon lacquered with golden fittings and trim.

"Arthur Conan Doyle to see Mr. Charles Dawson," he said from under his walrus mustache.

Mary ogled him. She was an insatiable and fanatical reader of the Holmes stories, serialized in the *Strand* magazine. That she stood before the resplendent creator of the world's greatest detective was as awesome as if she stood before her own.

"Are you deaf, child?"

Mary was only mute. Followed by Doyle, she backed away into the hall, forgetting the formalities the missus had drilled into her head. When she reached the door of Dawson's study, she reached for the knob, flung it open and cried, "Mr. Doyle," before retreating backward to the kitchen.

Doyle stepped into the room. Dawson, who had been engrossed in his work, looked up, paralyzed by the interruption.

"I'm Arthur Conan Doyle." He had once announced himself simply as Arthur Doyle, but since the success of Sherlock Holmes, he had taken to using his full name, feeling as justified in using it conversationally as he was sure other writers with triple-threat literary monikers did at first meetings, joining himself in his mind with the likes of Robert Louis Stevenson and George Bernard Shaw.

Dawson looked at Doyle and then at his desk top ablaze in the sunlight, each object hyper-real, glowing with incrimination. Apart from the movement of his eyes, Dawson was as still as a waxwork.

"The writer," Doyle explained, his tone implying that Mary's reaction had been more appropriate.

Dawson got up and scurried around the side of the desk putting himself between Doyle and it. One side of his mouth twitched in his effort at a friendly greeting. "I heard you had moved to the neighborhood."

"Yes. Crowborough."

Dawson responded with idiotic blankness, as if he had never heard of the town a short distance from Uckfield.

"I'm sorry to drop in like this. I'm disturbing you."

"Not at all," Dawson replied, trying to reconstruct a social manner, but his voice lacked conviction.

"I went to your office. Your chief clerk told me you were at home."

"Then it is a legal matter?"

"No. A matter of paleontology. I have been told you are the leading light of the Geological Society hereabouts."

Dawson pointed dumbly to the glass-front cases against the wall containing some of his specimens. As Doyle went toward them, Dawson changed position in relation to his guest, as if he were true north.

"It's good to have a hobby," Doyle advised. "I, unhappily, am a monomaniac. Literature is my whole life." He began to move around the room at random. "I haven't a clue what I'm looking at. Seems like a lot of old bits and pieces to me." He finally stopped, looking over Dawson's shoulder. "A paleontologist at work. Now that's interesting."

"Not in the least. The great things happen in the field," Dawson answered, sliding his behind against the desk, interjecting himself in Doyle's sight line.

"What's all that gear?" Doyle asked.

"What gear? Oh, that," Dawson foundered. "I'm writing a paper on the preservation of fossils. Many of them are terribly fragile, friable when exposed to the air." Dawson warmed to his subject once he'd found it, extemporizing in detail, hoping to distract Doyle's attention from the desk. "My findings will be the greatest boon to museum conservators all over the world."

"Does your method alter the physical appearance of the specimen? I mean that brown color. Is it original?"

"Absolutely. That's the beauty of my method. But I am trying your patience with all this. Come into the parlor where we'll be more comfortable." He maneuvered Doyle out the door.

"Would you like some tea?" Dawson asked.

"Do you have Critchley's Green Ceylon?"

"I really couldn't say. And Mrs. Dawson is out."

"There's only one shop in London that carries it. Oh, well, no matter."

Dawson felt no less easy when they were no longer in his study. He wondered whether Doyle's powers of observation were as sharp as his literary creation, Holmes, and whether Doyle might attach any further significance to the criminal still life on his desk. Dawson could read nothing disconcerting in Doyle's face or manner, yet his uneasiness persisted. "Do tell me exactly why you have come."

"While walking my property, I discovered some fossilized

dinosaur tracks. They're about this long," Doyle said with a fisherman's gesture.

"How many toes?"

"Three."

"Iguanodon. They were quite common in the neighborhood, and so are their footprints."

"The reason I came was not only to find out about my former reptilian tenants, but something more. After seeing those footprints I have become intrigued with the idea of writing a ripping adventure tale, set in the present, but in a lost world, an evolutionary backwater where dinosaurs and apelike men still live. I hoped you would help me, that I could consult you about my dinosaurs, their habits, their behavior. I mean to make my story sufficiently rich in detail that my readers will suspend disbelief for a few happy hours."

"I am a great believer in the suspension of disbelief," Dawson said.

"I knew I could count on you."

"You probably want the great thunderous dinosaurs. Brontosaurus; the magnificent carnivore, Tyrannosaurus Rex."

"That's the ticket," said Doyle.

"I'm not your man. But Ray Lankester is. Superintendent of the BM, South Ken. Rather a dinosaur himself, but charming. I have given many things to the museum, and I would be glad to write you a letter of introduction."

"Do you think he'll see me?"

"I should think he'd be flattered by your visit."

"I mean, after all, he's a serious scientist, no doubt. And one never knows whether such a person harbors prejudices toward a writer such as myself. Needless to say, the term 'popular' used in the pejorative sense is entirely misplaced. After all, the hoi polloi flocked to the Globe Theatre, and there were queues at the kiosks waiting breathlessly for Dickens' latest installment." Doyle went on, sawing the air with his brawny tweed arm, to clarify the timeless moral themes embedded in his own work—the maniacal conflict between good and evil personified by Holmes and Moriarty.

To Dawson, Doyle's voice was like the sound of a rusty hinge. There was a swaggering sportiness to the cut of his bespoke jacket even as he sat across from him, filling the space between the wings of the armchair where Helene usually looked almost lost in its breadth. His legs were crossed as if showing off one of his new wing-tipped brogans, a London bootmaker's version of a sensible country shoe. There was about him an expectation of deference that only fame could justify. And there was a grafting note of condescension to a bumpkin, a small-town solicitor who could be pumped for information about his little scientific hobby. Dawson listened with a show of interest, thinking it would not be long before Doyle would have every reason to be deferential to him.

"This new novel of mine will be a significant departure from my earlier work," Doyle explained. "It is set in the trackless jungles of Brazil, near the headwaters of the Amazon. My intrepid explorers will get into all sorts of jolly scrapes as they fight their way up river. The Indians are headhunters, you know. But apart from their decapitating their enemies and shrinking their heads to the size of a tennis ball, the Jivaro tribes are a most peaceful and resourceful lot. They use bright feathers of birds and iridescent beetles' backs to make the most extraordinary ornaments. They are masters of the river and the jungle and are consummate hunters."

"Bows and arrows, I suppose."

"Blowguns. Accurate to fifty yards. The arrows are tipped with a deadly poison. Curare. A poison of the alkaloid group of incredible virulence. It's a remarkable drug, really. In fact, it is used in modern medicine. It works as a muscle relaxant. Too much curare will relax you to death, but in the proper dosages, it's of enormous help in surgical procedures. Small amounts produce a tiredness, a lassitude."

"I see you haven't forgotten your early medical training."

"I am forever beholden to it. The original Holmes was a professor of mine at Edinburgh."

"Did you go to Brazil before or after medical school?" Dawson asked.

"Never been there in my life."

"You don't say," Dawson exclaimed with mock surprise.

"Good God, no. Traveling's not my sort of thing. Don't

care for it. Wogs begin at Calais,'' Doyle replied, Anglicizing the French seaport.

"Quite."

"Research, my dear fellow. I'm an awful magpie and notetaker. Research. And imagination!'' Doyle looked at the ceiling and began to improvise. "A fearsome spotted jaguar crouched in the foetid perpetual twilight of the rain forest. . . ."

Doyle would have continued, but Dawson said, "Surely you've been there."

"Put in enough detail and high adventure, and they'll believe it. The secret is giving them what they want."

"That's the ticket,'' Dawson agreed.

As Dawson was contemplating Woodward as a second choice to share his greatness, Woodward was methodically attending to his own business at the British Museum of Natural History. In 1908 he had been keeper for seven years, previous to that having worked his way up from a second-class assistant by building a reputation for fastidious research and for playing institutional politics strictly by the book. He read every memorandum from the superintendent that came across his desk and underlined its salient points with the same close attention he gave to scientific off-prints that arrived in the post. In fossil fish and museum etiquette he had no peer.

When not at his desk or rummaging systematically in the study collections of his department, he could be seen walking in a stiff, businesslike fashion through the hallways and galleries, his head slightly bent, preoccupied with the minute nuances of some administrative directive or puzzling over the morphology of a fossil ichthyodorulite. The guards in the galleries would automatically straighten up when he approached, whether or not he noticed them.

In the administrative hierarchy at the Museum, he showed proper respect to his superiors, and they approved. His curatorial peers tolerated him with something approaching respect because he appeared content with his geological fiefdom; he didn't seek territorial expansion in the exhibition galleries, nor did he denigrate other specialties or their keepers as less significant to the museum's purposes of research and education. Yet there was a feeling in the staff room that he was correct to a fault. Woodward had the best reputation among colleagues in other institutions who read his papers but did not have to work with him.

Woodward erred, perhaps, to those under him, to whom he was a humorless taskmasker, who never spoke of, or seemed to think of, anything but the museum. In 1902, when all of England, including those at the museum who gathered in the halls in excited groups, thrilled to the victories of Kitchener in Transvaal, Woodward went about his work as if nothing had happened. And once, when he hurried through the galleries on his preoccupied way, he collided with an exhibition case and broke his leg. His departmental underlings were overjoyed that they might have at least a week's respite from Woodward while he rested at home, his foot on a hassock. He appeared the next morning on crutches without skipping a beat in the relentless march to which everyone under his command kept perfect time.

Those who remembered when he'd come to the museum decades before said he looked exactly the same. Every institution has its myths. At the British Museum of Natural History, it was said that Arthur Smith Woodward had been born wearing a goatee and gold-rimmed glasses, and instead of crying lustily when the midwife smacked him on the bottom, he announced he had to go to a meeting.

The Victorian Romanesque pile of the museum set back from Cromwell Road was opened to the public in 1881. Two towers pierced with grouped arched windows and terminating in pointed steeples flanked an impressive arched entranceway, and two wings to the east and west formed the principal exhibition galleries and offices. The west wing housed the collections pertaining to living things. To the east, separated by a grand central nave of heroic arches and colonnades, was the kingdom of the remote past, geology and fossils. Careful observers noticed the carved decorations of the capitals and archways of each wing—to the west the familiar birds and animals of the present, to the east the creatures of the past, weird basilisks and extinct monsters peering down, more fabulous than imaginary gargoyles.

Woodward's office was under the slanted roof on the third floor, the two rounded windows separated by a slender colonnette closed against the hum of traffic in the road below. He had carefully worked his way through a memorandum from the reference librarian complaining that keepers failed to return books and was beginning to draft a reply that he was entirely innocent, when a porter knocked on his door.

"A gentleman to see you, sir." His manner was tentative, as he knew Woodward's strict rule about seeing no one without an appointment. "The gentleman says he's come all the way from China." By way of making a further excuse, he gave Woodward a calling card. It read: Edmund Trelawny Backhouse, Bt. Fingering the engraved coat of arms on the card, Woodward decided to make an exception.

The man who entered was tall and thin, with the fragile look of a recuperating invalid. His skin had a mutton fat jade pallor, and his thinning hair was practically colorless. The slight hook of his nose was a knife edge in his face, and it was difficult to read his expression behind a pair of octagonal rimless spectacles. He appeared to be of uncertain age, although he was thirty-six.

"So good of you to see me," he said softly.

"Sir Edmund," Woodward said, extending his hand over the top of his desk. Backhouse's hand was limp as Woodward took it, reminding him unpleasantly of touching a cat whose bones could be felt sliding under its fur when caressed.

"May I sit down?" Backhouse looked as if he might faint away if he did not.

"Please," Woodward urged with some concern.

"I have had a very long trip. The heat through the Suez was unrelenting, quite enough to drive one straight around the bend."

"I expect you'll soon feel your old self again once you've had a taste of our temperate English weather."

"My old self is gone. The climate of China has ruined me forever. China is justly famous for its recondite subtleties, but its weather is blatant."

"What is your business in China?"

"I have no business there. I have a knack for languages. For the past decade I have supported myself as a scholar and amanuensis. In the years after I was graduated from Oxford, I learned Russian and Chinese, which my family thought impractical." Backhouse leaned his elbows on the wooden arms of the chair and held his long fingers together to form a little white gazebo. He spoke so softly that Woodward could barely hear him. "But that interest in languages proved to be my salvation, financially at least. My inheritance, on which I had counted, was gone owing, I am afraid, to my father's mismanagement, not to put too fine a point on it. Fortunately, through connections, I went out as a protégé of Sir Robert Hildreth," he continued, not bothering to identify his protector further. "Through his kind recommendations and those of satisfied clients, I have been able to eke out a respectable living doing translations for the foreign legations and making myself useful in a small way, having acquired more than a passing knowledge of Manchu, Mongolian, and Japanese. And I have certain intimate associations in the Forbidden City, which are occasionally valuable, diplomatically, that is."

"How interesting."

"Not really. It is a poor existence. I am an exile in the City of Dreadful Dust. My greatest comfort is my scholarly work. My library of Chinese manuscripts was known even at my alma mater and was thought to be distinguished, only because the Bodleian had virtually nothing. It was my only extravagance. When they offered to buy it from me, I was sorely tempted, as it would have relieved my financial distress considerably. I use the past tense, because it was all destroyed in the Boxer uprising. Years of work gone. The lot. My house was in the Tartar City and that section was leveled to the ground."

"You were in Peking?"

"For each of the fifty-five days of the siege of the legations." Backhouse closed his eyes and told of the merciless shelling, the wild cries of the Boxer troopers outside the barricaded walls of the legation enclave, the final days when the hostages had been reduced to eating cats and worse, and after, the appalling wreckage and vengeful atrocities by anti-Boxer Chinese as well as the Allied troops who occupied the city.

Woodward wondered what had brought the frail expatriot and scholar to the museum. Whatever it was, it would be revealed by a circuitous route. But he was fascinated with Backhouse, hoping he would continue.

"When we were released, I went to visit my old friend, Ching Shan, a well-known courtier and confident to the Empress Dowager, Tzu Hsi, to see how he had fared." Backhouse pressed his thumb and forefinger to the bridge of his nose underneath his glasses. "I was hopeful for his safety when I approached the house in the British sector outside the Imperial City. The undisturbed facade was but an illusion, for inside was the corpse of my friend, his throat cut from ear to ear, his wife and children wailing in grief and terror, and a party of marauding Sikhs looting his possessions. His papers and books were scattered on the floor, but while those thugs from Baluchistan were tearing at the silk robes in his closets and smashing priceless K'ang-hsi porcelains for the sheer joy of destruction, I was able to save a few manuscripts, one of which, after the briefest perusal, I realized to be of the utmost importance." Backhouse took the thinnest pastille of a gold watch from his pocket, flicked open its cover, and said, "But I am taking too much of your precious time. I really should get to the point."

"No, no," Woodward protested. "What was in the manuscript?"

Backhouse complied. "It was the personal diary of Ching Shan, containing the most dramatic revelations about the rebellion, revealing thoroughly unexpected aspects of the intrigues and politics of the court at the very highest levels."

"How amazing. But why hasn't it ever been published?"

"Well, you see, there were things in it most unflattering, even seriously compromising, to certain members of the court, including the Empress Dowager herself. To reveal such information would have put me in danger, not only the threat of expulsion, but—and I don't mean to melodramatize—a threat to my life. There are those in Peking, and I mean Europeans as well as Chinese, toward whom I feel no enmity, who fancy themselves my enemies and who would intrigue against me."

It may have been only a sudden glint of sunlight on Backhouse's glasses, but Woodward thought he saw a spasm of energy, a momentary glimpse of another personality revealed.

"But last year the Old Buddha, as we fondly called the Empress Dowager, died," Backhouse said, returning to a soft, diffident tone, "so I no longer felt threatened, and I have collaborated with a dear friend, the journalist John Bland, in writing a new history of these last years of the Manchu dynasty, including Ching Shan's diary as its centerpiece, translated for the first time by me."

"How remarkable. When will it come out?"

"First I must find a publisher, which is why I am in London."

"I shouldn't think you'll have any trouble."

"Perhaps. But I cannot imagine that my book, about the rebellion, about what other historians now call, however erroneously, a little skirmish in the annals of Imperialism, will have wide appeal. I am hoping to bring this information to light to satisfy my obligation as a historian and a scholar; I have no fantasy of being inundated by a shower of gold, as if I were Danaë wooed by Zeus." Backhouse sighed. "Which finally brings me to the reason I came to the museum."

"Yes?"

"My personal needs are simple: a roof and a bowl of rice. My library, however, is my demanding mistress, and I cannot foresee the pittance from my own literary efforts will go far to relieve my continuing financial distress. But I have found a way that could be helpful to me and beneficial to you, to the museum. Chinese apothecaries dispense powdered dragon bones, which are said to have magical curative powers. These bones, we know, are dinosaur fossils. They positively abound in China. There is one Dr. Schildkraut in

Peking who has been regularly sending consignments of fossils to the museum in Frankfort, and I understand they have been extremely pleased with their acquisitions. I propose doing the same for you, acting as your agent in China.''

"This is an intriguing proposition," Woodward said. "Our collections of Asian fossils are as sparse as the Bodleian's manuscript holdings. We have never had a dig in China.'' Woodward had a serious concern that this baronet, however erudite, was no paleontologist. He could collect specimens, but the value to the museum of crates of old bones, without geological context was, at best, moot. Still, Backhouse seemed the sort of person who exuded possibilities. He could not be dismissed out of hand. If he could not be useful in one way, he might be useful in another. Someone sympathetic to the museum's interests in China, with his connections, might come in handy. It could be worthwhile to deputize him for a nominal retainer, whatever he might come up with, a small price for a friend at court if the museum decided to finance an expedition to that far-off land. That he, Woodward, had introduced such a person to the museum would not go unnoticed. "I would like to bring your proposal to the attention of the superintendent," Woodward said.

"Too kind," Backhouse murmured.

"But this is not the sort of thing that can be decided immediately. Will you stay long in London?"

"It is hard to say."

"I suppose you have many friends in London, friends who are eager to see you again."

"Had many friends. Again, the past tense. The curse of the historian. When one is away, one is forgotten. I am a ghost," he said, holding up his pale hands before his face. "Only yesterday I passed an old friend in Bruton Street who looked straight through me as if I were ectoplasm."

"The reason I asked," Woodward said, "was that Mrs. Woodward and I are having a tea tomorrow. Our teas are a little famous in scientific circles. Only the most distinguished of my colleagues are invited. It is very short notice," Woodward apologized, "and very short acquaintance," he apologized again, "but if you find yourself free tomorrow at six o'clock, we would be honored to receive you."

Maud was in a perfect frenzy of delighted anticipation at Backhouse's visit. She made Woodward tell and retell Backhouse's history, making sure he hadn't left out a single detail, clucking at the mention of his lost fortune, and holding her breath as she heard the horrors of the seige. She worried that her own watercress sandwiches might not be what Sir Edmund was used to, or that he might find her usual brown taffeta an affront to his taste. She concluded privately that since no refreshment she might serve and no rag in her wardrobe would satisfy Sir Edmund, her only recourse would be to throw herself on the mercy of his noblesse oblige. To Woodward she announced she had no intention of doing anything special for Sir Edmund, first, because they were quite good enough to receive him without embarrassment, and second, that she didn't want anyone to think they were putting on airs for a baronet who, from what Woodward had just told her, was poorer than they were.

The tea was attended by the usual gaggle of geologists, paleontologists, and scholars in the related natural sciences. Dawson, up from Sussex for the day, was among them.

Since Dawson had nominated Woodward and Arthur Keith as possible partners in his project, he decided to have a closer look at his candidates from his present point of view. He had called on Keith at the Royal College of Surgeons that morning on the pretext of discussing the finer points of a paper he meant to write on Neolithic finds, including some skull fragments he'd found on the estate of the Duke of Richmond. Keith gladly showed him examples from the reserve collections at the college, where Dawson made a visual reconnoiter of the storage areas, noting where the comparative specimens of the great apes were filed. He was most favorably impressed with Keith's quick intelligence and authority when speaking about his specialty. Dawson's initial feeling that Keith would do admirably was confirmed. And it was reconfirmed after visiting Woodward at the British Museum in the afternoon, where Dawson found him more than usually tiresome considering him as a prospective partner in crime.

When Woodward invited him to tea Dawson accepted only because there would be others from London's scientific community who he saw too infrequently.

Dawson knew or had a nodding acquaintance with everyone in the room. After making his rounds among the guests he'd had his fill of scientific gossip and came upon Backhouse sitting somewhat apart, contemplating the cabbage roses in the carpet.

"I don't believe we've met," Dawson said.

As Dawson sat beside him, Backhouse explained how he had come to be invited. "Dr. Woodward is a paragon of hospitality," Backhouse concluded.

"He is a paragon indeed, and has always been renouned for that quality, not only as a host, but as a scientist," Dawson said. Woodward might make a boring accomplice, but since Dawson was drinking his tea, he felt he ought at least to acknowledge his virtues. "He is universally admired for his thoroughness and his unfailing attention to detail. He is indispensible to science," Dawson said, thinking of the cataloguers, the listmakers, organizers, classifiers, the ones who sent two paragraph notes on this or that with two pages of footnotes to scientific journals he never had the patience to read.

"This is my first encounter with scientific society," Backhouse said.

"And what is your first impression of us?"

"Your universal fondness for gray suits."

"You wouldn't think it to look at them, but behind that apparent uniformity there is an immense range of backgrounds in this room. Scientific society is wonderfully democratic. Darwin's father was a country doctor. Newton's family were Lincolnshire farmers of no distinction whatever. And our own genial host is the son of a silk dyer from somewhere up north. Arthur entered the museum at eighteen by competitive examination with little education and no credentials."

"And here he is, a distinguished keeper at the museum with a villa in Fulham. A heroic rise."

"If you like."

"What is your own social saga?" Backhouse inquired.

"Utterly lacking in heroics. I'm a country solicitor with a few discoveries to my credit. I don't even belong here, technically, as I have not even a shred of academic parchment nor belong to any august institution. I am an amateur."

"Then we have much in common. I am also self-taught."

They began to amuse themselves in quiet tones about the pretentions acquired by those with formal degrees in Chinese studies and paleontology.

Maud had taken her usual place at a small tea table covered with her embroidered tea cloth, pouring and offering sandwiches, extracting a portion of conversation in return from those who came to her. From where she was she could see Backhouse and Dawson sitting across the room. By what perversity of social accident, abetted no doubt by Arthur's negligence, could her baronet have been found and monopolized by the one person in the room without academic status, an interloper, a scientific adventurer? Maud decided that as a conscientious hostess she could only do her duty by rescuing Backhouse, although it meant leaving those of her guests who were thirsty to their own devices. Rising, she smoothed down the front of her dress, approached the men and tapped Backhouse lightly on the wrist. As he rose she drew him away to a settee.

"I hope you don't find this chatter about tatty old bones and things that leap and crawl too trying, Sir Edmund."

"Trelawny," Backhouse replied, pleading for further intimacy. "I always ask my friends to address me by my middle name. Edmund wsa the name of a particularly formidable and austere great uncle. We are Quakers, you see, and my greatavuncular namesake had fundamentalist views of life to which I never subscribed. If I had, I would be sitting on a simple chair in a simple place in simple contemplation of my sins, rather than drinking tea with a charming lady."

It was only the austerity of Maud's face that stood between her and a simper. Backhouse captivated her beyond his baronial coat of arms. His every gesture spoke refinement. The arch of his eyebrows, the sculptured curve of his mouth were perfection. His nostrils, she noticed, were translucent as they flared with what seemed to her a mutual attraction. She wished she had a fan to indicate her indulgence.

"How I envy you knowing another culture so intimately; we English tend to be so insular, although we pretend to be cosmopolitan imperialists," Maud said.

"Most foreigners in China are just as shortsighted as their bourgeois counterparts at home. The men rarely go anywhere except for work and the women for shopping. And they only learn enough Chinese to order their servants about. I have taken a different view; my rewards have not been pecuniary, but I have learned a little something about the Celestial Empire."

"My husband tells me you are known at court."

"I have certain connections. The court is like one of those curios that are so popular nowadays—those ivory openwork nests of boxes, one inside the other. Few barbarians have been privileged to penetrate to the innermost chamber."

"Have you?"

"On several occasions I was called into the presence of the Empress Dowager Tzu Hsi, the Divine Personage, the Dragon of the North. If I were to recite all her titles, we would be here until tomorrow morning."

Backhouse's voice was so musical to Maud she would have happily listened to him read the death notices in the *Times*. "And what was she like?"

"I am told she was as ruthless as Machiavelli, Talleyrand, and Metternich combined. But from where I stood in the audience, all she looked like was a beautiful effigy, her face caked with rice powder and wearing the most divinely embroidered robes of state. She wore a jet black wig with gold butterflies and mythical birds stuck in it and a sort of jacket that covered her shoulders and bosom, a net made of pearls, each one the size of a mothball. She was a goddess, as she was believed to be. I saw her on another occasion, at a court theatrical—she loved dress-up—all decked out as the female incarnation of Kwan Yin, the Bodhisattva of mercy. And she was famous for that quality. In all her official acts of vengeance, she never once decreed tortures or lingering deaths that are so common in the lower echelons."

"What then?"

"Beheading or the ultimate in Oriental generosity—compulsory suicide."

Maud would have wanted to develop this theme of official and unofficial bloodletting, but she felt that her Trelawny might think her morbid. So she responded with a thoughtful and tolerant silence to his report of barbarism that passed for justice.

"She was well-loved by her people," Backhouse continued, "although in South China, particularly Canton, where the Manchus were barely tolerated, it was said that she was a monster of unparalleled depravity. But in my opinion, those were scurrilous rumors about *la vie intime* of the court."

"What rumors? About what?"

"Oh, you know, the usual things," Backhouse said. "Unnatural appetites, strange practices, opium, orgies . . ." He caught himself midsentence, suggesting that the list of indecencies was as long as a complete recitation of Her Majesty's titles.

"But she was an old woman," Maud said.

"Admitted to eighty-six the year she died," Backhouse said, informing her with an oblique slyness that age was no bar to corrupt pleasure.

Maud was silent again, seeing that her Trelawny was a man indulgent of human frailty and a cultural relativist of considerable experience.

"Do I dare to ask you something that has always intrigued me about China?"

"Dare to dare, dear lady."

"Eunuchs," she whispered.

"Her Majesty's chief eunuch, Li Lien-ying, was a particular friend of mine. He 'left the family,' as is said so charmingly, at sixteen. It was said that Li's ambition to be a eunuch was so great that he performed the operation himself. And it was said that his power and his wealth was exceeded only by the Empress Dowager herself. One had to know him to get anything done—and he took a squeeze, a bribe, from everyone for his favors. He could be very kind, providing you didn't rub him the wrong way, so to speak. Not that I am making excuses for our friendship; I was flattered, considering I was a barbarian and he had been honored with the rank of the Sixth Grade and the decoration of the Crow's Feather, which is like a dukedom and the Garter rolled into one. But he was an exception. The ordinary sort of court eunuchs are corrupt, vindictive, cruel, and sensual," Backhouse said. "I expect it is their sense of—well, deprivation, that makes them so ill-tempered and greedy. They have been part of court life from earliest times, as we know that Confucius refers with disapproval of their baneful influence. Her Majesty issued hypocritical decree after decree announcing the reform of the eunuch system, saying they were low creatures fit only for sweeping the floors, but they flourished for the whole of her reign, and their excesses were, and still are, flagrant and unconcealed."

"Can't somebody do something," Maud said with resentment. "What about our missionaries?"

"Our missionaries have no power in the Forbidden City. And even if they did, one cannot kill the elephant of tradition with a peashooter of indignation loaded with pellets of good intentions."

"These eunuchs," Maud began. "How do they . . . what do they. . . ?"

Backhouse sat in a relaxed pose, one arm on the back of the settee, the other dropped in his lap, waiting patiently as if for a stutterer to complete his thought. At last he said, "How-do-they, what-do-they? My dear lady, do not be ashamed of your curiosity; children are unabashedly curious. That is their charm, and we should never lose that part of our innocence, however cynical life makes us."

"Your wisdom exceeds my courage," Maud replied.

"The intimacies between eunuchs are what one might expect considering their lacunae. One must commend them on their inventiveness, I suppose. There are those who, I am sorry to say, allow themselves to be used by men who are *intactus* in a vile way. Do you speak Latin?"

"I regret I do not."

"Don't regret it for a moment. It allows me to speak to you openly about such matters without offending your sensibilities. *Pene in os recepto, ita ut commovendo, ore meo offecerim, ut is quem cupio,*" Backhouse began. Maud attended with eyes like steel rivets, as if attention alone would extract meaning from his unintelligible lecture on Oriental sexual curiosities. She was so engrossed that one of her guests who came up to her to say goodbye, a botanist who did understand Latin, stood for some moments, blushed scarlet at Backhouse's recitation, and withdrew in confusion and embarrassment without Maud's having even noticed him.

Eventually a general movement to dispersal among the guests intruded on Maud's tête-à-tête. She offered her courtesies and began to clear the tea service from the cloth.

"I want to thank you for a most enjoyable afternoon, Mrs. Woodward," Backhouse said, being one of the last to leave.

"Before you go, Sir Edmund," she said, now that they were again among those who were not admitted to their intimacy, "I wonder if you would do me the honor of adding your name to my tea cloth. As you can see, it has been autographed by many of our scientific friends. My needlework preserves the signatures for posterity."

"What a singular piece of work," Backhouse observed.

"The signators are all men of science, but since my husband has told me that you are to be the museum's bone man in China, it would not be inappropriate for you to sign it."

"I am more honored than I can say."

"Arthur, give me your pencil."

Maud held the cloth taut on the table. Instead of writing out his name, Backhouse inscribed a Chinese ideogram. "This is grass script," he explained, "an informal calligraphic style, two characters held together by a ligature. It is a phonetic transliteration of my name. An affectation, perhaps, but I use it in all my personal correspondence."

Maud folded the tea cloth and put it over the arm of a chair.

As Backhouse was taking his leave, Dawson said to him, "I wish you luck in your search for dragon bones. Perhaps you'll even find a dragon."

"Never underestimate legend. Schliemann discovered Troy."

Dawson extracted a personal card from his case and gave it

to Backhouse. "If you are ever in my neighborhood, let me know."

Looking at the address, Backhouse said, "I expect to be in Sussex quite soon."

When all the guests had left, Maud immediately opened her tea cloth up again and began the difficult and important task of deciding exactly what color her Trelawny was.

Edmund Backhouse was a baronet, the scion of a distinguished Quaker family, had attended Oxford and had gone out to China with his knack for languages, studied Chinese culture, wrote and did translations, and survived the Boxer siege of Peking.

Edmund Backhouse was also a compulsive liar. He would lie for the sake of the lie itself, to witness the credulity of his audience, and for the satisfaction of withholding the truth.

If he was late for an appointment, he would invent a fantastic encounter that had delayed him, described in minute and dramatic detail, rather than simply explain that he had been dawdling over the knot of his necktie. If someone admired a manuscript in his collection, he would enthrall the admirer with a convuluted tale of negotiations with the wiliest antiquarian in Peking, rather than say that it had been brought to his house for sale by someone who hadn't realized its value, even though the truth would have shown his connoisseurship to better advantage; he would make that sacrifice of forgoing self-aggrandizement for the sake of the lie. They were wonderful—lies—so much more vivid to him than ordinary truth, and more plausible to him because the lie was part of his own alternate universe, over which he was absolute ruler. When challenged in a discrepancy that cast doubt on his frankness, Backhouse would face his accuser with an expression of such pained offense and offer such an ingenuous explanation, that his challenger ended by explaining that he meant to cast no doubt, but rather sought a clarification.

Backhouse had no great-uncle Edmund, and his family's Quaker beliefs were relaxed to the point of atheistic indifference, but Backhouse could not resist lying to Maud, even in such a small thing.

It was true that he had attended Oxford, but he never

graduated, had no degree. His fortune was lost to him, not because of his father's financial pranks but because of his own. Having reached his second year at university, he had run up colossal debts of £22,000. Backhouse was rich enough but insisted on behaving as if he were very rich and very spoiled. Several dozens of shirts were ordered when an extravagant dozen would have done handsomely. When Backhouse announced that Ellen Terry was the most beautiful woman on the stage, he booked half the stalls at the Haymarket Theatre so his friends and acquaintances could share his delight. He never developed an affectation or obsession that wasn't conspicuously expensive; he began collecting jewels, became bored, and impatiently sold them at a loss to begin another collection—Greek gold coins. Finally, having airily declared himself a bankrupt, Backhouse upped and disappeared. His long-suffering father, a director of Barclay's Bank, was left to sort it out. Sir Jonathan, sensible man, put his incorrigible son on a small allowance with no further access to family money.

It was true that Backhouse had acquired a library—a small collection containing only a few important Sung manuscripts, and that during the siege his house had been destroyed. And it was true that he had begun again. His now-splendid collections were made by looting the homes of pro-Boxer sympathizers and innocent bystanders—a common activity in the days following the Allied liberation of Peking. Everyone joined in, even consular diplomats who justified their thefts by reasoning that whatever they could pilfer would be saved from being burned or trampled underfoot.

He had written a history, *China Under the Empress Dowager*, with J. O. P. Bland, and it did contain the diary of Ching Shan. That revelatory manuscript was unique in Backhouse's current collections. It was neither legitimately acquired nor illegitimately looted. It was a forgery of Backhouse's manufacture. Like all of his lies, this one hung on a peg of fact. Ching Shan had lived and died, and as comptroller to the Old Buddha was privy to state secrets. Mute in his grave, he could neither confirm nor deny Backhouse's version of those confidences, whatever they may have been, if any. The dead were the best accomplices; they could never lose nerve and betray you. It was not that Backhouse, beneath the soft, even gelatinous persona, had nerves of steel. It was simply that his belief in the credulity of others extended to himself. He thoroughly believed in his own lies. Bland was his unwitting accomplice, who looked on the Ching Shan forgery with the ready enthusiasm of a journalist, for whom the scoop was the Holy Grail.

It was partially true that Backhouse had come to London to find a publisher for his book, thinking that his lie might infiltrate thousands of minds, rather than the few people in his small world; it gave him an immense rush of power, almost omnipotence. He would read the diary that he meant to foist upon history with a feeling of wonder that he had rescued it from the wreckage of Ching Shan's house; that sense of wonder and accomplishment, however illusory, far outweighed the even more impressive, if perverted, accomplishment of having invented the diary in the first place, in all its convincing detail, and then forging the calligraphy of the Manchu official whose other genuine papers might turn up as a challenge to the false autobiography.

Backhouse had come to the museum specifically to see Woodward. The proposal about the dragon bones had nothing to do with his actual purpose. In all things Backhouse could not take a direct route. He enjoyed putting his quarry off guard, even when he was certain he had an unassailable position. That was the reason he had accepted Woodward's invitation to tea, and why he had played at charming Maud, like a cat poking and scratching at a wounded mouse, with the inborn instinct of a predator, seemingly tame, but giving in to the least stimulation.

Woodward was unsettled when Backhouse presented himself at the museum again the following day.

"I haven't had a chance to speak with the superintendent about your proposal," Woodward said. "First I must send him a memorandum; I'm afraid there is rather complicated protocol here at the museum."

"I didn't expect any decision so soon," Backhouse said. "I came personally to thank you for a lovely afternoon."

"Not at all. Mrs. Woodward was quite taken with you."

"I did not intend to give you any cause for jealousy," Backhouse said, smiling gently.

"I will certainly let you know how your proposal is received by the powers that be, and in the meantime, if there is anything further I can do for you, please don't hesitate to ask."

"There is something else I meant to speak with you about, which almost slipped my mind."

Woodward prepared himself for a series of tacks before Backhouse came to port.

"You already know of my continuing financial distress, and I will not bore you with pathetic tales of deprivation. But my finances are connected to the matter I want to discuss with you: a manuscript."

"Is it Oriental?"

"It is of English origin, unique in my collections, and I don't intend to offer it to the Bodleian."

"I would be glad to direct you to the keeper of English Manuscripts at the British Library," Woodward offered. "Is it something of historical interest that perhaps has descended in your family?"

"It is not an heirloom, but it has great historic interest and something you ought to know about."

"A scientific work?"

"A social scientist, perhaps, might think it a significant document."

"I'm afraid I don't have any relations with the social sciences."

"We all have relations with the social sciences. After all, we live in society and assume attitudes society imposes on us, and that is the stuff of social science."

"I stand corrected, but I have no professional relations in that area."

"The manuscript in my possession would be of interest to the social scientist concerned with the aberrant rather than the conventional. I for one believe that the unexpected, the astonishing, the shocking makes for a delightful inconstancy in life. What would history be without its eccentrics and its scandals? A boring pavane instead of the sprightly gavotte it is. Don't you agree?''

"Entirely." Woodward found himself wishing Backhouse would get to the point.

"I knew you would. Everyone loves a scandal, not only because there is something delicious about discovering other people's secrets, but because there is a painful pleasure in the awareness of one's own indiscretions. The ordinary man who reads in the newspaper about highfalutin adultery in Mayfair will relive his own shabby peccadillos, thinking that the swells are no better than he, and that he is just as good as they.''

"You are a psychologist as well as a historian.''

"I am put in mind of one scandal in particular. You may recall it. It was one of the most notorious episodes in the darker history of Victorian London. It was in all the papers. I am speaking of the Cleveland Street Scandal. In 1889 a certain house at number 19 Cleveland Street was exposed as a homosexual male brothel." Backhouse paused to take a reading of Woodward. He saw him swallow, his Adam's apple rise and fall in his throat. "Two lads who worked at a nearby post office were questioned by a superior as to the source of what seemed like more money than they ought to have had. They admitted having earned it having sexual relations with gentlemen at the house on Cleveland Street. From that small admission the scandal bloomed like a weed in summer. The procurer, Charles Hammond, fled England before he could be prosecuted. The boys testified at Scotland Yard, and it became known that the clients at Cleveland Street included prominent members of the aristocracy. The boys' evidence was suppressed, but not before Lord Arthur Somerset, whose perversion was known to all, decamped to the continent, much to the delight of the popular press, which trumpeted every bit of gossip, innuendo, and hearsay concerning the den of iniquity. But you know all this; you must have followed the accounts in the press with unusually avid interest.''

Woodward made no reply.

"I am not living vicariously when I tell you of these events," Backhouse said with his usual diffidence. "As a young student of sixteen, it was roaring good fun rattling down from Winchester on the train during the weekends and holidays, to do for money what I had been doing for free. I worked on a piecework basis, so to say; I was always short of pocket money, even then, and it was so nice, for a time, to be able to buy all the sugar buns I wanted, though they were bad for my complexion. Gave me spots. I was an oddity, even in that place, because of my background, but the boys were good chums. A bit rough around the edges. I remember two in particular, not for their beauty, but for their names— Newlove and Thickbroom. I couldn't help imagining them as characters in a Restoration comedy.'' Backhouse stopped to chuckle. ''I was especially in demand by those clients who preferred my aristocratic demeanor to the rough barrow boys and postal messengers who were my coworkers. Which is probably the reason I never encountered you in one of those dank bedrooms with stained and dirty sheets. That, and your special tastes, which I did not and do not share.''

''You have insulted me and my hospitality,'' Woodward said. ''Leave here at once.''

''You may recall,'' Backhouse continued, ''that at the time of the scandal, there were rumors in the press that there had been a ledger kept by the procurer Hammond, in which the boys had seen him entering the names of clients, boys engaged, acts performed, and fees paid. It was never found, but I myself helped Hammond add up his accounts, as he wasn't at all good at arithmetic. And I managed to acquire the ledger in the confusion of his hasty departure for Paris.'' Backhouse reached into his inside jacket pocket and took out some papers. ''This is a transcript of certain pages of the ledger.'' He adjusted his glasses and began to read. '' '3 March 1886. George,' that's the boy, 'Arthur Smith Woodward, tied and whipped, twenty shillings.' ''

''Stop it.''

''We are all in bondage to something: beauty, truth, science, money.''

''Get out,'' Woodward commanded. ''Those papers don't prove anything.''

''I am glad to see that you are concerned with the question

of proof, instead of attempting denial. I can invite you to inspect the original holograph at my bank, Grindley's, St. James's.''

''You are completely morally corrupt.''

''To be morally corrupt is nothing compared to being financially defunct. I can do nothing about the former, as it has been my nature, even as a boy. But I intend to rectify the latter. I am here on a matter of blackmail.''

''You'd do better looking to others who could better reward you for your efforts,'' Woodward said with contempt. ''What could you expect from me? It is hardly worth your while.''

''If you plead poverty, I as a poor scholar can sympathize. But I will make no exceptions. The others I have already visited were reluctant at first, regardless of their station in life, but to a man, they have agreed.''

''I won't pay,'' Woodward said. ''I'll go to the police and tell them what you're doing.''

''And expose yourself in the bargain? I think not. Besides, you have no proof this conversation ever took place.''

''The police will believe me.''

''Possibly. But to get satisfaction, you will have to charge me and make public the reason for this alleged threat.''

''You are remarkably arrogant, considering you put yourself in a position of being exposed as a prostitute.''

''I live far away in China. The Chinese are much more relaxed in their sexual attitudes. They do not look askance at me. And they would not look askance at you for being a sodomite and a disciple of Sacher-Masoch. If you do not pay me, you may have to think seriously of emigrating.'' After a full stop, Backhouse said, ''Ten pounds a month.''

''I won't pay you, regardless of the consequences,'' Woodward declared, getting out of his chair.

Backhouse took a card from his case. He had written the name of a hotel on it. ''You can get in touch with me any time this week, when you have changed your mind. If I do not hear from you, I will be at the museum again a week from today to get my first payment.'' With that, he rose and crossed to the door where his hand rested on the knob. "Good day."

Woodward heaved a terrible sigh of defeat and sank into the chair Backhouse had sat in. He looked at his desk and, seeing his own place unoccupied, got up and quickly sat behind the desk as if protecting his territory. Backhouse had the power to make him disappear; behind that light touch and pale fragility was an implacable demon. Neither reason nor pathos would affect him. Exposure would mean his immediate dismissal from the museum. He would be cast out of the world of science as a freak and a pervert. And Maud. Woodward dreaded to think how she would react to his disgrace. His playing victim to her tyrant was their own affair. She had never asked him the source of his fantasy, nor had he tried to find the origin of hers; theirs was an unspoken bargain. Backhouse surely counted on the effect of disclosure to his marriage, although he couldn't have imagined how it would upset that delicate balance. The whole ritual was based on choice, or so it seemed to Woodward. Maud would choose her moments to humiliate him, and he accepted that. Now she would loathe him unrelentingly, or worse, she might leave him altogether.

Woodward pulled at his stiff collar, suffocating from hopelessness and rage, and then got up to open the window. The traffic slid by on Cromwell Road. A taxi stopped in front of the museum and a woman got out. Then two small boys clambered onto the pavement and raced ahead of their mother to the museum entrance. They were going to see the dinosaurs, no doubt. Everything and everybody in the world was bound together in a mesh of the ordinary, indifferent to him as he stood apart from it, alone.

There was a knock at the door. Woodward started and turned from the open window. The knock sounded again.

Woodward braced himself against the windowsill. "Yes?"

The porter came in with a tray. "Eleven o'clock. Your tea, sir." He put it on a corner of the desk and left.

Mechanically, Woodward poured the hot tea through the metal strainer on the rim of the cup, set it aside with the dregs, and added his milk and two lumps of sugar. His stomach churned, but he sipped at the tea, trying to take his place again in the ordinary world.

The nameless proprietor of the house on Cleveland Street, whom Woodward came to know from the newspaper reports as Charles Hammond, had met him at the door the first time and at every subsequent visit. His manner was completely neutral. It was the strangest thing, Woodward had thought—this impartiality that went beyond tolerance—because he was always in a nervous state of expectancy and arousal.

There were periods, months, when Woodward thought he had mastered his shameful desire, when he thought of nothing but work. Then it would begin, a tiny flicker at first, like a delicate guttering flame lighted to kindling, the sight of a particular stranger in the street, a photograph in a magazine of a man that touched his erotic center. He would make a show to himself of resisting, of redoubling his scientific endeavors. But the pain of the struggle only intensified and distilled his urgent need until he accepted the inevitability of his powerlessness to resist.

He would never go directly to the house. Instead, he would appear to stroll aimlessly in Tottenham Court Road, glancing in shop windows, thinking that soon he would go through the door where he would be not himself, but another person, as a dreamer sees his familiar self acting in unfamiliar ways and knowing afterward that the imagery was of his own creation.

To rid himself of the irrational and demanding urgency of his desire, he would have to gather all his strength in a great effort of will, to go up the two steps to the door between the spear-point iron railings, put his hand on the knocker, and wait the endless moments before the door opened to receive him. He could never get over the feeling that the other people in the street who glanced at him on the threshold knew what he was up to, and that those who took no notice of him were purposely avoiding looking in his direction, the way he might avert his eyes with disgust and pity from someone with a monstrous deformity.

Often he would wait in the street some distance from the entrance to see who went in and who came out, to justify to himself that there were others like him and to see whether there was anything about their appearance, dress, walk, physique that marked them. Sometimes there would be a young man of military bearing, perhaps a guardsman out of uniform, or two of them laughing and chatting as they waited at the door. There were well-dressed men who looked as if they'd come from their clubs, who pulled at the brims of their beaver hats. And there were ordinary men like himself, for whom Woodward could invent no life. He would watch as long as he dared without seeming to loiter, taking the measure of men who walked by, making bets with himself whether they would stop at number 19 or pass it on their way to some other destination. Then he would make his decision, cross the street at an oblique angle, telling himself as he waited an eternity at the door that he was a fool to concern himself with the good opinion of complete strangers who passed by, but caring nevertheless. And there was always a chance—yes, there was—that someone he knew would see him. He pretended to cough and covered the lower part of his face with his hand.

Woodward followed the progress of the scandal in the newspapers, buying his copies at the stand in Parson's Green underground station and throwing them away at South Kensington. "Criminals in this case are to be numbered by the score," he read under the headline "West End Scandals," including The Earl of Euston and Lord Arthur Somerset, whose whereabouts were unknown. There were veiled references to members of Parliament and to a royal person. The scandal not only pounded at the door of Lord Salisbury's government but threatened to invade the Palace itself.

When some of the boys came to trial, one of the picture papers ran sketched portraits of the defendants, and Woodward looked at them trying to recognize which ones he'd been with. The courtroom artist had made them all into the same generic youths with slicked down hair, who might have been posing for shirt collar advertisements.

Woodward lived in a state of constant anxiety, but had his greatest fright when the existence of the ledger was rumored. The police denied its existence, and he was not alone in thinking that Scotland Yard was suppressing evidence that would compromise reputations at the highest levels of society. He was glad that the English vice was oblivious to class. Until Backhouse's visit, he had occasionally thought that the ledger was in some secret file, or burnt, he hoped, if it had existed at all.

The tea had gotten cold. The neat stacks of papers and boxes of index cards with color-coded tabs he had devised mocked him with their futile neatness. His adamant declaration to Backhouse that he wouldn't pay was a hollow bluff. He would pay, just as all the others would. But he would wait the full week's time before capitulating; at least Backhouse might think for a while that he'd had the courage to resist.

Chapter V

ANYONE TRAVELING FROM PEKING TO EUROPE WOULD BE-gin by taking the rattling train toward the coast fifty or so miles southeast to Tientsin. If one were traveling first class, it was necessary to go considerably further by rail along the prongs of either the Liaotung or Shantung peninsulas that pinched the Gulf of Chihli, to Port Arthur or Tsingtao, where the Cunard and French Lines had ports of call. There one would wait in perfect comfort in a grand luxe hotel, taking refreshments in a palm court or attending to the bruises acquired on the train while the ships made ready to set out toward the Yellow Sea.

If one were indifferent to luxury, or could not pay for it, the traveler needed to proceed from Tientsin only a few more miles to the port of Taku at the farthest curve of the gulf, where smaller vessels of obscure registry called. There, they dropped cargoes and picked up others, bauxite or nitrites, and took on passengers of no great distinction, missionaries on leave, low-level diplomats, and those who would not say where they had been and couldn't say how far they might be going.

Taku crouched on the shore of a swampy coastal plain at the mouth of an estuary that led to Tientsin. On one bank stood the grim walls of Taku fort, an empty boast since it had fallen to the Allied forces on the first leg of their march to

Peking. All along the shoreline, massive piers jutted out into the water, raised on bundles of black pilings painted with creosote. Under the tin roofs were offices and godowns where customs officials and brokers made out papers and stamped them for endless consignments of wooden crates, boxes stitched into jute coverings, and scuffed luggage being moved by sweating coolies. Behind the docks were warehouses and depots of stained, mud-colored brick or rusting cast iron and a hodge-podge of weathered wooden sheds.

Front Street, as the Europeans called the dirt esplanade facing the wharves, was set with one- or two-story buildings, once whitewashed, the offices of a few branch banks from Shanghai and Peking, shipping companies and chandlers selling ship fittings and spare parts. A noisy procession of western and Chinese entrepreneurs, tradesmen, and merchants filled the street, threading their way between coolies in blue cotton tunics, bearing swaying baskets of fish and vegetables on the ends of long shoulder poles, rickshaw drivers, ragged beggars, and street vendors shouting their wares in repetitive high-pitched diphthongs.

Commerce is an ugly thing, Backhouse thought as he stepped out into Front Street, squinting toward the bay littered with steamships, some with bare auxiliary masts, gunboats and cruisers, seagoing junks, whose high square outlines and reed mat sails hadn't changed in form for a thousand years. A permanent colony of sampan crowded against the shore.

Backhouse put his hand as a visor to his eyes and saw the *Higashi Maru* from Osaka sitting low in the water. In the evening it would begin the long voyage to England. He had gone on board with his luggage and, not having been satisfied with his accommodations, had taken himself to the office of the Matsuoko Line to explain that he was going to England for medical treatment and could not think of imposing the indelicate symptoms of his malady on a fellow passenger who was to share his stateroom. He had been near swooning when they had at first refused his request for a single cabin, but they had given in when he advised them that his family solicitors would certainly hold them responsible for anything they did that exacerbated his condition.

In 1908, Backhouse had completed his manuscript with John Bland and was setting out for London to find a publisher, not being willing to entrust it to the mails, and wanting to be there to answer any question that might be asked, particularly about the Ching Shan diary. He loved answering questions, as it gave him the opportunity to elaborate his lies like a lace maker, passing the bobbins of spurious facts effortlessly under and over each other to make intricate webs and arabesques.

He was looking forward to his visit in London, but the trip would be tiresome enough without sharing his cabin with some junior-grade person from one of the legations who, although they had never met, would insist they had a multitude of friends in common. There would be the inevitable maiden sisters on their once-in-a-lifetime trip around the world, and a preacher with his whey-faced family on leave from their discouraging posting in the hinterlands, still firm in their beliefs, but loose in their bowels. And besides, on top of everything else, the six weeks of the journey with few landfalls would be a period of forced celibacy, which he knew would make him neurasthenic. These last hours before his departure would be his only opportunity for an encounter, a little adventure, which memory might be as pleasant as the sea air during the day and might lighten the restless hours in his berth alone at night.

Behind the ramshackle facade of Front Street, which at least enjoyed the purifying wind from the bay, the rest of the town was a slum of stinking alleyways with small bars and brothels, where the smell of garlic, incense, and the ubiquitous miasma of human excrement seemed to have been trapped for centuries. Whatever swatches of sky that might have been seen between the buildings had been patched over with long, hanging signs of calligraphy or laundry hung on lines across the narrow streets. Wedged between the small shops, opium dens, and disreputable businesses were Taoist shrines and crib-sized Buddhist temples where whoremongers and shopkeepers took a moment to honor an ancestor or leave a joss stick in the fragrant ashes at the feet of Lord Buddha.

Backhouse was no stranger to Taku and walked through the winding streets, knowing at each turn whether the port was to his right, left, or back. He ignored the pluckings at his sleeve by the prostitutes. At the entrance of a bar he heard the scratchy whine and jangle of Chinese music on a gramophone, and the deep-throated, unmistakably Western laughter. Looking in, he saw a gang of Russian sailors, some drunkenly dancing with one another while others clung unsteadily on the necks of barely adolescent Chinese girls. He passed on, prowling, bored and expectant.

At a turning was a souvenir shop, its windows filled with bits of trashy china, dolls with miniature wigs and Mandarin robes, packages of incense, and herbal elixirs making fantastic claims as aphrodisiacs. A merchant seaman carrying a duffel stood at the window. He was wearing a knit hat, work shirt, and denims. As Backhouse approached, the seaman glanced sideways at him, then returned his attention to the window, but the brief contact was an acknowledgment, as if they had given a secret, fraternal handshake. They stood together at the window.

"What's your ship?" Backhouse asked.

"The *Shasta*, out of Seattle."

With those few words they pegged each other by their accents, a high-tone bigwig and a common East End cockney.

"Long live the King," Backhouse said.

"Nice to meet a fellow Limey."

"Are you looking for a souvenir? Something for your Aged P.?"

"My pee's not aged and neither is my tool."

"The direct approach. Most fellows would ask for a drink and then pretend to be a little drunk."

"What's the point. Here we are, two chaps far from home, and who'll be the wiser?"

"I know a bathhouse nearby where we can be quite comfortable." Backhouse led the way further down the narrow street into an alley.

"There's one thing," said the seaman, "I'd be much obliged for a pound or two."

Now that it came to a question of payment, Backhouse looked at his companion more carefully. He was a little old, perhaps, and there was a definite venal cast of his eyes. Still, he was white, and while he was no spring lamb, Backhouse, after so many uninterrupted years in China, would not quibble too much over the price of good English mutton. They settled on thirty shillings.

An attendant led them to a small room with a bunk, gave them two towels, and left. As they took off their clothes, the seamen said, "What's your name, mate?"

"Morley Ratcliffe," Backhouse said, naming the head of the British legation in Peking. "What's yours?"

"Charlie Hammond."

Their sex was nothing that would supply Backhouse with a vivid memory during his long voyage, but serviceable enough, considering the circumstances. They bathed in a large wooden tub and returned to the room draped in towels. Backhouse ordered several bottles of rice wine and Hammond gulped at the sweet, mild-tasting liqueur while Backhouse sipped at his.

"I'm a bit down on my luck," Hammond said. "Wouldn't have asked you for a farthing if I didn't have to."

"You give value," Backhouse said lazily, bored again. He was lying head to toe with Hammond on the bunk, his head propped up on one hand and patted him indulgently on the thigh with the other. "I suppose you have been very popular with your shipmates, ever since the days you swabbed the deck as a strapping young lad."

"It's my first time as a seaman."

"Seeing the world. The lure of the Orient."

"I don't care for all that do-this, do-that, and be-quick-about-it. I'm used to working for myself."

"So I see."

"Been away eighteen years now. America. Seattle. Plenty of money in that town if you know how to get it, and I did, mark my words, if only the coppers would leave one alone to do a bit of work."

"So you lit out to conquer new worlds."

"You could say that."

"I just did."

"Before I left London, I had all the money I could use." Hammond refilled his wine cup again and drank it off.

"And what has kept you so long from the source of your great wealth?" Backhouse inquired.

"Statue of limitations," said Hammond.

Backhouse suppressed a smile, imagining a suite of classicizing marble nudes in niches embodying Faith, Hope, Charity, and Limitations."

"They're looking for me," Hammond continued. "Those high-and-mighty blokes. They'd like to get their hands on what I got." He thumbed at his duffel lying on the floor.

"What is it?" Backhouse said without interest.

"A book."

"You're a bibliophile."

" 'Ey, mind your tongue. I ain't no biblio . . . whatever you said. I'm just as good as you or anybody else." Hammond's words were slightly slurred, and his voice had taken on a winey truculence.

"Better than most," Backhouse replied.

"Everybody's the same when they got that bulge in their trousers," Hammond observed. "But some blokes think they was born with advantages. Maybe they were, but I got my advantage, right there in that bag. When I said I'd tell what's in that book, a certain gentleman gave me eight hundred quid to stay out of sight."

Hammond began a rambling tale of his adventures after leaving Cleveland Street. He'd gone off to Gravesend and then, when a warrant for his arrest was issued, he managed to get to Paris. There, he consulted his ledger and estimating that Lord Arthur Somerset was one of the richest and easiest marks, being equerry to the Prince of Wales and having much to lose apart from the money, he arranged through intermediaries with Somerset's solicitor, Arthur Newton, for the blackmail. Hammond's proximity on the continent had been unacceptable to Newton, who arranged for the money to be deposited in New York and supplied Hammond with a first-class ticket on board the *SS Pennland*, Red Star Line, from Antwerp to get there. The rest of the story was a litany of transcontinental misadventures and treacheries that eventually landed him in Seattle.

"Lord Arthur wasn't the only swell who patronized the establishment," Hammond said. " 'Course, they never said who they was, but I found out easy enough. I had a little army of chaps; they'd follow everyone to find out where they went. Then my chaps would chat up the porters at the clubs or kitchen maids taking a breather in the street, and I'd put it down in my book. And one of these days, I'll make my way back to London and put the touch on some others, like I did his Lordship. It's never too late, I always say."

"And so you should," Backhouse said. He had listened to Hammond's story, becoming increasing attuned to its possibilities. He rang for the attendant and spoke briefly to him in Chinese. "I've ordered us some food. Your tale of derring-do has made me quite famished."

"There's more gold in that bag than anybody ever found in the gold fields of California," Hammond bragged. "I think I'll jump ship at Hong Kong and bide my time; they speak bloody English there, instead of this yap-yapping."

Backhouse filled his wine cup again while waiting for the food. Hammond's scheme of spending his declining years in comfort as a mass blackmailer was too good to waste on him. These things had to be managed carefully and with a little style, and Hammond would be clumsy; the police would be onto him in a thrice, and the ledger would be as worthless as fool's gold.

The servant entered the room and put down the tray of food.

"You should try the pork *shu-t'ing*. The boy says they do it particularly well here," Backhouse advised.

Hammond ate greedily at first, then noticing that Backhouse was nibbling at a bowl of stir-fried vegetables, he offered to share his pork.

"I have lived in China for many years and have become a Buddhist and a vegetarian."

"Blimey," Hammond said between mouthfuls. "Gone native.'' As his first hunger subsided, he slowed down. Suddenly he shot a look of confusion at Backhouse, then panic as his vision became blurred, his tongue and fingers numb. His mouth fell helplessly open as he reached toward Backhouse, and then he fell headfirst with a clatter among the dishes.

Backhouse rose and heaved the duffel onto the bunk. The book was black, a medium-sized bookkeeper's ledger with leather corners, quite worn. He began reading, occasionally looking at Hammond, his damp hair tangled in a platter of *lo mein*. It was an amazing document, a Debrett of English homosexual society. Backhouse smiled as he flipped through the pages. Then he dressed quickly. Hammond's clothes lay in a heap on the floor. Backhouse nearly succumbed to the temptation to retrieve his thirty shillings, but Hammond had given value, and Backhouse congratulated himself on his fairness.

In the corridor, Backhouse tipped the attendant for adding the special condiment to the pork and, with the ledger tucked under his arm, went out and was immediately lost in the teeming street. The voyage to England would not be as tedious as he had anticipated, now that he had something sensational to read.

Chapter VI

WITHIN A FEW DAYS OF BACKHOUSE'S VISIT TO THE British Museum to deliver his blackmail ultimatum to Woodward, Backhouse sent a short telegram to Charles Dawson in Lewes, saying that, as expected, he would find himself in the neighborhood, and unless otherwise advised, he would be very pleased to call at Castle Lodge.

After having listened to Woodward's absolute refusal to pay the blackmail, Backhouse admitted that things were not going as well as he had predicted when he had first sat on the deck of the *Higashi Maru* making lists of potential victims, the Sirs and Honorables in one column, the ordinary folk in another. Hammond had remarked that it was never too late, but upon arriving in London, Backhouse learned that some of his richest aristocratic prospects had died. Others had simply shrugged off the threat to expose what their families and fellow club men would regard as youthful indiscretion or ancient history. Some of this insouciance proved to be bluff, and the price had been paid, but those who responded to Backhouse's threat with "Go right ahead" and meant it, were completely safe, and Backhouse knew it. Should one of his intended victims go to the police and accuse him of attempted blackmail, it might be his word against one of theirs. But two or more would corroborate each other, and Backhouse would stand to lose what he'd already got as well as the possibility of what he still might get from others. He knew he would have to rely solely on conveying the sense of destruction of reputation and the disgrace of social ostracism. With the aristocracy he'd had only little success; it was in the fields of the middle classes that he found his most arable soil, particularly those who had risen in the world in the last eighteen years, for whom reputation had been hard won, for whom respectability was highly esteemed. The clerk from Selfridge's who had become a managing director had been properly dismayed.

Backhouse got off the train at Lewes in the late morning, still irritated at the surprising boldness of Woodward's refusal to knuckle under. Leaving his small portmanteau at the station—he would be continuing his journey that day—and after looking at a map on the station wall showing points of historical interest, he climbed the steep hill of the High Street and caught his breath at the Castle's barbican. After several weeks in the grime and cacophony of London, the half-timbered houses and old brick storefronts of Lewes had a reticent quaintness that momentarily distracted him from the purpose of his visit.

At Castle Lodge, Dawson satisfied Backhouse's curiosity about some of his specimens before the host settled in his desk chair with his visitor opposite.

"Do you find it as difficult as I," Backhouse asked, "to keep your work and your pleasure separated? Often when I am translating the most preposterously banal decree from the Palace for one of the legations, I find myself thinking of an exquisite line of Sung poetry."

"And when I am checking a title deed, I sometimes find myself standing with Darwin on the forward deck of the *Beagle* plunging through the seas to the Galapagos. But I am only an armchair adventurer, except in this green corner of Sussex."

"The Chinese say that man travels farthest in the mind."

"That was certainly true of Darwin—his theory of evolution. It has taken us farther from our former view of ourselves than any other idea in the last fifty years. It is only an idea; one can't test it. But what an idea! What a leap of imagination!'' Dawson exclaimed.

''Imagination. That is the most human of all human qualities. The mind imagines itself imagining itself. A dog doesn't know it's a dog.''

''If it did, would it be content being a dog, I wonder?'' said Dawson.

''Imagination breeds discontent. One always wants to be something different, which some call being better. But one can be neither different nor better, although a great deal of effort is expended in pretending to oneself and others one has changed or improved.''

''Living in the Orient has made you a fatalist.''

''My theory is true even of your dear friend, Woodward. He has made a long social and professional journey, but you may be assured that his original nature remains intact.''

''Perhaps you are right. I don't suppose Arthur has changed or improved. He's just gotten more so, distilled, concentrated,'' Dawson said. ''But if what you say about him is true, then it is true for you as well. Theories of human behavior must apply equally to all individuals.''

''My theory is particularly applicable to myself, as I have never tried to be better,'' replied Backhouse. ''But it doesn't signify, because my theory is probably completely specious. Perhaps it is true, perhaps not. I only made it up as an excuse for being immoral and beyond redemption.''

Dawson looked at him with amusement. ''Surely you say that merely for effect.''

''I don't expect you to take my word for it. But I will convince you, as I convinced your friend Woodward.''

Dawson's smile faded as he continued to look questioningly at Backhouse. ''Under what circumstances did you reveal this aspect of your personality to him?''

''Would you be distressed to know that everything your esteemed friend and indispensible scientist Woodward has achieved is hanging by the slenderest thread?''

''Am I correct is surmising that you are in possession of a pair of scissors?''

Backhouse snipped the air with his middle and forefinger.

And then, without a scintilla of feeling, he set forth the cause and terms of his blackmail scheme and Woodward's reaction. "As a homosexual, erstwhile or otherwise," Backhouse continued, "Dr. Woodward has no choice in the matter, although at present he doesn't see his situation in that light. He is letting his pride stand in the way of sound judgment. I have come to implore you, as his friend, to make him see reason. I am implacable in my resolve to expose him if he does not. I dislike being thwarted."

Dawson pondered the matter for some time, looking with intense concentration at Backhouse, then out the window of his study to gather his thoughts. Turning to Backhouse again, he said, "I am a solicitor. In my small country practice I have always advocated practical solutions to practical matters."

"You are quite right," Backhouse replied, coming forward slightly in his chair.

"Where is this document?"

"In a vault in London."

"I assume you know that a photographic copy of this document has no value as evidence."

"I have not attempted to make a copy."

"I don't have to believe you for the reason I have just stated. It would be useless to you in this contemptible enterprise of yours. You are correct in saying that Arthur is a proud man. If I went to him and did what you suggest, then he would know I had knowledge of his past follies, and I will not be the cause of further embarrassment to him."

"Then you have to live with the knowledge of contributing to his ruin when you had a chance to save him."

"How much are you trying to get from Arthur?" Dawson asked.

"Thirty pounds a month."

"Nonsense. I know what Arthur makes at the museum and you probably do too, approximately. You know he couldn't afford that; you probably asked closer to ten."

Backhouse was noncommittal.

Then Dawson said, "Now, then. Arthur would have paid you a hundred and twenty pounds in the coming year—if he had agreed. I am prepared to offer you one hundred pounds, cash, when you hand over the ledger pages to me.''

"That is not acceptable.''

"I attach a condition to this offer," Dawson said, as if ignoring Backhouse's refusal. "And that is, that once you give me those pages, you have no further contact with Arthur Smith Woodward. I will destroy the pages, and he will assume that you believed his refusal to be victimized and slunk away with your tail between your legs.''

"What an odious image. I have never been known to slink, although I do not deny I might have a tail. I repeat, your offer is unacceptable to me.''

"This is not a negotiation, Sir Edmund. This is my first and final offer.''

"An ultimatum is meaningless unless it has the force to compel. But nothing will happen if I do not accept.''

"Precisely. You get nothing from me, and chances are you get nothing from Arthur. You have wasted your time. I see that you are not a businessman, Sir Edmund, and blackmail is a business. If you accept my offer, your own account book will show a healthy profit.''

"Then I accept," Backhouse announced in a voice of good cheer.

"Where is your vault?''

"Grindley's, St. James's.''

"I will meet you there the day after tomorrow at precisely twelve o'clock. Do not be late, as I wish to devote as little time as possible to this revolting affair into which you have drawn me. I take satisfaction in having saved a good and honest man, whatever his private shortcomings may have been, but I truly regret I shall have to meet you one more time.''

Backhouse congratulated himself as he proceeded to his next stop in the neighborhood. The hundred pounds in ready money would make his stay in England immeasurably more pleasant. Having been able to live in Peking on his modest income at a luxurious level by Chinese standards—a good house and servants—he disliked living in England on the cheap. With this windfall, he could find some well-appointed rooms in London while attending to the publication of his manuscript and calling on his other intended victims. He had planned to spend the night in the country at whatever modest lodgings he could find, but having reached his destination, he allowed himself the extravagance of a tourist hotel that had a proper lounge and fresh flowers on the dining room tables.

The next morning the sun was shining on the lovely village of Crowborough, and Backhouse, feeling refreshed and optimistic, hired a horse trap at the village hall and proceeded to Wildesham, the home of Arthur Conan Doyle.

Backhouse hadn't expected a country cottage, but he was not prepared for the size and pretentions of Wildesham. He began to think his fortune was made. Two massive wings, obviously new additions, were set at right angles to the old house, matching its white-trimmed windows and gray shingles. Two gardeners among the profligacy of the roses along the oval driveway looked up, touching the brims of their hats as he passed.

Backhouse was greeted at the front door by a manservant, who stepped outside briefly and made a dismissive gesture to the horse-drawn trap. "You are to be driven back in one of the cars," he explained. "Please come this way."

They crossed the expanse of a Persian garden carpet that Liberty had patterned after one belonging to the Shah of Persia, and Backhouse was shown into a room occupying the whole of one of the added wings. "The Billiard Room," said the major domo, and withdrew.

Walking the length of the room was an expedition. There were more Oriental carpets and the skins of tigers and zebra on the polished floor. At one end of the room was a rosewood grand piano in the baroque style draped with a Spanish shawl set in a jungle of potted palms that looked to Backhouse like a beast of the forest, grinning with a lot of white teeth, just arrived for a costume ball. The embossed leather walls were hung with animal trophy heads looking pleased that they had been killed, and there was a full length, life-sized portrait of Doyle in evening clothes by a fashionable painter, possibly Boldini. The green billiard table in the center of the room seemed to be there only to give the room a name.

"Sir Edmund? Arthur Conan Doyle," a voice boomed.

Backhouse walked half the length of the room toward the figure at the door. The writer was a country fashion plate in plus fours and a Norfolk jacket. "I am always delighted to receive members of the press."

"Your home is palatial," said Backhouse.

"I am the most highly paid writer in England," Doyle replied. "Let us go to my study, where we will be comfortable."

That room occupied only half of the other wing, and its comparative intimacy was enhanced by the mess of work in progress. It looked almost as if there had been a burglary; oak file drawers were open, spewing papers, and piles of books were thrown haphazardly on the floor and tables. "I know where everything is," Doyle said, as if to answer a question about his filing system.

The walls were flocked with a claret red-on-red design of overblown cartouches, the wainscoting and paneling dark walnut. Scattered on tables and on top of the low bookshelves were photographs in heavy silver frames of Doyle with various other celebrities, and a collection of chocolate brown Barye bronzes of predators dispatching their prey. Doyle removed some books and papers from two armchairs and sat to be interviewed.

Backhouse was not at Wildesham under entirely false pretenses. He did, in fact, write occasional pieces for the Peking *Mail* and had a loose arrangement with the *Times* correspondent in China, and when Backhouse had written to Doyle from London with a somewhat inflated curriculum vitae, Doyle was only too eager to publicize his works and himself in even so remote an outpost as Peking.

Backhouse scribbled on a pad while Doyle lost himself in the pleasures of self-praise.

"I think my readers would be interested in some biographical information," Backhouse said.

"I cannot say my life has been dull as ditch water, but Sherlock Holmes is far more interesting than I."

"That cannot be. You and he are one, by definition."

"Holmes has a life of his own. I killed him once, but my readers forced me to bring him back to life."

"Our lives twist and turn, perhaps not as melodramatically as Sherlock Holmes's. Yours, for example, beginning as a doctor and ending as a writer. A difficult transition, perhaps?"

"My way was clear once I had my first success."

"A reporter must do some preliminary research, and I found something that, on the face of it, seems to contradict what you have just told me. *A Study in Scarlet* and *Sign of Four* were published, and yet"—Backhouse began consulting some jottings in his notebook—"I see that in 1890 you left England for more than a year to pursue further medical studies in Berlin."

"A crisis in self-confidence," Doyle said. He stirred restlessly in his chair.

"I have a theory about crime," Backhouse said. "I'd like your opinion."

"Theorize away."

"Well, I believe the nature of crime is determined, is defined, by the spirit of the age—the *Zeitgeist*. Each age has its particular, characteristic sort. Times of war are times of treason; only in periods of religious devotion, such as the Middle Ages, do we find the crime of heresy. Our own era, so passionately committed to manners, propriety, and appearances, will, I think, be remembered by historians of crime as the age of blackmail."

"I have used it, in *A Scandal in Bohemia,* for example."

"Ah, yes. Irene Adler and Wilhelm, Grand Duke of Cassel-Felstein. But I am not talking about fictional crime, Mr. Doyle. I am speaking of fact. I ask you to cast your mind back again to 1890, the year you left for Berlin. Your departure was not noted in the press, but another's was: the sudden flight of Lord Arthur Somerset to avoid testifying at the trials surrounding the Cleveland Street Scandal."

"Never mind the rest. I now understand the purpose of your visit."

"Good. But before we come to terms, I must advise you that the ledger rumored at the time to be in possession of the authorities at Scotland Yard is now in my hands. Your name appears."

"How many times?"

"Once. May twenty-sixth, 1888. You were there in the company of the late Mr. Oscar Wilde."

"Someone could have used my name. And Mr. Wilde is dead, deservedly so, in my opinion. You have no corroboration."

"You were not so famous in 1888 that someone would have impersonated you. And reflecting on the subsequent career of Mr. Wilde, your friendship with him . . ."

"I was not his friend. We met only once."

"Your friendship with him," Backhouse continued, "might be corroboration enough, at least in the eyes of your adoring public who, if their subtlety of mind matches their literary taste for the obvious, would tend to jump to the grossest conclusions."

Doyle rose slowly and paced the room while Backhouse enjoyed the way he had sprung his trap. Then Doyle moved behind Backhouse's chair and quickly brought his brawny forearm across his throat, exerting a slow steadily increasing pressure as he spoke.

"You are wrong on two counts, Sir Edmund, in both your theory of crime and its practice. There is one crime which is characteristic of every age: I am speaking of murder." Doyle bent forward, increasing his pressure, watching Backhouse's pallor darken with blood and listening to the awful rasping and gagging in his throat. "With my medical knowledge I could suffocate you without leaving a mark—it would take some time—increasing and decreasing the pressure, a half hour, perhaps, but the autopsy, if one were performed, would reveal a pathology identical to apoplexy. The servants are about, but they wouldn't be a problem." He increased his pressure as Backhouse's breath rattled. "I tried to revive you, but in vain. I no longer keep digitalis. But one must never attempt a crime, be it blackmail or murder, unless one is in perfect control of the situation. Luckily for you, I am not." Doyle suddenly released Backhouse, and he fell gasping to the floor. "You came out from the village in Old

Jesse's trap. He's a chatty sort, and so are you. Perhaps you said something to him that could be troublesome later, something that might give me a motive to murder you.

"A murderer must have a logic. What I would logically do is go to the police and complain that you tried to blackmail me, that you told me you had a document purporting to compromise my reputation. In order to deny that you had attempted blackmail, you would also have to deny that the putative ledger existed, for there would be no other reason for your having told me about it than to force me to pay. You couldn't say you'd told me about it for amusement's sake.

"If you were blackmailing me, I would have had a reason to kill you—to prevent you from exposing me. But having established that the attempted blackmail was a bluff—remember you told the police no compromising document existed—when I do murder you, no one could say I had a motive. Why would I want to kill a harmless crank?

"Finding you in London wouldn't be difficult; it is a small town, especially when you have a brush with the police. I should mention that I have many friends at Scotland Yard who would not take kindly to your attempt to harass me. But I would be magnanimous and tell them to leave you alone. You would have to go about your business in an ordinary way, so as not to arouse further suspicion, but you would otherwise have no sense of danger, not knowing that I was stalking you, waiting for my opportunity. A perfect crime, even a perfect murder is quite easy to accomplish. A friend at the Yard told me that only three percent of the murders in London are ever solved.

"Now, how would I do it? Shooting, stabbing, bludgeoning, poison? Planning a murder is as difficult as shopping in the Burlington Arcade. There are far too many choices." Doyle went to a file cabinet and took out a large folder. "I have my secretary keep this up to date." He said. "M for murder. Everyday he goes through the London papers and takes cuttings. We save the interesting ones. As a writer, I never know when I will need a good murder. It is such a good way of disposing of characters whom one has grown to dislike or are no longer required for the plot. Only last week there was a jolly good one,'' he said, turning the pages. "Ah, yes, 'Headless Corpse in Pimlico.' That sounds right for you, considering you are a man with an evil mind. You are feeling unwell, so I will not add to your distress by reading the account, but if I murdered you within the next week or so, in the same manner, the police would assume they were dealing with a serial killer. That, of course, was their mistake in the Ripper case. But the police, once they have a theory, hold onto it like grim death, which is why they solve so few cases and why Holmes, with his agile and questioning mind, solves them all.

"The press cutting doesn't say what sort of knife was used—a butcher's knife, carving knife, hunting knife, perhaps an Arabian scimitar such as I have hanging there, which would do the job in one swift blow,'' he said, indicating a fan of weapons on the wall. "But the police do not have the forensic skills of Holmes, and it wouldn't matter what I used.

"As far as an alibi is concerned—so much is made of alibis in detective fiction—since the police will assume one murderer for two corpses, I am perfectly in the clear, since the night of the first murder—good murders always take place at night—I had a large dinner dance in the Billiard Room, where hundreds of my guests will say they saw me.'' Doyle smiled with satisfaction. "Here now, Sir Edmund, let me help you into a chair.''

Doyle bent down and grabbed Backhouse under an arm and flung him into the seat like a sack of meal. "What I have outlined is merely a sketch, not even a first draft. If only you could stay, we could polish it some more, get deeper into the characters. Or we could try another murder. Would you prefer to be shot?'' He leafed through the file and, as if losing interest, dropped it onto a table. He went to the door of the study and yanked at the bell pull. Presently, Jennings appeared.

"Sir Edmund has changed his mind. He will not be staying for lunch.''

"Shall I get out the Morris or the Rolls?''

"Neither, Jennings. Sir Edmund has been having a respiratory episode, and he agrees with my suggested course of therapy. A long country walk.''

Doyle took Backhouse firmly by the forearm and led him to the front door. The two men stood briefly at the threshold.

''Good-bye, Sir Edmund,'' Doyle said as warmly as he had greeted him. ''I do not think we shall meet again.'' He watched Backhouse trudge around the curving gravel drive and disappear behind a hedgerow at the side of the road.

Chapter VII

IN THE DINING ROOM OF LANGFORD'S HOTEL NEAR PIC-cadilly Circus, Dr. Arthur Doyle sat to the left of Robert Townsend, the editor of *Lippincott's* magazine, recently arrived on literary business from Philadelphia. Townsend had printed Doyle's first Sherlock Holmes story, "A Study in Scarlet," which had been published in England with modest success, and he had invited Doyle to dinner to discuss Doyle's writing another Holmes adventure for his magazine. Townsend hoped to kill two literary birds with one dinner. The other bird, whose plumage was more exotic than Doyle's, sat at his right. Oscar Wilde had arrived late in a cloud of patchouli, declaring that punctuality was the thief of time.

In 1888 Doyle still lived at Southsea in suburban Portsmouth, caught between boredom and pessimism over his unsuccessful medical practice. He had published one novel, *Micah Clarke*, a historical romance in the manner of Walter Scott, which had taken a year to find itself a publisher and which was near to sinking into oblivion. He had been excited to receive Townsend's letter with its offer, since it was the first time he'd been asked to write anything; while he would certainly oblige by finding another case in the papers of Dr. Watson, he also had another historical novel brewing in his mind, a magnum opus. He had dressed carefully for the occasion. Not wanting to seem doctorish, he had passed over his gray worsted for a suit of Harris tweed that spoke the formality of a disciplined writer while the heathery wool whispered of outdoor adventure.

The waiter was removing empty dessert plates, the last act of a five-course dinner of overorchestrated sauces and gargantuan portions fit for divas and Italian tenors. Wilde's heavy-lidded eyes were more than usually somnolent after the Black Forest cake. His long chestnut hair was parted in the middle and fell in lazy scallops from his forehead and met the collar of his jacket, prune velvet with matching satin piping. His loose shirt collar was tied with an oversized, flowing bow tie. He toyed distractedly with an opal ring on his finger, looking into the intricacies of its blue fire. *The Picture of Dorian Gray* had recently appeared to cries of, "Genius!" and "Degenerate filth!" Townsend hoped to secure the serialization rights for *Lippincott's*.

"I am not sure we can come to financial terms, Mr. Townsend," Wilde said.

"I am an optimist, Mr. Wilde. I am an American. I'm sure we can come to a reasonable understanding. We Americans are absolutely reasonable. I think that is our distinguishing characteristic."

"How dreadful," cried Wilde. "I can understand brute force, but brute reason is quite unbearable. There is something unfair in its use. It is hitting below the intellect." He thrust out his fleshy lower lip in a pout and, picking up a fork, began drawing parallel lines with its tines on the heavy damask tablecloth.

"I believe you were speaking as Lord Henry when he lunched with his Aunt Agatha in Berkeley Square."

"Nowadays my characters are the only quotable people in London."

Doyle had read *Dorian Gray* and wondered whether Wilde had read *Micah Clarke*, but didn't ask. Wilde would undoubtedly demolish him with a withering and paradoxical comparison between the deep-chested Micah flailing at his enemies with a broadsword, and Dorian in ecru linen, listlessly reclining in a wicker chair inhaling the perfume of spring lilacs in Basil Hallward's garden. Doyle sat listening to Wilde wrangling with Townsend over money. Neither of them mentioned the amount that Wilde intimated was paltry, but Doyle suspected it was more than Townsend had offered him in his letter, an offer which he had readily agreed to during the lemon sorbet between the fish and meat course. If Wilde was the grand aesthete, the paladin of art for art's sake, then Doyle's suspicions were correct. These literary dandies who looked as if they'd been brought up in a hot-house in Kew, who minced and attitudinized, who sneered at commonplace decencies, were nothing but fakes and posers. Wilde was no better than a common peddler in Threadneedle Street, trying to flog shoddy goods at an outrageous price. It was unjust that Dorian had created a sensation while Micah had all but vanished.

The hour was late as the tired waiter cleared the coffee cups, while others began removing the half-eaten chocolate bombes and glistening fruit tarts from the dessert stand. The muscular caryatids supporting the gilded cornice of the ceiling were equally exhausted at their work. The three men left the empty dining room and went into the hotel lobby, where Doyle got his Inverness cape and Wilde his long black coat with a wide mink collar.

"I'm so pleased," Townsend said to Doyle. To Wilde he said, "I hope you will reconsider your position."

"I've quite forgot what it was. Perhaps you would get in touch with me again to refresh my memory."

They all shook hands, and Townsend went away to the gilded cage that would take him up to his room.

Outside, neither Doyle nor Wilde had any intention of continuing the evening. In the fog the street lights glowed with gaseous mandorlas, hundreds of little shrines in the night. Without Townsend, they stood on a corner like two diplomats from different countries who had lost their interpreter.

"Well," said Doyle.

"Quite," said Wilde.

At the instant they were about to take their awkward leave of each other, a young street tout accosted them. He was thin, barely thirteen. Even in the dim lamplight his face had an unwholesome paleness, but his eyes were alert, and he moved with irrepressible energy.

"Evening, Guv," he piped, flashing out one of his oversized advertising cards to Wilde. The boy looked directly at him with a streetwise expression that only left his face in sleep, when he could reclaim his innocence for a time. "I don't give my cards to just any gent I see," he said.

Wilde studied the card then handed it to Doyle.

"I say, 'Poses Plastiques,' " Doyle read.

"*Je ne parle pas le français,*" Wilde replied with the worst tourist accent he could manage.

"It's ladies dancing and taking off their clothes," Doyle explained.

The boy laughed. "That's right. We got to be awful careful. Poses plastics ain't against the law. It says that so's we won't get pinched. But if you got other things on your mind . . ." He licked his upper lip, then the lower one.

"You provide unlawful pleasures?" Wilde said with exaggerated shock.

Doyle looked at him, the softness of Wilde's face and his full mouth, so dark it looked rouged. In the dimness his gender seemed to fade into androgeny, and once again Doyle seethed with jealous anger. He would see if the self-proclaimed knight errant of art could enjoy the full-bodied, manly pleasures of life.

"How about it, old man," Doyle said. "I believe you rank pleasure above all else. You won't regret it."

"No civilized man ever regrets a pleasure, and no uncivilized man ever knows what pleasure is." To Doyle's surprise Wilde took him by the arm, saluted the boy, and set off with Doyle as if they had been lifelong companions in debauchery. They went up Shaftsbury Avenue toward Tottenham Court Road. Soon they left the avenue and were walking through the narrow streets of Soho. As the neighborhood became more disreputable, Wilde's mood became more expansive.

A prostitute stepped out of a doorway blocking their path. "What do you fancy? How about some French? I'll do you any way you like."

"What gorgeous servility!" Wilde said, laughing, and reaching into his pocket, gave her whatever coins he had before walking on. "She was so low," he explained to Doyle. "For the genuinely vulgar, no price is too high. The real tragedy of the poor is that they can afford nothing but self-denial."

Doyle wished he knew whether Wilde made up these paradoxes on the spur of the moment or whether he collected them in a file to be read from memory at the appropriate moment.

They walked on past ragged bodies of children sleeping in doorways, wraithlike women standing under street lamps, half hidden in the fog out of which came drunken mutterings and indeterminate cries.

A few dull lights from the wards of Middlesex Hospital showed in the gloom at the end of the street. They skirted it and turned onto Cleveland Street, passing a line of row houses, some stables, and a darkened shop with medical supplies and disembodied prostheses in the window. At number 19 Wilde seemed to hesitate. There was only a faint light coming from the narrow windows on either side of the door.

"Never judge a book by its cover," Doyle advised as he stepped boldly to the door and knocked.

Charles Hammond opened the door. He looked at Doyle, then Wilde, who was standing on one side behind him and who quickly put a finger to his lips, signaling Hammond to silence.

"Come in, gentlemen," he said. They were in a narrow hall that led to a flight of stairs. Two naked gas jets flickered on walls the color of wrapping paper.

"But this is charming," Wilde said, as Hammond led them up the stairs.

"Where's the music?" Doyle inquired.

"Upstairs. There's plenty of music. Plenty of everything," Hammond said to Doyle.

They were shown into a small room facing the back lot of the house, its windows covered with the shreds of gray curtains. Hammond plumped up the pillows on a small sofa, adjusted the wick of a lamp, and went to a player piano, where he set the mechanism in motion. An outdated sentimental tune began, the keys of the piano seeming to be played by a ghost.

"To drink?" Hammond asked.

"Champagne, of course," said Wilde, throwing himself into a chair while Doyle sat on the couch.

"It doesn't look too promising," Doyle observed. He had imagined that behind the blank front of the house was a secret bordello, like the seraglios of the Orient with Turkish cozy corners and plush ottomans, fashionable rakes in evening clothes, and splendid women shaped like hourglasses, their talced breasts bursting in fleshy profusion out of whalebone corsets and their monumental thighs tapering to the slimmest ankles.

"Kept promises are like answered prayers; they lead to nothing but unhappiness."

"Well, now that we're here, I suppose we might as well make the best of it," Doyle said. "I say, old man. I think that since I was the one who brought us here, and it hasn't lived up to expectations—I think that you should have first choice."

Wilde put up his hand, fending off Doyle's generosity.

"No, really. I insist."

"Very well, then," Wilde said. "What is it you like to do in the way of sex?"

Doyle stared at him.

Wilde looked back with innocent candor. "Do you like to have your prick sucked?"

"I say. That's a bit much," Doyle harrumphed, coloring.

"I am addicted to it," Wilde said. "Don't you approve?"

"Actually, no." Doyle resented having to declare his sexual attitudes, but felt powerless to conceal them.

"That doesn't mean you don't like it. But whatever my own preferences, I never approve or disapprove of anything. It is an absurd attitude to take toward life. We are not sent into the world to air our moral judgments."

"I am not afraid to state my moral judgments," Doyle said. "There is nothing wrong in that. I am not embarrassed to say I believe in honesty, courage, the Golden Rule." He knew he sounded like an awful prig, particularly sitting as he was in a dingy brothel, but Wilde's pronouncements of what were supposed to be the most advanced ideas challenged him to take as extreme a position on the other side.

"Do unto others," Wilde said. "Then you believe in philanthropy."

"Naturally," Doyle answered, with some trepidation. "Philanthropy is a good thing."

"So is having one's prick sucked. It is pure philanthropy. One spends for a worthy cause."

First, this unspeakably shabby brothel, Doyle thought, and then being unable to avoid Wilde's epigrammatic trap. He felt oafish, seeing Wilde smiling brilliantly, as at ease as he might be in the best drawing room in Mayfair. Doyle's jaws worked wordlessly as his mind faltered with half-formed rejoinders, while the teeth of Wilde's wit held him by the throat.

The door opened, and a teen-aged boy came in with a bottle of wine and two glasses.

"This isn't champagne," said Doyle into his glass.

"And this ain't Buckingham Palace neither," said the boy. "But what's the use to complain? Don't be gloomy, sir. Look on the bright side." He set the bottle down on a rickety end table and sat himself down on Doyle's lap, wrapping his arms around his neck. Doyle struggled, but the boy nuzzled closer, giggling into his shoulder. Letting go his glass, Doyle took the boy's arms and forced them away, then giving him a terrific box on the ears. The boy gave a howl of pain as Doyle got up, dumping him on the floor.

Hammond burst into the room.

"He hurt me," the boy cried out.

"If you're interested in that sort of thing, mate," Hammond said, "we've got Georgie. Hey, Georgie," he shouted over his shoulder into the hall.

Before Doyle could respond, another boy entered the room, clad only in a yellowing towel tenting slightly in front.

"Oh, he's a big one," Georgie cooed, looking at Doyle. "I bet he's got a big one, too. Let's have a look, luv." The boy stepped forward.

"Sodomite!" shrieked Doyle at Hammond.

"Pot calling the kettle," Hammond countered, pointing at Doyle's large stomach.

Doyle was stupefied with anger as Wilde stepped between them.

"You may not talk to my friend that way. Perhaps you are not aware of who he is. A literary giant. You should be honored to be entertaining Arthur Conan Doyle, no less brilliant than the master detective he brought to light in the teeming pages of 'A Study in Scarlet.' "

"Look here," Hammond said to Doyle. "I don't care if you're the bleedin' Prince of Wales. Do you want Georgie or not? Georgie, give him a closer look, there's a good lad."

Georgie let the towel drop and came slowly toward him.

Bellowing like a wounded bull, Doyle rushed from the room and down the stairs. The sound of the street door slamming resounded through the quiet house. Wilde sighed and took a sip of wine.

"Well, we haven't seen you for a bit," Hammond said to Wilde. "Doesn't look like your friend fancied our chaps."

"He is a philistine," Wilde said, looking at Georgie.

Hammond withdrew and went to an upstairs room he kept for himself. He opened a ledger on the table and added another entry on the page for Oscar Wilde. In parentheses, he also wrote "Arthur Conan Doyle."

Chapter VIII

A S SOON AS CHARLES DAWSON CONCLUDED HIS BUSINESS
with Backhouse, he tucked the ledger pages in his
briefcase and went immediately to Woodward's office at the
Museum. Sitting behind his desk, the keeper was perfectly
composed, his goatee pointing precisely at the apex of the
inverted V of his high white collar and his tie tightly knotted,
with a carefully pleated cleft in the center where it began to
flare into his waistcoat.

Dawson couldn't prevent himself from thinking differently
about Woodward. Formerly he had appeared to Dawson as
sensually vacant; the idea of him copulating, even thinking
about it, was impossible. Some men were like that, and
women too, an accident of birth possibly, a temperamental
flaw, an acquired aversion, sad, in any case. Dawson had
tried him in each of those categories without being finally
satisfied, but did decide that Woodward probably didn't even
know what he was missing. Dawson felt a kind of wonder,
knowing Woodward's secret. His correctness took on a different meaning, an imposition on another nature, and Dawson searched Woodward's face for an indication of what he
might have seen a hundred times without realizing its significance. There was nothing. As to Woodward's particular sensual interests, Dawson admitted to himself that he didn't
understand, simply didn't understand. It was like some peo-

138

ple's love of pets. It was just plain silly, seeing somebody gushing and talking sentimental jibberish to a dog.

"I know what your situation is," Dawson said. "I had a visit from Sir Edmund."

Woodward's face twitched as if with a tic. "What did he tell you?"

"Everything."

"Why did he come to you?" Woodward said in a voice of defeat, as if he had no interest in hearing the answer to his question. He'd done nothing else but ask himself questions during the last days, trying to find an escape, and the imperative answer was always, "You must pay," and hope that the malignant Backhouse would be content to leave him alone.

"He wanted me to persuade you to pay him."

"He needn't have bothered you," Woodward said. "Of course I'll pay. I have no other choice." He nervously fretted at some papers, correcting their angle by one degree to bring them into line with the edge of his desk. "We have been friends and colleagues for twenty years, Charles. I am mortified that you should know this thing about me, but I hope . . ." He shielded his eyes with his hand. "Oh, God. I know I don't deserve your sympathy, but think, think of being in lifelong servitude to that wretched person, being reminded month after month of what he knows, of what I've been. Of what I am. My work has been the greatest boon to me. The order in it, the order in science. But that's over. I have had the most terrible thoughts these last days, even of taking my own life, however worthless it is."

"Have you told Maud anything?"

"Of course not."

"Good. And there won't be any need for desperate measures. I have just seen Sir Edmund, and I negotiated to buy the ledger pages for a hundred pounds. They are now in my possession."

Woodward felt that a strong hand had wrenched him back from the edge of a crumbling cliff a split second before he would have fallen away into the raging sea. He tried to choke back a cry of relief, but the force of his emotion and the sudden realization he'd been saved broke through. His body was wracked with sobs. At last, he was breathing heavily, wiping his eyes, and blotting at his nose with a large linen handkerchief. "I haven't cried since I was a boy. Then it was tears of grief when my mother died; now it is tears of joy for your having rescued me." He put his glasses back where they belonged. "Now that you know about me, can I still call you my friend as well as my savior?"

Dawson indicated he disclaimed any credit. "You know, Arthur, since Sir Edmund's visit I have revised my opinion of you considerably. I didn't know you had such a capacity for secrecy. That is a great quality, to be discreet."

"You are fortunate. You can afford to be frank."

"I have my secrets as well. We all do."

"But you have never had to ask yourself, 'Why am I as I am?' "

"I have so thought about that," Dawson said, a little put out that Woodward thought him so shallow.

"And what did you conclude?"

"I concluded that I was lucky."

Woodward burst out laughing, "I'm sorry," he said. "I've been under such a strain."

"Your capacity for secrecy interests me very much," Dawson said, returning to his former subject. "Because I am going to tell you something that will test all your powers of discretion."

Woodward looked puzzled. "You can rely on me absolutely."

"In the near future the world will learn of the discovery in England of the oldest hominid fossil ever to come to light. The public will undoubtedly call it the Missing Link, but for those of us who understand human paleontology, it is a transitional creature dating to the Pliocene or early Pleistocene that vindicates the concept of human evolution through cranial development—an apelike creature with a nearly modern man's brain case."

"Who has discovered such a creature?" Woodward asked excitedly.

"I have." Dawson put his briefcase on his lap and as Woodward watched with astonishment, he took out several small packages wrapped in cotton wool and tissue paper. "I have only brought a few specimens from the find," he said. First he unwrapped a small skull fragment and placed it on Woodward's desk, then a flint and several mammalian teeth, all stained dark brown. Dawson sat back as Woodward examined the pieces, taking each one in his hand, carefully turning it over, and then screwing a loupe into his eye, looking at them under high magnification.

"These are remarkable objects."

"Aren't they beautiful?"

"Yes, they are. The thickness of the skull, the mineralization, and the flint, obviously the work of human intelligence. The site must be very rich in iron salts, judging from the color. Where did you make this discovery?"

"In the Wealden gravel beds at Piltdown, near Uckfield."

"Practically in your backyard."

"All of Sussex is my backyard, geologically speaking. But they had to be somewhere. It has been an article of faith among English paleontologists ever since Darwin's time."

Woodward picked up the skull fragment again. "How much more of the skull have you found?"

"Enough to show human morphology positively. And he's not a Neanderthal."

"If the animal teeth are Pliocene, the skull's got to be that old. It couldn't be Neolithic," Woodward said, as if answering an unspoken criticism.

"They are Pleistocene," Dawson said.

"I don't mean to be a killjoy, but even so there are those who might say that unless you've got more of this creature, he's still largely theoretical, a tantalizing probability."

"Well put, Arthur. You're being your old careful self again. What do you think would do the trick?"

"Well, this is not my field. I don't know. A jaw, I suppose."

"Apelike, but with human dentition, clearly transitional. I'm going to find one. There will be a jaw."

"I suppose anyone who digs has got to be an optimist."

"It is tedious work, but not without its rewards," Dawson said. "But in this case, I didn't really have to dig," Dawson said, indicating the specimens.

"Were they surface finds?"

"Yes. And the jaw will be too."

"I don't understand how specimens of this age could be surface finds, except possibly at an eroded site. Is that it?"

"Look at the specimens again, carefully."

Woodward examined them again and then looked with puzzlement at Dawson. "Is this some sort of test?"

"Yes," Dawson replied. "And you have passed with flying colors. This hominid from Piltdown—I have created him."

"Created him?"

"Not a fantastic Golem," Dawson said in a hoarse whisper. "He is mine, this ape-man with a human brain. The first Englishman."

"You created him?" Woodward said again, looking at his desk again and realizing the significance of what he was seeing.

"I have only anticipated what someone else will eventually find."

"We must stop this discussion now. With the vestiges of my good conscience, I can still maintain that I have misunderstood what you have said—an overzealous interpretation of incomplete evidence, an enthusiastic though misguided lapse of scientific objectivity."

"You are not being scientific, Arthur. You are not facing facts. I selected the site myself, and I have forged those specimens. There it is. That is as clear as I can make it."

Woodward considered Dawson. "You have discovered my shameful secret, and now you freely offer this equally shameful secret to me. This is an odd bargain."

"What would you say if I offered you an opportunity to share this astounding discovery with me?"

"I would respectfully decline," Woodward said with a little ice in his voice. "And since I am so greatly in your debt, I would never say anything, nor comment on your specimens if and when you decide to announce this—whatever you call it—discovery. You have saved me, and now I can save you. Don't do this. It is sheer lunacy, Charles."

"You are the most careful scientist I know. And you

didn't have a moment's doubt about the authenticity of those artifacts. The other pieces are just as good. You ought to see them."

"I don't want to see them."

"But you shall. Because I mean to force you to join me in my enterprise. You haven't had time to consider, but once you realize that now I have the Cleveland Street ledger pages, you have as little choice in this matter as you had in the other."

The moment was forever set in Woodward's mind. He felt himself fossilized, caught in an attitude of eternal agony, like an ancient creature found in a tar pit.

"Don't look so glum, Arthur. It is far better to be black-mailed by a friend, particularly one who is offering you the world in the bargain. The advantages of joining me are obvious—fame, advancement, power."

"At the price of compromising everything that is sacred to the objective search for the truth. You talk of fame, power, but do you realize that you are taking away from me the one thing that gives me any sense of self-respect. I don't suppose that means anything to you. But think of the consequences to science, assuming you are successful."

"Assuming we are successful," Dawson corrected. "And that is more than an assumption. You proved it by seeing the specimens as genuine."

"But why do you need me? I won't say anything. That's the least I can do."

"That's not enough. I am a lowly amateur. You are a professional. I hate to admit it, but you will add an imprimatur. Your colleagues will be jealous enough, but not quite as jealous as they might be if a lone amateur bested them at their own game. And once the specimens are here at the Museum . . ." Dawson began.

"Here at the Museum?"

"Where else would they be? You helped me find them. Besides, put a paste necklace in the window of Asprey's, and who'd suspect for a moment they weren't diamonds. It's all in the interest of verisimilitude."

"Your faith in gullibility is extraordinary."

"I anticipated your objections, and that is why I negotiated with Sir Edmund. Now I have the power to expose you, and I will if you don't cooperate," Dawson said.

"Your terms?"

"You will be my academic champion, my 'bulldog' as Huxley was Darwin's. We will publish joint papers, which will be in great demand. But of more immediate concern are the specimens. As you yourself pointed out, my kit is not complete. I am still lacking the jawbone," Dawson explained. "I have decided on an orangutan's mandible, and you will get one from the Museum's collections. Don't look so frightened. I don't intend for you to do it on your own. I'll help you."

"Help me?"

"I'll make a plan. It'll be great fun."

"Fun?"

"Stop repeating what I say as questions. As we are to be together a great deal, I feel I ought to point out your annoying habits. And please feel free to do the same with me, so as to make our time as pleasant as possible."

"You are asking me to be a thief as well as a liar."

"Better to be a private outlaw than a public outcast. Better still to be proclaimed as the most eminent paleontologist of your generation, second only to me, that is. We shall be famous, thanks to our ape-man. I have already named him: *Eoanthropus dawsoni*," Dawson exclaimed. "Come on. Let's go."

Woodward could only look at him with petrified astonishment.

"Where?"

"To the other side of the Museum. Come on. England, the world, is waiting!"

They went across the central hall of the Museum to the west wing of living animals. In the hall of the great apes was a stuffed gorilla in a glass case balanced on his knuckles, majestic and powerful with a lordly cast to his black face even with glass eyes, a family of chimpanzees gathering wax berries from bushes with silk leaves and delousing each other, and an orangutan, long-haired and foolish, relaxing in the fork of a tree. The installation included photographs and artists' renderings of forests and mountain jungles, complete skeletons for comparison with human proportions and diagrams of evolutionary lines from earlier monkeys.

"That's what I want, Dawson said, pointing to the massive jaw of a skeletal orangutan. Seeing Woodward's anxiety, he added, "I don't mean that specific one, but there must be duplicates in the reserve collections."

"I don't get to this side of the building, so I don't know anything about the reserve collections. But I do know that some years ago Sir Ray issued a memorandum requiring that every specimen—every snail, every single metatarsal in the Museum—had to be cataloged."

"Perhaps they're not as conscientious over here as you are."

"This is insane," said Woodward.

Dawson was studying a map of the Dutch East Indies showing the orangutan's habitat in Sarawak marked in red. There was a painting of the apes lolling in a dense jungle and next to it a photograph of some tribal peoples dressed for a ceremonial occasion.

"It's a pity we can't go to Sarawak. You'd look very smart in a topee and walking shorts. But since we can't go, we'll just have to find what we need right here. We'll simply take a jaw from this side of the building and bring it over to the other side, with a short detour to Piltdown."

"This is insane," Woodward repeated. "It is impossible!" he said, trying to keep his voice down.

At the doorway to the gallery, there was the sound of voices and shuffling of feet, and a flock of ten-year-old schoolboys in gray pants and blazers were herded toward the gorilla. A few of them escaped to inspect the great ape's nether regions before they were returned, shrieking with laughter, to the fold by their teacher and the Museum's docent, who began to explain that the gorilla was a vegetarian, quite intelligent, and mild-mannered despite his appearance. The natural history of the orangutan came next. "This great ape is especially important to the natives of Sarawak," the docent said, pointing to the photograph. "This fellow here is holding a shaman's staff decorated with orangs' jaws, which are supposed to have magical powers. Something about the spirit of the jungle. They are much prized by the natives, because they confer status and power, and as a result the orangutan is much hunted in this region. Over there are the chimpanzees. No running!''

Dawson looked closely at the photograph and then said to Woodward, ''I've always wondered if these educational programs for the masses really had any value. But now I am entirely convinced of their efficacy.'' He indicated the ceremonial staff. ''That's even better than this nice, clean specimen you've got. I'd say this one in the picture might have some age; part of the work's already been done. And if it confers status and power on him, it will do the same for us. It says here in the caption that the artifacts in this picture are in the Everett Collection.''

''The Everett Collection is not here.''

''Where is it?''

''In Bloomsbury. All the ethnographic collections were left there when we moved here in 1882.''

''Let's go have a look and see.''

''Now?''

Outside the Museum Dawson hailed a black, boxy taxicab and pushed Woodward in, as if he were abducting him. The engine ground and sputtered as Dawson climbed in. As they reached the center of the city, the traffic jammed the streets, and Dawson drummed his fingers impatiently on his knees as Woodward looked gloomily out the window.

''They'll miss me at the Museum,'' Woodward said.

''Everybody knows you're an absolute fiend for work. They'll think you're in some nook somewhere. Look, if you're going to be any good at this, you've got to understand several things. First of all, nobody cares two damns what you do or don't do, at least for now. I'm not attacking your sense of self-importance, because I'd say the same for myself. After we are famous, of course, things will change, and we will have to deal with that when the time comes. Second, nobody knows what's going on in your mind simply by looking at you. You are opaque. And third, nobody could

possibly imagine that we were going to the British Museum
to plan how to steal a specimen from the ethnographic collections, just as it is inconceivable that two men of science, such
as you and I, would be involved in this affair to begin with.
You must make the assumption that other people see you as
the same hard-working, thorough scientist of integrity. It all
becomes easy when you realize that other people are doing at
least half the work for us by needing and wanting to believe
that God's in His Heaven and that things are what they seem.
Bear that in mind, and you will feel quite safe.''

The cab arrived at the gate of the British Museum in Great
Russell Street. There Dawson pulled Woodward toward the
Palladian portico, jostling their way through the visitors and
tourists at the entrance. Once inside, they climbed the stairs
past the pink granite colossi from Aswan and through the
galleries of Celtic treasures and Gallo-Roman silver. The gigantic labyrinth of objects jogged to the right and left and up
several staircases until at last Dawson and Woodward entered
the ethnographic collections. The Everett Collection occupied
a small alcove. The glass cases against the wall contained
objects of daily use and mannequins dressed in costumes
showing various styles of weaving, ornaments of shell and
bone. Masks and ceremonial objects were in a separate case,
and among them several shamans' staffs, the tops tied with
strips of animal skin and orangutan mandibles.

"Awful stuff. All those bits of string and hair and God
knows what," said Woodward.

"But it's exactly what we want. There's got to be more,
great boxes full of it. Everett probably went in and cleaned
out a whole village."

"How could he bear touching it?"

"Do you know the cataloging system here?"

"It's the same as ours. The first number's the year of
accession, then the number of objects acquired, and then the
object number within the group."

Dawson looked at the label. "There are four hundred and
thirty-five pieces in the collection. So this is only a small
fraction of it. The question is, where is the rest of it? If you
were a fetish, where would you go?"

"I'd go and have a wash," Woodward said.

"Where's the catalog of the collection?" Dawson asked.

"I don't know."

"Yes, you do. Don't be difficult."

"I suppose it's in the Department of Ethnography."

"Could there be a catalog of the collections in the Museum general research library?"

"There are duplicate cards for each specimen, one in the specific department and one in the library."

"Ah, the joys of scholarship," Dawson said, pulling him along.

The library was in a different wing of the Museum, and they had to pass through at least a dozen cultural zones in time and space before they arrived at their destination. Inside the library Dawson noticed another recently arrived visitor signing a register at a reception desk where a librarian sat.

"Don't sign your right name," Dawson whispered. As they came to the desk, Dawson took the pen, scrawled in the book, and then gave it to Woodward.

"Could you tell me whether you have the catalog of the Everett Collection here?" Dawson asked.

"Yes. You'll find it under General Inventory, down at the end," the librarian said. "Are you with this gentleman?" she asked.

"Yes."

"Did you sign, sir?"

"No." Woodward had a glazed look.

"You'll have to sign the register."

Woodward slowly dipped the pen into the inkwell and poised the nib of the pen over the page.

"Is anything wrong, sir?" said the librarian.

"Wrong?" Woodward echoed. He looked distracted, almost drugged. "No." And then he signed the register.

"Come along," Dawson said.

They made their way down the rows of library tables lighted by polished brass lamps.

"What got into you?" Dawson said between his teeth.

"I couldn't think of a name except my own," Woodward said with angry embarrassment.

"What name did you use finally?"

"Never mind."

"I'll look in the register if you don't tell me."

"I signed your name," Woodward said. "I couldn't think of anything else."

In the middle of the quiet reading room, Dawson could only redden to express his exasperation. Woodward followed him to the end of the room, and they searched the faces of the small oak file drawer until they found the Everett Collection. Removing the drawer, they sat with it at an isolated table.

"They're making it quite easy for us," Dawson said, leafing through the cards. He pointed out that below the catalog number and description was a storage location. "I suppose these are duplicates of the department's catalog, so they can locate objects, and so can we."

There were fourteen shamans' staffs, of which two were designated as on exhibition. Dawson quickly copied down the catalog numbers and locations in the reserve collection storage area.

After sliding the drawer back in the file, Dawson led Woodward back to the entrance, stopping again at the librarian's desk.

"Can you tell us who is in charge of the Everett Collection?"

"Dr. Sudbury, Department of Ethnography."

Dawson and Woodward walked some distance from the library doors when Dawson stopped a guard.

"Excuse me, but I seem to be terribly lost. We are supposed to meet Dr. Sudbury at the ethnography reserve collections. Could you direct us?"

"Through Ancient Near East," the guard began, and after having to ask several times more along the way, Dawson and Woodward found themselves in front of a door.

"Locked," Dawson said, trying the knob.

"Of course it's locked," Woodward said.

A guard appeared at the end of the corridor. "Can I help you, gentlemen?"

"Yes. Have you seen Dr. Sudbury?" Dawson said.

"No, not today."

"We have an appointment to meet him at the reserve collections. Perhaps we've made a mistake. Is there another entrance?"

"From the department offices. That's probably what he meant. Just go down to the end there and turn left."

The next set of doors that presented themselves had glass windows that gave a view of the outer office of the Ethnography Department. A young woman sat typing at a desk.

Woodward looked in, then backed away from the door. "We couldn't get past her without being seen. Besides, we don't know where the door to the reserve collections is. It can't be done."

"I suppose we could hide somewhere in the Museum—in a sacrophagus, or something—until after closing, and then come back. But this door would be locked then," Dawson said. "Or we could come back in disguise: two anthropologists from I don't know where. Do you do any accents? No. I can see from your expression that won't work."

"We can't go in there," Woodward said.

"Why not?"

"We're not invisible."

Dawson brightened. "Thank you, Arthur."

"For what?"

Dawson pulled Woodward through the doors.

"Good afternoon," Dawson said to the secretary. "I am Charles Dawson of the Sussex Geological Society, and this is my colleague Dr. Woodward, keeper of fossil fish over at South Kensington."

"Good afternoon," said the secretary. "I am Miss Tuthill."

"I'm just up from the country for the day, and I asked Dr. Woodward if he could make an appointment for us to look at some specimens in your reserve collections. He said he'd bring me round personally, and I said that it would be terribly rude barging in like this, but he insisted. Didn't you, Woodward? Professional reciprocity and all that. I feel terribly embarrassed, but Dr. Woodward positively dragged me here. In any case, here we are."

"What is it that you're looking for? If you'd like to see Dr. Sudbury, I can tell him you're here."

"Please don't," Dawson said. "I feel we have imposed upon you enough already. Still, I only have today. Dr. Woodward and I are collaborating on a paper. It will deal with the use of fossil fish teeth in African fertility fetishes. I noticed a curious specimen in the Museum at Hastings that was part of a collection of artifacts donated by one Dr. Morrison, a missionary in British East, and I feel certain that it is part of a larger and hitherto unstudied group of the utmost importance. The rest is rather technical, but if we could just have a preliminary look at the reserves, we might know whether we ought to continue our investigations."

The secretary opened the drawer of her desk and took out a bunch of keys. "The collections are arranged by geographic location and tribal groups. If you come this way," she said, getting up, "I will show you where the East African specimens are located."

Dawson noticed how nicely the secretary's breasts filled her white shirtwaist, and as they followed her down a hallway, he saw that she also had a lovely bottom. "We shall be forever in the debt of this young lady for being so civil and helpful to two louts such as we," he said to Woodward.

The secretary worked her large key into the lock of the storage area, and with the last door opened to them, they entered a silent, cavernous space. There was row upon row of deep open shelves, like library stacks, with wooden objects on display. There were small armies of tribal sculptures, earthenware and calabash cooking pots to fill a thousand hearths. They passed bins full of carefully folded textiles and masks with fearsome or comical expressions.

"What a remarkable collection," Dawson said.

"This is all Africa," said Miss Tuthill with pride.

"And what's over there?" Dawson asked indicating the farther reaches of the storeroom.

"New World cultures, then India, Southeast Asia—only the tribal collections. The Hindu and Buddhist works of art are in Oriental Antiquities." Stopping in front of a bank of shelves, she said, "Here we are."

"So we are," Dawson said to her as she stood next to the shelf. After a moment, he said, "You've been so very kind."

The secretary smiled back but did not move. "I'm supposed to stay with you."

"That won't be necessary."

"Well, I really should."

"But why? You must have a thousand things to do. I'd bet that Dr. Sudbury is just like Dr. Woodward, always dictating too many letters that say absolutely nothing."

The secretary giggled, glancing at Woodward.

"We won't be long. I mean, after all, we're not going to steal anything."

"Well, all right. But please, if you remove any specimen, put it back exactly where you found it."

They stood at the shelves, watching her make her way to the door.

Dawson handed Woodward the paper on which he had written the catalog numbers of the Sawarak shamans' staffs. "Go find the Dutch East Indies section, and be quick about it."

"Where are you going?" Woodward asked like a frightened child.

"I'm going to look at these specimens. Go on, go on," he said, shooing him away.

Woodward scurried down the aisle, almost blind with panic; the numbers on the paper he held seemed to him incomprehensible hieroglyphics as he stumbled up one line of bins and down another, trying to match them with the catalog numbers that were inserted into brass holders attached to the shelves. He felt as if he were lost in a maze, and he was running from an invisible chimera. He stopped to catch his breath and then went on, each aisle looking exactly alike.

"Where are you?" It was Dawson's voice.

"I don't know," Woodward replied.

Dawson appeared at the end of the aisle. "Not over there, you idiot. Over here."

Quickly scanning the shelves, Dawson saw what he was looking for. He pulled on the handle of the shelf, easing it out. A dozen staffs were neatly arranged on the baize. They were about three feet long, wooden staffs with various objects tied to the top—animal hair, little leather bags filled with precious substances, small images of wood and shell, and on some of them, orangutan jawbones.

"The mother lode!" Dawson said. He made a quick selection of a mandible that still had a few teeth attached and began pulling at the rawhide thong that attached it to the wooden staff. "Damn! It won't come off. Can you find a knife anywhere?"

Woodward stood helplessly, looking blindly at the shelves. "There aren't any," he said.

Dawson took the mandible in his hands, still attached to the staff, he raised his knee and brought the jaw smartly down over his thigh. It split in two.

"Just at the midline. That's good," he said, returning the staff to its shelf. "We've only got bits of the skull so this will do as well. And they'll never miss this piece. Look, that one's broken too." He put the half jaw in the pocket of his jacket. "We've got to get back to British East Africa. I took some bones from a fetish over there to substitute for this one, but now I don't need them. No sense in taking more than we need."

When Dawson took Woodward's arm to lead him back to the Dark Continent, he could feel a tremor through his coat sleeve. "Chin up," Dawson said. "We'll be out of it soon."

They arrived at the East African shelf, and Dawson replaced the few bones he had removed.

"Good afternoon. I'm Sudbury." A tall, thin man in rumpled tweeds was striding toward them. "My secretary told me we had visitors."

"Charles Dawson." They pumped at each other's hands.

"Dr. Woodward. I believe we met some years ago at a Museum function," Sudbury said.

Woodward blinked through his pince-nez glasses.

"Arthur is quite speechless at the extent of the collections."

"Miss Tuthill said something about teeth and fetishes; I couldn't quite make it out. Did you find what you were looking for?"

"Partially," Dawson said, looking briefly at Woodward, and casually putting his hand in his pocket.

"Jolly good. Could I get you some tea after your safari?"

"I really must get back to the Museum," Woodward said.

"I quite understand. A museum doesn't run itself," said Sudbury.

They left the storage area, and Sudbury showed them to the door of the department's offices.

Once again in the public galleries, Dawson turned to Woodward. "Ha! We did it!" he said. He was flushed with excitement, and his face was split with a triumphant grin. Woodward took out his handkerchief and was mopping his brow.

"Gentlemen?" A guard was standing at an archway a few feet from where they stood.

Woodward lowered the handkerchief to his mouth and bit down hard.

"The Museum is closing," said the guard.

Dawson could hardly keep up with Woodward as he hurriedly followed the signs and arrows to the exit. "You're acting very guilty, Arthur."

"I don't have anything in my pocket. I'll say I don't even know you."

"That's a bad lie. It would only prove that you are guilty."

"Leave me alone."

When they got out of the Museum, Woodward leaned against one of the columns of the pedimented entrance that faced the large courtyard in Great Russell Street.

"I thought you said we were just going to have a look."

"You've got to learn to take advantage of opportunities. You gave me the idea—hiding in plain sight—and now we've got what we came for," Dawson said, starting to take out the jawbone from his pocket.

"Put that thing away. And stop saying, 'we.' "

"You'll get used to it."

"I think I would have preferred paying Backhouse ten pounds a month for the rest of my life than go through that insane and reckless escapade."

"But didn't you feel more alive, as if something was happening?"

"Something dreadful."

"Something vivid and unforgettable. However, from now

on, I can promise you quiet days in the country. When are
you coming down?''

"What for?"

"To dig."

"For what?"

"For the jaw."

On a cold Saturday morning Woodward took an early train
from London and arrived at the station in Uckfield, where
Dawson was waiting with a horse and buggy.

Under his dark wool coat Woodward was dressed as if he
were going to the museum, full three-piece suit.

"We're going to dig," Dawson said. He was wearing a
battered jacket, old trousers, and boots.

"I don't have any country clothes," Woodward said in a
sullen tone as he climbed into the buggy.

The road to Barkham Manor from Uckfield wound from
three miles between gentle hills past well-kept cottages and
farms, open fields and through stands of massive oaks and
elms on either side of the road whose branches met overhead.
Even late in the fall, when day lilies and Queen Anne's lace
were memories, after the goldenrod had withered and the
milkweed had burst leaving empty bronze husks, when the
countryside had gone purplish and brown, the landscape had
no look of ruin, but rather a calm complacency at having
accomplished its task, resting under the gray coverlet of the
sky. Occasionally the quiet was disturbed by raucous crows
coming to glean the stubble of the meadows or gunshots of
men after pheasant, quail, or snipe.

Dawson snapped the reins along the horse's back. "We'll
only have a few Saturdays for digging until the weather gets
really bad. The site will get too soggy, and there will probably be flooding in the pit."

"How long have you been at this?"

"I started in August, and I've been out virtually every
weekend since then. The Kenward family at the Manor has
been very nice, and it will be good to have them see us there.
Mabel, Bob Kenward's daughter, has taken quite an interest
in my work."

"You just go out there and dig for nothing all day long?"

"I can see you've never been a great one for field work. It's not as if one were digging for potatoes. Every spadeful of earth had to be sieved and washed, and the spoil heap has got to be resieved, in case something is missed the first time. And the finds must be recorded, their position relative to the surface and to depth, and in relation to each other. I didn't think I'd have to teach you all these procedures."

"Sometimes I have the impression you really don't know the difference between what is true and what is not."

"Two witnesses in court, one for the defense and one for the prosecution, both give testimony describing what they saw the defendant do; both are telling the truth, but each story is different. Both witnesses are unshakable under cross-examination. In the end the jury has to decide which truth they believe, or more to the point, which witness. It is as much the witness testifying as the testimony itself that determines the truth in a court of law."

"You're begging the issue, as usual."

"Am I? If the jury believes you did murder, you will be hanged. How many men have gone to the gallows screaming they are innocent? Surely some of them were telling the truth, for all the good it does them. At that moment there is only one truth: They will die."

At the turn into a lane that led to Barkham Manor was Piltdown Pond. White swans sailed gracefully, and men with fly rods cast for small perch and occasional trout.

The property of the manor began about a hundred yards from the house, which was approached by a perfectly straight avenue lined on each side by tall, dark spruces planted in doubled rows when the manor house was built in 1820. Just beyond the trees a scrub of hawthorn and briar had been allowed to grow into a natural boundary to the meadows, which subsided in the distance into thick woods. As they drove toward the house, only its red tile roofs and chimney clusters were visible beyond a high screen of hedges and between towering pine trees, black and dense in all seasons, which had been there long before the land had been cleared for the house, its outbuildings, and its gardens. Pine cones were gathered regularly from the clipped lawn to burn as fragrant kindling in the fireplaces of the manor. The house itself owed its reputation not to size, but to the restrained elegance of its proportions, the perfect matching of red brick and warm gray limestone, and its self-assured and self-effacing obedience to the seventeenth century. The lawn ran straight to its foundations, giving it the look of a jewel displayed on a swatch of green velvet.

Halfway to the house, Dawson reined in the horse. A short distance away was a caretaker's cottage and beside them in a ditch at the end of the road was an irregular shallow pit.

Woodward got down, looked at the pit and then at Dawson. "This is absurd. Why did you pick this place? Why not over there, or there?" he said, gesticulating.

"This is where the workman found the first bit of the modern skull that gave me the idea. Anyway, there's a nice big tree here, in case it rains, or the sun gets too hot. Come along, I keep the shovels and all the other gear in a shed in back of the cottage."

Dawson tramped along the edge of the ditch with Woodward following a few paces behind. The ground was soft from a recent rain.

"My shoes," Woodward said.

He waited outside the shed while Dawson handed him a pair of shovels and a measuring stick. Dawson carried the sieves, two wood frames with wire mesh that could stand like a lean-to on the ground, and a couple of hand sieves with finer holes. He filled a pail with water at an outdoor spigot.

The pit was three feet deep. "You see," said Dawson, pointing, "I've already reached the Wealden gravels, that dark stratum. I've matched the specimens to that color." He jumped into the pit and gathered a handful, giving them to Woodward who stood at the edge of the hole. "Well, what do you think?"

"It doesn't matter what I think," he said, dropping them back in the pit and wiping his palms together.

"Hand me a shovel, then," Dawson said. "You can sieve for a while."

Woodward set one of the sieves at an angle to the ground,

and Dawson scooped up a load of gravel, flinging it against the mesh.

"What a ridiculous waste of time," Woodward muttered as he shook the wire mesh.

"I'll let you dig after a while."

"I can hardly wait."

"After a half hour they switched places. The shovel crunched against the gravel as Woodward excavated. "I can't do this," he said.

"Open your bloody waistcoat. Put your shoulder into it."

"That's not what I mean."

"Well, what do you mean?" Dawson asked, refusing to acknowledge Woodward's misgivings.

"You know perfectly well that you are forcing me to participate in the grossest and most damnable lie—a scientific forgery."

"A duchess sells her emeralds to pay for her lover's gambling debts and has fake ones made to wear to the opera. No one suspects they aren't real. The duchess's friends still envy her emeralds, and the duchess still takes pleasure in their jealousy. What has changed?"

"What is it like having no morals?" Woodward asked.

"The same as having morals and acting otherwise," Dawson replied.

"If you are referring to the ledger, I knew I was wrong. That is the difference between us."

"But you must have known that, if you were ever found out, everything you had worked for would be lost. Yet you risked everything. In that we are alike."

"You are wrong. I had no plan. I could not help myself."

Everyone can help himself, Dawson thought, believing completely in his own autonomy, but he wouldn't tamper with Woodward's helplessness. "And you can't now," Dawson said, "so let's be about our work."

Toward the middle of the afternoon, a woman appeared in the distance between the hedges surrounding the manor house and came toward them on the road.

"It's Mabel Kenward." Dawson said. "Sometimes she comes out to see what I'm doing."

Mabel was in her middle twenties, lithe but strongly built, with a sensible look to her, her dark hair pulled back and impatiently wrapped in a bun at her neck. She held a crocheted wool shawl to her bosom and carried a jug and a pair of stoneware mugs.

"This is my friend Woodward from the British Museum," Dawson said.

"Bringing in the heavy artillery, I see. I brought you some cider. It doesn't look as though you'll have much more time," she said, looking at the gray sky. "There are oilskins in the cottage if you must press on in spite of the weather. What is your specialty, Dr. Woodward?"

"Fossil fish."

"So that's it. Mr. Dawson, you are forcing me to be a detective." Mabel turned again to Woodward. "He won't tell me what he's been looking for or if he's found anything. It's all so deliciously mysterious. We talk about it at the house. Papa thinks there's Saxon treasure in that hole. And I thought it had something to do with a skull, because that's what the workmen found that day; remember Mr. Dawson? But now it seems we have old fish in there. Papa will be disappointed, though it still must be terribly important if you've brought Dr. Woodward all the way from London." Mabel looked into the pit and the spoil heap of stones they had sieved. "I've often had a mind to have a go at digging when you're not here, to solve the mystery. But I know I might disturb something—the strata. You see, Dr. Dawson, you have taught me something. I even went to the library in Uckfield and read, or read at, Goldthwaite's *Geology of East Sussex,* just as you told me. It's difficult to imagine that our dear little corner of the world ever looked the slightest bit different than it does today. It is so peaceful here, and geology makes it all so restless, what with the earth heaving and tossing and turning."

"The earth sleeps. Occasionally it has a bad dream," Dawson said.

"Don't tell Papa I've been to the library. Not that he minds my reading, but he's not modern in his thinking. He would be most distressed if I told him those gravels were laid down five hundred thousand years ago, because, you see, he's quite convinced of Dr. Abernathy's view at the rectory that the earth was created in six days, lock, stock, and barrel in 4000 B.C. His face gets red as a beet root when anyone mentions Darwin. I myself find it rather fun to think of us all having distant cousins covered with hair and swinging through the trees.''

Mabel left the cider and went back to the manor.

''Poor Bob Kenward may have to change his thinking by the time we're through,'' Dawson said.

Woodward flung another shovelful of earth at the sieve, and stabbing the blade into the soft earth, he pressed his knuckles against the base of his spine and arched his back painfully. ''I'm going to be crippled tomorrow, and my shoes are ruined.''

''I've brought some lunch.''

They climbed up on the seat of the buggy, and Dawson brought out a small wicker hamper. Helene had packed some oatmeal bread with wedges of local cheese and some shiny apples. It had been more years than Woodward could remember since he'd picnicked out of doors. The distinct and heightened pungency of the cheese and the tang of the apple tasted wonderfully good to him, so much so that he reproached himself by forcing his thoughts back to the dark purpose of the visit to Barkham Manor. He had sweated from the work, and he felt almost feverish as the cold wind raked his coat.

''Mabel Kenward is a charming young woman,'' Dawson said, his mouth full of bread and cheese.

Woodward sat morosely looking at his mud-caked shoes and moving his wet toes, which were beginning to be numb.

''She's a perfect witness,'' Dawson added.

''It is amazing how you see everyone in the world as your accomplice.''

No more amazing than your seeing everyone in the world as your accuser, Dawson thought.

''Do you ever think of all the people who will be misled by this great discovery? Mabel will be one of them,'' said Woodward.

"I didn't bring you into this to act as my conscience. You've got plenty to do what with looking after your own. But suppose Bob Kenward decides to get rid of that medieval nonsense in his head and becomes an enthusiastic convert to Darwinism. Ask any missionary who's made a convert—whether it's with the bribe of a sack of glass beads or promises of life everlasting—and he'll tell you it's a good thing, it's the will of God."

Woodward shook his head impatiently. "You see people who are credulous, trusting, as if they were at fault, as if they deserved to be exploited. I wish I had a trusting nature. It is terrible going through life continually looking over my shoulder."

"I call that being realistic."

"Call it what you like," Woodward said. He looked at Dawson, who took no notice of the sharpness of the weather. He sat hunched over, his forearms across his thighs, a half-eaten apple in one fist, bread and cheese in another. The color was high in his face, and the ends of a workman's blue bandanna knotted around his neck fluttered in the wind. He tossed his head to get the hair out of his eyes and took a large bite of the apple, working it in his mouth and spitting some seeds out on the ground below. His eyes squinted into the middle distance.

For Woodward, Dawson seemed just then the embodiment of power at rest. He saw Dawson in minute detail, the coarse hairs on his wrist and the ropey veins on the back of his hand, his even white teeth as he bit into the apple, the tip of his tongue as he licked his lips. Woodward watched Dawson's jaws working as he chewed and imagined the muscles across his broad back as he hunched over in his seat. What must it be like to be this man? Woodward wondered, cursing himself for succumbing to what he saw in that unaffected and secure presence, a natural glamor that excited him to admiration. For all Dawson's guile and cynicism, he looked to be untroubled in his immorality. But how did his brain think? Where did his universe begin and end? Woodward thought of biographies of great men, whose lives from infancy to death were depicted on a single track: Alexander dreaming of world conquest at his mother's breast. Perhaps whatever Dawson was had been inborn, obeying a Darwinian law, that would carry him, mindlessly, through to the end. Or maybe his mind was a bin filled with disordered and uncataloged specimens of self-interest, aggression, and the will to exploit. What a marvel of simplicity Dawson was. Woodward came to the momentary conclusion that the key to Dawson was extraordinarily primitive.

Dawson turned, sensing he was being closely observed. "What is it?"

"Do you ever regret anything?" Woodward asked.

"What for?"

"Did you ever trust anyone?"

Dawson returned his gaze to the barren fields, his eyes narrowing to penny slots. "No. I never trusted anyone. I don't know why. I don't remember anything happening that made me feel that way. I don't remember any betrayal or disappointment, any moment when I lost my innocence. I can only think that I have always been that way, but then I don't remember very much about my childhood. I don't think I ever was a child in my thoughts and feelings. Except that I accepted the idea that adults were powerful and arbitrary. I didn't disobey them; in fact, I was a model child and respected in their eyes in my childish work of lessons and sport. But I knew there was another person, a true self in me, and that if I ever revealed it, it would be taken away from me without explanation. I could not give up the pleasure I got from the world's approbation, and in fact those pleasures were sweeter for the contempt I felt at the world's credulity that I was simply as they saw me. How easily the world could be fooled, because it never knew my power secretly to resist. I began to know that my way in the world was not to regard it as distinct from myself, but that each person I encountered existed to the degree that I could possess him or her—not possess in the ordinary sense of friendship and love, my friend, my lover—but only to have an effect. I felt the keen satisfaction of seeing others believe what I told them only because I knew what they wanted to hear. That is why we shall be successful here at Piltdown.

"I have been reasonably good at what I have done and in the various roles demanded of me. But it has been a gray existence. I have thought so often about leading a more brightly colored life, but for someone of my nature, my detachment, the way has been difficult to find. It isn't that I didn't dare for fear of disappointment, as I would try despite that inevitability, but rather I despaired at finding someone who would not be seduced and who would be incredulous of me, someone who might see right to this true self in me, and tell me what it is."

"Don't you know?"

"I must have known once, but I think I have forgotten. I suppose it is rather like a green plant. If you don't put it in the sunlight and air, it will die." Dawson pulled a piece of dry grass from the leg of his trousers and let it blow away.

"But all that has changed," he continued. "I don't mean to say that I have changed, nor did I find that incredulous phantom. Instead, I have found a woman who purely and simply desires me, and who has awakened my lust in the most miraculous way. It doesn't matter whether she believes me or not, not to her, not to me. All that is simply beside the point. I am entirely governed by lust, not only for its own sake, but because in lust there is hope. There is a sharp and wrenching reminder that I am alive, a delicious longing, moments of brightness and sensation, and a feeling of renewal. I cannot get enough of her now, but I will. The treasures we will tell the world we have found here will allow me to possess this woman once and for all, and who knows, perhaps a seed from my lost true self isn't dead. Perhaps it will grow again, and I will discover for myself what it is."

Chapter IX

D URING THE BLEAK, WET MONTHS OF WINTER, DAWSON busied himself in his study, completing several more pieces of the Piltdown skull and addressing himself to the orangutan's mandible. He knew that the ape's condyle wouldn't fit into the head, so he broke it off and used the condyle fragment as a test piece for staining, having to alter his recipe to suit the somewhat different structure and porosity of the anthropoid bone to make it match the human cranium.

He started a correspondence with Woodward, beginning with a letter dated to the previous August, confiding to Woodward, and urging the utmost discretion, that he believed some few finds at Barkham Manor indicated a hominid individual of the greatest importance. By the end of the fall, after Woodward's first visit to the site, they had found nothing further, but Dawson dictated letters that Woodward wrote to him, copies of which Woodward kept in his files at the Museum, in which Woodward expressed cautious optimism on the basis of the specimens Dawson had brought to London. Dawson wrote to Woodward frequently, saying that he had visited the manor, but that any further excavations were impossible until the spring, not only for the sake of the correspondence in the Museum's files, but to remind Woodward of his obligations.

Dawson's archaeological excursions were curtailed by the

weather, but he still got out into the countryside on legal business. There was scarcely a view that did not remind him of an idyllic summer afternoon with Arabella. Going toward Framfield, there was a wooded grove, now bare and lifeless, but its leafy bowers had once shaded their naked bodies; there was a small stream near Five Ash Down where they had laughingly splashed each other like naughty children. Arabella was everywhere in the countryside and in his thoughts. Each time they met on the Channel coast, in the resort towns that were shuttered for the winter, shabby and disconsolate in the sallow light, Dawson returned to Lewes satisfied that each day brought him closer to his moment of complete fulfillment. For her part, Arabella bade him good-bye with a sense of fulfillment already achieved.

In the spring, when there was a yellowish-green swarm of new leaves in the woods, but when it was still too cold for lovemaking, the fine days seduced Dawson from his duties as a solicitor to search for fossils. The limestone quarries at Hastings, the place-name known to every English schoolchild, was for him an inexhaustible source of specimens embedded in the sedimentary layers of rock faulted and warped by the upheavals and subsidences of the earth's crust. The whole of the coast was a gigantic shelf of limestone and chalk, ending at the sea as if a sculptor had cut it into nearly vertical cliffs with powerful blows of a chisel.

After years of prospecting at the quarry, Dawson was known by the workmen, who welcomed his visits. He tipped them for letting him dig and for setting aside pieces of stone that looked as if they contained fossils.

The quarry was near the cliffs. When the wind blew from the Channel, he could hear the strident cries of the white gulls as they floated in the updrafts and the chirping of the thousands of starlings that nested in the crannies of the chalk escarpment.

Dawson expected the usual cheerful greeting from the dusty foreman, but he looked disgruntled as he climbed up toward the lip of the quarry.

"There's a fellow down there looking for bones, just like you," said the foreman, thumbing at the jagged cliff of buff-colored limestone that had been blasted and carved into the side of the rolling downs. "But he don't give us nothing." He reached into his pocket with a chalky hand and showed Dawson two shillings. "I'd call that nothing."

Dawson promised to see what could be done and made his way along a wood scaffold and then down some workmen's steps that had been cut into the face of the quarry. The man who was the source of the foreman's irritation was working on a broad ledge, standing with his back to Dawson, intently chipping away at the stone with a geologist's hammer and pick. The brown jacket he wore was stretched across his spare back and protruding shoulder blades as he gently tapped at the limestone wall in front of him. The back of his head was narrow too, barely wider than his neck, with his hair closely cropped. He was completely engrossed in his work, unaware that Dawson had come within a few feet of him.

"Anything interesting?" Dawson asked.

The man turned quickly in surprise. His long, thin face matched his angular body. It was only then that Dawson saw his black shirtfront and white clerical collar.

"I don't know yet. I have not been working long enough." He spoke with a rich French accent.

"I don't mean to invade your territory, but there is a problem with the foreman: the size of your tip. If you're here on holiday, as a kind of geological tourist, I think you ought to know that four shillings would be about right. Did you come over from Dieppe?"

"For the moment I am living in Hastings. At the Jesuit seminary at Ore Place. I am a novice there."

"Charles Dawson." He thrust his hand out.

"Dawson," the novice repeated, wrinkling his brow a little. "Pierre Teilhard de Chardin."

"That's a lot more French than I can manage. Couldn't I just say 'Father?'" Dawson asked, thinking it was ridiculous, considering his youthful face; about thirty, he estimated.

"Teilhard will do. It is easy, and I am not yet ordained."

"Let's see what you've got." Dawson stepped closer to the wall of stone. "That's a nice vertebra. But from what I can see it's an isolated specimen."

"I know. But I have other pieces of this creature, and I am hoping to complete the spine."

"It is quite common to this stratum." Dawson said.

"Yes. That is why I am exploring this ledge. They have already cut it away on the other side, which is where I started. One week it was there, then it was gone."

"Then you come here often."

"Not as often as I would like," said Teilhard.

"A decade ago this hole was hardly bigger than a bathtub." Dawson looked across the quarry, carved in bold geometric patterns like the side of a fantastic building cut from living rock without doors or windows. It was at least fifty feet deep where the dusty men were hacking with picks and preparing holes for explosives. "Over the years I've found some of my rarest and most complete specimens here, most of which are now in the British Museum."

"The Dawson Collection. Of course. That is how I know your name. But you are very famous." Teilhard was now smiling eagerly. He stuck his hand out again to shake Dawson's, but he was still holding his hammer, which Dawson shook.

"Do you sleep with it?" Dawson asked.

Teilhard fumbled with the hammer and grinned with embarrassment. "Please excuse me, but I am so pleased to meet you. I have been at the Museum several times, especially for the East Sussex fossils. I admired very much the *Plagiaulax dawsoni*," he said, referring to an early mammal in the collection discovered by Dawson. "Where did you find it?"

"In the High Weald in some fine gravels near the Ouse."

"I do not know that part of Sussex. Not yet. My obligations at Ore Place take up most of my time. But I intend eventually to get my advanced degree in paleontology."

"Won't that conflict with your other . . ." Dawson hesitated searching for the right word. "Concerns," he said at last.

"There are many Jesuit scientists. I intend to be one of them."

"Then you must finish your work," Dawson said. "Let's see if there's anything for me here."

Dawson followed the various strata, running his fingertips over the rock. There were fine, buff-colored virgin layers and others thickly set with fossil shells, bivalves, and bullet-shaped belemnites like thick slabs of stony head cheese.

The two men worked on the ledge for several hours, Dawson occasionally glancing at the young priest. In profile, he was scarecrow thin. His nose was prominent in his face, slightly splayed at the end. A deep premature crease extended from his nostril engraving his flat cheek, and his thin lips were slightly parted as he concentrated on freeing the vertebra from the matrix. He tapped at the rock with a light, sure touch with the pick and hammer he held in his long elegant fingers as if he were carving instead of excavating. From time to time he would rest, rotating his neck and shaking the stiffness from his shoulders.

"What have you found?" Teilhard said to Dawson.

"A trilolite. I have several, but this is particularly large and well-preserved."

"Your collections must be extensive."

"They are threatening to dispossesses me from my study."

"And you must have explored everywhere in Sussex."

"I'm presently digging near Uckfield, a gravel layer."

"What period?"

"Pliocene and Pleistocene."

"I am envious. I have the feeling my interests will lie in the later periods. Until now I have only had some experience in the Cretaceous, like these limestones. Before I came to Hastings, I spent several years in Cairo teaching physics and chemistry, which I know very little about, I must admit. But there was much to learn geologically in lower Egypt, in the Fayum, that contained mostly early marine deposits." He spoke of what he had collected near in the marshy lakes of the oasis and also of the tall papyrus where white herons strutted, the dense flocks of coots and duck that covered the water, and how the sky turned opalescent when the sun set behind the distant violet hills. "A hundred meters from the lakes there was nothing but sand, and the stillness. It was as if one were carried back to the time when no life existed on the earth."

After each of them had respectable specimens, they climbed out of the quarry and sat in the grass at the edge of the cliff. Its profile undulated along the coastline like a white frill at the hem of a green garment, and they could see the roofs of Hastings off to one side. Beyond was the shimmering Channel disappearing into the haze. Teilhard looked toward France.

"Did you read that a man flew from France to England across the Channel in an aeroplane?" Dawson said.

"Yes. The seagulls must be jealous. I saw an aeroplane a few weeks ago. It was one of the finest things I ever saw in my life."

"I should like to try flying." Dawson thought that would be how he would escape with Arabella, sitting on his lap between the struts of a biplane, her hair blowing wild as they hurtled through the air at forty miles an hour.

"What a century to be living in. There will be great changes and many challenges." Teilhard fell silent, as if he took the thought and soared with it to a private place. He checked to see if Dawson was observing him, and he was relieved that Dawson was watching the gulls wheeling overhead. "Sometimes going home is a welcome respite. It is like a holiday in the seventeenth century. There is hardly a building later than that."

"Where is your home?"

"To the South, in the Auvergne."

"I assume from your name that your family is well-connected." Dawson had already observed that Teilhard had a natural distinction, that there was a certain finesse to his spare physique.

"You would call us landed gentry, but life in the French provinces is quite plain, rustic. We still have the Thursday market in the square, and the country folk are no different than they were three hundred years ago. Motorcars are seldom seen and are looked on with great suspicion, and there are many who will not have their photographs taken for fear of losing their souls. It is all wonderfully medieval."

"Did the local alchemist introduce you to science?"

"It was the landscape. The Auvergne is a savage country, with many extinct volcanoes. When I was very young, I asked my father what they were, and when he told me, I could hardly believe him, but he was my father, and so I did. I asked him how old they were, and he said millions of years, which amazed me. I began to ask him the age of everything—the Romanesque church, the trees in our orchards, even the clouds. The moment I became curious, I became a scientist. And the first thing I wondered about was why some things lasted while others perished. As a child, I never imagined that I would ever die. But one evening my mother sat me by the fireplace in the kitchen to cut my hair, and one of my curls fell into the fire and was consumed. I remember the terrible smell and the awful revelation that one day all of me would be ashes and dust. I cried so bitterly that even my mother could not comfort me. Then I began to look for something I thought was everlasting, and I began collecting bits of iron, carrying them about in my pocket, feeling the hard cold metal. Although my family was very pious, for five years I worshiped my own secret god, my god of iron, my *dieu de fer*. But then one day I saw an old plow in the garden—I suppose it had always been there without my seeing it—and I was horrified to see it was covered with rust. Again I was in despair, until I discovered stone. Stone was truly imperishable, and I began to collect pieces of it on my walks in the country. I thought a great force had destined me to make this discovery, since I had been named Pierre. I had my god of stone, my *dieu de pierre*.''

"So you began life as a pagan," said Dawson.

"Yes," answered Teilhard cheerfully. "I never met a child who wasn't. The Church is correct, I think, to insist that children receive a strict religious education, learn their catechism, and all of the rest. But it does not mean anything until later. I knew I was Catholic, but no one could have convinced me my god of stone was not everlasting and omnipotent."

"Your god of stone is older than Christ. We have seen that in the quarry."

"Only older than Man. But not older than Christ. Our Lord is eternal. He only became known through Man."

Teilhard wasn't preaching. He spoke matter-of-factly, as if what he was saying was self-evident, even trite.

"And is that revelation the reason for the evolution of Man?"

Teilhard raised his shoulders in an expressive Gallic shrug.

"Does that mean you don't know, or that you don't care?"

"It means that the design of the universe, including Man, and the reason for its existence are unknown to me. But I believe the advent of Man had a purpose," Teilhard replied.

Observing Teilhard closely, Dawson thought: The advent of this man has a purpose. This young priest was heaven-sent, with a finely honed mind and a passion for science. He spoke with an open sincerity that engendered immediate confidence. Even the sun placed itself behind him, making a light radiate from his head. The effect was not infelicitous.

"We have known each other only a few hours," Dawson began in a benevolent tone, "But I have the feeling you are destined for a life of considerable distinction. When I was a lad at St. Leonards-on-Sea, I was fortunate to have found a geological mentor in S. H. Beckles. He was a splendid old gent who took me on my first expeditions on the Weald. And when he died, I cataloged his collection and, together with what I found, made my first gift to the BM. By the time I was twenty-one, I was a Fellow of the Geological Society. I don't say that to boast, but only to acknowledge old Beckles's help. I would like to help you if I may, in memory of an old friend, and to bring you into the world of science."

Teilhard lowered his eyes like a shy girl.

Teilhard had first arrived at the seminary at Ore Place on a rain-soaked day that reduced the buildings and wooded park to a gray monochrome. It was situated outside the town of Hastings and was reached by a road that wound high on a hill that gave the south windows of the administration buildings and dormitories an unobstructed view of the town and expanse of the Channel. Even in good weather, when the sea sparkled in the distance, Teilhard felt he had first seen Ore Place in its most authentic mood. The main mid-Victorian building of gray ashlar blocks reminded him of an orphanage or madhouse. Behind it were the dormitory, classrooms, and chapel, institutional boxes with scarcely more than a grudging show of a classical order. The seminary was reached by a winding driveway from a front gate, so that the buildings were approached suddenly, without warning. Thick plantings of dark green, polished holly and unclipped privet, and tall, ancient oaks pressed close in on the buildings and narrow lawns. Teilhard's heart sank a little each time he returned from the outside world. He knew that, for most of his classmates and for his teachers, Ore Place was a retreat, a sanctuary where progress toward God could be measured day by day. But for him there was also danger.

It was a dangerous time for anyone but the most orthodox. The new Pope, Piux X, and his curia of old men sent out papal spies, a secret network rooting out modernists and subversives. A casual remark, the wrong question asked, would be reported in Rome. Antimodernist oaths were required of teachers and students alike. Teilhard knew that his interest in science made him immediately suspicious. He felt watched. Perhaps his teachers observed the careful way he answered questions in biblical studies and exegesis, responses that lacked the quickness of a parroted reply or the ingenous enthusiasm of those for whom doctrine was life's breath.

If Teilhard had been called to revolutionary politics instead of the Church, he would have been a secret agent. In family photographs as a boy, he stood slightly apart from the others, obviously pretending to belong, not yet having mastered the act of incognito. There was a reticence about him that some of his fellow students at Ore Place rightly ascribed to social and intellectual snobbery. His spiritual educators had a suspicion that, despite his fastidious submission to the rule of obedience, Teilhard was implacable and unreachable. In this they were correct, but for all his dissembling, Teilhard's spiritual life sprang from a principal of perfect simplicity that none of his superiors could argue with: faith in the universal dominion of Christ. Before Him, Teilhard felt limitlessly humble, tractable, and pliant as a child.

He had thought more than once about leaving the order. But each time he had been drawn back by an unassailable wonder that he had found the essence of the indestructible, that his mystical Christ inhabited every atom of matter in his own flesh and in the silent infernos of the most distant stars, even in the emptiness of the infinite universe. When he contemplated his vision, he offered absolution to the doddering formalism and politics of the Church.

Teilhard had thought that, if he had lived at the time of the early church of the Evangelists, he would have chosen the life of a desert hermit, gazing at the sun until his eyes were scorched sockets, blind to everything except his ecstatic vision of God. But as a man of the twentieth century, science would be his hermitage. Instead of a cave in the wilderness, he would seek his God in the world of men. It did not seem to Teilhard that piety and worldly ambition stood at odds. That was one aspect of his temperament with which the princes of the Church, with their crucifixes hanging on golden chains and their feet shod in brocaded slippers, could take no exception.

At vespers that evening, Teilhard's mind wandered. He had changed into his black cassock and looked indistinguishable from his brothers as they bent their heads in prayer. The chapel was cold and dimly lit, purposefully spartan, bare and ugly. Darkly varnished paintings of saints hung high on the walls, and a cadaverous Italianate crucifix behind the altar. If by some feat of imagination, Teilhard could have transported himself to the twelfth century chapel near his home, with its Romanesque marvels of sculpture, he would have felt no less imprisoned. As soon as he completed his novitiate, he planned to travel as far into the secular world as he would be permitted to go. To that end he needed lay friends. And he determined that Charles Dawson would be one.

"Don't be such a worry wart," Dawson said to Woodward. They were closeted in Woodward's study. The guests for tea would be arriving shortly.

"It's not a good idea to get a third person involved in this. Why didn't you discuss this with me first?"

"Because I knew you'd say no."

"What have you told him we've found?"

"The skull fragments, the jaw, the animal teeth. What's the matter with you? Are you getting dotty in your middle age? Don't you remember the specimens from your own excavation?"

"I don't like it. It only complicates things."

"He's absolutely safe. I told him not to say anything to anybody, and he won't. I want you to be sure to introduce him to everyone as our protégé, a most extraordinary and promising young man. "And he is extraordinary," Dawson continued. "I don't know how he's found the time to be so current in the literature, unless he reads under the covers at night, but I suppose that's a far sight better than what his other brothers are doing under the covers."

"Really, Charles."

"Poor bastards. But this one looks quite chaste, even virginal. If he ever finds himself in Hell, it will not be for lascivious thoughts but intellectual disobedience. He has taken me up as his intellectual confidant, and he has been quite right not to discuss his theories at the seminary. It's not just Darwin and the old chestnut about science and religion; if they ever knew what was going on inside his head, they'd put him on the rack."

"This thing is bad enough without having to be wet nurse to your protégé. What is he going to do at Piltdown, lie about praying that we find something?" Woodward said.

"I certainly hope that he will be praying that he finds something."

Woodward responded with silent incredulity.

"But that's the whole point," Dawson said. "It's a master stroke. He's going to find a specimen at Piltdown. There isn't a single person in the world who'd question its authenticity. Would a Jesuit priest be a conspirator in a despicable fraud? Especially this priest. Wait till you meet him."

"What's he going to find?" Woodward asked in a resigned monotone.

"I'm not going to tell you. I want to keep you in suspense,

so you'll be genuinely surprised. Just as surprised as I'll be," Dawson said, striking an attitude of astonishment.

There was a knock at the door. Maud put her head in. "Dr. Soames is here. Don't be long."

Woodward got up. Before leaving the room, he turned to Dawson. "Has it ever occurred to you what you're doing to this young man?"

"I am launching his brilliant career," Dawson replied. "He's like Piltdown Man. He was meant to be discovered."

"What if . . ."

"There is no 'What if.' Besides, he is innocent. And I intend to keep him that way."

Dawson moved about the room, introducing Teilhard to other guests, allowing him a brief conversation, and then taking him off to another encounter. They finally reached Woodward.

"This is my young friend, Arthur," Dawson said. He acknowledged another guest's greeting and left Woodward and Teilhard on their own.

"I've read papers by many of your guests. It is an honor for me to be here."

"I hope we shall see a great deal of you. And I hope you will stop in at South Ken. Our reserve collections of East Anglian fossils are excellent, thanks in part to Charles's generous gifts."

"Mr. Dawson is an extraordinary person."

"That point I will not argue."

"I think it is remarkable he has taken an interest in me."

"Charles's motives are not always easily read."

"He's an inspired teacher. Not only the way he speaks about the geology of Sussex, with such authority and personal experience. There is something else. It is his integrity, his passionate seeking after the truth."

"You are touched by Charles's attention. I can understand that." Stepping closer, Woodward gently turned Teilhard so that they faced away from the crowded center of the room. "He has told me of taking you into his confidence. This is an extremely important site, an opportunity that would ordinarily occur in your career many years in the future, after your degree, after years of fieldwork. This may not be the right time. You must consider carefully. You have led a sheltered life, if I may say so. The politics of science are formidable. They must be learned, just as one must learn scientific skills. A young person of promise is one thing; a young person of eminence is another. You will be the target of jealousy, even hatred. All the people in this room loathe each other. You ought to . . ."

"Arthur. Stop monopolizing our friend," Dawson said, bustling toward them. "You'll have plenty of time to talk on Saturday. Come along, Teilhard. There's someone you must meet."

On Saturday the three men dug at Piltdown. Dawson thought it wise to find nothing that time, as well as on the four following weekends. At last, Teilhard found an eolith. The crude flint was the final piece of evidence Dawson felt he needed. He told Woodward that as soon as they organized their notes and drawings and drafted a paper they would be ready to present formally the remarkable package to the British Museum.

Chapter X

AFTER THE RECEPTION CELEBRATING THE DISCOVERY OF the Dawn Man of Sussex, Dawson stepped out of the gates of Burlington House into Piccadilly. The last of the omnibuses lumbered by, and a few taxicabs prowled for fares as he set out to walk to his hotel in Knightsbridge. The night had a cold fine edge, but Dawson felt the mulled wine and the exhilarating glow of victory. He was too elated to sleep. Everything had gone exactly as he had planned, and his date book was filled with appointments for interviews that would spread his name far beyond the confines of learned societies and scientific journals. The next morning he was expected at the offices of the *Illustrated London News* and the *Telegraph* in the afternoon. Grafton Elliot Smith's attack had been a feeble one, easily deflected; Dawson had anticipated naysayers. Scientific controversy was entirely proper concerning such an important discovery, and desirable, as it would keep the Piltdown Man before the public with Dawson as his champion. He strode to Hyde Park Corner at a brisk pace, stopping in front of Apsley House. Looking up at the hawklike profile of the Duke of Wellington astride his horse, Dawson felt that their victories were not unalike. They had both vanquished the French. Piltdown was the Waterloo for French eminence in hominid paleontology. What a ruffian their Neanderthal was compared with the first squire of Sussex. He decided to recall these night thoughts at the next day's interviews.

Continuing onward up Knightsbridge Road, Dawson felt as if he had taken a powerful stimulant; he breathed quickly, every nerve ending eager and receptive. The cold wind in his face was as fresh and bracing as if it came straight from the sea. He unbuttoned his coat to feel it against his body, pulling his tie away from his neck and taking out his collar button. He was walking parallel to the park and had a sudden impulse to be in its darkness, alone, away from the Christmas tinsel of the shop windows, monuments of bronze and stone, the works of other men and the landmarks of history in the grand and powerful city. Dawson stepped across the soft cinders of Rotten Row, heading into the stretches of deserted lawn. The tracery of bare branches of the towering plane trees and elms were blacker still than the sky. Dawson's elation expanded in the space that surrounded him, moving with the city behind him deeper into the park. He kept off the pathways, wanting to feel the softer turf underfoot.

Dawson imagined everyone in London asleep, their collective consciousness obliterated. For each Londoner the city ceased to exist; even they themselves dissolved into the trough of the night between the past and the future, outside time and place. In his imagination, the whole of England succumbed to the benign plague of forgetfulness. Battles, dynasties, empires were nothing. Only Dawson, the Dawn Man, protean and alone remained. *Eoanthropus*. Man of the Dawn. The sun of the young earth would bring forth a gorgeous display of color, mauve and blue first, then a procession of reds and oranges to herald the first day of man, like the fluttering silk pennants of royalty yet born, an augury of color foretelling a glorious future.

Soon he was near the black water of the Serpentine, marked with shifting corrugations on its polished surface. He walked past the boathouse, where the rowboats were chained together upside down for the winter, toward the bridge further on, stopping between the two structures so that they dissolved in the darkness, the park again a wilderness. He could hear the leafless branches above him tapping and whispering when the wind gusted. On such a night the Dawn Man must have roamed, master of the dark.

Dawson breathed deeply, the cold air filling his lungs, and then began to make low guttural noises at the back of his throat. The Dawn Man crouched in the forest, looking toward the lake with his keen night vision. He felt as if he were in the thrall of an uncanny transformation, part man, part beast; the Dawn Man was his creation, and he would live for a brief moment in the night.

Looking around him, Dawson saw a planting of low bushes. Inside the thicket, he slipped out of his overcoat and took off the rest of his clothes until he stood naked. He raised his arms to the sky, stretching out the knots and cramps of civilization. The Dawn Man was the only naked creature on earth. Although dangerous carnivores might catch the tantalizing and new odor of humanity or see the paleness of his body, he felt heroic, invulnerable in the power of his intelligence and cunning. He got on his hands and knees, feeling the cold, wet ground and digging his fingers into it, took two divots and rubbed them on his skin, sniffing the sweet earthiness. The dampness heightened the bite of the cold, but his body responded with a rush of warmth. He rose, hardly visible against the murkiness of the night surrounding him with a tremendous sense of freedom and mastery and trotted at a low crouch, dropping on all fours behind the massive trunks of the trees to watch, get his bearings. He then went toward the Serpentine and pausing briefly at the edge of the lake, leaped with a shallow dive, swimming under the perfect blackness of the water for as long as his breath would hold. Emerging in the middle of the lake and gulping the air, he plunged again into its depths. After the first shock, the water was warm, and he swam for some time, diving and surfacing, buoyant and alive. He reached the edge of the lake again, and clambering out, loped back to the bushes. When at last he began to shudder with the cold, he took his shirt and vigorously rubbed his body dry, and then, putting it on, he got into the rest of his clothes. With his overcoat collar turned up tight against his neck, Dawson headed out of the park once again into the world of men.

The months following the official announcement were hectic for Dawson. He ricocheted between London and Sussex, giving interviews and having his photograph taken, either formally or at the site. He was an indefatigable tour guide at Barkham Manor for visiting scientific dignitaries and reporters who put up with the raw dampness of the weather to get a look at England's most famous gravel pit. The reporters took to Dawson's easy manner and responded to his evident vigor; he was as far as possible from their preconceived notion of a frail and stuffy scientist. He avoided dreary technicalities and pedantic lecturing, but rather spoke of the backbreaking work and the thrill of discovery, and he could make their pulses race when he declaimed on the subject of nationalist pride: "We are standing at the birthplace of man and the British Empire!"

Every reporter or paleontologist with whom Dawson or Woodward met asked to see the actual specimens. Requests from newspapers or magazines were summarily refused, although they were given official photographs of the fragments and a restoration. Scientific professionals were asked to put their requests in writing, as well as to include a scholarly biography, a list of publications, and a detailed proposal justifying their access to the most precious fossils in the world. Woodward personally reviewed each application and invariably wrote back saying that whatever they hoped to learn from the bones could be gained from an inspection of casts. The cast maker at the Museum had produced a masterwork of accuracy, every crack and crevice exactly as they had appeared on the originals. Dawson and Woodward convinced the superintendent that changes in temperature and humidity, not to mention the possibility of accidental breakage, were irresponsible risks to the Museum's most priceless possessions, and so the bones and implements were secured in a vault deep in the basement. Everyone in the field seemed to accept the sacrosanctity of Piltdown Man's remains. All future research would be done with fine casts of the specimens. The conversation workshop at the Museum set up a cottage industry, supplying Piltdown casts to universities and museums all over the world, and human paleontologists set to revising their textbooks. It was a new era for British natural sciences. Even those scholars whose interests did not touch on early man drew new energy for their own studies, and those fortunate enough to be nearer the riddles of human evolution looked for ways to associate themselves with the great find. Arthur Keith, the expert on fossil skulls, insinuated himself into Woodward's and Dawson's good graces and busied himself with a new variation of Piltdown Man's cranium, restoring it to enlarge the brain capacity, which found unanimous acceptance among his colleagues, who, to a man, believed in the superiority of English intelligence, being English themselves.

In the late winter, Dawson received a note at his office from Arthur Conan Doyle, asking for a private viewing of the site. Doyle arrived at Uckfield in a new car, a Daimler roadster, and was dressed for motoring in a twill coat to his ankles with a nutria lining and collar.

"I have much to thank you for," Doyle said as Dawson climbed into the car. "When we last met, you were kind enough to give me an introduction to Sir Ray Lankester. I did meet him and found him a striking character, just as you said. So much so that he is, in fact, a character. He served as the original for my Professor Challenger in my novel, *The Lost World*." As Doyle let out the clutch, the car jolted forward. He hunched over the wheel, keeping his eyes fixed on the empty road and making vigorous steering motions even on the straightaways. To Dawson he was an oversized boy to whom indulgent parents had given an overly expensive toy. For all the steering, Doyle was oblivious to the ruts which he crossed and recrossed as they jostled to Barkham Manor.

"I don't know why my chauffeur doesn't like me to take the car out by myself," Doyle said.

They came to a dramatic and abrupt halt at the gate to the private road and walked on the tree-lined avenue to the site. Remembering their last meeting, Dawson was surprised that Doyle listened with close attention to his explanation of the structure of the strata and questioned him on the fine points of the dig. "I would invite you to sieve a spadeful of gravel, but Dr. Woodward and I are not digging just now. You see there is flooding in the pit.''

"When will you resume?''

"In the spring, after the weather turns.''

"I've followed your career since the discovery was announced,'' Doyle said. "Got quite a bunch of cuttings. You must send me offprints of your articles so I can keep abreast. This Dawn Man of yours holds a great fascination for me. In fact, you seem to be something of a Dawn Man yourself. When I first met you in your study . . . Well, fame seems to agree with you. You have expanded.''

"I have found my place in the scheme of things. Natural selection. I have found my niche, albeit a large one.''

"You have made your niche. So did I. Sherlock Holmes, for instance. He wasn't an inspiration. He was a calculated exercise. Crime was nothing new, and neither was deductive reasoning. I simply pitted the former against the latter, in the person of Holmes, because I knew that people are deeply satisfied when the mysterious yields to intelligence and reasoning.''

"As in science.''

"Ah, science. Everybody loves science, not because it solves mysteries, but because of its practical applications. We can light the world with electricity because of science; we can get places faster, even though we don't know what to do once we get there. Science gives us what we want.''

"Can you say that of Darwinism? The greatest idea of the nineteenth century was the greatest insult to men's view of themselves.''

"Not at all. The reason why Darwinism has been accepted so quickly is that it is glamorous, so alluring. The idea of survival of the fittest allows men who have no interest in science to perpetrate the most terrible crimes against their neighbors with complete impunity; they are simply obeying natural law, which has had such authority since the enlightenment. Except now it is the law of the jungle. It suits us to a T, just as your Piltdown Man does. What luck you have found him for us. Think of the astronomical odds against finding him, and right exactly there," Doyle said, indicating the pit. "If you'd dug there . . . or there . . ." He shrugged.

"It is extraordinary," Dawson admitted. "On the other hand, I have been digging in Sussex my whole life. Looking back to the first indications that this might be an important site, the odds were greatly reduced by my intuition. The geology of Sussex has been my life. No doubt there was luck, but there was intuition, which is to say, the senses sharpened by experience. This place smelled right." Dawson picked up some brown gravels.

Doyle took one out of his hand and held it to his nose. "My intuition tells me there are more mysteries here then meet the eye." He put the pebble into his pocket. "A keepsake."

"I have solved only one," Dawson replied. "Over there or over there," he said, "there are mysteries for botanists, ornithologists, and every other sort of naturalist you can name. They will solve them too."

"Speaking from the literary viewpoint," Doyle said, "mysteries are written backward. You must know the solution before you start. You must be sure how it's going to turn out so that everything your characters say and do, each aspect of the plot point inevitably to the true facts of the crime—and the criminal—in the end."

"But there are no criminals in science. Only answers."

"Anyone can find an answer to anything. The trick is to find the right one. What about those who say there is no Dawn Man, that you found two disparate fossils, an ape and a man?"

"I see you have been following all of this closely," Dawson said. "That is not an answer. That is an erroneous theory, which Dr. Woodward and I have dealt with on the basis of the facts, the evidence."

"You have a positive attitude," Doyle remarked.

"That is necessary in every endeavor."

"And what is next on your agenda?"

"Whatever the earth has in store. One can coax a woman, but with the earth, one learns patience."

In the early spring, Dawson and Woodward began their

Saturday digging again. Dawson had no plans to find anything else, much to Woodward's relief, but the expectations
in scientific circles of possible future discoveries demanded
that they proceed with further excavations for the sake of
appearances.

With the countryside still wet from spring rains, Woodward had bought himself boots and workman's overalls,
which made Dawson howl with laughter the first time he
appeared as a ditchdigger. Maud had never seen him in this
laborer's outfit; he left for the country early in the morning,
before breakfast, and when he returned, he hurried upstairs to
change before presenting himself.

Teilhard was a less frequent participant than formerly. The
official announcement at Burlington House preceded the final
months of his studies at Ore Place and preparations for his
ordination. His superiors were aware of his intention to continue his scientific studies in Paris, and he thought it best to
assume his most obedient and humble manner, although he
was itching with restlessness to be free of the drudgery of
studying the nuances of dogma he found so stultifying and
beside the point.

The three men had not been working long at Barkham
Manor before Robert Kenward approached them from the
house. He was a big man with a loose, shambling gait,
wearing brown corduroys and leggings. His face was broad
and flat, with two perpetual streaks of high color on his
cheeks and generous mustaches and whiskers all-of-a-piece
that were as carefully trimmed as a show terrier's. As chief
tenant, he had authority over the cottagers who lived on the
large property and the daily workings of the farm, but he did
not shrink from pitching in or mucking stalls. He was popular
in the neighborhood though he was a blusterer and a scold.

"Hallo, Dawson," Kenward shouted with a loose-limbed
wave of his arm.

Dawson got out of the pit to greet him. "You know
Woodward, and this is Father Teilhard."

Kenward nodded in their direction. "I've been reading
about you in the papers. Mabel says we've become the most

famous spot in England. Thank heaven it's a private road, or we'd have every Tom, Dick, and Harry gawking at us.''

"There's still a great deal of work to be done," Dawson said. "And we'll be digging for the foreseeable future. I hope you won't be inconvenienced.''

"It's not my place to say. As long as Sir Percy has no objections," Kenward said, referring to the owner of Barkham Manor, "it's all right with me." He glanced disparagingly into the pit and sent a baleful look at Teilhard. "I don't want to take time from your work, but there are a few items of manor business I'd like to take up with you.''

"As soon as we finish up, I'll meet you at the house," Dawson said.

As Kenward walked away, Woodward said, "I don't think you've made a convert to Darwinism.''

Kenward's visit seemed to be a malign visitation, for soon afterward large gray clouds scudded over the fields, and the diggers fled in the drenching rain to the house.

At the manor Woodward and Teilhard settled themselves on a faded chintz couch in the cluttered, high-ceiling library to dry out and wait for Mabel to bring tea, while Dawson sat with Robert Kenward in a more obscure part of the house.

"I won't beat about the bush," Kenward said. "It's not manor business. It's that hole in the ground.''

"What about it?"

"I'm a God-fearing man," Kenward began, with what would have been a non sequitur except that Dawson knew Kenward's stance regarding evolution. "I'm not saying you're not entitled to your opinion. I'm the last person to put a muzzle on any man," he continued, trying to reconcile his yeoman's sense of fairness with his outraged religious scruples. Taking into consideration Dawson's stewardship and relationship to Sir Percy, as well as his genuine regard for Dawson's legal talents, Kenward cited instances of Dawson's Solomonic wisdom in manor affairs. At last, after beating around the bush he had said he wouldn't belabor, Kenward declared, "But you're wrong. It's against the Bible." Dawson might be entitled to his opinions, but the excavation at Barkham Manor was a territorial invasion, bringing pernicious secularism right to his front door. "I'm not the only one. Dr. Abernathy," Kenward declared, marshaling the highest ecclesiastical authority in the immediate vicinity. "We've known each other for a long time, Dawson, and that's why I can speak to you as a friend." Kenward lowered his voice. "It's that priest, that Jesuit." He was confiding information of the greatest importance.

"Yes?"

"And he's French," Kenward said, clinching his argument.

Dawson remained silent, unsure that he would make the right connections between Kenward's observations that emerged like tiny islands in a muddy sea of unspoken prejudices.

"You can't trust them. You never know what they're thinking. And you never know what they're doing. I know you're one of those ev-o-lu-tion-ists," Kenward said, "but it just won't stand up against the word of God, the Book of Genesis, and that's a fact." The smudges of color on his cheeks became more intense. "You don't see what's as plain as the nose on your face. That French Jesuit is trying to make fools of all of us. That's no bloody ape-man you found in that hole. God made apes, and He made man, and that's as true as I'm sitting here. Whatever you found—that priest put it there. They're not fossils. They're fakes!"

"I have the greatest respect for your religious beliefs, Kenward," Dawson said. "And I am sorry that our discovery causes you such discomfort. I know you are not alone in these views, and that your conclusion concerning the Piltdown fossils evolves, if I may use that term, from a literal reading of the Bible. But as far as Father Teilhard is concerned, I must tell you that the first finds in the gravels were made by Dr. Woodward and myself, considerably before Father Teilhard joined us in the digging. He could not possibly have put the fossils in the ground, since he didn't know where the site was."

Kenward fell into a pensive study. Then he said, "What about this Woodward fellow? Is he trustworthy? What do you know about him? He's gotten pretty famous, quite the celebrity now, from what I've read. Some men have that kind of ambition, liking to be pointed out."

"Are you suggesting that Dr. Woodward planted the specimens here?"

"Why not?" Kenward said with some belligerence.

"I feel I must tell you that I, too, have become famous. Do you suspect me as well?"

"You? You're a solicitor. You won't get any more business from this. And if you want to know the truth, you might even lose some. It was all well and good poking around for this and that as everyone knew you did. But a so-called ape-man is a different matter; it's not good business to argue with the Bible. Maybe it is in London, but not hereabouts."

Dawson climbed into the driver's seat of the buggy beside Woodward with Teilhard behind. As the horse trotted toward the gate of the manor, Dawson said, "You were right, Arthur. He's no convert. In fact, he came to the startling conclusion that the specimens we found were fake." He looked at Woodward mischievously. "But what can you expect? After all, he is a biblical literalist. I might have come to the same conclusion starting from that premise." Dawson looked over his shoulder at Teilhard. "He is also as dedicated to anti-Catholic bias as he is to the Book of Genesis. Teilhard, you're the culprit—an evil agent provocateur sent from Papist France to hoax the good Anglican British. But when I demonstrated that was impossible, he turned his attention to you, Arthur."

"I hope you defended me," Woodward said dryly.

"He wanted to know all about you, if you could be trusted, as if he were hiring a butler. I gave you a good character."

"That was kind of you."

"Both of you will be happy to know that, as far as Kenward was concerned, I was above suspicion."

"At least he was right on one count," Teilhard said.

It was still early afternoon as Woodward waited on the platform at Lewes for the train to London. The charade of digging at Piltdown, before the great announcement and after, had displaced his former Saturday routine: waking up a half hour later than his weekday morning and after breakfast being obliged to take Samson for a long walk. As Maud's surrogate, Samson tugged and yanked him on the green until his arm ached. The silence of the late morning dwindled into the late afternoon as Woodward worked on his papers, and as the shadows lengthened and grew emaciated on the carpet, the ticking of the clock got louder. Maude served high tea and held him prisoner with the week's neighborhood gossip.

That had changed when Dawson forcibly enlisted him as his accomplice. Woodward told Maud that Dawson was offering him an extraordinary chance at fame. Power, Maud corrected, and gave her consent, not without commenting that Dawson's promises were likely to prove worthless. Having been proved wrong, Maud took more complete charge of Woodward's professional life, so that he might wring the last drop of academic advantage from the discovery, and was scarcely aware that Woodward was enjoying a new freedom of movement. He was off to Piltdown on Saturday mornings before she got up and arrived home at unpredictable hours of the evening.

Woodward arrived back in London hours before he would be expected at home. Walking out of the iron shed of Victoria Station past the ticket windows, he caught a glimpse in a mirror of a middle-aged workman with a goatee exactly like his own. He stopped, sizing up his twin in dirty overalls, who raised his hand to adjust his pince-nez glasses at exactly the same moment. Both of them said, "Sorry," to the man who bumped into them when they stopped unexpectedly.

Ordinarily, Woodward would have gone directly down into the underground, but his twin, whose reflection he followed, stepped into Terminus Place and after a few blocks seemed to be waiting for him inside a pleasant pub, peering out at him from the plate glass window with a quizzical but friendly look.

At the Golden Hind a few elderly regulars occupied a table at the rear near the dart board, where the afternoon light, feeble as it was, was less intrusive. Some workmen looked into their lagers at the bar. The lull would quicken in an hour or two, but in the meantime no sense of anticipation disturbed even the motes of dust suspended near the window.

Woodward approached the bar, where a barmaid listened

attentively to a patron at the other end. She was fat enough to
be ageless, made up for a music hall turn, and was smiling
crookedly, showing a few gold teeth, until she exploded with
a swooping laugh at the patron's rude joke. She was still
laughing as she came toward Woodward.

"What's your pleasure, Duckie?"

"Half pint of bitter." In his workman's clothes, it seemed
to Woodward that he had stepped magically through a looking glass into the world of ordinary men. He rested his dirty
hands with their black fingernails on the mahogany as the
barmaid took a thick glass mug and pulled on a polished
brass handle.

"Got you working on a Saturday," she said, commiserat-
ing, as she waited for the head to subside on the beer and to
fill the mug with a full measure.

"Yes," Woodward felt deliciously understood. "I've got
no choice."

"I hate them bosses. Where're you working? I bet you've
got no choice about that neither!" She looked at his hands.
"Digging?"

"That's right."

"Poor dear. No rest for the weary." She set the glass
down before him. "Here's a bit of cheer. You're looking a
little pale."

"I haven't worked outdoors much."

"I could tell right away you weren't the rough sort. Lost
your position, right? When a man's out of work, he's got to
take whatever he can get."

"It's not that exactly."

"Nothing to be ashamed about." She leaned confidentially
over the bar. "See Ralph," she said, signing with her eyes.
"He gets discharged every two weeks."

"Poor fellow."

"His missus helps out. Does yours?"

"She does needlework."

"Very nice—don't have the hands for it myself, but I do
know how to pour an honest drink," said the barmaid,
splaying her stubby, dimpled fingers. "You're lucky to have
a good and loving wife—a helpmate. You'll be all right. I'm

never wrong about these things.'' She took a moment to look at Woodward and said, ''What's your name, luv?''

''Arthur.''

''Arthur. What do your friends call you? Artie?''

''Artie,'' Woodward repeated.

''I bet back in school they called you Farty Artie,'' the barmaid said.

'' 'Ey, Ethel!'' Ralph was signaling from the end of the bar with an empty mug.

''Well, Artie,'' Ethel said with a broad and optimistic grin, ''keep your pecker up.'' A laugh gurgled out of her throat, and winking at him she moved down the bar.

A few other regulars came in, and some transients like himself, as Woodward stood with one mud-caked boot on the brass rail, sipping his bitter, and thinking of the sad predicament of the man Ethel imagined him to be—a clerk perhaps, who'd been sacked and who'd lowered himself to manual labor, clinging to his respectability while trying to make ends meet. He thought of Maud stitching away at a piece of finery for some grand lady, the picture of beatific resignation in her love for him, unshakable in her faith in him and her optimism, surpassing Ethel's, even Mrs. Micawber's that things would turn out for the best and that he would prevail. There must be people like that, he thought, not only existing in sentimental fiction, but in real life. He was one of them as far as Ethel was concerned. He marveled at the way he could be so radically redefined by a stranger's fantasy.

For him to have achieved the heroism and pathos of the life Ethel invented for him, he would have had to be different in his elemental nature. He would not have decided, as a young man, to find his way out of the dingy house in the workman's row where he was born. And later, he wouldn't have gone to provincial theaters to hear Shakespeare and practiced reading aloud from books to remove the north country cadences from his speech. It would not have been necessary to control his sexuality, and to build out of small pieces of self-control and artifice the persona he knew was the butt of jokes at the museum. Being laughed at was the price of being mildly feared and respected. He was seen as neuter, but that was the price of his sexual disguise. Each part of his persona was paid for. His marriage to Maud was expensive. "We shall never touch," she had said. It was not an ultimatum; she was simply stating a fact, without risk, because somehow she knew he would agree, and they never asked each other the reason for her condition or his acceptance. It was the best sort of bargain struck between two willing partners, each of whom knew they'd made an unlikely, fortuitous deal. It was the closest to love he had ever come. Woodward sometimes thought that her bold statement was a revelation of herself which no other man had ever heard. What man, other than himself, would have presented himself as potentially so completely acquiescent to such an outlandish condition? There was something in him, something about him that made Maud confident—more than that, had given her power right from the beginning, a power she had never relinquished. Maud never told him she was a virgin, but he knew that no one had ever touched her, and although he hadn't ever had a woman, Woodward could at least pick through the spoil heap of his furtive and guilty experiences, finding little grains of sensual gold. They glinted for him, especially the pleasures of Cleveland Street, where guilt and lust had come together with a special poignancy and which he had re-created with Maud by combining the reality of humiliation with the remembrance of pleasure. His memories of Cleveland Street had been only tiny golden flecks until Dawson had coerced him into the Piltdown conspiracy. The sacrifice of his scientific ideals was real enough, and his fear of exposure excited authentic dread. But he could never have imagined how those sexual adventures could have led to professional fame and eminence that the rest of his colleagues had been unable to achieve. Everyone who deferred to him had failed to achieve what he had because they had not been bound at the wrists and beaten on the bum—buttocks—by a naked boy who frigged—masturbated—him; Woodward had never been able to decide how to describe those episodes to himself. The pornographic was exciting, but the medical made him less guilty. Either way, his sexual and temperamental perversions had been the making of his scientific fortune. It was too absurd, Woodward mused, watching the bubbles rise from the bottom of his half-finished beer. At that moment, however, his fame meant as little to him as the barmaid's awareness of it. It was Ethel's vision of him, caught in an everyday tragedy, that had a lucidity and reality. That, and her optimistic prophesy and her bawdy acceptance that he was like everyone else. He wished it were so.

Chapter XI

B Y THE MIDDLE OF 1913 DAWSON HAD AN EXTENSIVE
collection of newspaper and magazine cuttings about himself and the Piltdown discovery, which he had pasted into a
large scrapbook. Sitting in his office, he turned the pages
quickly, noting with pleasure how his name leaped again and
again from the page as if in boldface. He put it under his
arm, slung his geologist's rucksack over his shoulder, and set
out on foot along the road to Barkham Manor. The sunlight
on the green countryside was as bright as his expectations.
After about a mile he saw Arabella's cart on the road next to
a spangled pond. He followed its banks to the far side and
went a short distance into the woods, where he knew she
would be waiting.

Arabella had seen an Impressionist exhibition at the
Watercolour Society in London and had become converted to
that style. The landscapes went quicker than the manner of
the eighteenth century she had previously followed, leaving
more time for lovemaking and requiring less for the work of
art that was her alibi. By the time Dawson found her she was
already lying under a tree. Her hair was loose and the tiny
pearl buttons of her dress scattered with printed violets were
partially open at the bodice.

"Raise my skirt over my face and don't take off your

trousers. For something different. Come. I'll do your buttons.'' She made little clutching motions with her fingers.

"Oh, lovely,'' she purred.

"My mistress, my whore.'' Dawson breathed into her fragrant petticoat.

"My beloved.''

"My God!'' Dawson cried, and she cried out too, echoing his pleasure.

He shrank away from her, falling off to one side and lay on his back. Arabella looked at his penis with satisfaction and stuffed its limp dampness back into his trousers, doing up each button of his fly with a kind of motherly affection. "Sweet thing,'' she said, patting him on the crotch.

Dawson gazed up at the shuddering canopy of leaves above them and again, yet again, breathed the aphrodisiac scent of the woods. Arabella's passionate availability still amazed him, her inventiveness dazzled him. Taking his own pleasure, she made him feel generous.

"I have two things to give you, my love,'' Dawson said. He reached for his jacket and taking her hand put into it a small brown flint. "The rest of these belong to England. You are the only person in the world to possess a specimen from Piltdown. It is one of the pieces I excavated myself, and the moment I found it, I knew that I would give it to you.''

Arabella closed her fist and threw her arms around his neck. "You are the most wonderful man in the world,'' she cried. "My own dear flint. I wish I could have it set in gold and wear it around my neck on a chain. But I'll find a place to keep it safe.'' She slipped it into the cleavage between her breasts and did up the last few buttons of her dress, clasping her hands over her bosom and closing her eyes, as if singing the last dramatic notes of a romantic aria.

Arabella had been too single-minded to notice that Dawson had come through the woods bearing a large book, but as they lay together on the moss and ferns that were their mattress, he showed it to her. She pressed against him like a small child being read a fabulous bedtime story. '' 'Dawson's Dawn Man Revolutionizes Paleontology,' '' he read from the *Telegraph,* and then the lead. " 'Charles Dawson, an amateur geologist from Lewes, Sussex, with his colleague' . . . blah, blah, blah, and so forth . . . 'the greatest discovery of the century.' " He turned the pages and selected another extract. "From the *Guardian*: 'It is time we overcame our prejudice against amateurs, whose passion and dedication to science matches, if not surpasses, the more traditional *bona fides* of university-trained professionals. Charles Dawson . . .' and so on and so forth," he said, impatiently searching for another telling quote.

"You are the wonder of the age," Arabella said. "And you have a lovely cock."

"You are quite right. But where did you learn such dreadful language?"

"I'm married, in case you have forgotten. Colin and his friends tell the filthiest stories in loud whispers to each other, and they think I'm deaf, because I am a woman. There's the one about the soldier billeted in the farmhouse, and the farmer has three daughters. . . ."

"I know that one."

"You swine."

"You slut."

"We are well-matched. Fuck me again."

"Will you promise to listen to me seriously if I do?"

"You know I would promise you anything, even that," Arabella said, pulling up her skirts.

Later he reached for the scrapbook again.

"You are too vain for words."

"I am famous. My discovery is the talk of England, Europe, the world. There is nothing to stop us now."

Arabella was suddenly attentive.

"We'll go abroad—I'll write; not all those dull scientific articles, but vignettes in the life of early man. The *Illustrated London News* has already asked me to do something. And I have a wonderful idea for a popular lecture. Not just a slide show of old bones, but pictures of Piltdown Man as he actually lived on the Sussex downs. I'll be the technical advisor, but you'll do the pictures: Piltdown Man hunting, making flints, that sort of thing."

"You know I don't do figures," Arabella said.

"The public will love it."

"But is it dignified?"

"What twaddle! I'm tired of being dignified. I'm ready for adventure. I used to think that Sussex was big enough, but now it is only a prison. The world is out there waiting for us. Oh, my dear Belle, I've worked it all out. Helene will be more than comfortable with what I've put by, and my share in the firm is worth quite a bit. Hart will buy me out. With that, and what I get from my public life, my scientific projects, we need never worry. I know I can get financial backing for an expedition. We can go anywhere. We'll go fossil hunting in Java, then we'll go to Africa."

"All that traveling."

"I've thought of that. We'll take a house somewhere, in Germany perhaps, near a university where I could use the library, but somewhere beautiful, in the Rhine valley, Cologne. You could paint."

"You make it sound so wonderful," Arabella said, wrapping her arms around his neck but turning away from him so he would not see her anxiety. As he spoke quickly into her ear, she was thinking frantically of how to extricate herself from the powerful embrace of his plans.

"We'll start by taking the boat-train to Paris," Dawson said. "I want personally to rub some French noses in my discovery. And we'll have lots of champagne and oysters to keep us fit and randy." He drew away from Arabella, expecting to see her face radiant with his vision of their new life. "What's the matter? Don't you like my plans? We can change anything. We'll do whatever you like."

"Your plans are wonderful, my darling."

"Then what is it, my love?"

"It's the Bulgarians."

"The Bulgarians? What are you talking about?"

"Or the Serbs, or the Croats, or whoever they are," Arabella said tossing her blond mane. "Anyway, it's the Balkans. Good heavens, Charles, don't you ever read the papers except when it's about you? There's a war in the

Balkans. It's the second one this year. Colin says there's no telling what will happen."

"Damn Colin."

"All of Europe could go up like a tinderbox. Colin says . . ."

"Damn Colin and damn him again."

"Charles, please. Be sensible."

"For God's sake, Arabella," Dawson shouted. "This is what I've been working for." He grabbed the scrapbook and got to his feet, holding it aloft as Moses held the tablets on Mount Sinai. "This. All of this. This is what I have done for you, every moment thinking it was for both of us. A new life for you and me. You have been my inspiration, my light, my soul. All for you, Arabella!"

It was thrilling to see his romantic desperation, to hear that he was so completely hers. She rose and went to him, allowing herself to be embraced, hoping to obliterate the future. She spoke with her cheek against his shoulder. "We've waited this long. Surely we can wait a little longer."

European politics continued to worsen, and Arabella became a serious student of current events. The czar was being unspeakable, the kaiser incorrigible. She was passionate over the question of Serbian independence. Dawson raged that, just as the whole world was opening up to him, it was conspiring to keep him prisoner, but he admitted that the situation on the Continent was unstable.

Not being one to wait passively while events beyond his control did or didn't shape themselves to his convenience, Dawson embarked on a new phase of his discovery, one which would keep him and his works in public view. Scholars frequently wondered what future finds would reveal about Piltdown Man. First on everyone's list of desiderata was a canine tooth. It would enhance the picture of the human aspects of the jaw's dentition. Now that Arabella had put him off again, and the world seemed to be her ally, Dawson began preparing and staining a canine specimen from the orangutan's jaw for discovery in the near future. He had not troubled Woodward with his prediction of a new treasure.

On the eve of his ordination, Teilhard stood at some distance from the classroom building and dormitory at Ore Place, alone among the rhododendron and holly, looking out past the rooftops and pinpoint lights of Hastings toward the Channel, toward Paris. His thoughts were already sailing toward the freedom to pursue his scientific studies full-time. His applications to graduate institutes had been sent, and he had been taking every opportunity to slip away to London to solicit letters of recommendation. Remembering Woodward's advice, Teilhard was careful to present himself deferentially, as a student of paleontology with much to learn, and when Piltdown Man was mentioned, he was at great pains to say he'd only discovered a flint, one of several found. Privately he wished he had come up with a piece of bone, which would have put him even closer to the great English hominid.

As Teilhard stood watching the clear lapis lazuli sky deepen to black, he chided himself for not being more moved by his being ordained. He had little more than a mild affection for the rituals of the Church and the day-to-day miracles over which he might preside as a priest, though he did not denigrate their importance. The next morning, in the punitively drab and cheerless chapel, when he received the chalice and paten that allowed him to administer the blood and host, he thought of Bernini's levitating Saint Theresa; that was he didn't know how many thousands of pounds of Carrara, but how many hundreds of thousands of pilgrims each year in Rome were convinced that her transfigured agony was genuine, that she floated weightless in ecstatic pain.

Teilhard had no hope, no inclination to mend the tear between himself and the orthodoxy of the Church, knowing that his argument that the Christ of dogma and his private Christ of the limitless universe springing from the same faith were therefore synonymous, would fall on ears as deaf as those of the marble sculptures in Rome. If they would only listen, they would see that he was not implacable, but rather open to ideas generated in free discourse. If only he could make his spiritual soliloquies public. He grew tired of his loneliness, even bitter. He wanted a sign and was angry with himself for not being strong enough, for wanting to fall back into a primitive world of visions and stigmata, when he knew his destiny would not reveal itself in that way.

That destiny would be revealed through science. It was no longer light enough to see the distant quarries at the edge of the green downs just before they broke off into the sea, where he had met Charles Dawson. Perhaps that was his ordination, with geologist's pickax and brush as tokens of investiture. Was that merely an accident, or was destiny unfolding not as pure chance but with some partiality toward him? Dawson had said from the beginning that he was marked for distinction, and although Teilhard was flattered, he did not forget himself and behave foolishly. Dawson was his chance, and Teilhard held onto it. Teilhard was used to playing the novice. He had spoken his private thoughts to Dawson only to the extent that they would reveal him as a subversive, sensing that Dawson, as a scientist, would be put off by an unquestioning mind. As to the broad sweep of his ideas, Teilhard concluded early on that Dawson was as earthbound as the fossils he discovered. Teilhard recognized a connection between Dawson's generosity and his immense egotism and thanked him for his many kindnesses until Dawson had to beg him to stop.

Woodward he couldn't read at all. When they had first met, Woodward had appeared almost fatherly in his concern, but as they had dug at Barkham Manor, before and after the announcement, Woodward had withdrawn. There was no trace of resentment of him as an interloper, no personal dislike, but rather a pervading detachment, sometimes, it seemed to Teilhard, from the entire project. Teilhard had hesitated asking Woodward for a letter of recommendation, but Woodward agreed. On the official letterhead of the Department of Geology, British Museum of Natural History, he had uncharacteristically expressed a surprising warmth, almost a fondness for "a young man of unusual talents and unquestioned integrity."

As the time for his departure for France approached, Teilhard once again regularly joined Dawson and Woodward at the excavations at Piltdown. The co-conspirators worked at a phlegmatic pace in the sultry afternoon, and their thoughts were elsewhere. Dawson was depressed by affairs in Europe that lurched from crisis to crisis. During the calms and diplomatic reconciliations, his hopes rose only to be dashed again by reports of increased armaments and the ranting of ministers, princes, and generals making accusations and counter-accusations of duplicity and bad faith.

Woodward mused about Ethel and the Golden Hind. He had been stopping in whenever he returned from Lewes, regardless of the hour. Its good-hearted, stale coziness, the smell of beer and tobacco, Ethel's unfailing optimism, were a haven. If it was busy, he was content with a greeting from her and kept mostly to himself, listening to the laughter and the conversation around him. When he arrived at an off hour and Ethel had a few minutes, they would stand at one end of the bar and chat. He was careful not to lie to her and told her that he didn't mind his present work that much, the physical part, but that the man he worked for—the job foreman, Ethel concluded—was very tough on him. The bleedin' bastard, Ethel declared. When he couldn't think of something true to tell her about his present life that she could interpret in her own way, he would talk about his childhood, waking long-dormant memories, which he began to view not with his usual distaste, but with a sweet sadness of nostalgia. When she went off to serve another customer, he would run them like the flickering reels in a nickelodeon: the undersized boy he had been at six, trotting on the wet cobblestones clutching his tiffin sack on the way to school in the sooty winter dawn, or the thin-chested twelve-year-old shivering in bed, wondering.

Teilhard was a dozen or so yards away from Dawson and Woodward. He had a sieveful of gravels and was washing them in a tin pail of water before taking them to the spoil heap.

"I found something," Teilhard shouted.

"Probably a stone," Dawson murmured.

He and Woodward threw down their shovels and approached Teilhard. He was bent over the pail, washing something with both hands. They all looked into his dripping palm at a small brown object.

"A canine tooth!" Teilhard exclaimed. "Look, you can see the roots there, and the wear on the surface is exactly what was predicted."

Dawson took the tooth from Teilhard and examined it closely. "It's remarkable. Remarkable," he said with perfect candor. He gave it to Woodward, who aimed a killing look at him.

Woodward looked at the tooth with intense concentration. "Yes. Positively remarkable."

"I was digging over there," Teilhard said, indicating the far end of the pit. "There, just where my shovel is."

"I don't think you'll have any trouble passing your examination in field work for your advanced degree," Dawson said. "You are as unerring as a truffle hog."

Teilhard radiated excitement. "I hope I can get away from Hastings next week to come up to London to see how it fits," he said to Woodward. "Let me see it again."

Woodward dropped the tooth into his hand and looked back at Dawson whose expression told him nothing.

"Do you think it will be a perfect fit with the jaw?" Teilhard said.

"Probably not," Dawson replied. "The tooth is very eroded. Most of the roots are gone."

"But there can be no doubt that it belongs to the jaw," Teilhard declared. He looked from Dawson to Woodward and back again, as if waiting for one of them to give him a diploma.

"Congratulations, Teilhard," Dawson finally said. "This is a momentous discovery. Brilliant, if I may say so. Wouldn't you say so, Arthur? You shouldn't be so reticent." Returning to Teilhard, Dawson said, "Were you praying for this? If you were, I should have to give up my atheism."

"Have no fear. I would not tamper with your beliefs, as you have not tampered with mine."

"What a good lad you are. I say, well done and all that, but there are a few hours of work left, so would you fetch some more water from the caretaker's house? Who knows, we may end the day with a bicuspid."

Smiling, Teilhard took up the pail and went toward the house, a lanky sorcerer's apprentice. When he was out of earshot, Woodward turned to Dawson. "How dare you put this tooth there without telling me?"

"Idiot," Dawson hissed. "Does this look like my work?" He examined it again. "It seems to be painted. I didn't want to upset you, but I am making a canine, even as we stand here. It's in an acid bath in my study, but it isn't ready yet."

"Oh, my God," Woodward whimpered, and he began pacing back and forth.

"I didn't tell you because I knew you'd get as hysterical as you are now. Get a grip on yourself." Dawson looked toward Teilhard filling his pail at the spigot.

Woodward took a deep breath. "Someone wants to discredit Piltdown Man. One fake specimen would spoil the whole, even if the others were genuine. Everyone knew how important a canine would be. One of our beloved colleagues salted it."

"No self-respecting scientist would do that," Dawson said.

"You're impossible," Woodward said. He looked down at the gravel pit for a moment, then turned back to Dawson, his face the color of congealed lard. "Somebody suspects. Somebody knows."

"That's absurd. If somebody suspected the fossils were fake and we found the one he'd put in the pit, he would know we'd never report it. As far as the rest of the world would be concerned, we'd never found it."

"But Teilhard found it."

"Exactly. How could somebody know he'd be the one?"

"They took a chance. One out of three."

"Only you could think up a plan as stupid as that. And I am assuming you didn't put the tooth there."

"Then who did?"

"It wasn't the tooth fairy," said Dawson, turning toward the gate house. " 'I found some-sing,' " he said in a snide imitation of Teilhard's accent. "That ungrateful little bastard. That conniving Popish bugger. We have been nurturing the Macbeth of paleontology."

A week later the trio of excavators met at the British Museum, where Woodward confirmed that after careful study, the canine tooth unquestionably belonged to the Piltdown jaw; it was a near duplicate of the plaster one that Arthur Keith had supplied in his new reconstruction of the skull, one that would now be replaced by a cast of the new discovery. Teilhard's canine had already joined the other priceless treasures in the basement.

"I must caution you not to discuss this with anyone," Dawson said to Teilhard. "Not until Arthur and I have collated our notes and drafted a paper for publication. It would not be at all proper, and it would be altogether too sensational to announce this informally."

"How long will it take you to complete your paper?" he asked Woodward.

"Several months, at least."

"But I'll be in France by then. I had hoped . . ." Teilhard began.

"There, there," Dawson said. "I'm sure your French colleagues will be just as pleased and excited as all your friends here."

As they left the museum, Dawson glanced obliquely at Teilhard, pleased to see the traces of sulkiness around his mouth. Dawson and Woodward had no other choice but to accept the tooth. If they said nothing about knowing that Teilhard had planted it, Teilhard, who absolutely believed in Piltdown Man would assume he'd duped them into thinking the tooth was a genuine specimen, like the skull and the jaw. It was the best of a bad bargain, they concluded. If they accused him of planting the tooth and rejected it as a forgery, Teilhard would insist it was a legitimate find; if it were a fake, someone else had put it there, not he. While Dawson was convinced Teilhard had salted the tooth, Woodward held out the possibility that it might be someone else. If they mistakenly confronted Teilhard with the forgery of the canine tooth, that might start him thinking; he might even suspect that an unknown perpetrator had salted something else, possibly everything. The possible mess over the canine tooth might lead to an ever bigger one. Dawson and Woodward concluded they would say nothing, but it rankled Dawson that Teilhard had bested him and had advanced his own career. Dawson could only have the small revenge of postponing the announcement until Teilhard was out of the way.

They walked toward Kensington Gardens, where they ambled in the dappled sunlight under the plane trees. Little boys romped with balls and hoops while girls in Kate Greenaway smocks played at serving each other tea.

"I have wonderful news," Teilhard said. "Professor Boule has granted me an interview. He wrote to me asking to see him when I arrive in Paris."

"I have no doubt that you will convince him of your dedication to your chosen career."

"Marcellin Boule is the greatest physical anthropologist in France," Teilhard said.

"He's competent, for a Frenchman."

"Would it be too much to ask you to write him a letter recommending me to him?"

"Far too much."

Teilhard looked as if he had been slapped in the face. "I don't understand."

"Am I a cornucopia endlessly spewing favors?"

"I have often been embarrassed at the bounty of your generosity." The patches of shadows on his face looked like bruises.

"And how have you repaid me? With treachery. Betrayal. Oh, don't look the martyr, for God's sake."

"What do you mean? Whatever I have achieved I owe to you," Teilhard protested.

Dawson turned on him with savage contempt. "How many nights have you lain in your bed wondering at your good fortune? And how you might take advantage of my mis-

guided interest in you. You have the soul of a traitor. You do
not even know how to be loyal to your order, not that I give a
damn about your subversive heresies."

"I am only looking for the truth."

"Spare me your solemn disquisitions on the music of the
spheres. Your brothers will accuse you, as I accuse you now.
They will see behind that mask of pious innocence, and see
what I see—the corrupt face of an ambitious schemer."

"If you would only tell me what I have done to displease
you so. I would do anything . . ."

"There is your precious truth. Yes. You would. That is the
first honest thing you have said to me. You would do anything to further your own selfish ambitions. You've done
more than enough. You were nothing when I found you in
that quarry, pecking away at the rock like a little blackbird.
Do you think your Professor Boule would have answered
your letter if it hadn't been for Piltdown? If it hadn't been for
me? I was your mentor. I will not be your victim!" Dawson
strode angrily away without a backward glance.

Some weeks later Dawson came up to London at Woodward's urgent request and met him at a quiet pub near the
Museum.

"It's Elliot Smith and his Manchester cabal," Woodward
said anxiously as Dawson sat down with a pint. "I met him
at a conference last week, and he was particularly cordial, so
I knew something was afoot. Then I heard he was getting his
forces together. He's up there in that godforsaken mill town
plotting our destruction. A Piltdown symposium. All in the
interest of science. But the idea is to promote the two-
individuals theory. He's determined to prove there is no
Piltdown Man."

"Who's supposed to speak?"

"We are. And his people, of course. One of them—one of
his spies at the Museum—fortunately decided I could butter
his little academic slice of bread better than Smith, so he told
me what's going on. We're going to be invited, but it's like
being invited to your own hanging. They will have formidable arguments."

"How much time do we have?"

"That's just it. None. A month. Smith is spoiling for a fight, and we will be on the defensive."

"I'm not worried," Dawson said.

"Well, I am. You live in Sussex, not the Groves of Academe. I do. It's crawling with vipers, and Elliot Smith has the sharpest fangs of the lot. He's pure poison."

"Pure poison," Dawson repeated. "What an interesting notion."

"For heaven's sake, Charles. Stop being cryptic and listen to me. We've got to say no. Piltdown Man is not debatable. That's our position."

"Anything in science is debatable. I, for one, welcome disinterested scholarly exchange. Piltdown Man may be debatable, but fortunately he is irrefutable."

"Really? Suppose this is a ploy by Smith? A smoke screen. He's almost as devious as you. Suppose he suspects something? What if this is an excuse to demand detailed tests of the specimens? Nobody's thought of that yet. But suppose Smith wants to? I may not be able to keep them locked up in that vault. There may be pressures I can't deal with. They aren't fossils. They're forgeries."

"How can you say that, Arthur? I was there when you found the jaw—up to your elbows in gravel, you were. How exciting it was, and how modest you were about the discovery, telling me if I hadn't found the cranial fragments, you wouldn't have even known where to dig. That was very sweet of you. I've dined out on that story a thousand times."

"Sometimes I think you were born without a fully developed autonomic nervous system. Even a chimpanzee knows instinctively when he's in danger."

"You may consider yourself an anthropoid. But I am a descendant of Piltdown Man. An Englishman. Practical. Reasonable. There is a solution to every problem. There is no reason why we shouldn't encourage Smith's enterprise, even if it is a waste of time. To argue against Piltdown Man is like debating the validity of the British Empire. Those who argue against us are doomed to failure."

"A fine speech, but what you're saying is that we're giving in, that we accept their doubts," Woodward said.

"Not at all. I am saying that we accept their jealousy." Dawson slowly put down his glass of beer and heaved a sigh. Then he closed his eyes and put his hand to his forehead as if testing for fever.

"Are you ill?" Woodward said.

"I don't know. I haven't really been feeling well these last weeks. I haven't had my usual energy. I'm all right, and then suddenly I seem to have used up all my strength."

"Have you seen a doctor?"

"Doctors don't know anything. They look at your tongue and send you a bill."

"Don't be foolish, Charles. You can't afford to be sick."

"I suppose not. Especially with this symposium Smith is concocting. Don't look so worried; I probably need a tonic."

"I still think we should respectfully decline Smith's invitation."

"You've only to make sure that your slides and data are ready. I'll take care of the rest. I always have."

"You will promise to see a doctor when you get back to Lewes?"

"Without fail."

Shortly after Dawson returned home, he consulted with his local physician. His feeling of tiredness increased, and he complained of a pervading listlessness. The doctor's diagnosis was severe anemia, and he insisted on bed rest and iron tonic. Dawson rebelled against the boredom of being bedridden, but the doctor was adamant, advising Helene that she must enforce his orders. Dawson kept in touch with Woodward by letter; both of them had received formal invitations to Smith's symposium, but since Dawson was unable to attend, the meeting was postponed once, then again. Dawson had written to Smith, apologizing for the inconvenience he caused, promising to participate as soon as his health and his doctor's orders permitted.

Arabella was continually in Dawson's mind. He managed to rebel against the doctor's regimen once. A clerk from his office at Uckfield came weekly with a packet of letters and documents that needed his attention. Dawson dictated a letter to Mrs. Spence, advising her that he had given further thought to the legal matter they had discussed, and he would be pleased to see her at his office Wednesday at three o'clock.

Dawson sat at his desk, not wanting her to see that moving about cost him an effort.

"Do you know everything in these books?" Arabella said, waving at the thick legal texts that lined the walls. It was the first time she had visited his office. She was dressed for town in a sedate tweed suit buttoned high at her throat. "You're a solicitor. I've missed you, so be solicitous to me."

"I wish we could be at Brighton. But I'm supposed to be ill."

"You look quite well to me," she replied. But there was something definitely off about him, the way he sat in the chair holding his head slightly to one side, as if it weighed too much. "A little tired, perhaps. But you must look after yourself. Soon the weather will be fine, and I shall start painting again." Her mouth curved in a maenad's smile. "If I were the doctor in charge of your case, I would recommend fresh air."

"And plenty of it. I can assure you, I have no intention of spending the summer in a sickbed," Dawson said with finality.

Arabella took another turn around the room, as if to a slow waltz, and pirouetted into a chair across the desk. She began methodically, with studied provocative amusement, to unbutton, then peel back one of her fine leather gloves, revealing the white skin on the back of her hand, then her long slender fingers.

"I will take you on the desk," Dawson said.

"Oh, do, Charles," she purred.

There was a knock at the door, and Arabella quickly withdrew before a clerk entered with a file of papers, laid them next to Dawson's blotter, and went out.

"The real world," Arabella complained. "It always intrudes. Look at the war. Colin says it's not going at all well. He says there's going to be a battle at the Somme River, and no one knows how it will turn out."

When the war had broken out in Europe, Arabella's first reaction had been relief, an admission of the selfish thought that history had contrived to thwart Charles's vision of their life together on the Continent. The raging fires of battle seemed so distant from her small green corner of Sussex, but men had gone off from Uckfield, and some already would never come back.

"Damn Colin," Dawson said.

"It may be years before the war is over."

"Damn the war."

"Let's think of the summer," said Arabella.

"Belle, my beauty," Dawson said. "I have been thinking about after the war."

"Europe will be such a mess, nothing but a graveyard."

"I know. That's why I have another plan. America!" He beamed at her. In Europe Arabella might think of herself as a permanent tourist; in America she would be an immigrant. She conjured a distressing vision of skyscrapers and red Indians waving human scalps.

"However the war turns out, America will be completely untouched, even if they decide to get involved," Dawson said. "I've seen pictures. There are parts of Boston and New York that look exactly like London. And they speak English; well, some sort of English, anyway. I'll write, lecture, just as we'd planned. And there are wonderful things to be done scientifically. Do you know that no hominid remains have ever been found in the whole of North America? They've got to be there." Dawson excitedly told Arabella of the ancient land bridge that had spanned the Bering Strait, a passageway from Asia similar to the one that had connected England and Europe, once crossed by Piltdown Man. "My intuition tells me we'll find something in California. We'll go to San Francisco."

"Don't they have earthquakes there, darling?"

Dawson dismissed the threat of natural catastrophe. He was

confident of his success. If the earth of the New World did not give up its secrets any more readily than the gravels of jolly old England, Dawson saw no reason why he might not again anticipate an inevitable discovery. He had heard that Americans were great enormous children and had a reputation for boundless credulity.

Arabella was about to make other objections, but she saw the way Dawson's eyes shone with excitement and how the ruddy glow reappeared in his cheeks. Perhaps the expectation of a trip to America might help him to get better. Besides, there was the war. No one could predict when it would be over. There would be time.

Woodward arrived at Castle Lodge in response to a note from Dawson asking to see him. Helene met him at the gate. She was gaunt with anxiety.

"Charles is not at all well. There seem to be complications. The doctors are doing tests on his blood, but he's not responding to treatment," Helene said.

"He's strong as an ox." Woodward patted her hand.

"Not anymore. I'm worried, Arthur. There's been a slow decline these last weeks."

Woodward was shocked to see Dawson propped up in bed on a pile of pillows. Since the last time they'd met, Dawson had shrunk, and there was a waxiness to his skin, a passivity to his hands as they lay on the bedclothes.

"You're looking better, Charles."

"You're losing your talent for lying."

"I never had it. I learned it from you. There's a new idea that the human animal learns responses according to rewards and punishments, just like laboratory rats or dogs. Conditioned reflex, I believe it's called."

"Then you admit you've been rewarded," Dawson said.

"It's not as simple as that. You've held me hostage all these years."

"Have I?"

"When you left my office at the Museum that day, I realized how sure you were that I'd agree. I not only stood to lose what I already had, but I'd lose the chance at a great career, assuming I was willing to compromise my ideals. And if I didn't, I'd have nothing except my ideals—no work, no life. Would you really have exposed me?''

"You want me to say yes so that you can justify to yourself what you have done, because you feel guilty that it hasn't been half as bad as you thought it would be, because you've enjoyed it, as I have. You've been a willing victim, right from the start. I knew that when I read the ledger pages.''

"So you wouldn't have exposed me?''

"No. How could I? If I had, you would have had nothing to lose by exposing me, and then I couldn't have achieved my goal. If you had rejected my kind offer, you could have gone on with your little career, and I would have found someone else.''

"Who?''

"Arthur Keith. He was my first choice. But then there was Sir Edmund.''

"Keith,'' Woodward said. "And he hates me so. If he only knew.''

"He's been a great help anyway—with his endless puttering with the endocasts of the brain case. He's always down here chatting me up about it. Think, Arthur, if I'd given him the first specimens, you would have spent your life hating me for not bringing them to you.''

"I've hated you anyway,'' Woodward said. "But that's all passed. I don't even hate Backhouse anymore. You know, he sent Maud a copy of his book on China. I'm sure it was just to torment me. She takes it out of the bookcase now and then.''

"Have you ever told Maud?'' Dawson asked.

"About Piltdown, or the other?''

"Have you ever told Maud anything?''

"No,'' Woodward replied. "Have you told Helene?''

"Don't be ridiculous.''

They looked at each other and began to cackle like two old women.

"Helene will hear us,'' Woodward warned.

"What of it? You're doing just what you should be doing: cheering up a sick friend."

"I was just remembering the night of the announcement at Burlington House," Woodward said. "How petrified I was before. As I began to speak, I looked out at the audience and thought, 'My God, they believe everything I'm saying.' You know, I almost believe it myself."

"Not 'almost.' You do believe it," Dawson said with a missionary's conviction. But he began to laugh again. "What a time we've had, Arthur."

Dawson's laughter brought back some of his old animation, but as he settled again into the pillows, Woodward could see the ravages of his illness.

"I have come up with a solution to the unresolved problem of the Piltdown symposium," Dawson said.

"I hope it's something sensible."

"It's May now. In a few weeks time your academic friends will be leaving for holiday or field work somewhere, so they won't be able to get together until the autumn. And by that time, nobody will see the need for a symposium."

"Why is that?"

"Piltdown Man is a representative of his race. A race is not one person," Dawson said, stating the obvious.

"Charles. Please!"

"In for a penny, in for a pound," Dawson said, enjoying as he always did Woodward's distress when he made an audacious move. "I've often thought our man at Piltdown would have been lonely without a neighbor. Someone to chat with over a stile. At Sheffield Park. Not two miles from Barkham Manor. I've still got pieces from the Nubian skull. And my staining notes. And I have the canine tooth, the one Teilhard preempted with his own forgery. We have only to find another Piltdown Man. Not even our skeptical friend Smith would be able to stand up to that. Sheffield Park is a lovely spot. Our creatures may have been hominids, but they were English, and no doubt sensitive to the beauties of the countryside—not the dark, Wagnerian habitat of Heidelberg Man or the excessively exotic abode of Java, but the temperate Sussex downs."

"If there are questions about Piltdown, there will be questions about Sheffield Park."

"Not necessarily. I've been thinking about it. Not if other specimens are found at Sheffield Park under controlled excavating conditions—a joint team from the BM and the Royal Society. Your colleagues will be falling about trying to join this dig. Some of them will even go as far as to give up their holidays. Look what Piltdown did for us. For Teilhard."

"I'm not finding anything else," Woodward said. His mouth was set in a thin adamant line.

"Correct. Someone else will, as Teilhard found his damned canine tooth. But this time they will be my specimens. I've got to finish the staining."

"I'm not going near Sheffield Park."

"Yes you are. I'm sick."

"You're demented. Do you expect me to go out there in the dead of night with a pick and shovel, dig a hole, put them in and cover it up?"

"Not at all. The excavators will dig the hole for you. Then you'll put them in. Just as our Jesuit friend did in our hole. The lazy sod."

"They'll see me."

"No, they won't. There will be scores of people at the site, all poking about. We weren't twenty feet from Teilhard when he made his find. No one would expect you to do it, so no one will see you, even if they were looking straight at you."

"I won't."

"You're being obstinate."

"Why don't you write me some personal letters, backdated to 1913, giving details of the Sheffield Park finds. Then it wouldn't look as if we found them at such an absurdly opportune time."

"Why did you withhold the letters until now?"

"Because . . ." Woodward faltered.

"Because you're an absent-minded nit?"

"You've got to give me time to think."

"Think all you like, but I'm not writing any letters."

Woodward was silent.

"We'll do it my way," Dawson said.

"I wish you'd listen to me sometimes. We're in this together. I wish you'd acknowledge that. But you're always dealing from strength, so long as you have those ledger pages."

"What ledger pages?"

"Don't play cat and mouse."

"Suppose one day I was walking down High Street, got run over by a runaway lorry, and died. They'd go through my papers, and they'd find the ledger pages. It would be awkward, for you and for me, for my posthumous reputation."

"What have you done with them?"

"I burned them."

"When?"

"The day after the public announcement at Burlington House. That completely bound you to me and Piltdown."

"For God's sake, why didn't you tell me?"

"It wouldn't have made any difference."

"Not to you. But it would have to me, to know I was free. Why have you told me now?" Woodward asked.

"I was feeling old."

"I hoped it might be something else. These last three years, weren't you ever glad you weren't in it alone?"

Dawson held out his hand, and Woodward took it. Dawson's hand was so flaccid that later Woodward wasn't sure what the gesture meant. Sometimes he thought it was an affirmation; other times, a condescension.

Charles Dawson died of septicemia—blood poisoning—on September 10, 1916.

Woodward missed Dawson. In retrospect his hostage years hadn't been as onerous as they seemed while Dawson was alive. He remembered their weekend digging at Barkham Manor—Dawson's mock-serious sieving of each spade of earth, his bringing the ape's jaw to the site and insisting Woodward enact a charade of discovery. There were the heady times following the announcement. It had been the most exciting time of Woodward's life. Mixed with his nostalgia was fear; if something happened, there was no one to talk to, and no one with whom to share the secret of Piltdown. His mourning of Dawson was genuine. The staff at the Museum was surprised to see him openly depressed and distracted. It was so unlike him.

Fortunately for Woodward, Elliot Smith observed the proprieties of Dawson's death and did not immediately pressure Woodward about the Piltdown symposium, but Woodward knew Smith would not be deterred forever. He also knew he didn't have the nerve to face Smith and his hostile cohorts alone. He was convincing in print, but only Charles, with his zealot's belief, could withstand a personal confrontation. Dawson's plan of a second Piltdown Man at Sheffield Park was Woodward's only alternative. Lacking Dawson's boldness, he didn't organize a dig and salt the site himself. Rather, he selected specimens from Dawson's collection when he helped Helene sort out the contents of the glass cases at Castle Lodge. He picked out a fragment of a frontal cranial bone and a lower molar, which Dawson had finished staining. As for the canine tooth which Dawson had also finished, he destroyed it, along with Dawson's chemicals and recipes, fearing a second canine might invite comparison with the first locked in the Museum's vault.

Woodward's publication of the Sheffield Park finds was his usual careful physical description and analysis. No one was concerned with the sketchy chronology of the find or its exact location. As to the location and dates of discovery Woodward stated only that Dawson had made trial excavations at the site for several years, the last ones just before the onset of his illness.

The Piltdown symposium never took place. The two-individuals proponents had to admit that Piltdown Man occupied a significant branch of the human evolutionary tree.

Maud Woodward watched Arthur's mourning with considerable attention that approached empathy. That the death had left him so bereft came as a surprise to her, as Arthur had never spoken with particular depth of feeling about Dawson. She wondered about it, without being able to conclude anything. Maud had never quite known how to accommodate Dawson; he seemed amused by her and treated her as if she had no power. She admitted to herself that she was relieved Dawson was dead.

For a time, during Arthur's depression, Maud gave up her teas, contenting herself with contemplating her tea cloth. It was a pity she could not remove some of the pre-Piltdown signatures. The great discovery had allowed her to raise her standards, and some of her early guests, no longer invited, still announced themselves in chartreuse, aquamarine, and heliotrope. Sir Edmund's ideogram was there in jade green, a color he would have approved of. After receiving his book, she had written to him in care of his publishers, inviting a reply, but none ever came.

Chapter XII

PEKING WAS A PATCHWORK QUILT OF BROAD AVENUES, dirt streets, and malodorous alleys enclosed by twenty miles of high gray brick walls. The imperial citadel with its ceremonial gates and wing-roofed towers was visible for miles on the flat treeless plain of Northern China. The raking wind from the north was always hazy, and in the spring it pointed at Peking like an accusing finger, sending dust storms that scoured the barren countryside, reducing the monumental battlements to ghostly shapes, translucent as rice paper cutouts in the mustardy air. The summer's oppressive heat was unrelieved by the rains that turned the city into a quagmire of mud and night soil from flooded latrines. Now the fall was flirting with winter. It was the season of dry coughs and uneasy tedium.

The capital of Northern China was divided into two walled, abutting rectangles, the Tartar City and the Imperial City surrounding the Forbidden City, a historical misnomer by 1926. The hermetic, secret world of the Manchu court, with which Edmund Backhouse claimed to have an intimate diplomatic intercourse at the turn of the century, was a memory. The pavilions, the red and gold throne rooms, the scented bed chambers where the Empress Dowager and her retinue of eunuchs, lynx-eyed ministers, and concubines plotted, schemed, and debauched were empty architectural monuments. Coarse weeds had trespassed between the bricks on the walkways, and the artificial lakes were choked with unkempt lotuses. Ordinary young students in padded blue jackets leaned their bicycles against the railings of the white marble bridges and spat globs of phlegm into the greenish waters of the ponds, and old men with satisfied looks of entitlement walked within the precincts formerly sacred to the sons and daughters of heaven. The Chinese revolution that brought the Manchu dynasty to an end was fifteen years old.

But the Buddhist priests in their saffron robes and shaved heads who made up a funeral cortege as it threaded its way through the crowded streets were indistinguishable from those performing the same rite a decade and a half or a thousand years before; coolies still trotted other human beings through the alleys in rickshaws; young and old still scavenged for rags and bits of paper, and Marco Polo would not have been surprised at the sight of caravans of imperious Mongolian camels laden with baled merchandise and their nomad masters in long felt coats and fur-lined hats heading toward the great outdoor market. There, as they had for three times ten thousand days and more, their camels would sit down like slowly collapsing campaign chairs among the bullock carts and shaggy Chinese ponies, among the bags of coal and rice, crude straw baskets of lentils and wilting green produce, among the vendors hawking plum wine, honeyed tea, and stuffed dumplings, while acrobats and sleight-of-hand artists, whose skills had been handed down through generations of street entertainers distracted merchants and customers alike from their business as they had in feast or famine regardless of the winds of change.

Backhouse had become one of the minor oddities of Peking, a person to whom rumor attached in a city where rumor and gossip were taken in daily doses as one would take something or other for chronic diarrhea or dyspepsia. He was a fugitive character, altogether difficult to pin down, disappearing for months at a time without explanation and then reappearing, picking up a conversation where he had left off as if he'd never been gone at all. It was said that he had been a secret agent of the British during the war, authorized to buy rifles and ammunition from Chinese warlords for use by the Russians against the Germans—or was it the Austro-Hungarians?—that he had been involved in clandestine operations on behalf of the Foreign Office to buy cruisers and battle ships from the Chinese—or sell them to the Chinese?—and that the flotilla of gunboats had never drawn water except in the minds of the unlucky principals for whom Backhouse had acted as a commission agent—there were several versions of this story, each more improbable than the other, neither confirmed nor denied by Backhouse. There were rumors of forged contracts with the Chinese government negotiated by him as agent for the American Banknote Company—uncounted phantasmagorical billions, and trafficking in ephemeral curios including a nonexistent collection of pearls from the Empress Dowager's jacket. Those who claimed to know him well said that he was capable of anything. Those who were beguiled by his charm and erudition—what newcomer to China could dispute his interpretation of the arcanum of Taoist philosophy?—and by his unassailable reputation as a savant and scholar, simply invited the skeptic to inspect the man himself. Well into his middle years, Edmund Backhouse was still pale and fragile, as thin as a straight razor, and having grown a long wispy beard that was turning respectably gray, and having adopted the finely tailored black gown of a Chinese scholar, he looked to his Western friends to be as austere, unwordly, and benign as a monk. True, he was fanciful in some of his recollections, but when he chose to appear in public, he was unfailingly amusing, a quality highly prized in a small, tight community where boredom was as chronic a malady as dysentery, and more difficult to cure. To have achieved a reputation for eccentricity in Peking was itself an achievement; there were plenty of abnormal rogues—commercial representatives with empty sample cases, adventurers whose names were as changeable as their present addresses, diplomats who had succumbed to the blandishments of the exotic and permissive environment with all its unexpectedly diverse potentialities for addiction. Some people worked, some did not; some intrigued politically, for the sake of money or merely because it was their nature. Some gave parties because they were expected to, or because they were sociable and bored, or because a party was an opportunity to divide the world into those who were invited and those who weren't. All of them gossiped. There were stories about everyone, more or less colorful than those that swirled around the person of Backhouse. They were believed or not, depending on whether they were about an enemy of a friend of the moment.

The Legation Quarter pressed against the high traverse wall that demarked the Imperial and Tartar Cities, with Legation Street its main thoroughfare that served as a High Street, Main Street, Königstrasse, or Camino Real. The quarter's other walled flanks, which had proved to be almost fatally vulnerable during the Boxer Rebellion, had been reconstructed with a new, modern barrier, except for the bullet-scarred section near the embassy of the historically minded British, who left it exactly as it had been the day of the Allied liberation. The British had affixed a plaque to the wall which admonished, "Lest We Forget," presumably not forgetting the treachery of those Chinese who had the temerity to object to the importuning of missionaries and the venal ambitions of Western powers to carve China up into spheres of influence, or the carnage of innocents by the Chinese in the blood-soaked willy-nilly that Westerns still saw as a recurrent threat. No one in 1926, Chinese or foreigner alike, had a firm grasp on the reigns of China's future, certainly not the innumerable hooligans and warlords of the provinces who were laws unto themselves, not Sun Yat-sen, surely not the darling of the Russian Legation, Mao Tse-tung, or the sanctimonious Christian gangster, extortionist, and pimp from Shanghai, Chiang Kai-shek.

The relative merits of these and other pretenders to power were discussed with high seriousness within the world of the foreign legations and by the missionary factions, each of whom tried to persuade the others to support a loser in the inevitable power struggle to come. This exchange of information was an important function of the diplomatic party. The American minister confided to his wife that he needed to discuss Chiang Kai-shek with the British minister in a casual setting blurred by drink and social amenities. The compliant and bored American wife, who had just received a gossamer sheath decorated with a beaded design from New York, was only too happy to invent a pretext to satisfy her husband's diplomatic responsibilities while grasping at the opportunity within the sphere of fashion to affront the proletarian Russians and puzzle the hopelessly frumpy English, whose minister's wife, the daughter of a viscount, treated her like an upstairs maid.

The pretext for Madame Minister's soirée was an event whose importance she was only dimly aware of, but one which would have far-reaching scientific consequences. She had chosen to honor Dr. Davidson Black, professor of anatomy at Peking Union Medical College. Some months before, a team of American archaeologists and paleontologists under his direction had found two teeth, a molar and a bicuspid. In an abandoned quarry at Choukoutien, some thirty miles from Peking, they had discovered the first indication of early man in China, the most important find since Piltdown Man. At a symposium in Sweden, where the finds had been presented, there was universal acceptance of a hitherto unknown race, *Sinanthropus pekinensis,* Peking Man.

"I'm so glad you could come," said Madame Minister to Edmund Backhouse with genuine enthusiasm. That she had corralled a baronet, and such an elusive one at that, would, she hoped, equalize her social position with the viscount's daughter.

"One can never resist parties at the American legation. They are so democratic. One never knows to whom one will talk or who will talk to one," Backhouse said, strictly in the singular nominative case, keeping grammatically aloof while taking a glass of wine from a silver tray carried by a roving Chinese houseboy.

"One never knows, do one? Does one?" said Madame Minister, trying to agree.

"We find you Americans inexpressibly hospitable, so much more so than our own countrymen," Backhouse observed, switching to a more royal first person plural.

Madame Minister wondered whether she ought to drop or curtsy.

"I knew the Honorable Penelope in another life," Backhouse said, fixing on the wife of the British minister. "She used to be likened to the last cabbage in Convent Garden; she was quite wilted by the time she was bought. Her dear mother kept peeling off the bruised leaves, hoping to make her fresh for the next customer. Poor Giles," he continued, directing his gaze to the ambassador. "He was altogether taken in. Not that their wedding contravened tradition, however. There was a virgin in the bed that night." Backhouse withdrew from Madame Minister as she touched his arm. The wine was good enough for a second glass.

The guest of honor was Davidson Black. Having received his medical degree in Toronto in 1906 and having developed an interest in hominid paleontology, he went to England, visiting Grafton Elliot Smith at the University of Manchester in 1914, in time to witness the controversy that Smith was generating over Piltdown Man. After careful consideration of the evidence, he had cast his lot with Dawson and Woodward, and Arthur Keith with whom he spent many evenings discussing the casts of the inside of the brain case of the Piltdown skull, on the basis of which Keith had reevaluated the brain size of *Eoanthropus*. The new discovery, *Sinanthropus,* in no way contradicted the earlier find. Black was discussing this very point with his companion when Backhouse drifted into their ken.

In the sea of numbingly familiar faces, Black's chiseled handsomeness and the unexpected vocation of his friend had piqued Backhouse's curiosity. It was most unusual to see a priest at a legation party; missionaries of any stripe kept to a self-imposed asteroid belt, far from the glowing center of the foreign community. After making oblique inquiries about who the two gentlemen were, Backhouse contrived a gentle collision.

"My hostess was remiss in not presenting me to the honored guest," Backhouse said, introducing himself.

"Dave Black. This is Father Teilhard de Chardin."

"Welcome to our hopelessly provincial Sodom and Gomorrah," Backhouse said to Teilhard.

Looking around the room, Teilhard replied, "It looks as proper as the New Jerusalem."

"That is because you are a stranger to these parts. I was speaking only the other day to Monsignor Brissac—that is to show you that I am well-connected with your co-religionists—and he didn't tell me that anyone new was staying at the rectory."

"'I am not staying at the rectory.'"

"Are you here on a secret mission? It has often been rumored that Satan is Chinese. Some years ago a missionary, of the Baptist persuasion I believe, claimed to have seen him making obscene gestures on the roof of the Jade Pagoda, but it was only a chimney sweep."

"Father Teilhard has kindly agreed to stay with us at Choukoutien, at the excavations," Black said. "He is a paleontologist of international repute and a professor of geology at the Catholic University in Paris."

"I am on extended leave," Teilhard explained.

"Piltdown Man," Backhouse said.

"You astound me," replied Teilhard.

Backhouse said, "The discovery made an enormous impression here at the time. The Peking *Gazette* made quite a thing of it. Actually, I came here this evening with a sense of déjà vu because in 1912, the British legation had it own fossil fete, which I attended, for Piltdown Man. The party was memorable because it started out as a giddy romp, with everyone making bad jokes about being a monkey's uncle. But by the end they began to take it dead seriously, and with a great sense of pride, particularly the Foreign Office chaps who said that the antiquity of our superior race vindicated our present imperialist policies once and for all; the whole world could finally see we were meant to be in charge. Finally, somebody banged away at the piano at something that sounded vaguely like 'God Save the King,' and there was much unabashed dabbing of eyes and noses by strong men who rarely shed a tear in private or in public."

"I'm afraid that soon there will be more dabbing of eyes

and noses," Black said. "When we say good-bye to China. None of us will be here for long, at least not in our present status, with our enclaves and extraterritoriality. The revolution isn't over yet, but whoever wins, they'll kick us out by the seats of our pants—the Americans, the British, the French, all of us. I only hope I'll have time to complete my excavations."

"The only way to live in China is to ignore politics," Backhouse said.

"Is that easy to do?" Teilhard asked. "Although you may choose to ignore politics, politics may not choose to ignore you."

"You are French," said Backhouse. "The French are naturally political, because nobody in France understands what the politicians are saying to them. It's not just that politicians speak French, which is incomprehensible except for the little phrases the English have taken over, such as *comme il faut*. It's that the French are altogether too subtle when it comes to politics, which leads to too many political parties and a great deal of futile argument, which in turn misleads a great number of people into thinking they are politically sophisticated when they are merely confused."

"I know nothing about politics in China, but I was not ignored by them when I came to Peking by train from Tientsin," Teilhard said. "I was not disconcerted when I saw a half dozen armed soldiers climb on the top of the locomotive as we started out, since that was de rigueur, as the English would say, in Central Asia where I have traveled widely. But halfway to Peking, three of the soldiers were shot dead by bandits who attacked the train, while we passengers lay flat on the floor of the carriage. I was told that the murderers were mercenaries employed by a local warlord, Lin Chi. That is politics in action."

"I am glad you are here, alive, to tell the tale, Father Teilhard. But atrocities are as commonplace here as flies on a dung heap. I once met a Chinese friend of mine in Tung Chih Men Street, but he wouldn't recognize me, and all because of politics. All that was left of him was his head being paraded on a pike. The Chinese who watched that grisly procession cheered mightily, but the Westerners who happened to be on the parade route took umbrage.''

"Obviously they weren't French. We did the same thing, with the help of Madame Guillotine in our own revolution.''

"You see, you've got me talking about politics, about which I know nothing,'' Backhouse said. "I'd rather talk about paleontology, about which I know nothing either, but about which I yearn to know something.''

"You must come out to Choukoutien,'' Black said. "I'll show you around.''

"I do not get out much.''

"We can't bring the site to you, I'm afraid. But our supply truck comes into Peking regularly, and the driver will pick you up.''

"Perhaps,'' said Backhouse with a sudden weariness. "Are you with us long in Peking, Father Teilhard?''

"Indefinitely. It depends on the progress of the excavations.''

"So I do not have to rush into the country to see both of you again.'' Backhouse extended a dry, white hand to be grasped. Then he made a tour of the room and before leaving satisfied Madame Minister's palpitating curiosity by telling her that the virgin in the bedroom those many years ago was still unsoiled by carnal knowledge, at least according to conventional judgments about that sort of thing; he would say no more.

"Who was that?'' Teilhard said.

"Sir Edmund? One of our local community of exiles, a high-class remittance man of considerable intellectual accomplishment. A collector of manuscripts and calligraphy, and a good historian. His book on the last of the Manchus has become something of a classic. There's a story that he was the lover of the Empress Dowager, who was in her eighties at the time, but Sir Edmund probably started that one himself, like a lot of the other things said about him. But if only half of them are true, you have just met a very great sinner.''

Backhouse got into one of the rickshaws in front of the British legation, its collapsible canopy raised against the cold night, and was carried down Legation Street and through the gateway to the Tartar City. The streets were empty except for occasional clusters of men squatting around kerosene stoves, mummy bundles with pinched bronze faces. Sweepers worked with cramped movements at the entrance of the railway station, pushing the soot, dirt, and refuse in senseless configurations on the pavement. In the morning the city would be reborn, squalling with life, shrill with business, suffused with the rank perfume of squalor, but as Backhouse was taken through the deserted streets by his trotting coolie, Peking was a city of blank walls and forbidding silence, a necropolis finally abandoned by even the most ferocious warlord who had given up control of its dominion as a hopeless cause, as if the idea of the city belonged to the dead, distant past, along with the forgotten fantasies of law and philosophy, a dead civilization whose survivors, the beggers and scavengers huddling near the meager kerosene heat, the weak, the destitute, and the damned, had inherited the kingdom by default and without knowing what a glorious prize they had won.

Going down an obscure byway, Backhouse was let down in front of a wall pierced by a moon gate. After a few moments his knock was answered by a servant, and the master stepped over the threshold into a small courtyard. He had bought the comfortable house from a Chinese merchant and had made no Western improvements. Tubs of bamboo grew on either side of the doorway, sliding panels of geometric wood latticework backed with oiled paper, set back on a narrow stone platform with an overhanging tiled roof. Foreign ambassadors and minor diplomatic functionaries might have more up-to-date residences, but by Chinese standards the house was the envy of the neighborhood.

Backhouse took particular pride in the comfort of his life as he was met at the door by his factotum, Chang Ho-chai. In the intervening years since Backhouse had left England, he had achieved a measure of financial security. After having met Teilhard at the British legation, Backhouse was especially pleased with the spaciousness of the hall, the polished surfaces of the teak floors, which reflected the hardwood columns like a tranquil lake, and Chang who knelt to offer silk slippers to his feet. The whole of it, his languid view of

the world, his independence, had derived from his successful
blackmail scheme. The hundred pounds he had extracted
from Charles Dawson had been spent on minor extravagances
while he had been in London. But the rest of his victims,
those who hadn't seen the absurdity of his demands because
of their own guilty consciences, continued to deposit their
monthly payments to his bank in London, which transferred
the amounts to Peking.

He knew he was regarded by the foreign community as a
renegade of a distinguished family, paid off as an embarrassment, but his pride was assuaged by knowing that his income
was augmented by means that were, if known, more horren-
dous than any of his staunchest critics could imagine. But, he
argued to himself, the fault lay with his victims; he had
perpetrated crimes in China that would have left them also-
rans in the race to perdition, crimes that were known to all,
but no one had seriously dared to threaten him.

Chang followed Backhouse to the bedroom. He was too
old to be called a boy, as Backhouse's English friends still
designated him, but he had been a boy when Backhouse first
had his boots blacked by him in the street and when Chang
had held his foot by the ankle in a way that promised more
than a shine. Over the years, Chang had taken complete
control over the running of the house, particularly domestic
expenditures, and like other servants, extracted a squeeze for
every grain of rice and leaf of tea he bought in the market.
When his master was out for an evening, he would sit in the
large rosewood chair by the scholar's table, ordering the cook
to bring him tea and rice cakes while he leafed through the
volumes of manuscripts, knitting his brow, pretending to read
the columns of illegible squiggles of Sung and Ming poetry.

"Make me a pipe," Backhouse said. The bedroom was
dark, chilly, even though the coal braziers glowed near the
canopied bed.

"Master had one before he left."

"I am touched by your concern for my well-being,"
Backhouse said. "A pipe." He spoke to Chang in a gutter
dialect that was useful in the marketplace when he bought
curios in out-of-the-way shops, where the merchants would

talk among themselves about how they would cheat him without knowing he understood.

Chang helped Backhouse out of his formal black robe and into a loose Mandarin gown embroidered with peonies on a magenta background.

"Master is too thin."

Backhouse stroked Chang's smooth cheek and let his hand linger on his neck.

"Master is tired," Chang said, disengaging himself and, going to a wooden double chest, took out a long-stemmed pipe, a small crock of opium, and a brass tray with a charcoal burner. He gently heated the sticky node of opium and fitted it into the bow of the pipe, puffing to light it and offering it to Backhouse, who had stretched out on the silken bed cover, lying on one side with his head propped on a sausage bolster. Chang indulged Backhouse's occasional pipes, hoping he would become addicted, which would add another dimension to his, Chang's, influence. His hegemony of the flesh would wane, as it had in the last few years in direct proportion to Backhouse's age. But there were other ways of holding a master in captivity.

Backhouse smoked his pipe, holding the smoke deeply in his lungs. When he began to feel light-headed, he lay back on the pillows and looked at the writhing dragons and cloud scrolls carved into the canopy of his bed. Chang sat beside him, watching silently.

"I have been standing all evening. My toes are cramped."

Chang slipped down to the foot of the bed, removed the slippers and kneaded his feet.

"What have you stolen while I was out?" Backhouse said with put-upon resignation.

"Nothing, Master."

"That is only because you were sleeping."

"No, Master."

"If you have stolen from me, I will have your hands cut off; if you lie to me, I will have your tongue cut out. What is your preference?"

"What is yours, Master? What pleasure would you deny yourself?"

"Go away," Backhouse said, floating in another direction weightless and warm, thinking of Teilhard. The only sound from the street beyond the walled courtyard was the intermittent clacking of the neighborhood night watchman's wooden clappers, declaring that all was well.

Davidson Black had called Backhouse an exile, and Teilhard wondered how long he would also belong to that community. He had begun his studies in Paris in 1913 and had served as a stretcher bearer during the war. In that deadly fire storm that blotted out the sun, denuding the countryside of Belgium and France of anything that lived, it seemed to Teilhard that the earth was returning to its primordial state of molton seas and volcanic eruptions. He once said Mass in a little village church near Verdun. It was a bombed-out shell, fire-blackened, with its roof open to the sky, the tympanum of limestone saints lying shattered on the ground. The villagers had already begun with gentle reverence to gather up the disembodied heads, the piously gesturing hands and bits of fluted drapery as he had gathered up the dying and the dead from the battlefields. He was touched by the villagers' belief that one day things would be as they were. But he held no such faith in his church. He could find no answer to the question of why the Holy Father put his hands against his eyes. Surely, he said to himself, knowing the answer was a resounding no, the Church would see what everyone else knew: that there was something new unleashed in the world, still without a name, a new sort of chance that withheld judgment, a world without snobbery in some elemental sense, in which the scion of a family that could trace its antecendents to Phillip the Good could be, was, blasted to blood-soaked gobbets by a shell fire a thousand meters away, meant for no one in particular. Single combat, heroism, and honorable war were finished, species that had become extinct. Any evolutionist knew that extinction was forever. Surely the world that survived the war would need something new, a bold new synthesis, not a careful piecing together of broken fragments.

When the war was over, Teilhard returned to Paris, completed his degree, and began teaching at the Catholic University, where he was not surprised to learn that the antimodernist purges had not passed away with the hobble skirts and picture hats of the prewar era. He spoke out to students and wrote to Jesuit friends in an agony of mind after he was warned by his Jesuit superiors that, despite his protestations of piety and obedience, he was treading perilously close to heresy. Teilhard found that strangely exciting; the idea of heresy in the twentieth century was a fascinating atavism, knowing he could not be burned at the stake and wondering what his fellow Jesuits and the Holy Father might do to him now that burning or trial by ordeal could no longer be decreed with impunity. He would have his answer by pushing his enemies to the limit of their endurance. Exile.

Both his friends and his enemies urged him to confine himself to scientific endeavors, and he briefly capitulated, joining an expedition to Outer Mongolia and the Ordos in search of evidence of Paleolithic Man, until then unknown in Central Asia. But the vastness of the steppes and the lunar escarpments of the deserts only beckoned his thoughts further out into the universe. He had known the hospitality of nomadic tribes who knew nothing of Christ, and had been welcomed by Buddhist monks in monastery caravansaries which had taken in pagans, Christians, Hindus, whomever, along the Silk Route. Sectarian differences palled. Teilhard was not a missionary.

Returning to Paris triumphant, with cases of unprecedented specimens and artifacts, with the security of years of study and cataloging ahead, he pushed his theological luck too far; from his vantage point in Peking, he allowed himself to wonder whether his exile, the answer to the question "What could they do to him?" was not writ the moment he had set foot in Paris again. There were times he was convinced he had been entrapped: a note he'd been asked to write on the nature of original sin that had mysteriously found its way straight to the Vatican, and the inevitable and impossible demand for a recantation. If this episode was ever recorded in the history of the Church—Teilhard was not insensitive to the idea that his conflict might eventually have some significance beyond autobiography—he preferred to see himself as a prophetic apostate rather than a victim of circumstances. At the

moment, the fine historical distinction was immaterial, even
to him. He had been banished to China to pursue his paleontological interests, and he could preach his heresies to the
coolies, mangy dogs, and stray cats in the streets of Peking to
his heart's content. Teilhard's obedience and disobedience
knew no bounds; he kept a diary of his spiritual exercises,
jotted from day to day, that had the indications of being a
book he was ready to call *Le Milieu Divin* if anyone were
interested.

A nagging catarrh had kept Backhouse at home, even
bedridden, and knowing the dangers of the air in open country, he invited Father Teilhard to visit him in his convales-
cence. Backhouse had added hypochondria to his other
eccentricities.

Backhouse received his guest in his scholar's black gown
and a cashmere scarf wrapped several times around his neck.
Teilhard was wearing his cassock, not to be priestly, but it
helped with the cold.

"I spend my days here," Backhouse said as they stood at
the threshold of his study. The scholar's table had its requisite
brushpots, water jugs, and brushes, an inkstone and a number
of bibelots of rose quartz and rock crystal. Against the opposite wall were bins stacked with long wooden boxes for
rolled scrolls and shelves of bound manuscripts. Backhouse
went to the large translucent window that filled the room with
an even, grayish light and opened it a crack for Teilhard to
admire the view of the garden.

"The red maple and the bamboo are lovely in the spring,
and we have wonderful flowers," Backhouse said, then quot-
ing in adenoidal Mandarin and translating. " 'Everywhere
blossoms in splendor vying.' That is Chu Yun-ming, a Ming
poet and calligrapher, describing the arrival of spring at
Loyang, the capital of the T'ang dynasty."

"Do you have any calligraphy by him?" Teilhard asked.

"I am a poor scholar. I cannot afford such things. I must
be content with that," Backhouse said, pointing to a hanging
scroll of calligraphic crayfish that moved down the paper in
brilliant immediacy of brushwork. "That is by Ch'i Pai-shih,
who lives in Peking and who was kind enough to give me

lessons in the art, or I rather should say the poetry of the brush.''

"Would you give me a demonstration?''

Backhouse went to the scholar's table. With great ceremony he took a cake of dried black ink and ground it with water on the inkstone, discoursing on the history of Chinese ideographs, the idea of the rhythmic vitality of each character, and explaining the differences between formal court style and the eccentric variations of the Taoist literati tradition. Spreading out a long, thin piece of white paper, he seized one of the bamboo-handled brushes from the cylindral brush pot, and loading it with ink, began to whip the tip of the heart-shaped brush down the sheet. He inked the brush again and completed the column of five beautifully formed characters. "One drop of ink contains the world, an infinity of time.''

"Is that what you wrote?'' asked Teilhard.

"No.''

"What does it say?''

"Wonton soup. Five yen,'' Backhouse read. "Are you hungry? Would you like something? Tea?''

"Brandy, if you have it.''

Backhouse made a noise that started high in the sinuses, and Chang appeared instantly as if he had been standing unseen outside the room.

They went from the scholar's workroom to a gloomy saloon and settled into Ming-style chairs with tubular wooden arms and hard seats covered with finely reticulated caning. Chang moved a set of braziers near them. The smoldering soft coal gave off an unpleasant odor of petroleum. Then he brought in a bottle and two famille-rose wine cups.

Teilhard winced slightly at the taste.

"I should have warned you. It's made from sorghum.''

"It warms. It was very kind of you to invite me. The living arrangements at the dig are a little primitive. It is good to get away once in a while.''

"I understand there is plenty of room at the Catholic Mission guesthouse.''

"There is so much to do at the dig, it would be impractical to come and go."

"I have a suspicion that you do not find missionaries congenial. You are too cosmopolitan."

"They have their calling, I have mine."

"Exactly as I said. You are too tolerant to be a missionary. You are altogether out-of-character. I sense it. Every Catholic priest I have ever met immediately asked me what my faith was. I was born a Quaker, but for some time I have been attracted to Catholicism: the jeweled reliquaries of the Abbot Suger, the epiphanal arches of Chartres, Raphael's papal apartments."

"The eternal mystery of the creation, the belief in the Passion of Christ."

"Ah, the exquisite pain of Our Lord."

"The pain of Man."

"I wasn't prepared for Jesuit compassion."

"Our attitudes have been called Jesuitic, and sometimes for good reason. But we have one task: the redemption of Man."

"If I converted to Catholicism, I would have to confess all my sins," Backhouse sighed.

Teilhard agreed.

"I shouldn't mind confessing them to you."

"I haven't heard confession in many years. I don't care for it."

"But you go."

"Regularly. It is expected of me."

"I can't imagine what a Jesuit would confess."

"Come, now. You are being deliberately ingenuous. We are much the same as other men."

"Why don't you hear confession?"

"One confesses, receives absolution, and the next day one does exactly the same thing, knowing confession will wipe the slate clean again like a schoolroom blackboard that is erased every afternoon only to be written on the next morning. Confession is of no importance, except as a folkway of the Church, like St. Christopher medals. Freud, whose views I do not espouse, at least recognizes the value of confession without contrition, which is closer to what I do recognize and value: self-knowledge.''

''You have shocked me,'' Backhouse said. There was a touch of playfulness in his voice. ''I must have another brandy to calm my nerves.'' He filled his cup, then Teilhard's.

As Backhouse looked at his guest, he was reminded of a Chinese ancestor portrait, not in his weathered features—the deep creases in his cheeks or fan of crow's feet at his eyes—but rather, the stillness of the face, an unstated symmetry. Indeed the entire person of this finely wrought priest sitting in the chair appeared to Backhouse to have been formed around a spiritual plumb line, and he hated what he saw.

''Perhaps we ought to confine ourselves to science rather than religion,'' Backhouse said.

''I agree, as at the moment my concerns are largely scientific. If our hopes at Choukoutien are realized, the finds will be of great significance. The strata are extremely rich in animal fossils, and we are hoping to find not only the remains of a single human individual, but many—a whole race. You see, we already know that the two teeth we have found do not belong to the same individual; one is a juvenile tooth, the other is not.''

''Will it eclipse the finds at Piltdown?''

''It is too early to tell.''

Backhouse took a sip of brandy. ''You and I have a connection to Piltdown Man, apart from his being a distant cousin of sorts.''

''Really?''

''I was acquainted with Dawson and Woodward.''

Teilhard wondered why Backhouse hadn't mentioned that acquaintance at their first meeting, and he wondered why Backhouse sat quietly without elaborating further.

''How did you meet?'' Teilhard asked.

''We were introduced by a mutual friend.'' Again Backhouse invited inquiry by his reticence.

''Who was that?''

''Charles Hammond. His field was human anatomy.''

''I don't know him.''

"Did you ever go to the Woodwards' for tea? Maud Woodward. God, what a dragon. Did she invite you to sign her tablecloth?"

"Yes. But only a corner."

"My autograph was also solicited," Backhouse said. "My signature appears as ligature of two Chinese ideograms. You said you did not hear confession, but I must make a small one. You see, my name, Backhouse, in Chinese, has a rather rude connotation. In this land without plumbing, the combined ideograms for 'back' and 'house' mean privy. That small but essential structure is always behind the principal residence—in back of the house. A euphemism, to be sure, but an inescapable allusion to shit."

Teilhard laughed.

"You do not object to expletives."

"Not in the least."

"You are more worldly than I imagined," Backhouse said with a hint of condescension.

"You are disappointed."

"I'd hoped to corrupt you. Either you are incorruptible, or we have met too late."

In the months that followed, Choukoutien had begun living up to expectations. Two *Sinanthropus* skulls had been found. In contrast to Piltdown, there were scores of workers busy from morning until night at the site, which had been meticulously divided into two-meter gridded sections, both on the floor of the dig and the cliffs that rose steeply from the plains of the countryside. Teilhard was rarely away from camp except for occasional trips for supplies or to visit the Medical College, where Davidson Black had his permanent offices. From time to time he would receive a plaintive note from Backhouse detailing the congestion of his lungs, his depression at the thought of being a shut-in for the duration of the winter, a slight tremor in his right hand that denied him his chief diversion, calligraphy, and his despair at ever being able to visit the place that his friends who visited him all too infrequently said was yielding such treasures.

On his way from the supply depot at the college, Teilhard

detoured into the Tartar City and stopped at Backhouse's
residence, being sure to find the enfeebled invalid at home.
Chang had him wait in the columned hall and soon reappeared to usher him into the bedroom. Teilhard could see no
signs of the ravages of illness in Backhouse, but it was
difficult to tell since he lay in bed under a riotously colorful
embroidered silk coverlet and wore a voluminous damask
gown with wide sleeves.

"At last," Backhouse said, as if he had lived only for
Teilhard's return.

"I hope you are feeling better, Sir Edmund."

"I have good days and bad. My principal complaint is
ennui. Chang has his virtues, but they do not include the art
of conversation. While I lie here rotting in this bed, you, I
suppose, have been thriving."

"Very much so," said Teilhard, "if I may say so without
irritating you."

"I am not a jealous man. So this site will make you even
more famous than Piltdown."

"I am only one of many here. And the credit belongs
entirely to Dr. Black."

"Nevertheless, you apparently have a knack for turning up
at the right place and time. First Sussex, now Peking."

"In both cases I was told that the site had already proved
to be significant. I just went along."

Backhouse considered him for a moment. "What was
your relationship to Dawson and Woodward?"

"They were terribly important to me, mentors, really. I
was a young priest with scientific interests. When Dawson
invited me to dig with him, I was very flattered. I was a
novice; they were already well-established. Woodward was
knighted last year for his achievements. Dawson would have
been as well, but he died."

"And you do not miss England—the food, the weather?
Do not be afraid to tell me you don't, as I do not intend ever
to go back."

"Those years in England seem very far away. And I am
too concerned with what we are doing at Choukoutien to give
it much thought."

"I can see you are not a sentimentalist. You are too scientific. We English dote on the past. If I went back, it would shatter my vision of lace and blooming wisteria that is precious to me. Dear Victoria and Edward. This current George—well, we have had too many Georges. He became king accidentally, you know, since he was Edward's second son. Prince Edward Victor, Duke of Clarence, was meant to be king, but he died of influenza, they say, before he ascended the throne. It would have been an interesting reign," Backhouse said. "The whims of history. Suppose William the Conqueror had decided to stay in bed. Suppose you had decided not to come to China."

"I cannot imagine my being in China having any historical significance at all."

"Let us play a historical game. What is the connection between you and me, Dawson, Woodward, Prince Edward Victor, and George V?"

"You and I are here. We both knew Woodward and Dawson. Prince Edward Victor and George V were brothers, one of whom knighted Woodward."

"I see you are not a historian. History is meaningless without irony," Backhouse began. "Prince Edward Victor, Duke of Clarence, was a notorious homosexual, who frequented a male brothel in Cleveland Street, London. It was a great scandal at the time, 1889 to be exact. Not that Prince Eddy was openly implicated, as his escapades were hushed up by powerful friends. I mentioned that he would have made an interesting king, but it is particularly amusing to think that, as Edward VIII, he, rather than his younger brother George, would have conferred knighthood on Arthur Smith Woodward, because our Sir Arthur, who was also an ardent admirer of boys, had also made not infrequent visits to the very same brothel. Through fortuitous circumstances I acquired a ledger with visitors' names, and when in England in 1908, I confronted Woodward—and others—with the same poignant reminder."

"Blackmail," said Teilhard.

"When Woodward would not comply with my demands, I went to Dawson to get his friend to reconsider, but instead

Dawson paid me a lump sum for the ledger pages and saved him. A noble gesture. But I have always wondered about that. Dawson had bought from me an enormous source of power over Woodward, and I couldn't help thinking that, given the opportunity I had furnished, he would have used it. For what purpose, I do not know. Perhaps you do?''

"It is common to impute one's own motives to others," Teilhard said. "Others would not commit blackmail as easily as you. But I do not understand why you tell me these things, about yourself, about my friends. I know you do not seek absolution.''

"There is something about you," Backhouse said with sudden vehemence. "A goodness, perhaps. No. A certainty. It disturbs me. I've grown to hate it. I can suffer smugness, but not equanimity. I wanted to destroy that, at least with regard to your Piltdown colleagues. You knew them both well; imagine the power Dawson had," Backhouse's voice had become silken. "Not to extract money, but something else. What was it?" His eyes bore into Teilhard, looking for a reponse. "What was it? There had to be something, goddammit!" he shouted with frustration. "There's always something. Even in you, my saintly Jesuit!"

I am a pariah, a rebel, a subversive, an exile. How different am I from him? Teilhard thought as he left Backhouse. He is evil, Teilhard concluded, a tormentor living by inflicting pain and suffering on other men. A destroyer. He would step on a wild flower merely for the sake of crushing it. Irrevocably fallen from Grace, crouching in a corner of Hell as cold and dark as his house, never to see the face of God. But that is how they see me—they, my Jesuit brothers, the infallible Holy Father himself. I have obeyed, but I will not yield.

What could Backhouse have seen as my certainty? Teilhard wondered. My mask of obedience? My protestations of friendship. Lies. Half-truths. He at least told the truth. I hadn't the stomach for it. I can take comfort, at least, that for all his cynical contempt, his corruption—for all that—Backhouse is as ingenuous as he pretended to be, as credulous of me as a peasant woman who sees the Holy Virgin in majesty and roses blooming in the snow.

Teilhard remembered his own yearning for a miraculous sign that the Kingdom of the universal Christ would be revealed to him through science. Then he had found the canine tooth at Piltdown. God favored him for this secret thoughts. He had blessed him by revealing to Teilhard a treasure of knowledge from the earth. God was not afraid of Darwin's truth. Teilhard began to believe that the bit of brown bone he had found was the sign of divine approval he had hoped for. The young priest would go forward, reconciling the Passion of Christ with the awesome panorama of the universe as it was being unfolded by twentieth century science.

Now, on the other side of the world, Teilhard forced himself to reconstruct the whole of those Piltdown years. Backhouse had added a catalytic element to Teilhard's inert memories—Dawson's power over Woodward.

When Teilhard first met Dawson at Hastings, he could not have imagined how important that association would be. In those next years he had derived so much benefit from Dawson's friendship. How could Dawson believe he could be anything but grateful? On the eve of his departure from England, Dawson had accused him of overweaning ambition. Teilhard had pointed out to Backhouse the mistake of imputing his motives to others, but Dawson had done the same to him, and he wasn't far from the mark. Now it was clear to Teilhard that Dawson had been referring to the canine tooth. Dawson must have reasoned: I was ambitious; I planted the canine tooth and found it. But, Teilhard thought, that could also read: Dawson was ambitious; he planted Piltdown Man and found him.

Dawson must have been convinced he first planted the tooth and then found it to further his own career. That's what his accusation of betrayal was all about. But if Dawson thought that was so, there would have been no reason to accept it as genuine. Why did Woodward accept it too? Why add a spurious specimen to the authentic skull and jaw? Teilhard returned to Backhouse's revelation of Dawson's power over Woodward—to extract something—complicity in a fraud.

Woodward had tried to warn him that day at the tea, before he found the flint at Piltdown. Teilhard could see him once again, his expression of concern softening his features, before Dawson joined them and thought of Woodward's letter of recommendation. So Woodward had been Dawson's unwilling champion. Dawson must have known he couldn't do it alone. And Teilhard was also chosen to lend credence to the lie.

In his exile, Teilhard's position within the Church was precarious. To add a connection to a scientific fraud would result in a double exile. Both he and Woodward would be more than logical suspects. Everyone had been fooled by Piltdown. In Dawson's absence, both he and Woodward would be the obvious scapegoats for their angry suspicions. The wrath of science would be directed toward them, not toward a dead man, who could not suffer humiliation, protest in vain, turn this way and that, helplessly looking for allies. No one would want to believe they had both been Dawson's victims, although they were, for different reasons. Teilhard could never prove his innocence of complicity, and there would be no lack of malicious rumors of his guilt; Woodward had been right to warn him of the politics of science.

If the whole cloth of Piltdown began to unravel, Teilhard resolved at least to try to protect Woodward by saying Dawson had shown him finds from Piltdown Two in 1913; Woodward had nothing to do with manufacturing the specimens. As to the rest of it, he would continue to reiterate his affection for his two English mentors, and to maintain the impossibility that either of them, men of the highest ideals, could have been involved.

Perhaps I am a historian after all, Teilhard thought. The air around him teemed with irony. Dawson's early death and Woodward's knighthood. International paleontology led around by the nose. Dawson's indignant accusation of betrayal, his outrage, disappointment. What of Dawson's betrayal of him, Teilhard, and of science, the history of man? Teilhard could imagine Dawson's sly amusement. He thought of the Piltdown skull, that inestimable treasure, virtually inaccessible. Small wonder. As he thought of Backhouse, of the intense degree of premeditation he brought to everything he touched, everyone he met, Teilhard realized that even as they first met, Backhouse must have found the idea of revealing his involvement with Woodward and Dawson irresistible. But he would never know the scope of events he had inadvertently set in motion, the monstrosity he had helped to create. For a moment Teilhard longed to tell him. And he thought of the canine tooth, that lowly piece of bone, that bogus sign of divine approval that had given him the courage to challenge the authority of the Church, the beginning of a wide spiritual trajectory to the farthest radiant nebula, and a wordly exile to that windswept place in China where he had finally seen the shameful truth of Piltdown Man. The chill he felt was not only the cutting edge of the north wind, but the thought that, if the tooth was false, a mockery, so was his belief in God's love.

Chapter XIII

DURING THE DECADE AFTER THE ANNOUNCEMENT OF Piltdown Two, which had silenced Grafton Elliott Smith and his minions, Arthur Smith Woodward produced an impressive bibliography of articles and essays on Piltdown Man and his other specialty, fossil fish. Although he no longer had to fear dealing with hostile questions from disbelievers that a race of hominid Englishmen existed, Woodward was still reluctant to speak publicly on the subject; at scientific conferences concerning human paleontology, he preferred to play a gray eminence, amending or correcting what other men might say. After someone spoke, heads would automatically turn in his direction. He would nod, make a point, acknowledging his proprietary relationship to the great fossils locked in the Museum's vault and was looked upon as something of a high priest of those relics. Maud picked and chose his appearances with great care, and he was glad she had put the scientific world on short ration.

When Woodward received a letter from the Prime Minister offering knighthood, he brought it home to present to Maud before telling anyone else. She read it with the deepest satisfaction, reminding him that her management of his academic career and her direction of his alliances to powerful, well-placed scientific colleagues, who had made the recommendation to the Prime Minister, was in no small measure a contributing factor. In the six weeks before he would be called to Buckingham Palace, he had his fittings for the cutaway coat and striped trousers he would wear to the ceremony. With a silk top hat to complete the ensemble, he went by taxi from Fulham one morning, dropping Maud near Bond Street for some shopping, having agreed to meet her later in his new avatar at the Ritz. The taxi then circled the Victoria monument in front of the Palace, where the usual clutches of tourists pressed against the railing, wondering if the noses of the immobile guards itched. At the side entrance, other top-hatted gentlemen were getting out of cars and limousines as Woodward arrived. He was shown with the greatest courtesy to a magnificent audience room of ivory and gilt Georgian design, hung with flashing chandeliers. He was among seventy men destined for elevation that morning at nine o'clock, who were assigned seats on gold ballroom chairs in alphabetical order. Woodward had expected something more exclusive, and he thought that knights of the realm were as common as pigeons in Trafalgar Square. The palace functionary who rehearsed them in the proper way to kneel on the two steps before their monarch held the same view; his manner was courteous and aloof, not unlike Hammond, the procurer of Cleveland Street, whose memory had more than once invaded Woodward's thoughts during the morning's ceremonies.

Woodward looked around the room, not recognizing anyone. The man next to him was large and florid-faced, with white muttonchop whiskers. As Woodward glanced at him, he said, "Woodner—coal."

"Woodward—fossils."

"Woodner—coal" turned his attention back to the dais. Woodward was momentarily struck by the splendor of monarchy when an elderly but resplendent page entered from a paneled side door, thumped a great staff on the floor, and boomed, "His Majesty the King."

Sure enough, as if on cue in a costumed pantomime, George V entered with an entourage. He was exactly, no more, no less, as Woodward had seen him in countless photographs in the newspapers, on postcards, on souvenir plates, and he wondered briefly whether for such occasions the King, still in his bath, didn't send in a brilliantly made-up double to release yet another batch of elevated worthies into the world with the same indifference as a sea turtle deposited her eggs in the sand to be hatched by the sun. Only Woodward's sense of detachment allowed him to enjoy the moment. "Woodner—coal" must have also been thinking about all the explosions in the collieries and the children with black-lung disease with the same poignant sense of the ridiculous that Woodward had in his own subversion of the moral decencies of his age that had brought him, and perhaps many others in the room, to that place of honor.

Woodward was glad that he wasn't Robert Adrian, the first one to be called to the dais, who tripped on the first step as he knelt to be dubbed and who rose red-faced as Sir Robert. As Woodward sat, he was carried back to a graduation exercise, where the curse of the alphabet put him at the end. Having sat through sixty-nine brief recitations by his King of the services rendered by each new knight, Woodward responded to the call and did what all the others had done. The King was magnificent in a military tunic with a mass of gilded scrambled eggs on each shoulder and an extravagance of gold braid loops going every which way on his chest, a curved shield of tailoring. Woodward looked up at the King's face for a split second, and not wanting to appear worshipful, immediately lowered his head while his accomplishments, including Piltdown Man, were read. He furtively looked up long enough to see the monarch's hand, like any other hand he had seen, with a few liver spots, grasping the hilt of the sword of state, gold and encrusted with diamonds, before it rose out of his line of vision and tapped him lightly on each shoulder. The most vivid impression of the moment for Woodward was a surreal remembrance of the King's gold belt buckle, the most interesting thing at his eye level, an interlaced monogram in relief, set with tiny brilliants. Woodward was trying to count them when he heard George V say, "Rise, Sir Arthur," and he had a moment of irritation that he would never know exactly how many little bits of glitter were there, a piece of trivia he would have liked to be able to report to those who might ask him about the ceremony in the years to come. "Sir Arthur," he said to himself as he took his place in his chair and before a desultory royal congratulation was offered to the room and before he found himself out on the street at eleven-thirty. "Well, Sir Arthur," he said to himself, " 'That,' as they say, 'is that.' " It had been like paying tuppence to get into a fun house at an amusement park, and before having had a proper laugh, he'd been dumped out again on the midway.

At least a few people looked at him, so splendidly was he dressed with his top hat glistening in the morning light. Charles would have loved this, he thought. Charles would be doing cartwheels in the flower beds of geraniums. He would have been there with me. The service Woodward had renderd to his King, his Emperor, his Empire, had been all Charles's doing, Charles's vision, his madness. His immense nerve. He, Woodward, was an imposter, and he thought that Dawson would have enjoyed that, or at least would have had a wry appreciation of the idea, having been cheated by Death of his ultimate victory that was now being claimed by his victim. There was something in that, some meaning that Woodward thought he would sort out sometime. In the meantime, he headed across the top of Pall Mall past St. James's Palace toward the Ritz to act out the part Maud had written for him in her own ceremony of accolade.

Woodward followed her instructions as he entered the lobby of the Ritz, no less sumptuous than Buckingham Palace, he could now tell her with authority, and went to the desk of the hall porter.

"I was supposed to meet my wife here at eleven-forty-five," Woodward said, taking out his pocket watch in a stage gesture. "I understood her to say in the main entrance, but as she is unfailingly prompt, and she is not here, perhaps I have made a mistake. Would you be kind enough to page her? Perhaps she is in one of the public rooms."

He felt the perfect fool, but the hall porter, who was never astonished or annoyed by the eccentricities of the high and mighty, who would have on his own account simply either waited or looked in the lounges and tea rooms until he found that worthy female person, summoned a boy in scarlet livery and a matching pillbox. The youth wrote the name of the august female personage on both sides of a slate attached to a long pole and began to search the premises, turning the slate so that the tiny silver bells chimed in the lounges, in the various vestibules, in the alcoves, and finally in the dining room overlooking the verdant expanses of Green Park. A formidable person, dawdling over tea and a portion of crustless bread and butter sandwiches, responded with such fervor, "I am Lady Smith Woodward," that not a few other august personages and rich nobodies in the room turned in her direction to see who was making such a to-do. The kind of hats that used to give Maud a public authority had passed into fashion's history, as had the positive effect of the sharp angles and corseted curves of her physique. She looked somewhat costumed, rather than dressed, as she rose in the morning frock of brown crepe de chine amidst the snowy napery, bud vases of blushing carnations, and the clinking of hotel crockery to respond to the urgent summons and positively sailed out of the room.

The congratulatory excitement at the Museum over Woodward's knighthood faded away, and he became used to being routinely addressed as Sir Arthur. A year later the post of superintendent became vacant, and in spite of Maud's advice as to how to position himself to reach for the job, Woodward was passed over. He would not have thought himself a possible candidate before his becoming Sir Arthur, knowing how his colleagues viewed his narrow correctness and fussiness over detail, but he and Maud enjoyed an uncharacteristic agreement of acrimony at his rejection. He entirely concurred with her that he could not spend his remaining years at an institution that thought so little of him, even though he had private misgivings that leaving the Museum meant relinquishing control over the Piltdown fossils. As to that, he wrote a lengthy memorandum to the new superintendent recommending as strongly as possible that his policy of the last decade be strictly maintained. At the age of sixty-four, leaving his office bare of any sign of his tenure, Woodward retired in a huff to Haywards Heath, Sussex, not ten miles from Barkham Manor.

Before leaving London, Maud gave a series of farewell teas for those who had not shown themselves traitors to Woodward's candidacy at the Museum, and to extract the last signatures that would complete the cosmology of the multi-colored scientific constellations on her tea cloth. Those who begged prior engagements on one date were immediately offered another, or yet another, so that in the end Maud was satisfied that no one escaped her.

Then, slowly, the dark clutter of the villa in Fulham was packed in stout wooden crates for removal to Sussex. A few days before their final departure, on a late Saturday after-noon, Woodward adjusted his tie, shot his shirt cuffs from the sleeves of his gray worsted suit, and took the under-ground to Victoria.

When he entered the Golden Hind and his eyes became accustomed to the warm shadows, he could see that nothing had changed: the same etched glass, the trade signs for Guinness and Watney, the framed prints of dogs and coaching scenes on the cocoa-colored walls, sparkling glasses and the buttery sheen of polished brass. A few regulars still congre-gated at the rear, near the pockmarked dart board while silent workmen presented their backs to Woodward as he went to the bar. He looked anxiously for Ethel, who wasn't there, but presently she came in, broad behind first through a swinging door, a clutch of glass mugs in each hand, doing a graceful and practiced half-turn keeping the glasses away from the door. Woodward observed her as she set the glasses down and arranged them in a neat little platoon next to the tap. She was about to go into the back again when she noticed him.

"What's your pleasure, Duckie?" she said without a sign of recognition.

"Half pint of bitter. "

Ethel went to the tap and returned with a foaming mug. Woodward was looking at her so intently that she stopped, her penciled eyebrows askew with effort, and she slowly pointed a finger at him.

"Artie," Woodward said.

"Artie! Of course, you're Artie. Well, give us a kiss, then, luv." With her forearms on the bar, Ethel heaved her breasts over them and offered Woodward her fat, powdered cheek. She smelled strongly of lilacs as he touched her cheek with his lips.

"Your hair's different," he said.

"A girl's got to keep up. But, crikey, will you look at you. Got your position back, didn't you? And from the look of it, you must own the whole bloody firm. Didn't I tell you? Didn't I tell you things would work out? I'm never wrong about such things."

Ethel beamed at him, as if her prediction had been responsible for his change of fortune; she was as happy for herself as she was for him. There was a little more gold in her mouth and quite a lot in her hair.

"How are things with you?" Woodward asked.

"Can't complain. Me old mum died, but that was a blessing." Looking Woodward up and down she said, "So, how many years has it been?"

"Oh, before the war."

"I shouldn't have asked." Ethel primped at the ordered waves of her marcelled hair that was at odds with the rest of her fat, blowsy sensuality.

"Not that I haven't thought about you all these years. I have."

"You're a luv."

"I'd recognize you anywhere. Except for the hair."

"I have it done."

"Very becoming." Woodward's mind raced for bits of small talk that darted away like frightened minnows. Finally he said, "The reason I came in now is because I'm leaving London, retiring, to the country."

"Well, you deserve it, that's all I can say, after all you've been through. Couldn't have happened to a nicer fellow. Where are you going?"

"Haywards Heath. It's near Hastings. When I was working, those Saturdays, I used to look forward to coming here, and as I won't be up to London much, I wanted to say good-bye."

"You're a luv."

"Would you be kind enough to join me in a farewell drink?"

"Since you asked so nice, don't mind if I do."

A hoarse demand came from down the bar. "Eff'l."

She and Woodward turned. He saw Antinoüs in workman's disguise, with bunches of glossy chestnut hair falling in his face like grapes in an arbor.

"Hold off," Ethel shouted. "Can't you see I'm talking with my friend, Artie?" She gave Woodward's rival a look of ostentatious disdain. "These young blokes."

Woodward smiled shyly with a feeling of fierce pleasure at her preference for him.

As Ethel poured a whiskey for herself, Woodward glanced quickly down the bar toward the young man, and had a slight longing, the sensation itself, rather than the sense memory that was all he would ordinarily permit himself. His romantic imagination stirred.

Ethel held up a jigger, and they clinked glasses, and she tossed the drink down with a quick turn of her wrist. As she set the glass down, Woodward put his hand on hers.

She didn't move away. "Be careful, Artie dear, or you'll make me fall in love with you." There was a soft humor in her voice. She lay her other hand on his.

Woodward's eyes brimmed behind his glasses. He knew it was only a barmaid's flirtation, but those few seconds were the longest affectionate contact he could remember.

"I'd better see to that young fellow," Ethel said.

Woodward took his hand away.

Halfway down the bar, Ethel said, "Send me a postcard. From Hastings. With a picture of the sea. I love the sea."

He would send a card with a seascape to her each Christmas. Woodward finished his beer. As he drained the mug, he smelled the odor of hops and malt mingled with lilacs.

Once settled in Sussex, Woodward remembered his visit to the Golden Hind as his good-bye to London. When he and Maud left Fulham for the last time, they had wrestled with luggage, with Samson in his extreme dotage, missed the train from Waterloo and waited for another, a blurred leave-taking and a similar arrival at Haywards Heath with weeks of unpacking and arranging. The house was a former gatekeeper's cottage with two bedrooms, which nodded architecturally toward Tuscany. While Maud moved furniture from one place to another and hired and discharged three servant girls for impudence, sloth, and ignorance of cleanliness, Woodward worried over arranging and deploying his scientific papers, which would be his main occupation. Woodward had purchased a small motorcar and was at Maud's disposal for trips to town, where she quickly established herself with the local merchants as a customer who would not tolerate a bruised pear or loose button. When Maud was not scolding the local fruiterer or dressmaker, she attended to a flower garden and made much of the failing Samson, who still lay at her feet during the long, silent evenings and at the end of the bed through the night.

Woodward also used the car to go to Barkham Manor. It was remarked at the manor house that he had a wonderful dedication to the site; since the discovery of the canine tooth, nothing had been found. Still, sometimes, when the weather was fine, he would turn up to spade and sieve for a few hours. Piltdown Man's firm reputation did not necessitate his digging as a show of good faith in the authenticity of her fossils, nor did Woodward, his own reputation as secure, ever entertain the idea of adding anything to the specimens at the Museum. But he had never been entirely convinced of Dawson's conviction that Teilhard had salted the canine. From time to time, he would be seized by the fear, never entirely set to rest, that whoever had salted the canine had also put other specimens in the pit, waiting to be discovered. Then he would make the short trip and dig at the site as a therapeutic exercise, until he felt the anxiety subside. He was never finally certain that there wasn't something there.

Although the Woodwards had never been churchgoers in London, Maud thought they'd better conform to the ways of provincial life. None of the congregations of Haywards Heath suited her, so they drove each Sunday to Uckfield, where some of the ladies were closer to her high station and where the sermons assured her of salvation. While Maud had convinced herself that she was attuned to the sensibilities of life in the country, she had not reckoned with the local attitude that she would probably not live long enough to be considered anything but a newcomer. It was generally agreed among the congregation at Uckfield that she should have waited some few years before entering the church flower show, held on a Sunday afternoon after services. The jury decided that a potted hydrangea was a pushy flower and that the particular entry's too aggresively fuchsia color was caused, no doubt, by overambitious mulching. Maud's single long stem with its balloon of pink blossoms was awarded a third, and she was pleased with the recognition until she realized that every losing entry got a third, including a pot of pathetic nasturtiums. First prize that year went to Arabella Spence's yellow roses. They were displayed with the other entries in the center of a long trestle table on the lawn next to the rectory.

Arabella had kept her youth wonderfully. Her fine jawline and delicate throat had only slightly softened, and the aura of her hair and pale skin was undimmed. Only her aquiline nose and the luminosity of her eyes could be considered out of date in the flapper era. But the twenties had revealed to the world an aspect of her formerly known only to Colin and Dawson: her legs. She wore a short tawny silk dress that captured the sunlight, its hem grazing her lean thigh just above the knee, and sandals with Spanish heels. The effect was streamlined perfection. She might have been thought too modern for Uckfield, but she was not looked upon with disapproval. She carried herself like a satisfied matron, wearing her youthful appearance as if she took no credit for it, and as if she wouldn't miss it once it had gone. Besides, her family had always counted in the neighborhood and so had Colin's. They had begun their married life as a perfect couple and had remained so. Liam was in business with his father, and Mark was a cadet at Sandhurst. They had grown as tall and well-made as Colin and had inherited a suitably darker version of their mother's blondness. It was hoped they would marry locally, thought Mark was away and Liam went frequently up to London for weekends to dance and drink gin-and-French in places decorated with chrome and onyx.

Colin was off somewhere talking about cement as Arabella ambled with easy confidence in her beauty and her horticultural victory among the other contestants and townfolk. Like a viewer at a picture exhibition, she walked slowly along the trestle table, looking at each entry and the little cards with the flowers written in English and Latin, and the names of the entrants.

When Arabella read "Lady Smith Woodward," her memory opened like a morning glory in the sun. She hadn't had a lover since Charles. While men looked at her with admiration, no one had ever possessed her so viscerally and immediately with a single look. Arabella gazed past the fieldstone rectory and gardens, where her neighbors stood chatting in twos and threes, past the flowering shrubs toward the pastures and hills. On afternoons like this they had met, at the edge of a meadow where the cicadas strummed tunelessly to the rhythm of their damp and naked bodies, or in the woods where the leaves were like bed-hangings of verdure tapestry.

One of the flower show's jurors pointed out the Smith Woodwards to Arabella. She could see Maud in conversation with Jeanette Morris, with Woodward standing to one side. As she approached, she could hear Mrs. Morris discoursing on manure.

"What a smelly subject," Arabelle said, kissing the air next to Jeanette's cheek.

"I feel that the smell of a really good manure is just as sweet as a rose," said Mrs. Morris. "And congratulations, Arabella, yours are even better than last year's."

"Nature was kind."

"Do you know Sir Arthur and Lady Smith Woodward?"

"We haven't met, but I know Sir Arthur also digs in the ground. I am Arabella Spence, and I am a great student of your discovery."

"I am very glad to hear it," Woodward said.

"We've been trying to get Sir Arthur to give a small lecture one evening," Mrs. Morris said. "At the Town Hall. Nothing too technical."

"You must honor us, Sir Arthur."

"We are not entirely settled in, but as soon as we are, we will set a date."

"Lady Smith Woodward, since you and Jeanette have found a subject of common interest, could I borrow Sir Arthur for a few moments? There is someting I particularly want to talk to him about concerning the excavations at Barkham Manor."

Maud took a little step backward, and Woodward advanced a pace in a social minuet.

Arabella said to him, "It is a lovely spot, no dobut about it," as she took his arm and steered him down the brick pathway.

"I would like to go more often, but I am much occupied with my papers and do not get out of Haywards Heath as much as I would like."

"If I had known you lived nearby, I would have paid you a visit."

"It is unusual for a woman to be interested in paleontology."

"I have never studied formally," Arabella said, "but I was a particular friend of Charles Dawson."

Woodward broke stride. So this was the woman for whom Dawson had dared all. She would have to be that beautiful, he thought. Her beauty was all the confirmation he needed. My God, what did she know? he wondered, with a stab of nauseating emptiness in his stomach. He wished there were a bench so they could sit down. Woodward tried to appear only mildly interested as he studied her; for the sake of this woman, the whole world had been duped, this ripe and desirable local Eve. He felt for her a fascination and repulsion. Did she know what she had done, what she had caused? Here he was, strolling in a garden with her, who in the end, if all the tangled events of the Piltdown fraud were ever undone, would be found at the very center. There was an absurd inevitability, Woodward thought, to their having met. He dreaded what she might say. It was not too late for the whole structure of lies to fall to pieces.

"I have something most interesting to tell you," Arabella began.

Woodward forced himself to look directly at her, adjusting the glasses at the bridge of his nose.

"After the announcement of the Piltdown discovery, Charles

gave me one of the specimens he excavated—a small flint. I have never mentioned this to anyone, for fear that my relationship to Charles might be misconstrued. I was, of course, flattered beyond measure by that gift, as it is, in a sense, a national treasure. Since Charles's death, I have thought many times about getting in touch with you in London, but since there are other flints of similar manufacture in the Piltdown collection, I didn't think that mine would add anything significant to science's knowledge of that hairy old English gentleman. But my conscience bothered me, and now that we are neighbors, I thought it right at least to put you in the know.''

"This is very serious, Mrs. Spence, more serious, perhaps, than you think. I cannot presume to judge Charles's relationship to you, nor the sentimental value you attach to what you rightly call a national treasure. But I can tell you that withholding a specimen from a dig, particularly one as important as Piltdown, was a most deplorable breach of scientific ethics. Please don't think that I am maligning Charles; but if you knew him well, you would agree, I think, that to say he often acted on impulse would not be far from the truth.''

Arabella had never spoken to anyone about Dawson. All her dialogues had been with herself. Now she checked the impulse to relax into reminiscence, and only indicated she agreed.

"I must urge you," Woodward continued, "in the strongest possible terms to, shall we say, repatriate the flint. It could be done discreetly, anonymously, if you wish. I would be glad to see to it," he offered, thinking once it was in his possession, he would destroy it. "No one but you and I need ever know how your Piltdown flint came into the collection.''

"I couldn't part with it." There was something exciting to Arabella in the way Woodward looked at her. There was danger in the air, and her awareness that the small flint possessed a value beyond its prosaic appearance. "Let us be content to share the secret.''

"May I at least see it?''

"It is brown. This big." Arabella held up her thumb and

forefinger an inch apart. Woodward's eyes were locked on the blank space between her fingers, as if trying to will the thing there. "To be quite candid, Sir Arthur, I have the impression that if I showed you the flint, you would snatch it from me and then swear my story was false."

"Mrs. Spence, I am only trying to maintain the integrity of the Piltdown site and the reputation of my colleague and your friend, Charles Dawson."

"I apologize for my vivid imagination," Arabella said. "We must try to see each other socially, now that we have discovered we share a common interest. I mean flowers."

When Woodward gave his lecture, he spotted Arabella in the audience. Their social paths crossed from time to time, but the subject of Arabella's flint was never mentioned. It was often in his mind when he excavated at Piltdown.

Chapter XIV

ARTHUR KEITH HAD CONTINUED HIS POST AT THE HUNTER-
ian Museum at the Royal College of Surgeons and so
successfully associated himself with Piltdown Man that, when
the group portrait of personalities connected with the discovery was painted by John Cook of the Royal Academy, Keith
was seated smack in the center, cradling the skull he had
reconstructed in his hand. He had made it a point to go
frequently to Lewes and Uckfield to visit with Dawson,
discussing his own theories and Dawson's brilliance as a field
archaeologist. After Dawson's death, Keith maintained as
close a relationship with Woodward as that reserved colleague would allow. Keith had lectured and taught, had an
impressive bibliography of papers, and had published *The
Antiquity of Man,* recapitulating the history of human paleontology, of which Piltdown Man was the chief event. But just
as the post of superintendent of the Museum of Natural
History had slipped from Woodward, so knighthood eluded
Keith. He had never forgiven Dawson for bringing the Piltdown
specimens to the British Museum, nor Woodward for being
the lucky recipient. When Woodward was summoned to
Buckingham Palace, Keith began to grind his teeth again at
the thought that the new Sir Arthur might have been he. His
old jealousy unfurled like an umbrella, and he felt a deep
sense of deprivation and epic unfairness that invaded his

work, disturbed his sleep. Out of his brooding indignation he formulated a plan.

Spiritualism was all the rage in England. Never before had there been so many spirits from the Beyond so eager to be heard, and never before were mediums, clairvoyants, and spiritualist pundits in so great demand. Luminous clouds were conjuured up in front parlors, chests of drawers slithered about on the parquet, materialized hands carried flowers. Unaccountable rappings occurred in tables, which quivered as if taken with fits of the ague. Handbells rang when no hands were near and from no visible cause. It was fashionable, even for supercilious unbelievers in Belgrave or Russell Square, to entertain their guests after dinner with a séance, perhaps with a practitioner adept at automatic slate writing or a Ouija board. It was reported that Lord Abercrombie held a long conversation with his deceased wife in his own drawing room while the medium, a Mrs. Ashburnham, had tea at the other end of the room some thirty feet away; and the voice from the Beyond—magnified by a trumpet held to one of Lord Abercrombie's tin ears by a friend and witness—was continuous and distinct when Mrs. Ashburnham was unmistakably eating and drinking.

To be sure, there were regrettable scandals and frauds exposed by unregenerate materialists, but true Spiritualist believers maintained that the existence of occasional counterfeits did not negate, but rather confirmed, the existence of the real thing, which had been copied.

Hardly an evening went by in London when there was not a public Spiritualist event, a lecture or meeting of one or another of the societies that manifested and dissolved like the spirits they meant to promote and study.

Arthur Keith put aside his skull fragments and religiously attended these meetings to steep himself in the language of the occult and its theories, as offered to the here-and-now by the self-styled seers, prophets, and hucksters. The odious lectures he went to were mainly public events, designed to encourage private consultations. Within several months Keith had compiled a thick dossier of handbills and business cards that were handed out at the meeting rooms and small auditoriums, where he suffered to be told about life beyond the grave, of spirits in white robes holding anchors of hope, of brave soldiers lost in the Great War standing proud and whole in aureoles of celestial light. There were many women Spiritualist practitioners, but Keith confined himself to men; he was sure that a woman would be unable to absorb the scientific background necessary for his plan. He had private séances with a number of mediums, at the going rate of a guinea a sitting, to observe their techniques and styles of summoning, at his request, the spirit of his dead wife. He was finally satisfied that Dr. Joshua Haverstock was his man.

Keith returned to visit Dr. Haverstock in his modest rooms near Portobello Road, down the hill among the fruit and vegetable stalls. His lodgings were a step up for Dr. Haverstock, as he could be found at a permanent address, for the moment. His doctor's degree was neither medical, philosophical, nor divine. Until recently, Dr. Haverstock had been an itinerant actor whose mind-reading act enjoyed considerable success in the provinces, except for a troublesome episode with the police in Hull regarding a related confidence game, Dr. Haverstock, having been betrayed to the law by a confederate dissatisfied with the division of the take. It was time to try the Spiritualist game in London. He was a small, lean man, weasely in profile, unprepossessing, but Keith sensed in him a quick study and a hungry readiness to be coached.

"I want to communicate with someone else in the Beyond," Keith said.

"I have been blessed with the power," Dr. Haverstock murmured, raising his eyes to an unseen benefactor. "Another loved one."

"Not exactly."

"It can be dangerous to effect contact with a rancorous spirit. I cannot be responsible for the consequences." Dr. Haverstock's voice dropped to a theatrical rumble with the warning.

"I like that. That's very good. That stentorian tone."

"I sense a note of disbelief. But you cannot doubt that your dear, departed wife spoke through me right here in this room, not a week ago."

"I have no wife, dead or otherwise."

"Perhaps not in this life, but assuredly you had in your former life."

"Look here, I've taken a great deal of time and trouble, and I've seen a great many of you chaps. Last week my dear, departed wife appeared to me as a piece of dirty cheesecloth. So let us get down to business and not waste any more of your time or mine."

"Are you a copper, or what?"

"I should think, with your power, you would know. I am a scientist."

"If you're writing one of those scientific exposés, why don't you pick on one of those other chaps," Dr. Haverstock said with a note of pathos. "I'm just getting started in this line of work."

"You misunderstand me. I don't want to spoil your career. I want to engage you. I want you to preside over a séance."

Dr. Haverstock brightened. "I charge a guinea a head and expenses. Would you like globes and columns of light? Luminous vapors? The sound of harps? That'd be extra. Automatic writing in trance? Would you like a historical person? I've done Gladstone. Whole speeches from Parliament."

Keith interrupted and explained that the séance would concern his work as an anatomist and paleontologist, and in particular the circumstances surrounding the discovery of Piltdown Man.

Dr. Haverstock began making grunting noises.

"What in hell are you doing?" Keith asked.

"Piltdown Man. He didn't speak English, obviously."

"Obviously. But I want to make contact with one of the discoverers of Piltdown Man, Charles Dawson. He passed over, as you would say, without revealing information of the utmost scientific importance."

"To whom?"

"To the world of science."

"Which you want divulged?"

"Divulged. Yes."

"I shall divulge to your heart's content."

"There will be, I hope, two other participants in this séance, besides myself: Charles Dawson's widow, Helene, and Sir Arthur Conan Doyle."

Dr. Haverstock was mightily impressed and immediately began to think what an opportunity had presented itself.

For many years Doyle had been a passionate convert to Spiritualism. The advocacy of his voice had given the movement and many of its individual psychics and philosophers a wide hearing and respectability. He had devoted his literary talents exclusively to spreading the gospel, particularly the issue of communicating with the dead, and spent much of his considerable fortune in the promotion of Spiritualist ideas.

Keith inspected Dr. Haverstock's suit, gone shiny at the elbows. "Is that the only thing you've got to wear?"

"I'll give it a brush, don't you worry."

"When I've fixed a date for the séance, I'll run you over to Harrod's and get you fitted out."

When Keith arrived at Wildesham and was shown into Doyle's study, he assumed his most conspiratorial tone. "It was so good of you to see me." They sat opposite each other, Keith in the armchair where Doyle had nearly strangled Edmund Backhouse.

"Your communication was intriguing," Doyle said, and then read an excerpt of Keith's letter. " 'A matter of extreme urgency in the cause of Spiritualism about which I must talk with you personally and in the strictest confidence.' "

"I hope you don't object to my penning to you in longhand, but I could not trust my secretary at the college to know that I was writing to you in this vein."

"Your letter indicates a sympathy uncommon in the world of science, which had been so antagonistic to us, even in the face of incontrovertible evidence; I myself have spoken with eleven relatives who have passed over. Science will simply not face facts."

"Then you can understand my caution. But being here now, I can tell you of my complete conversion, my belief in the spirit world. A few months ago, quite by chance, I

attended a sitting at a friend's house. Of course, I thought the
whole thing a sham, and as a test, I asked the medium to
make contact with my brother, who died ten years ago. He
was the noted Sanskritist, Malcolm Keith, who taught at the
University of Aberdeen. He spoke through Dr. Haverstock,
the medium, and I immediately knew it was he. He talked of
my mother's lead crystal fruit bowl, which we broke as boys
playing tag in the parlor, and even recited the entire first
canto of the *Bhagavad Gita,* in Sanskrit.''

Doyle showed no amazement at Keith's anecdote, taking it
as an ordinary occurrence.

''Since then I have spoken with him many times; it is such
a comfort to know he is happy in the Other Life. And I have
read widely in the literature. Your great work, *The New
Revelation,* is my bible.''

''If you had brought it with you, I would have been glad to
inscribe it.''

''That is more than I could have ever hoped for,'' Keith
said, his voice catching in his throat. ''When I think of how
many years I have wasted in my materialist preoccupations!
But it is wonderful in a way, really, that I have spent the
greater part of my scientific life looking at the endocranial
markings of the human brain, without realizing that I was
looking at the vessel of the mind, that hallmark of humanity
that lives on in the shining ether of the Other World.''

''But now you have found the Path.''

''Yes, I have. And I have a vision. That is to bring the
worlds of science and Spiritualism into concurrence. They
are two sciences, in a sense, and they need not be at daggers
drawn, but rather ought to proceed arm in arm to a new and
higher truth. At first, I thought I would shout this joyous
revelation from the rooftop of the Royal College but I have
come up with another idea—of being a secret spokesman, a
disinterested witness, burrowing from within.''

''You would merely report what you see and hear without
prejudice.''

''That is correct. I am a man of science and always will
be.''

"And you have access to the editorial boards of the most prestigious scientific journals," Doyle said. He got up from his chair and paced the room in restless excitement. "There's no telling what could be accomplished. And your own public conversion might come after we had won over other men of equal eminence. I see nothing wrong in your taking the position you indicate."

"The greatest service we could do for Spiritualism and science is, in fact, to bring them together. Sciee expanded and enlightened in the Spiritualist context. I mentioned that much of my scientific life has been concerned with the morphology of the human skull, hominid skulls in particular and the Piltdown skull specifically. When Charles Dawson was alive, I visited him frequently, and he often spoke to me of your interest in the dig. I believe he sent you his papers on that subject."

"I was keenly interested in the site. Dawson once gave me a tour at Barkham Manor, and I have kept an extensive file of those exciting years."

"Then you probably know that there was a second site, at Sheffield Park, known in the literature as Piltdown Two, where Dawson and Woodward found the remains of a second individual."

"Yes. It was almost as astounding a discovery as the first."

"Then you also must know that we have very little information about Sheffield Park. Dawson became ill and then died before he set down any notes about the site, and Woodward, when he published the finds himself, said only that Dawson had dug there before his illness confined him to bed. It was a great loss that Dawson was unable to communicate what he knew, the position of the specimens in the ground, the circumstances of discovery, the exact location of the site. For all we know, there may be important things there, waiting to be found."

"I believe I know what you are going to suggest."

"That we make contact with Charles Dawson."

"Scientific information of the upmost significance revealed

through the power of Spiritualism. The first formal meeting of the two sciences. A brilliant idea."

"We speak with one voice," Keith said. "I would like to have Dr. Haverstock preside. He is a person of unusual power."

"I don't know him."

"You should."

"I trust your judgment."

"I intend to ask Dawson's widow to attend. Her presence will be crucial in confirming that the spirit is her husband's, when we make contact."

"I think that if we act in accordance with your position as a disinterested witness, it would be better for me to approach her and that I suggest it was my idea."

"I had hoped you would undertake that," Keith replied. "I do not wish to put myself forward. I do think, though, that we ought to hold the séance in London, at my house in Hampstead. I do not know Mrs. Dawson's views on Spiritualism, but if she is the least bit skeptical, I expect she would be reassured that the arrangements were scientifically controlled, and that the surroundings were unprejudiced."

"I have had many sittings here," Doyle said.

"Yes, but remember, there are those of our critics who would argue that this setting is not neutral."

"There is something to that," Doyle admitted. "Wildesham's congeniality to the Spirit World is well-known. We do not want to appear to be taking an easy way."

"Very well, then. London it is."

"One more thing. Since I have been an amateur of Piltdown these many years, there may be a question or two I would like to put to Dawson myself."

Helene Dawson still lived at Castle Lodge. Nothing had changed about the house or the massive medieval rubble and towers of Lewes Castle that rose behind it. The rooms were the same inside, except for Dawson's study. The furniture was still in place, but the vitrines were empty and the desktop and bookcases were bare since Woodward had helped Helene dispose of the flints, the boxes of bone oddments and fossils to museums in Hastings and Brighton, and she had donated his library to the local geological society. The house was more than big enough for herself, and she hadn't converted the study to any other use. It remained Charles's sanctum where she went sometimes to look idly out the window down into the courtyard of the Castle and the gate where tourists entered to climb up to the keep.

Helene went down through the barbican to High Street to buy one chop instead of two, and said grace aloud to herself now that Charles wasn't there to disapprove. She had taken comfort in religion, not fanatically so, but only because it helped. She had become pleasantly stout and wore mostly black, because it made her feel comfortable. Marriage having formerly defined her, she felt without being maudlin that her widowhood was the central fact of her life. When Helene spoke of Charles, it was with a quiet dignity, a calm acceptance of his death, and a pleasure to have been his wife.

When Doyle visited Helene at the Lodge, he had some small difficulties in persuading her to participate in the séance. While she had formed no rigid opposition to Spiritualism, it was hard to reconcile what little she knew of it with her own standard Christianity. Doyle pointed out that the two elements of lofty morality and intercourse between the visible and the invisible world were shared equally by religion and Spiritualism, and that Christianity would never dispute the existence of the soul's everlasting life. As to getting in touch with the dead, which gave Helene pause, Doyle argued the scientific importance of the meeting and that neither he nor Arthur Keith would ever contemplate involving her in anything improper. What they were suggesting was not faddist novelty, but was based on principles as old as Babylon. The séance he proposed would be the beginning of a new era, bringing further renown to Dawson and his life's work. The thing could be managed, Doyle said, without the least inconvenience to her. He would nip over from Crowborough, and the chauffeur would safely convey them to London in the new car, a dove-gray Bentley.

Keith outfitted Dr. Haverstock in a well-cut clerical gray,

and like many actors before him, once in costume, he entered fully into the part, like an unlikely, shirt-sleeved, rehearsal Hamlet who became melancholy to his fingertips once decked out in black doublet and hose and a paid performance in his pocket.

The performance would, of necessity, be something of an improvisation, but the bare outlines were set down by Keith after a brief tutorial in paleontology: The Piltdown finds at Barkham Manor—Piltdown One—the original skull fragments, jaw, flints, animal remains, and the canine tooth, were genuine. However, the ambiguous finds at Sheffield Park—all of Piltdown Two—were a conglomeration of evidence planted by Woodward. He, and he alone, had published Piltdown Two in 1917 after Dawson's death. Keith told Dr. Haverstock that Dawson's spirit would reveal that Woodward had discussed with him salting Piltdown Two as a way of settling scientific questions brought up by the proponents of the two-individuals theory, but Dawson had angrily refused to compromise his scientific integrity. After Dawson died, Woodward "found" the specimens allegedly unearthed at Sheffield Park to enhance his own reputation and to insure his knighthood. Sheffield Park was a phantom site invented by Woodward, and Dawson had been wandering in the mists of the Other World, waiting for the opportunity to set the record straight. This revelation of Woodward's ambition run amok and scientific calumny would destroy Woodward while preserving the integrity of Piltdown One—and Piltdown Man, undoubtedly genuine, a shibboleth of British paleontology and the cornerstone of Keith's career. In short, in answer to Dr. Haverstock's furrowed brows, Piltdown One was genuine while Piltdown Two was Woodward's invention. Dr. Haverstock was ready to divulge.

Doyle arrived in his car with Helene as evening was settling over Hampstead. Doyle had proselytized all the way from Lewes, and Helene could find nothing to argue with during the trip. But once in Keith's front parlor, the thought of being in the presence of Charles's spirit, however he might be manifest, made her edgy and highstrung. She shook hands with Keith and was presented to Dr. Haverstock, who didn't look at all like her Charles and was nothing like she expected; he was a ferret while Charles was more than a man among men. She whispered anxiously to Doyle, who pressed her hand in his large paw, reassuring her that everything was all right. "A medium is only a conduit to the Spirit World. Think of yourself as going on a journey to a far-off land, and him as Thomas Cook."

Helene did not appear reassured.

"All the arrangements have been made," Doyle said. "You are entirely safe in his hands."

Dr. Haverstock was fawningly attentive to Doyle, who took his attentions kindly. They spoke briefly in hushed tones about Spiritualist matters as Keith made sure everything was in readiness. There was a round rosewood table in the center of the room cleared of its wax fruit, around which were placed four chairs. The two men flanked Dr. Haverstock, who faced Helene.

"Before we begin," Doyle said, "I would like to make a few remarks concerning what we hope to accomplish here this evening." As he explained what he called the New Synthesis, spoken with capitals N and S, Dr. Haverstock, upstaged, fidgeted impatiently under the table. "And Dr. Keith has kindly agreed to be an impartial witness to these historic proceedings."

The opaline Gallé glass chandelier cast a dim, fleshy pool of light on the tabletop as Dr. Haverstock spread his palms flat, thumbs touching; the others did the same, forming a ring.

After some moments of total silence, there was a sepulchral moaning in the shadows of the room as Dr. Haverstock's eyes became glassy and his body rigid with energy from the Beyond. Inchoate sounds emanated from his throat finally forming into a horse whisper. "Helene!"

Helene looked tentatively at Dr. Haverstock, refusing to commit herself. His mouth worked frantically, as if struggling to communicate with her, struggling against the barrier she was putting between them. Breaking through, he croaked, "The gold locket." Every widow had a gold locket.

Helene's hand went convulsively to her throat. "What is the inscription?"

"There is no inscription." The odds were in his favor; they usually asked that question if there wasn't any.

"Charles! Oh, dear Charles!" Helene exclaimed.

"Do not grieve for me. . . . I am happy. . . . We shall be together again . . . soon," Dr. Haverstock crooned.

Helene began to speak, but Doyle intervened, addressing the spirit. "We would not have interrupted your eternal rest, except for the most pressing reasons," he apologized. "But in the earthly years since you passed over, certain problems concerning the discovery of *Eoanthropus dawsoni* have still to be resolved. . . ."

Helene had meanwhile begun to rock back and forth in her seat. Keith looked at her sharply, but she was oblivious. Softly at first, then louder, a keening sound of a widow's lamentation filled the room. "Why didn't you tell me?" she wailed, her pale face streaked with tears.

Keith was alarmed, but Dr. Haverstock never wavered. The question had been put to him before, and he had a ready answer. "Because I loved you."

"I don't understand," Helene moaned.

"You will, in time," said the spirit from the Other Side. "But now I must answer other questions. You must be patient."

"I can't wait. You must tell me now," Helene cried. She suddenly rose from her seat.

"You have broken the contact," Dr. Haverstock said severely in his own voice.

With an agonized cry she groped across the table for Dr. Haverstock who flinched backward, toppling his chair and landing on the floor.

Helene uttered another great wailing cry and collapsed senseless.

Doyle leaped to her. "Smelling salts! Brandy!"

Keith rushed from the room while Dr. Haverstock collected himself. "The spirits are especially strong tonight," he said to Doyle who checked Helene's pupils and began rubbing her hands.

Keith returned with a decanter and some glasses. He poured a measure for Doyle who held it to Helene's slightly parted lips, and he poured another dram for himself hoping to master his wrathful frustration.

Dr. Haverstock watched Doyle's ministrations, scarcely able to conceal his enjoyment of the melodrama. "We could try again. I feel the power particularly."

"Mrs. Dawson is in no condition to make contact again tonight."

Dr. Haverstock's face crumpled. "But she is very receptive."

"It was good of you to come, Dr. Haverstock," Keith said, indicating it was time for him to go.

Still Dr. Haverstock lingered, feeling his great opportunity becoming as ephemeral as a wraith.

"The spiritual atoms have been disturbed tonight," Keith said. "There is a surfeit of vibrations."

"I quite agree," Doyle said.

Dr. Haverstock withdrew a large business card from the inside pocket of his new suit and, after laying it on the table, reluctantly allowed himself to be shown to the front door.

Helene's eyes fluttered open, and slowly reviving, she allowed herself to be helped to a tufted davenport.

"It was Charles," she said.

"Of course it was,' ' Doyle replied. "Don't blame yourself for having been overcome. It often happens the first time."

"Where's Dr. Haverstock? I must see him again."

"There are other practitioners, somewhat more eminent, that I would like you to meet," Doyle advised. Then he turned to Keith. "I am still anxious to pursue this line of scientific inquiry. I'd like to arrange another meeting, this time at Wildesham."

"Of course," Keith said. "But we must see to Mrs. Dawson. Where are you staying?" he asked her.

"With friends in Bloomsbury."

"I will take you there, if you feel well enough to go," Doyle offered.

They sat silently for a time, each self-absorbed as the car

made its way toward London on the dark roads. At last, Doyle said, "I can't help wondering about your question to your late husband: 'Why didn't you tell me?'"

Helene glanced uneasily at the back of the driver's head. Doyle reached forward and securely fastened the glass partition. "You may be confident of my complete discretion," he assured her. It had been more than a decade since he had written a Holmes story, but Doyle felt, just then, as if he might be his own creation, urging a distressed female visitor in his rooms in Baker Street to reveal the details of a mystery.

"Charles's death," Helene began. "He had so little time after the great discovery, so little time to enjoy what he had achieved. The doctors said at first it was anemia, then there were complications, blood poisoning. But the doctors couldn't do anything; it was awful, seeing Charles's strength ebb away. He had a lifetime of work ahead of him. And he particularly needed his strength then, because I remember his talking about a symposium of some kind, about Piltdown Man. He said it was especially important that he attend. But the doctors insisted that Charles stay in bed. Of course he wouldn't; he said they were all idiots and quacks, and he continued to work on his specimens, his papers. Toward the end he could barely move, but one day I found him trying desperately to get into his study. It was as if that effort took the last of his energy, because after I put him back to bed, he stayed there and died soon after." Helene paused, as if gathering her own strength. "Until he died I had never been in the study alone. Charles was so particular; he was always in there when I tidied up, saying that he knew where everything was and not to touch anything. Well, for months after he died, I couldn't get myself to go in. But finally I did, and there were all his things. Arthur Woodward went through Charles's fossil collection and helped me sell the specimens. The personal things I kept, of course. There was a small portable writing box—inlaid wood, quite pretty. Nothing in it, but when I picked it up, I could hear something rattling inside. I examined it more closely, and I saw that there was a false bottom. I pried it open," Helene said, "and in the small space I found Charles's pocket diary, a little glass bottle, and a hypodermic needle.'' She reached into her purse and took out a florentine leather notebook and then a little vial, handing them to Doyle. The vial contained the remains of a brownish substance. Doyle began to read the diary entries— ordinary reminders, appointments.

"Look at March third," Helene said. "You see, there's a notation: five milligrams. That's the first one; there are others."

"Do the dates mean anything to you?" Doyle asked.

"They start about the time Charles first became ill. And they stop a few weeks before he died. Charles was taking whatever was in that bottle. It was a brownish liquid with a very strong smell. Charles became anemic and then got blood poisoning. When I found these things, I thought he must have been taking some kind of iron tonic and that he got the blood poisoning from the hypodermic. But I never heard of anybody taking a tonic with a needle. Early in Charles's illness, the doctors prescribed a tonic, and Charles made an awful fuss about the taste. I know he didn't trust doctors, but he must have realized what he was doing wasn't helping either. I can understand his not telling the doctors what he was doing, but why didn't he tell me? I don't understand."

Doyle unscrewed the top of the vial and held it to his nose. The dry remains were odorless.

"I wondered what was in there," Helene said, "but I didn't know how to find out. At first I thought I'd take it to the doctors, or the chemist in town, but I couldn't get myself to do it. I was afraid—afraid of what they might tell me."

"Do you know why you were afraid?" Doyle asked. "Think back. Try to remember."

"I don't know," Helene replied. "That is, I'm not sure. But when I found what was in the writing box, I thought back to that time I found Charles trying to get into the study. As if he were trying to get in without my knowing. I didn't say anything about it at the time, but I couldn't help wondering why he hadn't asked me to help him. After he died, when I was going through his papers, I almost hoped I might find something among them that Charles would obviously not have wanted me to know about. But there wasn't anything, not until I found the diary, the bottle, and the needle.''

''So you think that's what he was hiding and wanted to get rid of before you found out?''

''Yes.''

Doyle gazed thoughtfully out the window of the car at the familiar sights of central London. ''It seems to me that we could either find out what was in this bottle, or let matters rest as they are.''

''I think I'd rather know.''

''Then we can either try to have the contents analyzed, or we can make contact with your husband again and ask him.''

''I do want to contact Charles again, but if he didn't tell me about this while he was alive, I don't think I should ask him now. He said to be patient; he loved me. I think he was right.''

''I think you've made a wise decision. If you'll allow me to keep the vial, I'll have a chemical analysis made. And I'd like to borrow the diary so that I can copy the schedule of doses; there may be a connection between the amounts taken and its effects.''

Doyle dropped Helene Dawson in Bloomsbury, promising to return the diary and the vial with a full report by post as soon as possible, and went on to Brown's Hotel, where he spent the night before returning to Crowborough the following day.

A week later, Doyle received a trunk call from London: Sir Robert Bickford, chief of the Forensic Laboratory at Scotland Yard, at whose office he had left Helene Dawson's vial the morning of his return to Sussex.

''Bunny! How are you, old boy,'' Doyle said.

''Never better. What are you doing down there, Arthur? Digging up an old unsolved murder?''

''What do you mean?''

''That vial you left us. Nasty stuff, once we'd put it in solution again.''

''What is it?''

''Curare.''

Doyle reached across his desk and took up a sheet of paper on which he had made notations of Dawson's dates and dosages.

"Arthur?" Sir Robert said. "Are you on?"

"Sorry, Bunny. Just thinking."

"This stuff must be years and years old, but it's still quite virulent. I'm afraid I can't return it, even to you."

"That won't be necessary."

"Anything I can do?" Sir Robert asked. "Why don't you stop round. Inspector Lestrade was asking about you only the other day."

After hanging up the telephone, Doyle opened his writing folder and wrote a letter to Helene Dawson: "Dear Mrs. Dawson, I am enclosing herewith your late husband's diary. As promised I had the contents of the vial examined by a noted forensic chemist. I am unable to return it to you, as the remains were entirely used up in the chemical analysis. You will be relieved to know that your surmise about what it contained was correct—an iron tonic, which I have been advised is most effective taken by injection. After these last years of anxious uncertainty, I hope you will now set to rest whatever uneasy thoughts you may have had about the circumstances of your late husband's death. I would be glad to meet you again concerning Spiritualist matters, and I take the liberty of also enclosing a paper I recently delivered on the significance of ectoplasm. I am, believe me, Sincerely yours, A. C. Doyle. K.B.E."

Curare, Doyle thought. Dawson had been dosing himself with poison, the same poison they had talked about when Doyle had discussed his proposed novel, *The Lost World,* and its Brazilian setting. Dawson knew its medical uses, the symptoms it might produce. He wanted to be sick, but he was no suicide. He must have been convinced he could reverse the symptoms. The blood poisoning might have come from the needle, but more likely it resulted from the prolonged use of the curare; Dawson had raised the doses, probably in response to a tolerance factor, or possible to counteract medication he couldn't avoid taking. There could have been a chemical reaction between his medication and the poison. The doctors were powerless to deal with the septicemia, the resultant internal abscesses and hemorrhages. Helene's suspicion was correct. When she found Dawson trying to get into the study, he may have known it was too late and wanted to destroy the evidence of his misguided plan.

A self-induced illness with symptoms mimicking anemia; the blood poisoning had been a fatal complication. Helene had said there had been a Piltdown symposium Dawson wanted to attend, but that he'd been too sick. Dawson had faked his anemia in a way it could be corroborated by his doctors. He fooled them, fooled his wife. Even when he was dying, he never told her. Doyle was sure Helene was not withholding a deathbed confession. But it was clear that Dawson didn't want to talk about Piltdown and had gone to extraordinary lengths to put himself incommunicado.

Doyle crossed the paneled library to a bank of file cabinets, taking out one marked "Piltdown Man," and returned to his desk. There were press clippings about the discovery, a number of offprints Woodward and Dawson had sent him. Doyle re-read the contents of the file, particularly noting passages he had underlined, little check marks, exclamation points in the margins.

There was a satisfied look on Doyle's face as he pushed himself back from his desk, as if he had just finished a large meal. He left his study, passed through the dining room, through the kitchen to the mud room. Putting on a deerstalker hat, Burberry, and a pair of boots, he went out. In the garage, next to the Bentley, was a small, open Bugatti runabout, sapphire blue. Doyle wedged his girth behind the wheel, started the engine with a deafening roar, and careened around the circular drive onto the road. It was a spring day by Constable, every gracile willow, every virile oak quintessentially English. Racing along, Doyle breathed in the loamy smell of the freshly turned fields.

Dawson, you old scoundrel, Doyle thought. And he remembered as he had before, his unannounced visit to Castle Lodge: the dark brown fragments on Dawson's sun-struck desk, the chemicals, Dawson's evident embarrassment, as if he had been caught in *flagrante delicto*—while the crime is ablaze. Doyle had noted Dawson's behavior, but had not attached much importance to it until after the announcement of the finds at Barkham Manor and the newspaper descriptions of Dawson, his flamboyance and swashbuckling manner. Then, having met Dawson again at the dig site, the anxious manner of their first meeting could only have been a man in danger of exposure. The newspaper photographs of the reconstructed skull reminded him of the fragments and chemicals on the desk, as did the chocolate brown color of the fossils. Not quite "elementary"! But what if Piltdown Man was Dawson's creation. And if so, was Woodward a dupe or a co-conspirator? As Doyle sped along the road, he ruminated on his old suspicions about the fossils. He'd had a sense that he was right, almost from the beginning, but the information about Dawson's death added a final certainty. Dawson, the forger of his illness; Dawson, the Piltdown forger.

The afternoon turned gray under a bank of dirty clouds as Doyle slowed down at Piltdown Pond and pulled into a narrow path, where his car could not be seen from the main road. Then he walked to the gate of Barkham Manor, and continued up the tree-lined avenue to the gravel pit. A small tool shed stood to one side, beyond an area that had been roped off, and there were footprints and signs of recent excavation. He ducked under the rope and stood at the lip of the pit, looking down like a mourner at a grave site.

Years before, when he had thought of the possibility of Piltdown Man being a forgery, Doyle had decided to send an anonymous message to Dawson and Woodward, for their eyes alone, a message that someone had guessed the truth.

Doyle's thoughts were interrupted by the sound of a gunshot. It wasn't hunting season. Poachers, he thought. With the ire of a landowner, Doyle quickly went around the gravel pit and struggled through the dense hedges to use as a blind. If he saw who it was, he'd made a report to the local constabulary. From where he lay he heard another shot, closer this time, then the coughing and sputtering of a car's engine. The infernal thing was backfiring, Doyle realized. He was about to get up when the car pulled alongside the gravel pit and stopped. Doyle remained concealed.

Arthur Smith Woodward got out. He was dressed as formally as if he were going to his old office at the British Museum, the pince-nez glasses firmly in place. Doyle watched him go to the tool shed, unlock it, and take out a spade and an archaeologist's sieve. Next he put on a pair of mud-caked high boots and a pair of gauntlet-like work gloves. Once outfitted he looked as if he couldn't decide whether to be a banker or a buccaneer.

Woodward set up the sieve and began to dig. He worked slowly, with the crabbed movements of an old man. After each spadeful of gravel was placed on the sieve, Woodward shook through the dirt, carefully examining the remains. He would then trudge to the waste pile, throw away the gravel, return to the pit and dig again.

Doyle remained hidden, his cap pulled low over his eyes. He knew it was absurd to think that Woodward might do anything significant, but it was fascinating to watch him unobserved, to see him unguarded, absorbed in his slow, lonely work. Neither he nor Woodward were aware that the sky had gradually darkened with rain clouds until the first drops began to fall. Woodward looked up, took a reading, and prepared to leave. Before getting into his car he paused to look at the work in progress. Nothing in his expression conveyed what he might be thinking. Neither guilt nor innocence could be read on his face. Still looking at the gravel pit with utter neutrality, Woodward scratched his crotch. It was such an unaffected human gesture, Doyle thought, smiling. According to the rules of evidence, it meant nothing, but Doyle made up his mind Woodward had been Dawson's dupe. He was still excavating, hoping to find another memento of Piltdown Man, not knowing it was a hopeless quest. Poor bloody bastard.

So Dawson's my man, Doyle thought contentedly as Woodward drove explosively away, frightening whatever poachers or game might be in the neighborhood. Doyle rose stiffly to his feet and crashed through the hedge to the road. Looking back at the gravel pit, he repeated to himself: Dawson's my man, and then added aloud, "But I'm his."

Doyle could see the peaked roofs of Barkham Manor, jutting beyond the hedges and dark pines. The last time he had seen the house was a summer's night in 1913. He had parked his car in the lane beside Piltdown Pond and walked the rest of the way to deliver his message to Dawson and Woodward. There had been scudding clouds, a highwayman's moon. He'd used that description in one of his historical novels, and wondered briefly which one. But there had been enough light to see. Having visited the site and having listened to Dawson's spirited explanation of the gravel layers laid bare by the excavation, Doyle knew precisely where to put the canine tooth.

Doyle assumed sooner or later Dawson and Woodward had to find the tooth that all British paleontology had been waiting to be found, the tooth that he had colored with Van Dyke brown paint, an obvious fake and a ridiculous fulfillment of a prophesy—a message to the two that somebody out there knew what they were about. It would be deliciously unnerving, although Doyle would never have the full satisfaction of knowing their reaction to his purposely clumsy forgery. He had never imagined that Teilhard would find it, or that it would be accepted as genuine. That accident was even sweeter than Doyle's original plan.

It was obvious that Teilhard wasn't invovled in the forgery. If all three were co-conspirators, the find would never have been reported. Woodward was clearly innocent as well; otherwise his continued excavations at Piltdown made no sense. Dawson thought he had commited the perfect crime, but by accepting the obviously fake tooth as genuine, Dawson tacitly admitted that all of the Piltdown specimens were false. Teilhard never knew he had unintentionally proved Doyle's suspicions. Doyle wondered who Dawson thought put the canine tooth in the gravels at Piltdown. That was the question Doyle wanted to ask Dawson's spirit at the séance.

Having seen Woodward excavating at the site, Doyle was convinced he, the hapless dupe, could tell him nothing. There was no point in revealing his own part in the Piltdown fraud to Woodward, just as it was pointless to tell Helene Dawson the circumstances of her husband's death. She would eventually learn the truth, after she passed over.

As Doyle drove home, he decided to destroy his Piltdown file. All's right with the world, he thought, satisfied that he'd been a better forger than Dawson and that he had been able to bring to bear his old Holmesian logic to the Piltdown case. He drove on with the expectation of warming his toes at the great Jacobean fireplace as the Piltdown file burned to ashes while he sipped his tea and munched Cook's superlative muffins dripping with butter and slathered with strawberry jam.

Chapter XV

THE NEWS OF THE PILTDOWN FORGERY WAS A SENSATION in Uckfield. Even before the newspapers from London arrived in town, the revelation had been on the morning broadcast of the BBC. Men on their way to work, who usually passed the offices of Dawson & Hart without thinking twice about it, stopped to ponder the brass doorplate. Not a few were late for work after going into the offices, where the successors to the firm were amused that anyone thought they might have a clue concerning Dawson's involvement. Their amusement didn't prevent them from airing their own theories of the case. Later in the day the local pubs were jammed with Poirots and Lord Peter Wimseys, many of whom had known, or claimed to have known, Dawson. Some loudly vouched for him while others shouted with equal conviction that he had "dunit". Woodward, who had died in 1944, was also hauled into the dock and found guilty and innocent by turns. Conspiracy theories were rife. A carnival atmosphere prevailed and a perverse pride that the townsfolk of Uckfield had rubbed shoulders with one or both of the rascals who might have pulled the wool as thick as any Southdown sheep's over the eyes of science. One pub near the site called The Piltdown Man, which had entertained archaeological tourists, viewed the future with gloom until the owner got the idea of redoing the sign, which was painted and hung within a week: the reconstructed Piltdown skull with a silly, curling grin and winking eye.

Mabel Kenward heard the news and, putting on a rubberized trenchcoat, had gone to have a look at the pit. She remembered Dawson and Woodward digging there, the mugs of cider, the crocks of lager and stout she had brought out to them and how she'd never touched a pebble in the pit for fear of disturbing it. She remembered her father's anger and how she had listened indulgently to his conviction that the fossils were fake. Her father had died firm in his disbelief, and she was glad he'd been right, even for the wrong reasons. Mabel wondered whether the Nature Conservancy would come to take down the shed and the protective glass that showed the stratification. She thought about picking up a rock and heaving it at the glass panel, but her vandal's instinct was frustrated by not knowing at whom her anger was directed. The men she had known, whom she had trusted? The priest, Teilhard? Someone else? Mabel forced the heel of her boot into the earth at the edge of the pit until it crumbled away and fell to the bottom. Her fists were deep in her pockets as she went back to the house.

Arabella heard the news too, and read the stories in the papers when they arrived in Uckfield that afternoon. She was seventy-five and a widow. Colin had died three years before. Liam ran the business and lived nearby with his wife and two children, daughters. Arabella was glad for granddaughters. She could indulge herself and them in frilly dresses, and she knew they would never have to fight if there ever was another war. Mark had been lost in the North Sea when his cruiser was sunk by a German submarine. Her life was quiet and prosaic, tinged with grief, which was how she looked. The austerity of the war years had left its mark on her. The glow of her paleness had faded, and the fineness of her skin was marked with tiny wrinkles around her dark eyes and meeting the curve of her upper lip. She had grown thinner as she got older and kept her white hair cut short, almost mannish, and it curled enough to wash, comb and fluff without any further bother. Arabella still painted, but having gotten used to saving petrol during the war, she found that her garden still offered opportunities in its azaleas or holly-hocks. She didn't go into the country and was without thoughts of wilder shores.

After reading the news of Kenneth Oakley's announcement at the British Museum, Arabella climbed the stairs to the attic. The room, with its slanting eaves, was redolent of cedar and the sweet smell of old books; the memory of old-fashioned scents, verbena and roses, clung to the racks of her clothes that were out of date but too good to throw away. A feeble light came through the dormer windows, and she pulled on the cord of a single hanging bulb, which sent shadows swinging back and forth on the walls, gradually settling down. She moved crablike between the furniture and round hat boxes, luggage that hadn't been used since the thirties, to the portfolios of watercolors stacked against the wall. After finding one that contained her early efforts, she then searched for a large pasteboard box with old letters, postcards, and souvenirs. Sitting in an old rocking chair, she untied the laces of the portfolio and leafed through the paint-ings, looking for the one in which at Charles's insistence, she had depicted him as a tiny, barely noticeable figure. Arabella looked at the landscape, its color still fresh, seeing the sun-light and the wind rippling the grass on the slope as it fell away to the copse of trees. She remembered Charles as he had hailed her across the meadow and the power of her desire, increasing as he came close until she was in his arms; his mouth, his hands, his body. Could it possibly be over forty years? She caught a glimpse of her self in a dusty pier glass leaning against the wall, ghostly, but not bad for an old lady, she concluded.

Arabella put the box of souvenirs on her lap and found the flint from Piltdown Charles had given her. It was in a piece of tissue paper. The last time she'd had an urge to see it was when Arthur Smith Woodward had died, and she had looked at it, trying to figure out its significance to him, apart from the reasons he had given her.

As she held the small brown flint in her hand, she felt another tremor of romance, putting herself in the company of

Helen of Troy and Cleopatra, for whose sake men did wonderful and terrible things. Charles had told her how he had worked and striven only for her. Only now did she understand the extent of his daring, his reckless audacity for her sake. For a few moments Arabella almost regretted not having gone away with him.

But other thoughts invaded. The object she held was fake, as were all the other Piltdown flints, the bones, the lot. She couldn't understand why it had taken the British Museum so long to discover the forgery, since the evidence presented in the press stories—the limited penetration of the staining of the bones, the clear indications of the filing of the molars— was so overwhelmingly obvious to anyone who might have had a mind really to examine the specimens. The discovery of fraud might have come at any time. And where would she have been if they'd run off to Paris, Cologne, to America? Lost, irrevocably lost, living in abject, penurious disgrace, with no turning back for either of them. Charles had every right to risk that for himself, but not her, not without her consent. He had endangered her whole life with his harebrained subterfuge. The flint was fake, and so was his love for her.

Kenneth Oakley's weekend at Oxford had done wonders for him. He had forgiven Ian Carr for his surprise party, and the next two days they had worked closely and productively on pulling together the data of their joint paper. As Oakley strode through the Romanesque portals of the Museum on the bright Monday morning, he had resolved to put the Piltdown forgery firmly behind him. There was still some residual excitement in the offices on the third floor and a stack of letters waiting for him. He told the departmental secretary to weed out those that concerned ordinary museum business for him, but the rest, anything to do with the fraud, were to be filed away. Perhaps years hence he would read them, for amusement, when he would have a historical perspective on the whole affair.

Oakley made himself a cup of tea, watered a pet snake plant on the window sill, and sat contentedly at his desk. He had been working for only a few minutes when Miss Ogilvy came into his office with a small parcel and a letter.

"I'm sorry, but I thought you ought to see this one."

"Where's it from?"

"Uckfield, Sussex."

"What's in the box?"

"A flint."

"What's in the letter?"

"Whodunit," Miss Oglivy said, smiling.

Mrs. Spence's letter was vague about her relationship to Charles Dawson, but it explained that in 1912, shortly after the announcement of the discovery of Piltdown Man, Dawson had presented her with the flint as a token of his affection and esteem. He had personally excavated it at Barkham Manor. Years later, she had met Arthur Smith Woodward, who had retired in the neighborhood, and after having told him about the flint in 1924, he had urged her to show it to him and to reunite it with the other Piltdown specimens at the Museum, with neither of which requests she had complied. The news of the forgery had come as a great shock to her, greater perhaps than to the public, owing to her relationship with Charles Dawson. She had also read speculations concerning who the forger might be, and while the flint still had sentimental value to her, she felt it was her duty to reveal its existence to the Museum, so that it might firmly place the guilt for the Piltdown forgery on whom it belonged: Charles Dawson. The letter closed by inviting further inquiries from the Museum, if necessary.

Oakley studied the letter for some time and then turned his attention to the flint. It was brown and crudely worked, much like the other flints from Barkham Manor.

Interesting letter, he thought. The tone was so reasoned, straightforward, and frank. But good liars had a knack for credibility, just like the Piltdown forger, whoever he might be. She'd been clever to bring in Woodward but apart from his never having seen the flint, he was also dead and could not confirm that they had even met. Dawson must have done something extraordinarily hurtful for her now to take the opportunity to implicate him falsely. It was an odd sort of revenge for what he had done, or what she imagined he had done to her.

"I know you meant well, Miss Ogilvy," Oakley said, offering the bit of stone and letter back to her. "But you can file this with the rest. It's a crank letter; we'll probably be getting a lot of them for a while. Accusations, confessions, proofs of guilt of this person or that."

"Are you sure it's not important?"

"Absolutely. This flint has a superficial resemblance to our specimens. But after studying the Piltdown flints for five solid months, I am convinced that this flint is not part of the group deposited at the Museum by Woodward and Dawson. Every one of those is fake. This flint," Oakley announced, holding it up, "is a genuine paleolithic artifact."

"That doesn't make any sense," said Miss Ogilvy. "If Dawson was the forger, why would he give Arabella Spence a genuine artifact?"

"This is not one of your film scripts, Miss Ogilvy."

"He didn't give it to her," she said, pleased with her rewrite and ignoring Oakley's comment. "Then where did she get it?" Miss Ogilvy continued.

"How the bloody hell do I know where she got it?"

Miss Ogilvy became thoughtful. "Maybe she got it from Woodward. She said she met him."

Oakley took a deep breath to control his impatience; on the other hand he had to concede to himself that he too had once found the Piltdown puzzle irresistible. "Why would Woodward give her a flint?"

Miss Ogilvy started slowly, shaping the script as she spoke, her voice taking on the ring of authority as she spun out her synopsis. "Arabella," she began, already intimate with her character, played by Valerie Hobson, "found out something from Dawson about the dig and she became suspicious." Miss Ogilvy paused long enough to cast Trevor Howard in the Dawson part. "So she went to Woodward to see if her suspicions were correct—no wait—to confront him. Yes, she went there to confront him, since she assumed he was in on it too. Woodward gave her a genuine flint saying it was from Piltdown, thinking she might have it tested, and knowing that the test would come out right."

"If she got the flint from Woodward, for whatever reason,

you still have to explain why she lied in the letter and said the flint came from Dawson.''

''She must be protecting Woodward.''

''Why? From whom? From what?'' said Oakley.

Miss Ogilvy was thoughtful again. ''Well, I haven't worked out the whole plot yet.''

''Your gift of cinematic imagination is matched only by your gift of understatement,'' Oakley observed. His voice softened as he said, ''You are not alone in trying to solve this case,'' remembering some of the more convoluted plots he and Joe Weiner had invented. ''But you won't solve it and I won't solve it and nobody will solve it, with or without Mrs. Spence's flint. If you want to try, fine. But I'm getting back to work. And please, don't show me any more Piltdown letters of any kind, however intriguing.''

Alone in his office, Oakley began to work again. Dawson must have been an awful cad with Arabella Spence for her rancor to have remained intact all these years, Oakley thought, in spite of himself. Still, being a cad with a woman didn't make him a forger. But suppose he was the forger, Oakley continued; perhaps he'd been in love with this woman and given her a genuine flint, saying it was from the Piltdown dig; what if he feared that one day she might reveal its existence as she now had done? he thought, borrowing from Miss Ogilvy. If that happened it might be tested and, if so, be proved genuine, just as the other flints appeared to be. Oakley began to be irritated with himself, feeling drawn back into the bog of convoluted conjecture and speculation about identity of the Piltdown forger. Suppose . . . perhaps . . . what if? There were endless scenarios he could write out of the bits of information and suspicions he had. With an effort of will, Oakley turned his attention once and for all, he hoped, from the mysteries of scientific fraud to the mysteries of science itself.